ALL T

FIFTH IN THE 'HEART OF STONE' SAGA

ALL
THAT
GLITTERS

SHELAGH MAZEY

Matador
9 Priory Business Park,
Wistow Road, Kibworth Beauchamp,
Leicestershire. LE8 0RX
Tel: 0116 279 2299
Email: books@troubador.co.uk
Web: www.troubador.co.uk/matador
Twitter: @matadorbooks

ISBN 978 1800462 069

British Library Cataloguing in Publication Data.
A catalogue record for this book is available from the British Library.

Printed and bound in the UK by TJ Books Limited, Padstow, Cornwall
Typeset in 11pt Baskerville by Troubador Publishing Ltd, Leicester, UK

Cover image
The Diggers Rest Saloon and Diamond Dealer illustration at the Big Hole
Museum in Kimberley, South Africa.
Photograph by kind permission of Dirk Jacobs.

Matador is an imprint of Troubador Publishing Ltd

This book is dedicated to
My South African family members
My late brother Terry who was the pioneer
My late mother and father, Roma and Pat Farrell
My sister Bridget Overd and her family
My sister Maddy Sams and her family

I have visited them all so many times
Travelling to Johannesburg and north to Pretoria
and the Kruger National Park
South to Cape Town, the Garden Route
and the Stellenbosch winelands
I have driven with my husband across
the Great Karoo and visited the coastal towns
of Durban, Knysna and Port Elizabeth
This beautiful African countryside has enticed
the characters in my book and inspired me to write this story

CONTENTS

LIST OF CHARACTERS

Note that some historical characters are mentioned in the text, but are not included in this list of fictional characters.

PORTLANDERS
VIOLET STONE (1814) *Joshua's mother*
MATTHEW STONE (1811) *Joshua's stepfather*
REBECCA STONE (1838) *Joshua's sister*
BENJAMIN STONE (1832) *Joshua's half brother*
JEM STONE (1866) *Joshua's nephew*

THE IVELL CAST

THE DRYER FAMILY
ALVINGTON MANOR
LORD JOSHUA DRYER (1832)
LADY LOUISA DRYER (1833)
AURORA DRYER (1851)
GABRIEL DRYER (1855)
LYDIA MAY DRYER (1870)

ALVINGTON MANOR STAFF
HARVEY WOODFORD (1823) *Butler/House steward*
EDGAR PARISH (1830) *Footman*
JOHN MOORE (1827) *Head groom*
EDWIN PROCTOR (1841) *Groom*
PERCY SANDFORD (1810) *Gardener*
THOMAS HAWKINS (1831) *Gardener*
HENRY HODINOTT (1820) *Handyman*

JOHN BOUCHER (1809) *Gamekeeper*
RAYMOND HAWKINS (1832) *Gamekeeper*
RUTH PROCTOR (1820) *Housekeeper*
FLORA BOUCHER (1810) *Cook*
ROSA WARREN (1825) *Lady's maid*
LETTIE BOUCHER (1838) *Parlour maid*
ELSIE HALL (1833) *Chambermaid*
EMILY POTTS (1837) *Housemaid*
HARRIETT PROCTOR (1844) *Kitchen maid*
ELLIE PROCTOR (1848) *Scullery maid*
CHARLOTTE HODINOTT (1827) *Laundress*
BETH PUDDY (1835) *Nanny*
GRACE TWEEDY (1821) *Governess*

THE WARREN FAMILY SENIOR
HOME FARM
ISAAC (1792) & ELIZABETH (1795) WARREN
SIBLINGS: JACOB (1830) & BEATRICE (BUNNY) (1844)

THE WARREN FAMILY JUNIOR
HAMLET COTTAGE
MALACHI (1825) & ROSA (1825) WARREN
SIBLINGS: RUBY (1856), ELI (1858) & DAISY (1861)

THE SEYMOUR FAMILY
SUTTON BINGHAM MANOR
COL. JEREMY (1803) & MRS HELEN (1808) SEYMOUR
SON: RUPERT (1823)
DAUGHTER-IN-LAW: LUCY (1836)
GRANDSON: FRANKIE (1869)
GORDON ROBSHAW – *Steward*
MARY ROBINS – *Cook*
GLADYS TURNER – *Parlour maid*
MERCY MEREDITH – *Nanny*
TIM JEFFRIES – *Gardener*

CAMP ROAD FAMILIES
ESTATE WORKERS
RUTH PROCTOR (1820)
SIBLINGS: AMY (1838), EDWIN (1841)
HATTIE (1844) & ELLIE (1848)
MICHAEL (1800) & MAUD (1802) PORTER
HENRY (1820) & CHARLOTTE (1827)
HODINOTT
JOHN (1827) & SUSAN (1831) MOORE
SIBLINGS: LUKE (1851) & LILLY (1853)
PERCY (1810) & MARY (1812) SANDFORD
SIBLINGS: ROBERT (1830) & HARRY (1833)
JACK (1805) & MOLLY (1802) HAWKINS
SIBLINGS: FRANK (1823) & THOMAS (1831)

THE BOUCHER FAMILY
KEEPER'S COTTAGE, POUND LANE
JOHN (1809) & FLORA (1810) BOUCHER
SIBLINGS: LETTIE (1838) & TOBY (1846)

THE BONFIELD FAMILY
KNAPP COTTAGE, PRESTON PLUCKNET
ARTHUR (1808) & MARTHA (1813) BONFIELD

THE FAIRWAY FAMILY
CHURCH COTTAGE, STAIRS HILL, IVELL
AMBROSE FAIRWAY (1804)
DAUGHTER: CLARA (1834)
MISS MAUD CAVENDISH (1824) *Housekeeper*

THE MEAKINS FAMILY
SUMMERVILLE HOUSE
LADY ANNABEL (1797)
ALISTAIR (1802) & OLIVIA (1813) MCNAB
AGNES (SENGA) (1860)

THE TOMPKINS FAMILY
THE BOROUGH
MR & MRS TOMPKINS
SIBLINGS: HARRY (1834) & BOBBY (1835)

THE SOUTH AFRICA CAST
ON THE 'SYRIA'
LUCY SEYMOUR (1836)
FRANKIE SEYMOUR (1869)
ETHAN HART – *Diamond prospectors*
SIMON McCALLISTER – *Diamond claim salesman*
ROGER & DAVID MOSS – *Diamond prospectors*
ELLEN WEATHERALL – *Travelling to Durban*
MAISIE BARFORD – *Travelling to Cape Town*
MR & MRS PARTRIDGE – *Travelling to Port Elizabeth*

HOPETOWN
RUPERT SEYMOUR
TAMELA – *Rupert's Khoikhoi maid*
BERKO – Tamela's son
MOSES & SOLOMON – *Rupert's diggers*
BENTHE – *Waitress*
MR & MRS BUTHELEZI – *General Stores*
MRS ERASMUS – *Draper*
MAGHIEL – Frankie's school friend

ON THE FARM
LUAN AND HILDA VAN DER MERWE
SIBLINGS: FRIEDRICH, ANJA & MARTA

EUREKA ROW
NORMAN & BETSY NORRIS – *Grocers*
MR & MRS BEKKER – *Bakers*
MR & MRS JASPER COFFIN – *Chandlers*
LUIGI CAPELLO – *Barber*

IDAYIMANE ENCAMPMENT
KHUMO TSHWANA – *Xhosa diamond digger*
Sons: KOFI – Works for Thomas
ROELI – Frankie's playmate
MPHO – *San bushman*

MINERS' DEFENCE UNIT
STEFAN RENSBURG – *Landlord of the Diggers Rest*
LIEUTENANT ANDREW GREAVES
BRUCE ROBINSON
NORMAN NORRIS
JASPER COFFIN

KIMBERLEY
MERVYN McCALLISTER – *Businessman*
SON: SIMON McCALLISTER

THE AUSTRALIA CAST
BENDIGO

THE KELLY FAMILY
KAMAROOKA, WHIPSTICK ROAD,
EAGLEHAWK
SEAN KELLY (1816)
SAM (1836) & ANGELICA (1834) KELLY
SIBLINGS: CAMIRA (1863) & CONNOR (1864)

THE DAVIES FAMILY
MYRTLE STREET
HUGH (1808) & SARAH (1811) DAVIES
SIBLINGS: LEWYS (1836) & GWYNETH (1839)

THE THOMAS FAMILY SENIOR
BRECON HOUSE, WARATAH STREET
BRYN (1812) & NELL (1814) THOMAS
SIBLINGS: OWEN (1837) & RHYS (1839)
ALINTA – The maid

THOMAS FAMILY JUNIOR
WATTLE STREET
OWEN (1837) & FREYJA (1837) THOMAS

THE ZHANG FAMILY
BRIDGE STREET, DAI GUM SAN
ZHANG WEI – *Grandfather*
ZHANG LONGWEI – *Father*
ZHANG LING – *Mother*
SONS: WEIMIN, YINGJIE, JIAN
DAUGHTER: QINYANG

RESIDENTS OF SANDHURST
MR & MRS BRUNSVOLD – *Emporium*
JETHRO TULLY – *Landlord Eureka Hotel*
ARCHIBALD WOODBURY – *Postmaster*

THE PROLOGUE *(April 1871–March 1872)*

Mr Rhys Thomas
Brecon Valley Mining Company
C/O Bendigo Post Office
Sandhurst
Victoria
South Australia

15ᵗʰ April 1871

My Dearest Rhys,
    We have arrived safely back home in Somerset and it is with sadness that I put pen to paper to let you know how dreadfully I am already missing you and how I regret not being able to stay in Bendigo longer, so that we might get to know each other better. During the brief period we spent together I admit to being blissfully happy, but the time was far too short to be able to decide on the course of a whole lifetime. Cruel fate has decreed that we should be parted too soon; I dearly miss your strong arms around me, those wicked twinkling eyes and your loving kisses. Please write, for I feel it is important that we should keep in touch, for who knows what the future may hold.
    My mind has been going over and over what happened between us and how I involved poor Gwyneth in our conspiracy, and I fear that she too holds a candle for you. I hope that we have not unintentionally hurt her, but I do think you need to be aware of her possible attachment to you, Rhys, so that you might deal with her sympathetically.
    I must close now, as I also promised to write

to *Gwyneth* and *Camira*, but please remember I am
thinking of you always, longing to hear from you
and praying that one day we might be together again.

Your loving sweetheart,
Aurora.

xx

Mrs Lucy Seymour
Bingham Manor
Sutton Bingham
Ivell
Somerset
England
Great Britain

1ˢᵗ October 1871

My Dearest Lucy,

I am the bearer of good news in that we have
dug down and discovered a kimberlite layer that
looks promising enough to make all three partners a
fortune. Please do not discuss this with my father,
as I will be writing to him separately, but I am in
a position to fund both a fine ranch and your voyage
over here with young Frankie if you are so disposed.
I have befriended a Dutch builder who has already
constructed some fine homesteads in the area and he's
drawing up plans for me.

I am writing to you in the hope that you have
had enough time to give my offer serious thought and
I trust that by now you may have come to a decision.

I have been unable to get you out of my head
since we spoke together at Ashleigh's funeral and I
know we could have a wonderfully adventurous life
together, here in South Africa, if you are prepared to
leave your family behind and give us a chance.

If you are willing to come, I would recommend that you wait until the autumn, perhaps September, when Frankie will be over three years old, the journey by sea less hazardous and you will be arriving here in time for our summer. My ranch may well be completed by then.

Please let me know as soon as you have decided. I eagerly await your decision.

I realise we don't need to marry, as you already have my surname and we could continue with that pretence, but if you do join me, I would like you to do me the honour of becoming my wife.

With fondest wishes,
Rupert
xx

Rupert Seymour Esq
The Hopetown Hopefuls
C/O Hopetown Post Office
Hopetown
Pixley ka Seme
Thembelihle
Northern Cape Province
South Africa

14ᵗʰ March 1872

My Dear Rupert,
I have given your offer a great deal of heartfelt consideration and I am delighted to tell you that I am inclined to accept your proposal of marriage. I am honoured that you think I will make a worthy wife for you and thrilled that you wish to be a father to little Frankie. I believe it will be sensible for us to be betrothed as soon as I arrive, but not to make marriage plans until I am sure I will be able to

accept this new life and that both Frankie and I are happy with this arrangement.

You are quite right, my dear, it will be the making of the boy and I can't help but feel excited at the prospect of the journey to an unknown land and to a very different lifestyle.

I am, however, loath to break it to my family and especially reluctant to tell poor Clara. I think I will simply inform them I am going on a visit in September; in this way, I can disclose it to them gently over time.

I will start preparations for our emigration and eagerly await receipt of the tickets.

With fondest love,

Lucy

xx

CHAPTER ONE *(March 1872)*

THE DECISION IS MADE

Lucy Seymour posts the letter at the post office in Princes Street, and smiles, quite amazed she has summoned up the audacity to accept Rupert's suggestion to emigrate to South Africa. Since Ashleigh's death, she's been unhappy at Bingham Manor, while it's just her and her in-laws; they no longer entertain and, understandably, both of them have been dejected and defeated since their son's murder. With Rupert abroad in South Africa prospecting, they feel the loss of both their boys. Helen is constantly in a fog of laudanum and the colonel can't even summon up the energy to play with his only grandson. She shouldn't desert them, but her life is so dull now, and she wants so much more for young Frankie.

One of the first things she plans to do is pop into Whitby and Son's to see if they have any picture books about South African poisonous snakes, scorpions and spiders. She has to be sure Frankie is aware of the dangers.

The wind ruffles her skirts as she crosses the road and makes towards the ivy-clad shop, with its seven ornate pillars and four elegant plate glass windows, displaying a vast selection of books and other produce. She locates the nature section and searches for 'reptiles' and 'South Africa'. Mr Whitby comes to assist her. "May I help you, madam?"

"Yes please, Mr Whitby. I'm looking for an illustrated book about venomous snakes, spiders and scorpions, particularly with regard to South Africa, as I'm going there with my young son and I want him to be able to identify any creature that may harm him."

"I don't have a book particularly pertaining to South Africa but this comprehensive study, *Venomous Creatures*, published by A & C Black, may be of help to you. It does have good illustrations and it also shows their habitats and in which country they're to be found."

She takes the volume from him and glances through it, recoiling at the images of snakes' fangs and tarantula spiders. "That will do very well. Thank you, Mr Whitby."

She pays him and he wraps the book in brown paper for her. "I hope you both enjoy your visit and that you don't have any encounters with the subjects of your book."

She smiles. "Me too."

Outside the shop she turns towards the bootmaker's shop, noting that Ivell is particularly quiet today, probably owing to the smallpox scare. The doorbell jangles and the owner looks up. "Good morning, madam. How may I help you today?"

"Hello, Mr Summers. I'd like to be measured for a new pair of waterproof leather boots, please."

"Certainly, madam. Please take a seat. I'm sure you'll have heard that we make our boots of specially prepared, anhydrous leather to defy all weather conditions."

"That's exactly what I'm looking for, as I'm going on an expedition across the Great Karoo in South Africa."

"Well, my dear, that's very ambitious of you, and I can assure you that these handmade boots won't let you down."

He brings the footrest and sits down in front of her, before undoing her buttoned shoes and removing them. He quickly and efficiently takes all her measurements. Then she follows him to the counter while he gets his order book and writes down her address details. "How soon will you be needing these, Mrs Seymour?"

"Oh no rush, Mr Summers. I don't plan to leave until September. I thought I'd give you plenty of time. I know how busy you are."

"That's very considerate of you. If you give us a couple of weeks, then next time you're in town, they should be ready." He slides his pencil behind his ear.

"Can you give me some idea of how much they'll cost?"

She watches him as he does the mental arithmetic. "They should be about ten shillings and sixpence."

"Thank you very much, Mr Summers."

"Not at all; my pleasure. Thank you, madam."

She leaves the shop and climbs back into the gig. Rather than turn Dolly around in the street, she continues up to Fiveways to see the new, twenty-bed, hospital completed in January. An impressive building, the Kingston tollgate end of the structure has an open galleried turret with the main hospital development constructed behind it. The completed work sits well in the land allocated for it and she looks forward to telling her parents about it when she calls in to see them, before returning to Bingham Manor.

She hopes she can pluck up the courage to tell them the truncated version of her plans. They'll not think well of her, if they suspect her of contemplating the double sin of marriage with her brother-in-law, and her friend Clara's ex-fiancé, but will they believe that she only intends to visit and then return after a few weeks? They probably have no real conception of the distances involved.

When she arrives at Home Farm, she finds her sister, Beatrice, hanging out washing with the benefit of the gusty March wind. "Bunny!" She waves and her sister drops some wet bloomers into the wash basket and runs to embrace her.

"It's been ages, Lucy. What have you been doing that's kept you from us?"

"It's only been about a month, but it's lovely to see you. How is everyone?"

"We're all well. Malachi and Rosa have thankfully put behind them the trauma of his stay in Shepton Mallett Prison and the children are all more settled again now. Although it's taken some time for young Daisy to let our brother out of her sight without fretting."

"Ah, bless her."

"Come on, let's go in and find Ma."

They walk, arm in arm, through the scullery and into the farmhouse kitchen. "Ma, guess who I've found."

Their mother turns to them from her pastry rolling, dressed in her familiar blue gown protected with a crisp white corn-starched pinafore. "Lucy! What a lovely surprise! How are you? Where's Frankie?"

"Sorry, Ma. I didn't bring him this time, as I've been into town. I left him with Mercy."

"Oh! Never mind, it's so good to see you, I forgive you." Her mother kisses her cheek and hugs her, holding out her floury hands. Then she returns to laying the rolled pastry over the meat-filled pie and trimming it with a knife.

4

Lucy tells them, "I've just been up to Fiveways to see the new hospital. It looks very smart."

"And in the nick of time for the smallpox epidemic now rife in the town. I hear they've been busy vaccinating folk with Mr Jenner's vaccine," says Bunny.

Their mother shrugs her shoulders and scoffs, "I don't know why he gets all the glory. He may be responsible for producing the standardised vaccine, but old farmer Jesty from Upbury Farm in Yetminster had the idea, well before Jenner did." She washes her hands and dries them in her pinafore.

"Really, Ma?"

"Yes, it's been known for years in our farming community that milkmaids who get cowpox, from handling cow's udders, are then immune to smallpox. These folk can nurse smallpox victims without any fear of catching the disease. So when there was a smallpox scare, Farmer Jesty took the bull by the horns, so to speak, and took his family to an infected cow at a farm in Chetnole and, using a darning needle, he removed some pustular material from the cow and transferred it, by scratching the arms of his family members with the infected needle. They were thereafter immune to both diseases."

Lucy's impressed. "Well I never! Who'd have thought we'd an innovator so close to home?"

Their mother shakes her head. "He was pilloried by his neighbours though, poor man. For introducing animal disease into people, he was called inhuman and couldn't go to market without being jeered and hooted at."

Bunny says, "Well, I suppose he took a huge risk, didn't he?"

Their mother agrees, "Yes, but for him it was a calculated risk, which obviously paid off. Although I do believe his poor wife had a bad reaction, before recovering completely."

Lucy says, "Well, Ivell was much quieter today, presumably due to this epidemic."

Footsteps are heard approaching the back door. "That must be your pa and Jacob. Put the kettle on to boil, pet." Bunny does so, while Lucy gets the cups and saucers from the dresser.

Their mother puts her pies into the oven, clears the table of all her baking equipment and wipes it down with a damp cloth. They can hear the water pump and Jacob and his father laughing, as they remove their muddy boots. Then the door opens, and her father pops his head around it. "Thought it was your gig we could see from across the fields. How are you, lassie?"

"I'm well, Pa. How are the both of you?"

"We're in good spirits, thanks. We've just been muck spreading, so please excuse the rich aroma wafting around us."

"It doesn't bother me, Pa. I'm used to it."

They each look fit and well with rosy cheeks from working in all weathers. Her pa wears his old loose brown trousers with a matching waistcoat and jacket, and Jacob has on a pair of blue coloured overalls under his jacket. They each give her a peck on the cheek. She'll remember the familiar soft brush of their short beards. Her heart aches; she'll miss them all so much.

She asks them, "Where's Malachi?"

"He's gone over to his cottage to fetch the Peruvian guano he purchased the other day for us. He'll be here shortly."

Around the kitchen table they are enjoying tea and apple cake when, out of the blue, her pa asks her, "How are you doing, Lucy, over at Bingham Manor, now it's just you, the boy and the in-laws?"

"It's not at all what I'd envisaged, Pa, when I married Ashleigh, to be left so soon with young Frankie and no future to look forward to."

He wipes some crumbs from his mouth with the back of his hand. "Then you must take the initiative and make yourself another future. These things don't happen by chance, you know, love. You're still a young woman with your whole life ahead of you; too young to be a widow at any rate."

This is her cue. She hesitates. "Well... I was thinking of going on an adventure with Frankie."

"Really?" says Bunny.

"Well, yes. I was contemplating going to see Ashleigh's brother, Rupert, in South Africa. It seems he's been quite successful and is already building a homestead over there and he's invited us to visit him."

"Oh my! That sounds incredible," exclaims her sister.

"Incredibly dangerous," says her mother with a concerned frown. "Aren't you worried about young Frankie, running around with all those poisonous spiders and snakes and the like?"

"Yes, Ma. I'm concerned, but the natives have children over there, and they all survive. I'd simply be vigilant, if I did decide to go."

They hear Malachi in the outhouse, removing his boots, and Lucy gets up to greet him. He walks in and the room suddenly seems smaller.

"Hello, Sis. To what do we owe this honour?"

She grins. "I had to go into town, and I thought I'd pop in to see you all, on my way home."

"She has some news, Mal," says Jacob.

"Oh yes, and what's happened that's so exciting over at Bingham Manor?"

"Nothing's happened at Bingham Manor, for ages," she replies, "but Frankie and I have been invited to visit Rupert in South Africa."

"Well, I'm blessed! I hope you're not going to decline. I think it'll be the making of young Frankie and what an experience for both of you. Don't hesitate, Lucy. Tell your brother-in-law you accept and be done with it."

"You think so, Mal?"

"Most definitely. I'm envious. If I didn't have responsibilities here on the farm and a large family to care for, who I love beyond all else, I'd be off like a shot."

Jacob drinks his tea and then uncharacteristically adds his opinion to the conversation.

"I think so too, Lucy. There's nothing for you anymore at Bingham Manor, your life will be an excess of tedium. Take a chance and grab this opportunity. Who knows what good may come of it?"

"But we'll miss you so, darling," says her mother.

"It's only for a few weeks, Beth. What harm can it do?" says her father.

She blushes guiltily but doesn't disillusion them.

Now that she's made the decision, the days seem to pass more quickly into summer. Then in June, she receives a letter from Rupert. She picks it up from the salver in the hall and takes it upstairs to her room to read in peace.

Mrs Lucy Seymour
Bingham Manor
Sutton Bingham
Ivell
Somerset
England
Great Britain

14th March 1872

My Dearest Lucy,

I've taken the plunge and organised passage for both you and Frankie for 18th September on the Union Company's Mail Steamer, 'Syria', departing from Southampton and disembarking in East London. I hope that you're still keen to come, as your ticket cost me thirty-eight pounds, seventeen shillings and Frankie's was seven pounds three shillings, so no small sum at forty-six pounds in total. They brag that their route is the quickest passage out on record, with '1,000 miles' cruise along the Atlantic coast and a Cobb and Company Concord stagecoach trip through Kaffir-land'. They will leave on the first tide and so I suggest you arrive in Southampton the previous night, because it will be an early start. I'm so thrilled you've decided to come.

Our ranch is coming along well. Johan has some Tswana boys under his charge, and we've sited the homestead on a perfectly sized, raised plateau in the curve formed by the river. I think you'll be impressed. Jack Penberthy also has chosen his site further along and so we'll be neighbours.

How is young Frankie? Is he excited? Have you told anyone else yet of your plans? Please forgive me, but this missive must be brief, as I'm in haste to *catch the mail coach. I am, however, left here eagerly anticipating our reunion.*

With fondest regards,
Rupert

She's lost in thought – *It's really happening. I can't possibly go back on it, now that he's bought our tickets. Should I tell the colonel and Helen, or should I ask Rupert to break it to them? It probably won't matter much to them either way. Now that they're both so self-absorbed, they'll hardly notice we're gone.*

In July she invites Louisa, Rosa and Clara to take tea with her, knowing she'll have to tell them her plans, now she has the tickets and everything's arranged, but what will they think of her?

She hears the carriage arriving and goes outside to greet them.

"My dears, how lovely to see you all. Thank you for bringing Clara with you, Louisa."

"It's no trouble at all. Her papa delivered her to Alvington, enabling us all to set off together from there."

There's much kissing of cheeks and hugging. "Come on through. I thought we might sit outside, as the weather's so conducive. Robson has organised the cushions and parasol for us, like he did on your last visit."

The ladies follow her, via the drawing room, out through the French doors, onto the terrace, and into the sunshine. They all wear sun bonnets, but endeavour to sit in the shade of the parasol, to protect themselves from the scorching mid-summer heat. Bees are buzzing among the flowers and buzzards soar on the thermals above them, occasionally calling to each other with their characteristic soulful cry. Every now and then there's a plop sound from the water, as a fish jumps out for a damsel fly or some such tasty morsel. The scene is extraordinarily peaceful.

Once they're settled Lucy feels compelled to confess her plans. "I'm so pleased to have you all here together, as I've something important to tell you."

"Why the worried frown, Lucy? Surely it can't be that bad?" says Louisa, concerned.

She smiles at her friend. "No, it's not at all bad, but I'm afraid we'll miss each other very much."

"Why? Where are you going?" asks Clara.

"I've been invited to take Frankie to visit his uncle in South Africa. Apparently, he's completed the building of his ranch and believes the lad will benefit from the adventure, rather than being cosseted at home with just Mercy, myself and his grandparents." She lowers her voice. "Rupert knows how they've both gone downhill, since Ashleigh's murder, and thinks it will do both Frankie and me good to get away for a while."

"I agree with him, Lucy, darling," says Louisa. "You've gone through so much, you deserve a holiday and what an experience for both of you, to see all the amazing African wild animals and fabulous birds that we don't have here. Frankie's old enough now to remember it all too."

Lucy looks at Clara's wistful expression. *She's thinking that it should be her going*, but Clara looks up and smiles at her. "I think you're very brave, Lucy. I didn't have the courage to leave my dear papa, and commit to such a life, but I'd love to see where he lives and how he is. I did love him so." Tears fill her eyes.

Lucy feels her friend's pain and her own guilt

rips through her. She takes Clara's hand in hers. "Well, at least I'll be able to write to you and report back on his progress and describe his living and working conditions while I'm there."

"Yes, that's some consolation." She smiles.

Lucy sighs, relieved to have the blessings of both her family and friends and able to look forward to her adventure without feeling so culpable.

Rosa has been quiet, because Malachi told her about the trip, but she thought it only right that Lucy should be the one to break the news. Then she asks her, "How long will you be staying, Lucy?"

"Umm… I'm not entirely sure at present, but several weeks, as it takes such a long time to get there." She blushes, guilt flooding back for deceiving her friends once more.

"When are you planning to leave?" asks Rosa.

"Not until September, so that we'll arrive in their summertime." She changes the subject. "I'll just go and ring for our refreshments to be served."

Louisa looks at Clara's regretful expression. "Please don't be sad, my dear. It simply wasn't meant to be. You know very well that kind of life wouldn't have suited you and I'm certain that the good Lord has other plans for your future happiness."

"I do hope so, Lou Lou. I really don't want to end up an old maid. I was thirty-eight in April, so time's running out and, like the rest of you, I too would like to have children one day. I'm quite sure my papa would make a wonderful grandpa."

"He definitely would," says Louisa, "and you'd make a wonderful mother, Clara."

Rosa suddenly blurts out, "I actually know the perfect person for you. He's shy with women, but he's a hard worker and he's kind and considerate; you could do a lot worse."

Clara smiles self-consciously. "Who are you talking about, Rosa?"

"Lucy's brother, Jacob. I can see you two being together until you're old and grey, and he'd make a good and gentle father. I've seen him with tiny orphaned new-born lambs, wrapping them in oilskin and bottle feeding them, sometimes even keeping them warm in the oven, when they're near death from the cold. He's nice looking too, not quite as tall as my Malachi, but he has strong lean arms from farming, and they'd keep you safe from harm."

"I don't know what to say. I hardly know him, Rosa."

"That's easily remedied. Leave it to me."

"No… no please don't embarrass me, or him, by trying to matchmake. I'd far prefer a man to show his genuine interest than have it thrust upon him."

"Don't be silly, Clara. If time is of the essence, there's no harm in sewing the seed of an idea into his mind. Some men simply require a little nudge in the right direction."

Louisa encourages her. "Come, Clara, you can trust Rosa to be diplomatic."

"Oh, very well then, but please make it seem as if I have no clue as to what you're doing."

"Like I say, just leave it to me. I've no idea how long it will take for the seed to germinate, but I'm sure it will flourish in the end." She grins, the light of mischief in her eyes.

Once back at Alvington, and after Clara has left with her papa, Louisa and Rosa begin to plan a *bon voyage* party for Lucy at the manor.

"We must include the Fairways, and all of Lucy's family, so it'll be an ideal opportunity to begin our matchmaking plans," says Rosa.

"We ought to have some music, so they'll be obliged to dance together too," suggests Louisa. "We could ask the string section of the Ivell Town Band if they'd play for us, like they did for our Summer Ball. Do you remember?"

"I do and they played beautifully. It was just a shame that Lord Dryer invited that villain, Nathan Meakins, allowing him the opportunity to assault poor Becky and ruin everything."

"Joshua has always felt guilty that he didn't manage to protect his little sister from that trauma. But since the rogue's untimely demise, there's no fear of that this time. Besides, it'll be just close friends and I'm sure the band will be pleased to oblige Lord Dryer, for a generous fee."

Rosa smiles at Louisa, knowing she'll have to persuade her husband that the musicians will be a worthy investment. "When do you plan to hold the party, milady?"

"I don't know... Aurora's returning from France in time for her birthday. It's her twenty-first on the twelfth of September and we'd planned to have a party that evening to celebrate that milestone, so perhaps we could combine the events. I just hope that Aurora won't mind sharing the limelight."

CHAPTER TWO *(August–September 1872)*

IMPERIAL WORKS AND WORTHY KINGS

Violet's young grandson, Jem, is finding it hard to contain his excitement. Not only is his sixth birthday coming up on Monday the twelfth of August, but there's a huge celebration planned for Saturday the tenth to mark the completion of the construction of the first two arms of the harbour breakwater.

Yesterday, after school, they'd strolled together along Hamm beach and seen fifteen huge, five-mast, broadside ironclad ships already congregating in the harbour, and with Matthew's eyeglass, they could just make out the names of *Achilles, Agincourt, Hercules* and *Minotaur* along with the Channel and Reserve Squadrons. Tomorrow Albert Edward, Prince of Wales, is going to arrive, and Jem will be among the children chosen to sing for him. No wonder he's so full of beans.

Becky, her daughter, is expecting a second, long-awaited, happy event and for the sake of propriety she's decided it sensible to remain behind, working at her sewing in Fortune's Corner. Violet has, therefore, volunteered to accompany her grandson, as she too is excited to see this wonderful celebration, after the long years of hard work and the ups and downs of the construction.

She shudders, recalling the day when one of the piles gave way and an engine, four wagons and eight men were plunged into the sea. Amazingly, George

Evans and his stoker were able to jump free, but the other poor fellows were crushed under the stones and drowned. Unfortunately, in the early days while it was still under construction many vessels collided and foundered against the huge stone arms and metal pinning of the undersea wall. Their sad loss was part of the price paid to form this magnificent harbour of refuge, the largest man-made harbour in the world and a source of pride to her fellow Portlanders.

Today, they're both dressed in their Sunday best, as she takes Jem's hand and they walk down from Fortune's Corner to Castletown. Jem skips along the high pavement, as they mingle with more Portlanders, all travelling in the same direction. When they turn in to Castletown, Jem cries out with glee, "Look, Granny, he's coming; see all the sailors saluting His Royal Highness."

She notices the royal yacht *Victoria and Albert* entering the harbour and the various ships companies giving the royal salute, but she's shocked by the number of kimberlins, many dressed in their finery, filling the street, pavements and even the small beach.

"Please excuse me," she cries, unnerved, squeezing through the mass of people outside the chandlers. They hurry on, battling through the crush. She must get Jem to his teacher in time, so he too can witness His Royal Highness laying the final commemorative stone.

Finally, she can let go of his hand and Jem runs to join his friends, converging and settling on the grassy bank behind the Portland Artillery Band, who are ready and standing to attention in front of the Admiralty Offices.

At the appointed time, Prince Albert and the other dignitaries assemble on a large platform, specially erected for the occasion, at the end of the breakwater. When the ceremony is concluded, the stone is lowered through an aperture in the platform and everyone on land and sea cheers, as they witness the memorial stone being lowered into place. Animated chattering breaks out among the onlookers, as the royal barge conveys the Prince of Wales to the shore and the crowds proudly flutter their flags.

When he finally disembarks, the noise of the multitude cheering almost covers the sound of the band striking up, but they all calm down and listen and watch, as the dignitaries greet His Royal Highness.

Violet smiles encouragement to Jem, as he sings 'God Bless the Prince of Wales' along with his friends. When the children have finished their tribute, they all peel away back to their parents and Jem comes running to her.

"Did you like the singing, Granny?"

"Of course I did. It was beautiful." She smiles, for only innocent children could sound so pure.

The ceremony concluded, they turn to retrace their steps, threading through the kimberlins, Violet hanging tightly on to Jem with one hand and her reticule with the other. They pass the Jolly Sailor and then the Castle Inn. The drunken men hanging around the dockside pub remind her of something she's tried to bury for forty years and she trembles. She can never pass this place without feeling the chill damp September air swirling around her, smelling again the drunken sailors' filthy masculine body odour, their stale, smoky beery breath, and remembering their huge greasy hands pawing her body as they tried to ravish her. She pushes the haunting thoughts, and the dark shadows of what she did to defend herself, from her mind. Today is a celebration and she must keep smiling for Jem's sake.

A few days later Jem's father, Ben Stone, is reading the *Dorset County Chronicle* report of the event, while Jem's mother, Becky, is doing some ironing.

"It says here that the arrival of the Prince of Wales to declare the work completed was one of the greatest celebrations Dorset has ever beheld. Apparently, the commemorative stone slab is inscribed, '*From this spot on the 25th July 1849 His Royal Highness Prince Albert, Consort of Queen Victoria, sank the first stone of this breakwater. Upon the same spot Albert Edward, Prince of Wales, on the 10th August 1872, laid this last stone and declared the work complete. These are imperial works and worthy Kings.*'"

"Do you remember the first ceremony, Ben? How we kids sneaked under the platform and got soaked from the spray?" Becky giggles.

"I remember it well, my love. You were only wearing a thin summer frock and when you were drenched… well let's just say I realised you were growing up." He grins at her.

Jem looks up from his drawing book. "Were you and Papa naughty then, Mama?"

"Not really, darling. Lots of us kids gathered there, and no one got into trouble for it. We were just nimbler than the grown-ups."

Ben continues to read from his newspaper, "The east face is inscribed: '*James Meadow Rendel designed this work and directed its execution till his death in 1856. John Coode, the resident engineer from its commencement, then succeeded to its charge and completed it. J. T. Leather was the contractor for the work.*' Those families must be so proud of their achievement, as should all the poor convicts who laboured under them and hewed nearly six million tons of stone, over the last twenty-three years."

Becky spits on her iron to test its heat before continuing to iron Jem's school trousers, then she returns it to the range and continues with its twin.

Ben tells her, "Your pa and I enjoyed watching the ceremony from the boat. We slid in among those huge ironclads and observed the royal yacht's arrival and we saluted, as the Prince of Wales passed us by. Not that he'd have noticed us, but it was only respectful to do so."

"You never told us that!"

"No, well, we were playing hooky. We should have been working on Mr Atwool's lerret."

"Hmm, I wonder if Ma knows?"

"You'd both have only worried about us, in amongst those huge vessels, if we'd told you. But we had great fun."

Jem interrupts them. "Pa, do you like my picture?" He shows his drawing book to his father.

"Wow, Jem! That's very impressive. Well done! Show your mama." He turns to Becky. "Look, Becky, he's drawn a beautiful galleon."

His mother smiles. "That's perfect, darling." She looks back at Ben. "I told you he was really good at drawing."

"Well, I didn't think he was that good! He's only six and that's extremely detailed."

"Adam says I have to practice my drawing, if I want to be a stonemason, Pa."

"Oh, does he now? And there's me thinking you'd be joining me and your grandpa in the boat-building business, when you're old enough."

Jem looks uncomfortable. "Well, it'll be good to practice for that too, Pa."

"Hmm!" says Ben, frowning.

Becky wipes her brow. The heat from the iron and the range is too much on a summer day, in her condition. "I've had enough of this, Ben. I'll do the rest tomorrow."

"Why don't you get our Cassie to come and give you a hand? I'm sure she'd be glad of the pocket money. I'll ask Uncle Eddie if he has any objection when I see him later."

Back at Bingham Manor, Lucy selects her wardrobe for her trip. She's broken the news to Helen and the colonel, and they seem to be so pleased that Rupert will have visitors from home, that the loss of Lucy and their grandson pales to insignificance. This is a good thing for her, but of course they don't know that she doesn't intend to return to them.

As she fills the huge trunks with both Frankie's and her essentials, mixing them together in case one should go astray during the journey, a shiver of unease runs through her. *What if I'm making a huge mistake? Without my family's support, I'll be Frankie's only protector. If Rupert and I turn out to be incompatible, what then? I've no personal funds to be able to return home to Somerset.* She carefully folds the cream silk shawl that her mother crocheted for her twenty-first birthday, then closes the trunk and pulls back her shoulders. *We'll just have to take one step at a time.* It's a huge gamble but she knows she must follow this path into the unknown.

On Thursday the twelfth of September, Louisa has invited Lucy to Alvington Manor to celebrate Aurora's birthday. Robshaw delivers her to the manor and will return at midnight to collect her. She's dressed in a purple satin evening gown, trimmed with four scalloped flounces over the bustle, each edged with black lace ribbon, which also decorate the low-cut bodice, in deference to her late husband. Gladys has pinned up her ringlets into a coiffure with purple silk flowers, dangling cream lace and dainty black silk ribbons. This will be the last time she'll wear this ensemble; she'll have no need of it where she's going.

She feels self-conscious, all dressed up to the nines without an escort. It's at times like this she longs for another relationship, someone else to support and care for her.

The manor looks beautiful in the moonlight, with the flaxen torches lining the driveway and she's excited to see all her friends and family. She hears violin music wafting on the night air and recognises it as 'Tales from the Vienna Woods' by Johann Strauss II, one of her favourite melodies. Robshaw hands her down from the carriage and she enters the manor tentatively. Emily, the housemaid, takes her wrap and gloves and a footman, whom she doesn't recognise, shows her to the ballroom.

Joshua and Louisa greet her at the entrance. "Ah, Lucy, welcome!"

The ballroom is festooned with floral arrangements and suspended banners saying, 'Happy Birthday, Aurora', but also, to her surprise, 'Bon Voyage, Lucy'.

She smiles. "How kind of you both. I am overwhelmed."

"Well, we couldn't let you sail off into the African sunset, without marking it in some way."

Her nieces and nephew, Eli, come rushing over to welcome her. "Hello, Auntie Lucy, happy bon voyage to you," says Daisy. She gives them all a hug. "Thank you, darlings, I will miss you very much." They run off back to join Lydia May in their designated area for the younger ones, with Nanny Beth in charge.

She greets her own family members gathered together in one corner of the room. Then Aurora and Bunny come to draw her into their group with Luke, Edwin and Toby at their table. Once seated, she draws out her gift for Aurora from her reticule.

"Happy Birthday, Aurora. I hope you like it."

Aurora seems to glow, with the light from the wall sconces gleaming in her red hair and shimmering over her deep blue gown. Lucy watches her, as she unwraps her gift and exclaims in delight. She shows the others. "Look, it's a copy of *Middlemarch*, by George Eliot. How thoughtful, Lucy. I love it." She kisses her cheek. "Has Mama given you our present yet?"

"It isn't *my* birthday, Rora."

Louisa overhears her comment as she joins them. "No, but we thought you might like this for your journey." She hands Lucy a parcel and she carefully removes the wrapping.

"Oh my! How wonderful... I've heard this is an amazing tale. Look, everyone, it's *Les Misérables* by Victor Hugo... I'll certainly relish reading this on the ship, while Frankie's sleeping. How kind of you... Thank you so much. How strange we both chose books."

Louisa says, "Despite it being achingly sad, I really enjoyed that story and so did Joshua."

Lucy takes her hand. "Thank you. I'm sure I will too." She spots the footman showing Mr Fairway and Clara into the ballroom. "I was going to ask you, Louisa, who's the new footman? I was surprised not to see Michael."

"He's Edgar Parish and his family live in Cerne Abbas. He's replaced Michael Porter who's now retired, as has Gareth, who has, unfortunately for us, enticed Mrs Abbott away with him. Who knew they were so close?"

She's curious. "Where has Gareth gone with Mrs Abbott?"

"He's happily returned to the bosom of his family in Wales, with Mrs Abbott on his arm. It's quite romantic really, but we'll sorely miss them both. Michael and Mary Porter will be moving, as soon as they can find accommodation near to their daughters, who are in service just outside Exeter. So, Ruth Proctor has been elevated to the position of housekeeper and our new steward is Harvey Woodford over there." She nods towards Mr Woodford, currently in earnest conversation with Miss Tweedy.

Lucy is thoughtful. "So that must mean there'll be an estate cottage available soon."

"Yes, there will be, as both Harvey and Edgar are living in."

The musicians begin playing another Strauss waltz and people are soon dancing. Louisa says, "Please excuse me, I must find Joshua, as I'm longing to dance with him again," and she goes off to search for him.

Malachi arrives at her table and holding out his hand most politely, he asks his sister if she will dance with him and she is moved by his kindness. She smiles at Rosa across the room, for sharing her husband for a few precious moments, aware of people watching the brother and sister making a pretty partnership on the dancefloor.

Then he whispers in her ear, "I know your husband was killed due to his indebtedness, so I want you to accept the purse I won at my last boxing match. It's just a few guineas that I want you to keep hidden for emergencies."

He hands her the purse and she notes its weight. It's no small sum. "But you, Rosa and the children will need that money."

"Please don't argue with me, Lucy. It'll put my mind at rest, when you're so far away from us. We have all the family around us here, offering their support and I know that Lord Dryer will always look out for us; whereas you'll be unescorted, with a young child, until you reach Rupert and even then, I want you to have options. Besides, I've discussed it with Rosa, and she's in full agreement."

"Thank you, Malachi. I must admit, it's already eased my worries, with Frankie depending on me."

"It's my pleasure. Anyway, with luck, I'll probably win some more at the next St Leonard's Day Fayre in November."

She smiles at his renewed confidence, and enjoys the security of her brother's strength, held in his reliable muscular arms and expertly guided across the ballroom. He and Rosa are so kind to do that for her and Frankie. She'll miss them so much.

The piece concluded, they return to their table and Rosa sits down with them. Rosa wears her best, rose pink satin gown and looks radiant as always. Malachi can't take his eyes off her; at least one of her siblings has found true happiness.

"Malachi has just given me his purse. Thank you, Rosa, for agreeing to it. I promise I'll do my best not to touch it and bring it back on my return, but it does mean that I'm not totally reliant on Rupert, so I'm very grateful."

"You're most welcome, Lucy. It's also given us more confidence in your safe passage and return to us." She hugs her.

Luke and Aurora go off together for the Gay Gordons. Then Louisa returns, accompanied by Clara. Louisa's rich burgundy-coloured silk gown and Clara's ball gown of lavender satin, with gold trimmings, combine beautifully together. Everyone appears to be sparkling with elegance and it's most uplifting to behold.

Lucy spends the rest of the evening seated with Clara, the two unpartnered ladies. The music becomes louder as the evening progresses, along with the buzz of chatter. Luke comes over to say something to Clara, she can't hear what, as they're speaking confidentially and the music overlays it, but she notices, across the room, Aurora's frown.

Aurora is offended that Luke should be whispering with his boss's daughter, Clara. After all, she's so much older than he is, but they both seem to have a close bond. She watches Clara laughing with a twinkle in her eye and Luke smiling. *They must be flirting like this all the time, when he's supposed to be working. How could he humiliate me like this, in front of all my friends and family and on my birthday too!*

Luke looks up and sees her staring at him. He says something to Clara, bows and rushes to join Aurora. "What's wrong, Rora? You look cross."

"Is this how you and Clara behave every day, when you're supposed to be at work?"

"Of course not, I was simply telling her that she ought to be dancing with Jacob. Elsie has set her cap at him and if she's too reticent it will be too late."

"Well you certainly looked to be overfamiliar to me."

"Rora, please don't get on your high horse. We're friends who know each other well from being thrown together every day, but we don't have those kinds of feelings for each other. How could I, when I only have eyes for you."

"High horse? Is that what you think of me?"

"I just mean there's no need to get upset. Come on, let's dance."

Aurora takes his hand, and for form's sake, she sails onto the dance floor, but she has no intention of forgetting how relaxed and familiar he looked with Clara.

Clara and Lucy are sitting chatting together like old maids, when Malachi and Jacob approach the table. Malachi simply holds out his hand for his sister to join him, but Jacob is more formal. "Clara, will you do me the honour of accepting this dance with me?" He bows his head respectfully.

"It will be my pleasure, Jacob," says Clara, smiling and blushing.

She puts her small hand in his. It feels almost dainty, compared with his larger manly one. Her body is drawn close to him in the waltz and she can feel the heat of him against her and realises just how much she has missed this physical contact with a man. He smiles down at her and she smiles back. "Thank you for asking me to dance, Jacob. I've missed this, since Rupert left me."

"He was a fool to risk losing you, Clara. He didn't know how lucky he was."

She smiles. *Is he simply being courteous, or does he really feel this way?* "Thank you, kind sir."

Jacob flushes. "I've admired you from afar for many years, Clara, but you and our Lucy were both taken with those flashy Seymour boys and no one else got a look in."

"Well, times have changed, and we've each paid the price of our foolishness; both sitting on the edge of the dance floor like two old maids."

"Never say that, Clara. You're two charming women with your whole lives still ahead of you and although I'm just a simple shepherd, I'd very much like to be a part of yours, if you'll allow it."

Clara looks up at him, a handsome six-foot-tall man, with kind sparkling blue eyes, healthy tanned skin, a gentle smile and soft full lips and then he kisses her in full view of everyone.

She pulls away, the heat of passion running through her. "Please, Jacob, not here in front of our parents."

He replies breathlessly. "Then say you'll meet me tomorrow. I can't wait any longer to show you how I really feel."

Her heart races. "All right. Meet me at the cottage at Ninesprings. We can take afternoon tea there."

"That would be wonderful. I'll be there at three of the clock, and we can walk through the woodland, under the falling autumn leaves."

She smiles again. "You're a romantic, Jacob Warren."

"Of course, and a dreamer and now I'll be able to dream of our future together."

This may seem to be going far too fast, but Clara had given up on love and now it's music to her ears. They dance together for the rest of the evening, much to the delight of the successful matchmakers.

The following day is cool but sunny and Clara puts on a fetching purple walking costume and her sturdy buttoned boots to climb the hill through the trees to the little cottage. As she approaches, she sees Jacob standing on the wooden bridge over the stream, staring down the pathway. When he recognises her, his face lights up and she knows she has made the right decision.

He rushes to meet her and hands her a bunch of chrysanthemums that he'd hidden behind his back. "They're from our garden. I hope you like them?"

"Of course, I love all flowers. That's very thoughtful of you, Jacob. Thank you. I hope your ma didn't mind you stealing them from her."

"Oh no, I didn't steal them. I grew them. Besides, it was Ma's idea."

They walk up to the cottage holding hands and he draws out a seat for her to sit down. A young maid comes to take their order.

He asks her, "Would you like a pot of tea and a selection of sandwiches and cakes?"

"Yes please. That would be lovely."

The maid goes off to prepare their order. The birds are singing in the trees all around them and the little stream gurgles merrily, as it splashes over the rocks and down the hill. A chaffinch pecks for crumbs at their feet, while a robin comes to the next table, bobs and flies back up into the branches.

"This is such a tranquil place. It was a good choice for our first meeting, Clara."

"I love it here, and they serve such delicious food too."

"Do you like to cook, Clara?"

"I do and I especially like to cook freshly grown vegetables." She smiles.

"My pa taught me to grow vegetables and fruit bushes when I was a nipper and there's nothing like picking your own gooseberries or rhubarb. Ma makes some fabulous pies with our berries."

"I know, I've tasted her cooking many times. I've had no choice but to learn to cook for my pa, since my ma died when I was born."

"That's so sad." Jacob squeezes her hand.

"I know no different. Pa and I are so close now, which was why I couldn't leave him to go with Rupert and I was hurt that he'd expect it of me."

"I'll never want to leave you, Clara. In fact, I've had an idea. If all goes well with us, and I know it's early days, but Lucy told me there's a cottage coming available up on Camp Road, when Michael Porter and his wife find a place nearer to their daughters, and I could ask for it. I'm entitled, because I work on the estate and then maybe, when you feel ready, we could get wed and you'd still be near enough to your papa. What do you think?"

"Is that a proposal, Jacob Warren?"

He flushes crimson. "Is it too soon?"

"It is a bit, but nevertheless I rather like the idea." She grins at him and he kisses her surreptitiously, before being interrupted by the waitress.

Finally, the big day arrives, and Lucy and Frankie set off with all their belongings for their onward trip to South Africa. They've been dropped off at Penn Mill Railway Station and are now on the train taking them to Dorchester, where they'll change for the Southampton train. Frankie was thrilled to see the huge locomotive puffing and panting into the station and fidgets with excitement in their carriage compartment. Lucy tries to entertain him with the pictures in a sixpenny toy book, but he climbs up onto the seat to look out of the windows, delighted with the views of the farm animals, as they rush by with the smoke and steam billowing alongside them.

Robshaw handed their luggage to the porter, tipping him to keep it safe in the guard's van, and ensuring that it will be conveyed to the appropriate platform and reloaded onto the correct guard's van, when they reach the Dorchester West Station. Nevertheless, Lucy still worries about the transfer and intends to supervise closely. When the time comes, she checks her tickets and follows the porter to the right train at the Dorchester South Station. Once she and Frankie are settled in their compartment and their luggage has been transferred successfully, she calms down a little; she can now relax until they reach Southampton.

As the towns of Wareham, Poole, Wimborne, Ringwood, Brockenhurst pass them by, Frankie is lulled by the rhythmic chant of the wheels on the metal rails and he drops off to sleep, while she's lost in thoughts of her journey over land and sea and their life once they reach Hopetown. Finally, they arrive at Southampton West. She wakes Frankie up, gathers their belongings and steps out onto the platform, where she sees the porters are unloading their luggage. She'd tied purple ribbon to both their trunks, just to be able to recognise them, and is glad she did so, as there are several other trunks being unloaded for folk presumably also travelling by sea tomorrow.

She's reserved an overnight room at the Dolphin Hotel in the High Street, recommended by Joshua and Aurora. She tips one of the porters to convey their luggage to the hotel, and she and Frankie follow him, Frankie dragging his steps and wanting to be carried. She says, "Come on, darling, it's not far," but she knows that for his little legs it seems a long way, especially as he's so sleepy.

She orders room service and is soon asleep with Frankie beside her. She has booked an early morning call and it seems she has only just put her head on the pillow, when she hears the tap on her door and the chamber maid enters with a pot of tea.

She says, "Thank you," and gets up to pour the tea, before waking Frankie, still dead to the world. She glances at her timepiece. Five o'clock in the morning is early for her, but she drinks the tea, performs her ablutions and dresses, before rousing Frankie and washing and clothing him.

They go downstairs for breakfast, but she finds it difficult to eat, she's so anxious about getting on the ship. They both manage some scrambled egg on toast and fresh orange juice. Then she settles the bill and they set off once more to the dockside, with the hotel porter conveying their luggage.

They disturb a flock of seagulls, waddling along the road ahead of them, and she watches them fly up, screeching and wheeling above them in the bright early morning sunshine. The porter leads them to the dock gates where she produces their tickets and passes. They're not detained for long at the gates and from there they make their way to the steamer, moored on the opposite side of the docks. The dockside appears busy with passengers, sailors with their duffle bags, lascars loading the boats, and porters pushing trolleys, overladen with steamer chests and trunks and all jostling for position, as they make their way to their designated vessel.

Lucy points out their ship, painted black with a narrow white ribband around her, and she's struck by her elegance. Her porter heads for a sailor calling for 'first-class passengers for the mail steamer *Syria*' and she sees the collier ships coaling her up for the voyage. They cross a narrow footbridge to be delivered up beside her. The porter hands their luggage to the crewman who conveys it on board.

31

She tips the porter and the sailor helps them down the gangplank. Finally, they relax.

Syria is a handsome vessel, with a smooth deck of the finest teak, along which folk can promenade from bow to stern. She notes it has been swabbed so clean, you could eat your victuals off it. She and Frankie wait with the other passengers to be allocated their cabin and she watches with interest the people milling around her, because they'll be her travelling companions for the next few months. The majority of the passengers are single men and she wonders if they're prospectors like Rupert.

Her name is called, and they're shown to their cabin, which is light and airy and painted pale blue. There's a large square porthole which, when opened, will send in plenty of fresh air, a looking glass, wash basin and vessel for the wastewater, water bottle and tumblers, soap and towels, a bed and bed linen, and a place to hang her clothes. Frankie jumps up and down on the bed they'll be sharing throughout the journey. The cabin's lit by round glass lamps topping rows of marble columns, which are repeated along the cabin deck. Each column lamp lights the corridor outside and the inside of two cabins. The partitions of the cabin, although eight feet tall, don't reach the above decking, allowing light and air to circulate the whole deck. Impressed with the layout and happy they'll both be quite comfortable for the voyage, she unpacks their clothes, and they return to the promenade deck.

The time for sailing has arrived and the vessel moves to the locks, in order to receive the mail. The mail delivered, the ship readies to depart. The steamer gives a warning blast and moves off towards the dock entrance. All is accomplished efficiently, as the ship moves out of the docks and into

Southampton waters. The engines are then ordered full steam ahead, and their epic journey begins.

Lucy looks out at the calm seas and then back at the English shores and wonders when, if ever, she'll see the loving faces of her family again, and sadness overwhelms her. The waters ahead are calm, but she knows there will be rough seas to come and hardships to face in South Africa.

CHAPTER THREE *(October–November 1872)*

PRIDE AND SHAME

Early in November, Joshua receives a letter from Ben and Becky announcing the birth of their second child. He rushes to find Louisa. "I come bearing glad tidings, my dear. Our Becky has had a little girl. They're calling her Jessica. They say she weighed 7lb 2oz and baby and mother are both in good health."

"Oh, my dear, that's wonderful news."

"I was wondering if you might like to pay them a visit? It's Ma's birthday on the twenty-third of this month; perhaps it would be a good idea to combine the two events. What do you think?"

"I think that's a perfect idea. Write back and let them know."

"I will do." He kisses the top of her head and returns to his study.

Joshua arranges for the family to visit Portland on the steam locomotive from Penn Mill Station. They are all eager for a break in their routines and look on it as a short holiday. The wind-driven rain pelts the windows throughout their journey, the only break in the clouds is once they arrive in Victoria Square and disembark from the train.

Aurora and Gabriel are both excited to see the new baby and of course their grandparents, Uncle

Ben, Auntie Becky, and cousin Jem, after not having seen them for such a long time. Aurora grips two-year-old Lydia's hand firmly, while with her other hand she holds on to her hat, lest the wind snatch it away. Avoiding the large puddles, they make their way from the railway station up the hill towards Cove Cottages.

When the girls lag behind, Joshua turns back, picking Lydia up and carrying her. She gives him a kiss on his cheek, holding his face in her chubby hands. The impish wind continues to harass them, tugging at the ladies' skirts until they reach the sanctuary of their grandparents' home. Joshua tips the porter for conveying their luggage, as the rest of the family crowd into the small hallway to remove their mantles and jackets.

"Oh, how wonderful to see you all!" exclaims Violet at the sight of them.

"Happy birthday, Granny!" cries Gabriel, giving her a big hug.

"Happy birthday, Granny," says Aurora, hugging and kissing her. She removes her mantle and then helps Lydia with hers.

"Oh my! It's so wonderful to have you all here. Come on through, to make room for your pa to get inside the door and shut out that cold wind."

As they enter the living room, Joshua and Louisa both say together, "Happy birthday, Ma," and Joshua hands his mother their gift.

"Oh, my dears, thank you. That's very kind of you."

Matthew sits patiently in his armchair, waiting for the hullabaloo to die down as the visitors all disrobe, and Lydia's immediately drawn to him. She goes to him for a cuddle and he lifts her onto his lap.

"Hello, Gramps," says Gabriel. "How are you?"

"I'm fine, lad. It's good to see you all on this miserable day." Even inside the cottage they can hear the waves crashing against the shingle and the drawing sucking sound of the groundswell. Matthew sighs, nodding in the direction of the beach. "There'll be souls lost at sea somewhere in this foul weather. That there's the death groan."

"Come on, Pa," says Joshua, "cast away those worrying thoughts. This is a celebration of Ma's birthday."

His father continues, "It's a shame for all of you, to have to travel in this weather, but what can you do when her birthday falls in November?"

Violet smiles and gives a little shrug. "I'm sorry about that, but it can't be helped." She unwraps her present. "Oh, Josh! They're beautiful. Thank you so much, both of you." She kisses her son and Louisa and holds out her soft kid gloves to show Matthew.

"Try them on, they look perfect for you," Matthew says, smiling. "Just what you need for this time of year."

"Well, we have to do our best to support our local industry," says Joshua, grinning.

Lydia shyly toddles forward. "I've made a picture for you, Granny. It's of you and Grampa on the beach with the sun shining."

"Well, well. You are a clever girl. I'll put it on the mantelshelf for all to see. Thank you so much, my darling." She gives her a big hug and a kiss.

Then Aurora pulls a small package out of her reticule. "Here, Granny, this is from me and Gabriel." The enamel brooch they purchased from the peddler, who visits the kitchens regularly, is the perfect gift for their granny. They both wait for her reaction.

"Oh, how exquisite! Look, Matty, it's a dainty little lacquered violet in the perfect colours."

Matthew smiles at his grandchildren. "That's very appropriate. How thoughtful of you. You're so fortunate to have found it."

Violet removes the brooch from its box and pins it to the bodice of her gown. "It'll go well on my wraps too, my dears. Thank you so much."

"You're welcome, Granny," says Gabriel. "We couldn't wait to give it to you, because we knew you'd like it."

"I really do." She kisses both of them in turn. "Come on through to the parlour. I have some victuals prepared for you. Ben and Becky will be here any minute."

Gabriel is first through the door, always hungry. Matthew is last, anxiously looking out to sea beforehand, while the shutters rattle on in the November gale.

Moments later, Ben and Becky arrive with Jem and baby Jessica and the wind follows them through the front door. The ladies rush to greet the new-born and congratulate the parents on such a beautiful child. Lydia May, fascinated with the baby, follows Becky into the living room, gently taking the baby's tiny hand in hers, as soon as she's placed on some cushions.

Louisa gives her sister-in-law a warm hug. Then Jem passes her the birthday cake. "Ma made it and iced it for Grandma."

Louisa smiles. "I'll put it on the table for you, Becky. It looks beautiful and delicious."

Joshua hands his sister a package. "A present for Jessie."

"Thank you, Josh." She unwraps the gift, revealing a silver teething ring with a mermaid handle.

Ben says, "That's beautiful, mate. Thank you."

Josh grins. "How are you both sleeping now?"

"Well, she's only four weeks old, so Becky's still disturbed in the night, but she's very quiet, and they don't worry me too much."

Joshua says, "They grow up so fast. Just look at Lydia May, a proper little madam, now she's two and walking and talking."

They eventually return to the buffet and after they've had sufficient food, the candles are lit on the birthday cake and all sing 'Happy Birthday', while Violet blows out the candles. Afterwards they sit together around the fire in the living room and play parlour games, the women taking it in turns to nurse baby Jessie, while Matthew and Violet reminisce, their children and grandchildren listening in awe at their smuggling exploits.

On Sunday morning they awake to discover the appalling news that the five-man crew of the *Jane Catherine* have all drowned off Chesil Beach in the storm. Matthew is devastated, as both he and Ben knew them well as experienced fishermen, boatmen and friends and his heart goes out to their families. He and Joshua waste no time donning oilskin jackets and sou'westers to go out into the storm and help with retrieving the bodies.

A melancholic pall hangs over the household. Violet and Louisa prepare the vegetables for the Sunday roast meal. Once the joint is in the oven and the vegetables are ready, Louisa tries to cheer everyone by suggesting they have a game of whist, while Lydia's having her nap. Violet goes to look for a pack of cards. Aurora and Gabriel relax a little as the game progresses and their competitiveness takes over.

The following day the gales continue, rain lashes the windows and the fierce wind rattles the shutters. "Will there be no let-up? This must be the wettest November in living memory," says Matthew, dragging his tired limbs from his bed. He throws back the curtains to look out at the dismal day, brooding leaden skies and heaving grey sea.

Violet stirs and stretches. "I'm just thankful you never chose the life of a sailor. At least as a fisherman you know your area and are never too far from home."

"Maybe, but even us local men can be caught out by the unpredictable trickery of the weather, like those poor fellows yesterday. The sight of their womenfolk grieving for them on the beach yesterday was pitiful." He shakes his head, trying to dispel the haunting memory, and pulls on his dressing gown. "I'll go down and put the kettle on to boil. No rush, Vi, you stop there, till you're ready."

"What time is it?"

"Quarter past six."

"Matty, try not to wake Gabriel. Don't forget he's on the cushions downstairs."

That night Matthew again loans Joshua his spare oilskin and sou'wester, and along with Ben they wander down to the Cove House Inn to enjoy the relaxation of the ale and the banter, but after a couple of hours, their camaraderie is interrupted, when they hear, above the howl of the wind, a distress rocket and, as one, without thought for their own safety, they re-don their waterproofs and leave the bar and the warm fireside to go and render assistance. The fishermen in the lead, they make their way, with flaming torches, through the wind and foggy rain along the vast pebble bank.

Up at Cove Cottage, just after Lydia has fallen asleep, they also hear the sound of the distress rocket flare. Because all their menfolk are in the Cove House Inn, Violet is immediately concerned. The fishermen will be rushing to help, whatever the cost. She jumps up and pulls back the curtains. She can just make out the row of flame torches progressing along Chesil and knows instinctively that their menfolk are among them. Louisa tries to calm her, and Becky goes to brew a pot of tea, but all three women are trying to hide their worry from each other and praying all will be well.

Eventually Joshua recognises, through the fog, the outline of a large vessel rolling broadside, about twenty yards off the beach and the shadows of many local folk gathered on the shore. He knows that some will have sadness and empathy for the poor souls in jeopardy and be wanting to help, but fears that others will be after the ill-gotten gains, once the doomed vessel breaks apart.

They reach the spot, and he clearly sees, in the light of the flaming torches and blazing tar barrels, the foundering vessel, grounded and wedged on the shingle, but not close enough to the shore for salvation.

They join the fishermen, linking together and plunging into the chilly pitching waves, until they manage to get a line across. They are closely followed by the coastguard men who finally muster and fire their rocket-propelled lines towards the dangerously rolling vessel, until thankfully one is successful.

Unfortunately, the desperate crew on board are busy concentrating on rigging the fishermen's line, to attach the breeches buoy, when the line snaps and they have to start over again with the second line from the coastguard. In the meantime, Joshua hears the women on board crying and praying for deliverance, as they hang on for dear life to whatever's at hand to stop them from being washed overboard.

He observes two of the crew clambering over the side of the fracturing vessel in an attempt to jump and swim ashore. He watches in horror as they hang from the ship's rail, until a sudden breaking wave rolls the boat backwards, towards the open sea. The men rise up and cling on desperately, until, as she begins to roll forward again, they are hit by falling spars. Their arms exhausted, they lose their hold, each slipping into the churning sea to be crushed to death under the huge iron hull. There is a cry of dismay from the onlookers on the beach.

The crew on board eventually manage to get the second line fixed and initially all seems to be going well. Joshua and his fellow rescuers manage to haul five women and several men safely across the surging seas in the breeches buoy. Then, a woman mistakenly takes hold of the ship's main brace, instead of the rope to the breeches buoy. The cradle is pulled from beneath her and she falls into the swirling waves. The other passengers gasp in horror and, after witnessing that, the master of the ship cannot persuade anyone else to take courage and climb into the basket.

Joshua hears a desperate father on board, with two small children clasped tightly in his arms, begging someone to take them to safety. But no one volunteers, until the ship's master grabs one of the children and climbs into the breeches buoy with the child, to demonstrate its safety. The rain pelts down on them. Joshua's arms strain with the effort of hauling the captain and child safely to the shore. The child is handed to one of the rescuers. The poor captain then tries to get back to his ship but is stopped by the coastguards. Joshua watches the despondent fellow hanging his head in despair. "I thought we were making for Portland Roads, but the visibility was so bad we miscalculated and ended up in Lyme Bay. We tried to go about, but it was too late."

One of the coastguards responds, "They don't call this place Deadman's Bay for nothing, sir, but we're doing our best to save them, Captain. All is not lost."

"You don't understand. I've let them down. Those luckless passengers have left behind all their worldly goods to emigrate to Sydney, Australia, on my ship the *Royal Adelaide*, taking only their treasured possessions and now they'll lose everything."

However, once the master has crossed, the remaining people seem to understand the dire urgency. The ship is breaking up. They must realise if they don't get off now it will be too late. Joshua sees seawater surging through the sides of the hull and is relieved when finally, one by one, they haul the terrified passengers and crew over the heaving treacherous chasm between ship and shore to safety.

Then, above the noise of the howling wind and surging sea, there's a resounding crack, and the hull of the ship snaps in two. Joshua can still make out two adults and a child left on board. One young lady had hung back, reluctant to get into the precariously swinging basket, but now she has no option and clambers in, but as they haul her ashore, she's swamped by the waves and by the time they drag her and the basket onto the beach she has no life left in her. But they must go on, Joshua sees there are still two more souls to deliver.

The last fellow, a heavily built chap, bravely takes with him the little six-year-old girl whose parents are already onshore with the child's sibling. There are cheers from the beach as he climbs into the breeches buoy, but their combined weight is too great, the line breaks and all on the shore watch in dread as down they both go, to be lost forever in the bubbling cauldron of waves. The distress of the onlookers on shore is audible, and Joshua hears the unbearable hysterical screams of the child's mother and the other women trying in vain to comfort her. His shoulders slump in despair, but Matthew, seeing his desolation, reminds him, "Try not to dwell on it, lad. Just focus on all those we've managed to save."

According to the ship's master the only other person now left on board is a seventy-two-year-old lady, who has been bedbound since leaving the port of London. He tells the rescuers that, despite the desperate attempts of the passengers and crew to get her ashore, she's adamant that she's staying put in the bed and that the good Lord will decide her fate, which regrettably, he does.

Joshua, Ben and Matthew collapse, exhausted, onto the shingle and watch, through the pouring rain, the sixty survivors being taken away to the Victoria Inn, beside the ferry bridge at Wyke Regis. They realise that the other Portlanders have formed a line of bedraggled fellows making their way back along the beach towards the Cove House Inn. Exhausted from their efforts, they stagger to their feet and follow on behind them, leaving the soldiers and customs officers to their duties.

As the ship breaks apart, all manner of goods are washed ashore and within an hour the beach fills with the debris from the wreck, boxes and crates of cargo, sewing machines, furniture, clothing, personal items, money, livestock, kegs of spirits and basically everything left on board.

Looking back, they can see that despite the presence of the coastguards and the soldiers of the 77th regiment, who've been posted to guard the goods, a treasure hunt starts, as the locals pillage their bounty. Joshua can't help feeling saddened at the desperation of these folk. They must be poor to be out in this foul weather for the sake of grabbing whatever they can. The rush of looters is too overwhelming for the soldiers to control and they've no choice but to watch as many run off with their ill-gotten gains.

In the meantime, on their journey back they encounter a small runaway piglet that's survived the ordeal and is roaming free on the beach. Ben attempts to grab the animal, but it escapes his clutches, squealing indignantly. "Jem would love to have a pet pig."

"Come on then, let's catch him," says Joshua. His spirits rising.

And a farcical game of chase takes place with them slipping and sliding on the pebbles as the pig eludes capture, but the poor animal, exhausted from its efforts, on top of its traumatic experience in the sea, gives in to being caught. Ben tucks it into his oilskin coat and buttons it up, so the animal's safe and warm. "Jem will be so thrilled with this," he says, laughing.

"We could be arrested for this," says Matthew, grinning. "It takes me back to our smuggling days."

"I doubt Ma will be too pleased, though," says Joshua.

"I'll handle your mother. I'm sure she'll soon forgive us, because in the long run she'll be pleased we saved it from the butcher's knife."

The following day Ben pops round to tell them the latest news. "The *Royal Adelaide* was a modern iron vessel with iron masts and strong wire rigging. The coastguards had spotted her in the fog off Chesil, but she'd managed to turn and veer out to sea again and they thought all was well, but the fierce winds and tides had swept her back towards the danger of the beach. They'd tried to raise the sails, but the gale-force winds had shredded the canvas of the jib and main topsails, forcing them to heave the damaged sails down again. Apparently, even before they'd fired their distress rockets a huge crowd had assembled on the shore."

"It must have been terrifying!" says Louisa, tears brimming her eyes at the thought of it. "I can't help thinking it could have been you and Aurora on the *Delta.*"

"But it wasn't, and we both arrived and returned perfectly safely," says Joshua, kissing her on her forehead and hugging her.

"I doubt many of those on board could swim, either," says Aurora.

"I don't think in those tragic circumstances any swimmer would've survived, darling," says Joshua.

"I hope Lucy and Frankie aren't going through storms like that one," says Louisa, shuddering at the thought.

"I'm sure they're both fine. They're too far south by now to have been affected by this particular storm," says Joshua.

Ben continues his story. "The seven that drowned

were the first mate, who'd tried to get a line ashore before we arrived at the scene, the stewardess who fell from the breeches buoy, the two sailors who tried to swim for it, plus the elderly lady, who refused to leave the ship, and the poor man with the young girl."

Joshua shakes his head at the memory and Ben puts an arm around his shoulder to comfort him. "But remember, Josh, that we managed to save the other sixty souls who were in jeopardy that day."

"I know, I know, but it would've been better to have saved them all, especially that poor little girl."

"Well, that isn't the end of it."

"What do you mean?" asks Violet.

"Overnight the looters have cleared the shingle of most of the goods washed ashore and this morning unconscious bodies have been found scattered all over the beach. Men, women and children who'd helped themselves to the contents of the kegs of spirits lay exposed on the pebbles throughout the cold wet night and many are near death."

"Oh no! How shameful, whatever will the world think of us?" Violet sighs.

"Medical help has been called, as they were unable to rouse the lifeless bodies and they've been loaded onto wagons and taken to places of safety, like the Cove House Inn, where they've been laid out, stripped of their sodden clothing and covered in blankets and warm bricks to hopefully revive them. But it's believed that four of the plunderers didn't survive, from a combination of their drunkenness and exposure to the elements, but I don't recognise their names, as they're all from Wyke Regis or Weymouth."

"How terrible for their poor families," says Louisa.

Ben, continuing to read, begins to laugh. "Apparently, one fortunate fellow, called John Stone, had a narrow escape. He was rescued in the nick of time, after lying across the railway line!"

"'Tis the demon drink! It steals away all sense," says Violet, vehemently.

Matthew looks at the boys. "Do you think we should tell her now?"

"Well, she'll find out soon enough, when she next pays us a call," says Ben.

Joshua looks up and asks his mother, "Ma, you know the nursery rhyme, *'Tom, Tom, the Piper's Son'*?"

Violet looks confused. "Of course."

"Well last night it should have been, 'Josh and Ben the fisherman's sons, stole a pig and away did run'."

"You didn't?"

"We did. Well, we actually rescued it and took it home for Jem. It was about half a mile away from the wreck when we saw it, lost and frightened, and we rescued it. No one saw us and Jem was delighted this morning when he woke up and discovered it in the back yard."

"I bet he was, but he won't be so delighted if the animal's discovered and you're arrested for looting."

"Have no fear, Ma, it won't happen. We'd have had to be caught at the time; it's too late now. We're all quite safe."

"You men will be the death of me!" she says in exasperation.

Lucy and Frankie have settled into the ship's routine. They are seated every evening at dinner next to Mr and Mrs Partridge from Salisbury, who tells Lucy they are missionaries with the London Missionary Society, travelling to their mission station at Kuruman, an oasis on the edge of the Kalahari

Desert, in the Northern Cape Province. Mrs Partridge is a rounded cheerful lady with a pretty face and gentle manner and Mr Partridge is loving and deferential towards her. They are chatty, and she relaxes in their company. Mrs Partridge helps her to understand the French terms on the menu, for which she's grateful.

Mr Partridge tells her, "This vessel started life as a Peninsular and Orient paddle steamer and the Orient Steam Package Company converted her into the screw propeller ship we're so fortunate to be sailing on, with its modern and complete refit."

The other mealtimes are less formal. Everyone can choose who they sit besides, so Lucy befriends a Miss Ellen Weatherall. A young lady of around her age and she sits down next to her for their first luncheon. They soon become friends and she learns that she's also travelling to South Africa to be married. Her fiancé lives and works in Durban, producing sugar, and is doing so well he's decided to settle there and has asked her to join him in this lifetime adventure.

When they stop at Madeira for re-coaling, there are boats that come alongside. Lucy learns that you can hire them for one shilling to take you ashore. She decides that she and Frankie would like to go and so they take the excursion ashore with Ellen. At first Lucy is anxious about Frankie getting on and off the ship, but a kindly sailor carries him down into the smaller waiting boat and they set off towards the black pebbly beach. The stern is put towards the beach and she fears they'll get wet during their efforts to land, but the boatman expertly rides the groundswell and manoeuvres through the drawback until, on the largest roller, the boat is conveyed to the shore and they're landed safely above the tide line onto the pebble beach, as the water retreats. The boatman lifts Frankie and places him on the dry pebbles and then hands both ladies out. Lucy pays him the shilling and they set off to see the sights of Madeira.

They're hassled by the local men and bombarded with offers of a variety of tours of Funchal, but Frankie's excited by the oxen-drawn sleigh and as the roadways look so steep and pebbly, the ladies agree to be shown around the town in this manner. They half expect a bumpy ride, as the trap has no wheels, but they're agreeably surprised to discover there's less jolting than if the sled had wheels, as it skims across the roads made from the black pebbles.

The island is beautiful and, in this clement climate, flowers abound, from the high cliffs covered in myrtle and orange nasturtiums, to the gardens decorated with trailing purple and pink bougainvillea, colourful roses and red geraniums. They go up hill and down dale in their unconventional transport. Lucy notes the rows of jacaranda trees lining the streets and imagines how beautiful they'll look in April, with their mauve blossom and purple puddles of fallen petals, pooling on the ground beneath them. They pass many neat whitewashed cottages, and smart hotels, until in no time they're returned to the beach. They're conveyed back to the ship with the same boatman who delivered them, and he hands Frankie up to a steward who helps them on board.

As they up anchor and leave the little island, Lucy looks back from the promenade deck and admires the emerald isle with its dark forests and the pretty cottages cascading down the hill at Funchal, with the colourful boats in the foreground and the beautiful vines decorating the buildings. This has been their only excursion from the boat throughout the journey and Frankie especially enjoyed the break in the routine on board.

The following day the captain announces they're passing Tenerife, and in the distance they should be able to make out the Canaries. Folk make their way up on deck to see the islands, volcanic mountains rising up from the sea. They then pass Palma, Gomera and the island of Ferro, and are informed that this will be the last land to be seen until they reach the Cape Coast.

The next morning Frankie wakes early, fidgeting until Lucy feels the need to get up. They both dress and go up to the promenade deck to see the sun rise. The deck has been steam-hosed ready for the day. The quartermaster's checking to see that all's as it should be and collecting up any of the passengers' property left behind on the deck chairs. Lucy and Frankie enjoy the fresh breeze and lift their faces towards it and the gentle sunshine.

Soon the passengers begin to appear in their morning costumes ready for their breakfast. At half past eight the first bell rings and Lucy spots Ellen with another companion walking towards them.

She dips a curtsey. "Good morning, Ellen."

The ladies also curtsey. "Good morning, Lucy, allow me to introduce you to Miss Maisie Barford, she's travelling with her parents to Cape Town. We met last night, after you and Frankie had retired. Things became a little riotous didn't it, Maisie?"

"It did rather, but it was chiefly due to the influence of the wild young gentlemen, who are en route to the diamond fields."

Ellen agrees with her. "They were rather rowdy, but it was a stimulating departure from the norm on this boat."

"Why? What did they do?" asks Lucy, intrigued.

"They drank quite a lot and gambled and sang rude songs, which rather shocked the older folk present," replies Ellen, giggling.

"It's as well I'm obliged to take to my bed early with Frankie, then," she responds.

"The one with the freckles and gingery sandy hair was the ringleader. His name's Simon McCallister. He's rather good looking, don't you think so, Ellen?" asks Maisie.

Ellen looks wistful. "I preferred the dark-haired fellow who sang most heartily. He had a gorgeous smile."

"Oh yes," says Maisie. "You mean the prospector, Ethan Hart."

"Yes him. I think he wanted to buy a stake in the claim that Simon was selling on the Vaal River."

Ellen nods her head. "I think he'd got several of them interested in that, including the two brothers."

Lucy is thoughtful. "I'm not at all sure it's a good idea to do business deals with a person you've just met, especially when there's drink involved."

Ellen takes her arm. "I'm sure you're right, my dear, but boys will be boys," she says, grinning. "Come on, let us be first in the queue, so we can all sit together at the table." As they go towards the companionway, the second bell chimes, summoning them to breakfast. They select their favourite spot, opposite a port hole, and Maisie joins them.

As the other passengers file into the dining area, Maisie nudges Ellen. "There's Simon, Ethan and the others."

Lucy looks towards the young adventurers and can see they're all full of life and the vigour of youth. No wonder Ellen and Maisie enjoyed their company last night, but are they to be trusted, whether in romance, or in commerce?

CHAPTER FOUR *(November–December 1872)*

TO TRAVEL IN HOPE

During her journey, Lucy discovers the piano in the saloon is for the use of passengers and she enjoys playing most afternoons. In this way she is introduced to all those on board who are musical, including the dark-haired young man, Ethan Hart.

She soon shows that it isn't only classical pieces she can play when, reminiscent of the Black Panther Club, Ethan requests she play 'Champagne Charlie' and he sings along doing the actions of a toff and making everyone laugh. Lucy can't help but like him. She plays 'The Flying Trapeze' for him and then goes on to play other requests, like one from a cockney fellow asking for 'Pretty Polly Perkins of Paddington Green' and another lady who requests 'Walking in the Zoo'.

Then it's time for afternoon tea and Ethan joins them, along with Maisie and Ellen. Over their sandwiches, he tells them he's done a deal with Simon McCallister and purchased a full share in a section mapped out along the Vaal River and they all congratulate him; he seems so excited.

"This claim has cost me nearly all I have, but I've still enough put by to get there and to purchase some tools for the job."

Lucy tells him, "My brother-in-law has two claims beside the Orange River, not far from Hopetown, and he says he's doing very well. To start off with, he mostly discovered semi-precious stones like garnets, but there's still a market for them. However, since then, he and his partner have dug lower and discovered the diamonds."

"He's lucky to have a partner. I do feel a touch apprehensive, going it alone."

"Well, he was alone when he left home, but he met his partner, Jack, on their journey, and they enjoyed each other's company and decided to stick together. You may well have the same good fortune. There'll be hundreds of young prospectors to choose from, when you reach the encampment at Vaal River, I'm sure."

During the rest of their voyage Lucy regularly plays the piano in the afternoon and plays quoits with Frankie in the morning and they're invariably joined by their friends.

When they reach the harbour of refuge at Table Bay in Cape Town, a magnificent sight beholds them as they drop anchor. Table Mountain overshadows the small city, with its tablecloth shroud tumbling over it and concealing its flat top, accompanied by the smaller rocky summits of the Devil's Peak, the Lion's Head and the Lion's Rump.

Lucy, Ellen and Frankie huddle together against the ship's rail, along with other passengers, all jostling to get the best view of the famous mountain and the city at its feet. The land slopes down from the base of the mountain towards the bay and the settlement. Scattered among the evergreens Lucy can pick out the most desirable of dwelling houses.

From her complimentary map, she's learnt that the Blue Berg Mountains are a range that runs behind Table Mountain to the north-east and in between the two is a sandy neck of land which separates Table Bay from False Bay and Simon's Bay. She sighs with wonder at the beautiful sight before her.

For many passengers their voyage is over, and they leave, as others join the vessel to go around the Cape of Good Hope, into the Indian Ocean and up along the eastern coast of South Africa. Lucy and Ellen are saddened to say farewell to Maisie, and they all promise to keep in touch by letter. Maisie waves to them, as she and her parents disembark to their new life in this thriving young city.

After a short stay in Cape Town, the crew of the *Syria* prepare to leave. A single gunshot is fired, the signal that they can get underway and they're soon full steam ahead at about ten miles an hour. They pass the end of the breakwater and the lighthouse at Manille Point, then Green Point and Sea Point. Lucy and Ellen admire the properties with their grounds running down close to the shore. They want to stay on deck until they round the Cape of Good Hope. The weather is overcast and breezy as they approach Hout Bay and they can see in the distance Chapman's Peak before they pass Chapman's Bay.

"Look, Lucy. There's a river in the middle of those sand dunes!"

A nearby passenger, who must have boarded at Cape Town, because she hasn't seen him before, is leaning against the ship's rail and he comments, "That's the Kromme River. We'll soon be passing Cape Point lighthouse. You should look out for whales and the little African penguins, because they're prevalent in Boulders Bay. Would you like to borrow my eyeglass?"

"I'm sure my son would love to, sir. You're most kind, thank you. Do you hear that, Frankie? This gentleman's offered us the use of his eyeglass, so we may look out for penguins and whales."

Lucy looks through the instrument and, looking back at the bay, she spots the penguins among the sand dunes. She holds the telescope out for Frankie. "Look through the glass, Frankie, but be careful not to drop it. Can you see the penguins waddling upright on the beach and swimming among the waves?" She holds him firmly by the shoulders to steady him.

Frankie's delighted. "There are so many, Mama!"

Then the passenger continues in his slightly guttural foreign-sounding accent. "We'll be navigating around the Cape of Good Hope next. The lighthouse there warns of the treacherous dangers of the Bellows, the Anvil and Dias Rocks, which all need a wide berth." But the *Syria* steams on, navigating around the hidden dangers and they soon pass the Cape of Good Hope and continue sailing in a south-easterly direction, passing False Bay and Cape Hangklip, with their busy little fishing villages.

Ellen excuses herself. "I'm sorry, Lucy, but I've had enough of the wind blowing my hair about. I'm going to go below to the saloon cabin. I'll see you down there later."

She decides to stay because Frankie's enjoying himself. "All right, we'll follow you down there, once Frankie's had enough."

Then the helpful passenger tells them, "The next peninsular is Point Danger, where twenty years ago, HMS *Birkenhead* was lost, along with 436 souls. She was wrecked while transporting passengers and troops to Algoa Bay, but there weren't enough lifeboats and famously the soldiers stood firm and allowed all the women and children to leave on the lifeboats."

"How remarkably brave and chivalrous, sir." She lowers her voice. "Please, let us not talk of wrecks in front of the child."

Seeing some large creatures on land, Lucy changes the subject and asks the man, "Can you see those creatures, there?" She points towards them.

"Yes, that's an ostrich farm."

"Look, Frankie, can you see the ostriches? They appear small from here, but they're really big birds."

Frankie looks through the telescope again. "Yes, I can, Mama. Will we be able to have one, when we get to Uncle Rupert's?"

"We'll see."

The gentleman continues his guided tour. "The next rocky projection is Cape Agulhas, the southernmost point in Africa, so hold on to your hats, as this is where the Indian Ocean and the Atlantic meet, and the sea, at the very least, will be choppy."

The wind increases the nearer they get to the tip of Africa, and Lucy tells Frankie, "Give the eyeglass back to the kind gentleman now, Frankie, and hold on tightly to my hand." But the *Syria* progresses steadfastly onwards, its stern rising and falling through the rollers. As they lurch up and down amid the turbulence, she has complete confidence in their captain and crew and they soon pass Cape Agulhas and continue their journey around the base of Africa.

Lucy and Frankie finally excuse themselves, to go below to the saloon and out of the wind. As they step into the companionway, Lucy sees a man approaching along the passage. Stepping inside from the bright glare of the sunshine, she can't make out who it is, until he draws closer. It's Simon McCallister. They're about to pass each other, but he puts his arm across their path, with his hand flat against the opposite wall, effectively barring their way.

Lucy says, "Excuse me, sir. Would you please allow us to pass?"

He grins at her. His tongue wetting his lips. "Not until you've paid the forfeit."

"I'm not sure what you can mean, sir?"

He moves in even closer. "The price is a kiss."

She pulls back from him. "What do you take me for? I am no whore, sir."

Suddenly he lunges at her, trying to kiss her neck, plunging his hands between her legs. She struggles with him, until he gives out a loud howl and draws away.

Frankie has kicked him in his shin. "Leave my mama alone!" he shouts so the whole ship might hear.

Simon McCallister scowls and pushes past them. "You keep that brat out of my way! Do you hear?" He limps off down the corridor.

She responds equally forcibly, "No, sir. *You* keep away from me and my son."

Lucy bends down and says to Frankie, "Thank you, darling, you're a brave boy and you stood up for your mama against that horrid silly man. I'm proud of you." She takes his hand and says, "Come on, let's forget all about him and go and find Ellen."

They settle with Ellen, deciding to play a game of tiddlywinks, which Frankie goes off to find in the children's area.

"Are you all right, Lucy? You look a little pale."

"I've just had a most unpleasant experience at the hands of Simon McCallister."

"What do you mean?"

"He tried to molest me in the corridor when I was with Frankie. Thankfully, Frankie kicked him in the shin, which immediately put paid to his unwanted attentions, but he was rude and aggressive."

"Oh, my dear! How horrid for you."

"I know. It was frightening for both of us, but let's change the subject now. I don't want Frankie to worry about it."

The incident forgotten, they are soon laughing, as the small counters go anywhere but in the pot. Then Frankie gets bored and Ellen suggests they teach him how to play Happy Families. He soon learns all the different families.

"I like Soot the sweep best, because he's all dirty," says Frankie, clapping his hands in glee, as the game continues.

The ship stops off in Mossel Bay where there's another brief exchange of people. Then it's time for afternoon tea and they set off again. Frankie's napping with his head in her lap, when Ethan approaches them. "Lucy, if you will permit me, I'd like to have your address in Hopetown, if you've no objection. I know no one where I'm bound, and it'll be reassuring to have at least one connection with someone already established in the area?"

"Of course, Ethan, but aren't the brothers and that unpleasant Simon McCallister all going to the same area?"

"I'm not sure, but I believe there's some distance between us. The brothers are at a place called Klipdrift and I believe mine's further south at New Rush, but they'll all be in the same boat as me, starting out from scratch. Besides, I don't know them any better than I know you. I'd like to be able to contact you, if need be, as you're already established. In case of any problems I may encounter. I know there'll be all sorts of characters there, some God-fearing men and some out-and-out rogues, all fighting against the odds to survive."

"Well, I'm sure Rupert won't mind you contacting us, should you wish to visit at any time, and I'll certainly look forward to it, once Frankie and I are settled. I'll make a note of Rupert's address and give it to you at breakfast, but I'm pretty certain his claim will be off the beaten track. He'll be collecting us from the Hopetown Post Office, when we arrive."

"Well, I can always make enquiries there, if I need to. Thanks, Lucy."

"You're welcome."

Ethan then comments, "Can I ask you what you have against Simon McCallister?"

She flushes at the memory. "I'm afraid I don't like him. I believe he's an arrogant misogynist. There was an incident, which I'd prefer not to go into, but as a result Frankie kicked him in the shin and so he dislikes both of us now."

"I'm sorry to hear that, Lucy, as we'll most likely be travelling together to the diamond fields."

Her heart sinks. She hadn't thought of that. "Oh, that's most unfortunate. In that case I shall depend on you to be our shield and arbitrate over our differences, Ethan."

After dinner that evening, she says farewell to Mr and Mrs Partridge, due to leave the ship at Port Elizabeth in the morning, for their journey following a string of mission stations, until they reach their destination on the fringe of the Kalahari Desert. She wishes them well and, taking Frankie's hand, she leaves them and Ellen chatting with Ethan and the brothers, whom she has since learnt are called Roger and David Moss. She's quite glad to be retiring early with Frankie, because she can continue reading *Les Misérables*, which she's really enjoying, especially now that Jean Valjean has rescued Cosette from that despicable family.

She awakes the following morning to find the ship moored in Algoa Bay, the nearest town being Port Elizabeth. As she and Frankie prepare for the day ahead, she thinks about the kindly Mr and Mrs Partridge, who will probably have disembarked by now and will have a head start on the rest of them, crossing the African terrain.

They join their friends for breakfast and chat animatedly about their future prospects on the diamond fields, after which Lucy takes Frankie below to their cabin and begins to get all their belongings packed up into their trunks. They're nearing their own final destination, the port of East London.

In the meantime, Frankie's on the bed and looking through the port hole, as the *Syria* sets off again, passing a lighthouse built on the highest of a set of low rocky islands, surrounded in the air and covered on land by sea birds and aptly named Bird Islands. Frankie exclaims, "Look, Mama! Look at all the birds."

She obliges him, surprised to see so many varieties of gull and cormorant all congregating together.

Next, they pass Woody Cape, followed by nothing to see but ridges and hills of sand dunes until they go by the mouth of the Great Fish River. For a distance of about forty miles the coast has a rather wild appearance. They pass the Cave Rock and the land slopes down towards the sea, looking lush and green.

Their final destination is set on high land on the south-west side of the mouth of a beautiful river called the Buffalo. There's a breakwater under construction, which enables the vessel to enter the river and land the passengers with ease. It's at this point that Lucy has to say goodbye to Ellen who's going on to Durban to meet her fiancé. There are tears as they hug each other. This has been a better experience for both of them, because they've become good friends. They promise to keep in touch by letter, aware that the distance between them will be too great to visit each other.

"Good luck, Lucy. I hope this adventure turns out the way you'd wish it to."

"Thank you, Ellen. I hope the same for you. Godspeed, my dear. Maybe we'll meet up again someday."

"I hope so, Lucy. I'll miss you. Be sure to keep my address safe, in case you should ever need it, and take good care of Frankie. Goodbye, my friend."

"Say 'goodbye' to Auntie Ellen, Frankie."

"Goodbye, Auntie Ellen. I'll miss you."

"Goodbye, Frankie." Ellen kisses Frankie on the top of his head.

They wave as they go along the gang plank. Then Ethan, Simon McCallister and the brothers all hug and embrace Ellen and follow behind them, madly waving farewell to Ellen.

Lucy can't help but feel sorry for her, with all her friends abandoning her, but she'll be in Durban by tomorrow and in the arms of her lover.

Lucy is gratified that she's in the company of Ethan and the brothers en route to the diamond fields. The only problem being that Simon McCallister is with them as well and Frankie isn't happy about that, any more than she is. They are directed to porters, to convey their luggage to a reliable looking Cobb and Company Concord stagecoach. She and Frankie avoid McCallister and settle together beside Ethan in the comfortable seats, grateful for the four strong-looking horses that will convey them there.

They're soon in the countryside with its grassy hills dotted with thorn trees, and river valleys with thick clusters of trees and shrubby bushes. Simon McCallister, being South African born, knows the area well and takes on the job of guide, informing them, "The first place we'll pass through is a German village called Panmure where the industrious Germans produce fruit by the truckload, destined for East London."

After which they pass through acres of uncultivated land and Simon McCallister comments, "Just think of all the near-destitute agricultural labourers in England who, given the opportunity to buy up this barren land cheaply, could cultivate it into productive farmland, earning for themselves a good profit, just like those Germans have."

Tired of hearing his voice, Lucy says, "Perhaps you should be selling parcels of land for farming, rather than diamond claims."

"It doesn't have the incentive of easy money though, does it? Farming is hard graft."

"True, but I'd have thought that digging for diamonds is also hard graft, especially if you're unsuccessful."

"But that's the attraction for a gambling man," says McCallister, grinning at the men.

Lucy thinks of Ashleigh and Rupert. *Does this gambling gene run in the family?*

They pass through another German village called Jackson and here the folk are all busy at their work on the land, while attending their stock. Lucy notices a strange contraption being pulled by two oxen and McCallister tells them, "It's a spider, the name for a variety of homemade vehicles, constructed from anything that comes to hand, that will form a box-shaped container with four wheels." After that they pass many different varieties of spider all steadfastly drawn by oxen.

King William's Town is at the head of the Buffalo river. It's a garrison town and thriving with businesses. They stop there for some luncheon and a change of horses at the hotel in the market square. Frankie has a run in the park, behind the square, before they set off again to Queenstown, where they stay in the Junction Hotel for the night. Lucy has selected underwear for both her and Frankie, which she has in her tapestry bag, deciding to travel the whole journey wearing her travel costume, however dusty it may become.

Bordering the Orange River, just outside Hopetown, Rupert prepares for the arrival of Lucy and Frankie. He's in the process of supervising the construction of an extension to his homestead for his maid, so that Lucy will be able to occupy the second bedroom within the property.

He considers his maid's downcast expression and catches hold of her arm. "I'm sorry, Tamela, but I have to do this for propriety's sake. I'll make it comfortable for you. Berko can go and stay at the farm with your mother. There's no need to fret."

"But will I still be number one woman?"

"Of course, but we need to be careful. You must understand that what we've been enjoying together is illegal and so I need to develop an acceptable relationship for decency's sake. Please collect your things together, ready to move in. The lads are just fixing the windows for you. You can take your bed, and Berko's cot can go with him to the farm. I'm going into Hopetown now, as I have to refurbish the room suitably for Lucy and my nephew."

He can see she's not happy to be ousted by the interlopers, but she has no choice; *she's simply a Hottentot female servant and must do as she's told.*

After staying overnight in Queenstown, Lucy and her companions set off once more. After travelling for about twelve miles, they change horses at Schutte and have lunch at the Bushman's Rock Hotel under Stormberg Mountain. It's a beautiful area, abounding with buck and zebra. The next stop is at Burghersdorp where they stay overnight, arising early the following morning to keep their place on the stagecoach. They stop for breakfast and coffee at Sower Fontiene then, after their driver has in-spanned fresh horses, they set off again across grazing country towards the Orange River. Here they encounter row upon row of carriages, spiders, covered wagons, carts, all pulled by horses, mules, or oxen; as well as whole families with sheep and goats and all their household goods, queuing for several days for the punt to cross the river.

To Lucy's relief, the Concord stagecoach takes priority and goes straight to the head of the queue. She grips the side of the carriage when, despite the brakes on both hind wheels of the vehicle, the horses slip and slide on their haunches down the bank of the river, until, thankfully, horses and carriage are squarely upon the punt and setting off for the further bank of the sluggish, muddy-looking waterway.

When they arrive on the other bank, it looks almost impossible for any animal to pull a carriage up that steep slippery slope. All the passengers are requested to disembark and climb up the cutting. McCallister leads the way. Lucy is anxious, it's so steep, but Ethan comes to her assistance, by lifting Frankie up onto his shoulders and striding up the steep grassy verge. Roger and David chivalrously take her hands and help her too. Then they all stand at the top and pray that the horses, carrying all their worldly goods, will make it through the two-inch-thick slime to the top of the embankment.

The horses have done this before and prepare themselves for the challenge as the driver readies them with a cry and a flick of his whip. The animals can scarcely keep their footings on the slippery deck of the punt, but they gather themselves and with the second crack of the whip, away they go pell-mell up the slope, headlong through the churned-up mud, sliding and struggling, until with enormous effort they pull the wagon over the mound, panting and snorting and eyes rolling. The driver allows them to rest and recover for a while, before they continue on their way to Bathuie. Lucy feels sorry for all those left in the queue, who have the tiresome wait and then have to go through that frightening experience at the end of it.

She notices the countryside is rich in grassland and game as they approach the diamond fields. Frankie pinches her, excited to see antelope, springbok, zebra and ostrich, many grazing along the roadside, springing away as their carriage approaches. The carriage stops again at the post office in Fauresmith, established beside the banks of the river Modder. They stay overnight in a hotel where they're offered, 'bed, dinner, coffee and grog at 10s 6d'. The following morning, she and Frankie are downstairs in readiness for the early start, when she sees the boys are saying farewell to Simon McCallister, who's going on to Jagerfontein diamond fields to drum up some more business. Relieved he's leaving them in peace; she and Frankie keep out of the way until he's gone, and shortly afterwards, they're climbing up into their carriage for the next leg of the journey.

Days later, when the post-cart approaches the Dutoitspan camp, they join the congestion of the King William's Town transport, converging with traffic from Port Elizabeth, Cape Town, and Graham's Town all making for these diamond fields. Lucy's astounded to see the number of ramshackle homes, and a tented city of around 50,000 people, spread out over the area. There are shopkeepers, hoteliers, hawkers, traders, innkeepers, shebeens, gambling dens, brothels and diamond dealers all vying for trade, and of course the miners, frantically digging and sieving in the heat, dust and flies, and hoping to make another historic discovery. Through the carriage window wafts the amalgamating smells of all kinds of foreign food cooking, smoke from fires, the dusty earth, perspiring bodies, manure from the animals and unsanitary middens.

Above the noise of the busy streets she hears the cart-cabmen and omnibus conductors shouting out, "New Rush, New Rush," or in another direction, "Old de Beers." The post chaise, blocking the road ahead of them, delivers his bags, and their driver follows behind him, on the road to New Rush. They pass hotels constructed of wood and canvas, and a round, neat doctor's tent with the name 'Hermanus Pistorius MD' painted in black on the side of the tent, along with his surgery hours. She spots a dentist drawing teeth in the open air, beside his galvanised dwelling, his poor victim gripping his seat in terror.

There are hundreds of diggers in every kind of garment: canvas and cord trousers, brown moleskins, red, blue and brown shirts and jumpers. Some wear neckties and some have open collars. There are men in whole suits of buckskin and others wearing tweed, but all wear strong lace-up boots and headgear of some kind to keep the hot sun off their faces, the billy-cock hat being the favourite, and most wear a belt of thick brown leather, which, Ethan informs her, is a diamond belt, with compartments for diamonds and money.

Then they arrive at the New Rush encampment, spread out below the Colesberg Kopje and skirting the main road to Pniel. Ethan stands up to leave.

Lucy says to him, "Bye, Ethan, and good luck to you." She hugs him before he steps down from the carriage. "Thank you for looking out for us on the journey."

He's been a Godsend, always helping her with her trunks, until they could find a porter. Sometimes, if Frankie was sleeping, he'd gently carry the lad from the carriage, into the hotel and to their room without even waking him. He's a thoroughly nice fellow and she'll miss him and wishes only the best for him.

"We hope you're very successful. Don't we, Frankie?"

"Yes, Mama, we do. Bye, Ethan." Ethan kisses Frankie on the head, then steps down from the carriage. He looks back up smiling and says, "You take care, mind."

"We will."

David shakes him by the hand and his brother says, "I hope you discover another Star of South Africa diamond, mate." He pats him on the back. "You've got Simon's paperwork for the licence and the claim, haven't you?"

"Of course. A lot depends on it."

The carrier hands down his large carpet bag and he's off on his quest.

The stagecoach then sets off towards the riverside diggers' republic of Klipdrift, about twenty-three miles away. Frankie dozes, and Lucy fans herself as the hot December sun beats down on them, and it's mid-afternoon before they reach the settlement. Here they say farewell to the brothers, Roger and David, and the carriage turns south again towards Hopetown.

Lucy is relieved to finally reach the Cape Karoo coaching house in Hopetown where she and Frankie disembark and the driver hands down their luggage. Her clothes are crumpled and dusty and she's badly in need of a warm bath, but there's no sign of Rupert.

Outside the post office a barefoot, native post boy sits in the dirt, and as the carriage pulls away, she turns to the lad and asks him, "Would you be good enough to deliver a note to Mr Rupert Seymour at the claim of the Hopetown Hopefuls in return for this silver sixpenny bit?" She holds out the coin so that it glints in the light of the sun.

The lad nods his head, clasps the coin and makes off. She's not sure if he'll simply take the money and run, but what option does she have? She hopes that, being a post boy, he'll know where Rupert's claim is. The lad disappears into the distance and she and Frankie sit down on their trunks in the shade of the building. The small town is busy with traders, businessmen and prospectors but Frankie dozes, with his head resting in her lap. People stare at them as they pass by, but she's past caring.

CHAPTER FIVE *(December 1872)*

HOPETOWN

It's past six of the clock and dark by the time Rupert arrives, with the young Khoisan lad in the back of the mule cart. They halt in front of the post office and both jump down from the wagon. The young boy loiters. She sees the shock register on Rupert's face at the dishevelled state of them and is embarrassed. Watching his lean and supple movements, she's reminded of his brother, Ashleigh. His blond hair is longer and more unkempt than the last time she saw him. He takes up her hand and kisses it; then lifts Frankie, still sleeping, into his arms, while with his other hand he helps her up and onto the seat of the cart. She places her tapestry bag on the floor beside her. He deposits Frankie onto her lap and then attempts to lift up one of their trunks. He struggles, drops it back down again, and instructs the boy to help him. He chucks the lad a coin, which he catches adroitly, then Rupert clambers up beside her. He makes a clucking sound and the mules set off.

After a moment of silence, he says, "It's so good to have you both here finally. How was the journey?"

"The time on the ship was enjoyable. I made some friends which helped a lot, but the journey overland has been tiring for both me and Frankie, as you can see. The constant jolting over ruts and rocks was extremely wearying and of course we had to rise so early to claim our place on the stagecoach."

"Never mind, my dear. You're here safe and sound now."

"I didn't imagine the distance from the coast to be quite so great."

"Well, it's not far to our homestead and my maid has prepared your beds and some supper for us."

"Thank you. That will be most welcome."

The mules make good progress in the light of the lanterns fixed to each side of the cart and the animals seem to be familiar with the route.

Ahead she can make out the lights of dwelling houses and in places glimpses of the moonlight on water. They must be near to the river again. Then the mules are halted, and Rupert says, "We're here. You stay there, Lucy. I'll lift Frankie down and take him inside and then I'll come back to help you down, my dear."

She watches him take Frankie up the steps of the wooden veranda and disappear inside their new home. In the lamplight, through the open door, she can make out part of a wooden sideboard and a sisal rug and is pleased he's made some attempt to make the place homely.

He returns to help her down. She carries her tapestry bag into the home they're destined to share with him. Frankie has awoken and sits up looking anxiously about. He smiles with relief when he sees his mother. She sits down beside him.

Rupert says, "I'll just go and see if our food's ready."

The oil lamps flicker as he leaves the room through the side door and she takes in her surroundings. The room is made of timber, with walls and ceiling clad in boards. It's small and unpretentious, dominated by a stone chimney and fireplace at one end, then arranged before the hearth is the comfortable cowhide upholstered sofa, on which they're sitting, with two matching armchairs. At the far end is a wooden dresser, a small dining table, laid out with cutlery and rattan table mats, and four chairs with padded cowhide seats. On the sideboard is a potted plant of some kind, with bright red bracts in its centre. There's a wide window overlooking the veranda, but no curtains, and outside she can see the moon peeping through clouds. She gets up to look out of the window, but apart from the silver streak of water and the odd patch of firelight flickering in the darkness from across the river, there's nothing to see.

The door to the kitchen opens and Rupert returns with his maid in his wake. He's carrying a tureen of hot steaming stew, and she has bread and butter, which they place on the table. It smells delicious.

"Come and eat before it gets cold," he says, beckoning to them.

Lucy and Frankie sit at the table and Rupert introduces them. "Lucy and Frankie, this is our maid, Tamela. She lives next door, in the extension to the homestead."

Lucy observes the girl and replies, "Hello, Tamela, pleased to meet you. Thank you for preparing this food for us."

The girl dips a curtsey and then sits down next to Rupert to eat with them.

While they eat, Rupert tells her a little more about her surroundings. "This land, that Jack and I have built on, was purchased from Mr Van der Merwe, the farmer. We were lucky, in that we arrived here early on in the diamond rush, not long after a serious drought, and Mr Van der Merwe was struggling, having lost some livestock. Fortunately for us, he was happy to sell us this strip along the river at a reasonable price. We've more land behind the homesteads, suitable for cultivation, but at the moment we buy our milk, butter and cheese from Mrs Van der Merwe. Tamela fetches it whenever we are getting low. Their farmhouse is south of us and about a mile away. You may like to make friends with them. They speak English quite proficiently."

"Indeed, when I'm more settled, I'll certainly pay them a visit." She looks at Tamela. "Perhaps I could accompany you, Tamela. When you next go for our milk?"

The girl lowers her eyes. "Yes, missus."

Rupert changes the subject. "We're also fortunate in that this colony of Griqualand West is now officially British Territory."

"That is reassuring."

"Yes, it is. It all started when there was some trouble between the Boers and the Griqua chief, Nicolaas Waterboer. The Transvaal president intervened and declared the diamond fields Boer property, establishing a temporary government over the diamond fields. The administration of this government, however, wasn't satisfactory to the Griqua, the indigenous Tswana, the diggers, or the Boers. Tension escalated between them all, until a former British sailor, Stafford Parker, organised the disgruntled diggers to drive the Transvaal officials out of the area."

"Oh dear, the battle for control of the money, no doubt?"

"Well many at the Klipdrift settlement supported Parker and he declared the area to be the 'Independent Klipdrift Republic', or some knew it as the 'Diggers Republic', and Parker was named president. Klipdrift was then renamed Parkerton, after him."

Lucy tells him, "Two brothers who travelled here with me both purchased claims at Klipdrift."

Rupert nods, but isn't diverted. "Well, that's not the end of the story, Parker was actually a bit of a rogue and he began to collect taxes, often at gunpoint."

"That tactic must have been worrying for everyone?"

"Yes of course. Eventually, folk in the republic, uneasy with these methods, implored the British government to annex the territory. The junction of the Vaal and Orange rivers is land which the Griqua people regularly pass through, with their herds of animals, but in December two years ago, there were about 10,000 British settlers in the new republic, when Boer forces tried to regain the area through negotiation. The British Governor, Sir Henry Barkly, was asked to mediate, and he set up the Keate Committee to listen to all the evidence. Thankfully they decided in favour of the Griqua Chief, Nicolaas Waterboer, who then offered to place the territory under the administration of Queen Victoria, which, luckily for us, was accepted last year when the 'Griqualand West Colony' was proclaimed to be British Territory."

"That's heartening, Rupert. So, does that mean that Parkerton has become Klipdrift again?"

"Yes, it has, for now anyway." He laughs. "There are so many interested factions, who knows how long that will last?"

Lucy returns the soup spoon to her empty bowl. "That was very tasty and satisfying, Tamela. Thank you." She turns to Rupert. "Unfortunately, Frankie and I are both exhausted, after our long journey. Would you please excuse us this evening, Rupert? I fear Frankie will soon be asleep again at the table."

"Of course, my dear. I trust you'll both be comfortable."

She notes the look of understanding in his green eyes and says gratefully, "Thank you. I'm sure we will. I think tonight I'll sleep through anything." She takes Frankie by the hand. "Come on, darling, it's bedtime."

It's not long before they're in their beds and sleeping soundly.

The following morning, Lucy stirs with the dawn sun lighting up their room. She rubs her eyes. Suddenly she's wide awake. *We're here at last!* She gets out of bed with a new spring in her step and rushes to the windows to look out at their land, but what greets her is an ugly sea of mud between the homestead and the river. At the back of the house there's a lone sweet thorn growing, its pretty yellow acacia blossom now giving way to seed pods.

What a dismal place, no other shrubs or flowers to be seen. The place has been stripped of all vegetation; there's merely a series of humps and hollows to behold. To the north, beyond the banks of the wide sluggish river, there's an untidy tented community of diamond diggers and she can only imagine the unsanitary conditions there. Mercifully, it's far enough away to be beyond earshot.

She washes in the bowl, using the cold water from the ewer Tamela has left for them. How she longs for a hot bath, but she must make the best of things. She dresses in a fresh gown, combs out her hair and pins it up, before dealing with young Frankie. Once they're both dressed, she goes to find Rupert. She discovers a note telling her that he's gone to oversee Neville Frosdyke's claim, which, she remembers from Rupert's letters, is about six miles up-river and on the opposite bank. *He'll probably be gone all day. Well, in that case we've time to explore.*

Thankfully, she has Mr Summers' comfortable leather walking boots and she'd remembered to pack Frankie's little rubber boots too, so they set off along the river at the edge of the working area, to see if they can find Jack Penberthy's place.

The morning sun beats down on them and she's glad they both have sunhats. They wave as they pass Khoisan natives digging and sieving, working Rupert's claim and the next one, which she presumes is the colonel's. Then, sure enough, only about 500 yards away, they come across another homestead, out of sight from their own, because of the southward curve in the river.

As they approach, Lucy can see a man digging nearer to the water's edge with a Khoisan man sifting through the alluvial soil alongside him. The Cornishman is dressed in brown moleskin trousers with a loose-fitting cream shirt and a brown billy-cock hat. She waves in greeting and he discards his spade and makes his way towards them. He approaches her, removing his hat, revealing thinning hair, despite having the bushiest eyebrows and sideburns she's ever seen.

"Hello, I'm Lucy and this is my son, Frankie."

"Ah! Rupert's been looking forward to your arrival. Jack Penberthy at your service." He gives a little bow.

"We're just enjoying some fresh air and discovering the lie of the land."

"Well, there's not much to see, I'm afraid, apart from mud and dust. We've constructed a stone retaining wall to hold back the river and have dug down quite deeply all along it, about twelve foot and more in places, and we're now methodically working outwards and refilling behind us, to sift through the dirt as we go. We've both had some success which, as you can see, has enabled us to construct our homes, but not yet made our fortunes." He grins affably and Lucy is immediately at ease with him.

"It's such a shame that all the vegetation has to be sacrificed. I've been wondering if I might make a garden, behind Rupert's house, where my Frankie could play, and I could grow some vegetables?"

"You'd have to talk to Rupert about that, but it sounds like a good idea to me. We've a pile of discarded topsoil that could be used for your vegetable beds."

She's happy to have thought of a way to be useful and to spend her time with Frankie.

"Well, it's good to meet you, after all this time, Jack. You must come and have supper with us one evening."

"I'd love to. You take care, mind."

"We will. Bye for now, Jack."

"Goodbye, sir," says Frankie, holding out his hand to be shaken. Jack obliges and they're off on their walk again.

At the furthest boundary of the three claims, the landscape gives way to scrub, large rocks and thorn trees, but down by the river's edge are the wafting fronds of pale green willows, dotted with the hanging nests of weaver birds.

"Look, Frankie, can you see the little yellow and black birds, flying to their nests in the willow trees?" She points at them. "Look, darling, that one's still weaving his."

"Oh yes, Mama. He's clever, isn't he?"

"Very clever indeed."

"Oh! Look, Mama. Can you see the deer?"

"I can, my love, and it's called a springbok. There are probably rock rabbits hiding in there too. But, Frankie, this is important – you must never go into the wild area without a grownup with you, because there may be poisonous creatures in there that could harm you."

"Like lions?"

"No not lions, but small creatures like snakes, scorpions or spiders that might sting you and they can be extremely dangerous."

She might not be brave enough to take her son into this wild area, but she can't help but think how beautiful it would be to reinstate these trees along their stretch of the river. They retrace their steps and she decides to make a list of the things she'll need to purchase the next time they go into Hopetown.

When they reach the homestead, she's taken aback to discover a man seated on their veranda. Then delighted to see that it's Ethan. "Ethan! I didn't expect to see you here. You haven't encountered a problem already, surely?"

He stands up. "Hello, Lucy." He gives a little bow. "How are you, Frankie?"

"I'm fine, thank you, Ethan. We've just seen a summerbok."

Lucy smothers her laughter. "You mean springbok, darling."

"Yes, a springbok, Ethan."

"Well done, you."

Lucy opens the door and steps over the threshold. "Please, Ethan, come indoors and I'll get us some refreshments."

"Thank you." He leaves his baggage on the veranda and follows them inside.

"Frankie, go and ask Tamela to prepare us some cordial and biscuits, please." This appeals to the child and he runs off eagerly.

Concerned for her friend, she says, "Please sit down and tell me what's happened, Ethan. You look worried."

He slumps down into the nearest armchair and, his face flushing with suppressed anger, he explains to her his dilemma. "I am worried, Lucy. You were right about that rogue, Simon McCallister; he's fiddled me out of £150 for a non-existent claim!"

"Oh no, Ethan. I'm so sorry. I take no pleasure in being proved right. What are you going to do?"

"I'm hoping to get some work somehow to enable me to earn some of my money back, so that I can afford to purchase a genuine claim. But in the meantime, I'm left virtually penniless, with just my tent, a bedroll and my tools to my name. It was so embarrassing. I turned up at the licence tent at New Rush and handed over the paperwork, only to be told that the claim in question was owned by someone else! I accused the fellow of being a claim jumper, but he was the one with the genuine papers and I looked a right fool."

"Oh dear, you poor man. You must stay here with us tonight, as long as you've no objection to sleeping on the sofa, and when Rupert returns home, we'll see if he can help at all."

Tamela enters with a tray of glasses, a plate of homemade biscuits and an eager Frankie in her wake.

"Tamela, this is my friend Ethan and he'll be staying to supper tonight, so please make allowances when you're preparing the food."

The girl nods her head and says, "Yes, missus," before returning to her room.

The lemon cordial is refreshing, but the biscuits are hard and dry, not at all what Lucy and Frankie are used to and she vows to do the baking herself in the future.

When Rupert returns, he walks in asking, "What's that carpet bag and bedroll doing on the *stoep*?"

"Oh! I'm sorry, it's mine," says Ethan, standing up and holding out his hand to shake.

Lucy observes Rupert's indignant reaction to finding a strange man in his house. She tries to enlighten him. "Rupert, this is Ethan Hart, one of my companions on the *Syria* and on the journey to the diamond fields."

Rupert shakes his hand begrudgingly, and she continues to explain. "He's come here for our advice, because he's been swindled by a confidence trickster on the ship. The claim he purchased in good faith, for £150 at the New Rush diamond fields, turns out to be fraudulent and is already occupied by its rightful owner. He's, therefore, in dire need of our help."

Rupert studies Ethan critically. "How did you manage to find us?"

Ethan turns his hat in his hands. "Lucy gave me a rough idea of your address and I made enquiries at the post office. I'd nowhere else to go. Besides, there are no more claims available at New Rush now, it's proved so productive."

She steps forward and links her arm in Rupert's. "I said Ethan could stay here tonight, in the hope you might be able to suggest a solution to his problem, Rupert."

He peers down his nose at her. "That was hospitable of you, Lucy, but I'm afraid there's only the sofa available."

"That will be preferable to pitching my tent. If you're sure you've no objection."

"None at all. I'll go and see what Tamela has concocted for our supper."

Peeved by Rupert's brusque manner, Lucy is relieved when he leaves the room. She smiles and says to Ethan, "Please, Ethan, make yourself at home."

The poor man looks uncomfortable, as he sits back down in one of the armchairs.

This time Tamela doesn't join them for supper and Lucy is surprised when Rupert makes a suggestion. "I've been thinking about your predicament, Ethan, and I may have a solution."

"Really?" Ethan looks surprised.

"Yes. I'm responsible for a claim about six miles up-river, owned by my sponsor Neville Frosdyke, and between you and me the logistics of working our claims here and that one, which is also inconveniently sited on the opposite, northern bank of the river, are not the most efficient. If you're interested, I could employ you to manage Frosdyke's claim. It would free me up to concentrate on mine and my father's claims."

"That would be most agreeable, sir."

"I haven't told you the terms yet, Ethan."

"Beggars can't be choosers, and I'm extremely grateful for your help."

She looks at Ethan and can't help thinking, *Don't be too hasty to accept, Ethan. Rupert wouldn't offer this unless it benefitted him the most.*

"I can offer you a basic retainer and then it'll be up to you to make a profit for Neville and take a small percentage for yourself."

"Let's be frank, Rupert. What will be my allowance and what percentage would be acceptable to Mr Frosdyke?"

"Well, I'm entitled to twenty-five percent but, as I'm also employing you, I think that I can afford to reduce that to fifteen percent and give you the remaining ten percent of any discoveries, which would also be fair to Neville."

"And my retainer fee?"

"Would £10 a month be acceptable?"

"Yes, sir. Thank you." They shake hands across the table.

The following morning Rupert takes Ethan to Neville Frosdyke's claim. Lucy has persuaded him to let her go with them, with a view to going into Hopetown afterwards to get some shopping. Not yet comfortable leaving Frankie behind with Tamela, even though that's what Rupert suggested, she insists he comes too.

She holds her parasol over them in the front of the cart, to protect them both from the heat, while Ethan bounces up and down in the rear. They go into Hopetown and cross the River Orange via the ford. Then follow the river eastward, until they come to the diamond fields situated in the alluvial triangle formed by the Orange and the Vaal rivers. This field, although smaller than the others she's seen, is still a mass of ramshackle, rickety dwellings, tents and covered wagons, with multiple humps and bumps in the sea of dirt. Now close up, the squalor and stench of the settlement is overwhelming. There are open trenches sited randomly amid the shacks and tents, serving as public middens, with flies swarming along them.

They pass through the central wagonway, causing a cloud of dust to follow in their wake, until Rupert locates the claim. Then he and Ethan jump down, and Rupert introduces him to his native workers, all with bare feet and dressed in torn scruffy shirts and rolled up trousers. Lucy remains with Frankie in the mule cart, handkerchiefs held over their mouths as they watch the two men. *Thank goodness Ethan was able to find them, otherwise it doesn't bear thinking of what might have befallen him.*

She scans the township, observing the dust, the sweating working men and the flies. A costermonger trundles along one row with his cart of provisions, including a large barrel, possibly wine, and in another row, the waterman fills up ewers and buckets as he passes with his water-wagon.

Rupert returns with an expression on his face that suggests he's rather pleased with himself. He grins down at her and then says, "Right then, let's go into town and show you off to the traders."

"Well, Rupert, if you plan to show me off, then I think I ought to visit the bathhouse first," she says smiling.

"Well, that can be arranged. I can take Frankie for something to eat and drink, while you go and pamper yourself."

Rupert drives the mules through the ford and along the main street and pulls up outside a corrugated iron building, which serves as the bathhouse. Lucy's apprehensive, not knowing what to expect, but he encourages her to go in. When she enters, she finds that one side is for men and the other side is for women and she relaxes a little. She pays the attendant, who gives her two bath towels and a tablet of soap, and she's led to a cubicle containing a cast-iron bath full of fresh warm water. She strips off her clothes and her jewellery, removes the pins from her hair, allowing it to tumble onto her bare skin, and steps in, luxuriating in the warm soapy water immediately relaxing her. She soaps her skin all over and scrubs away the dirt, then ducks her head under, to wash the dust from her hair. She'd like to linger longer, but she doesn't want to leave Frankie too long with Rupert, in case he gets upset. She steps out eventually and dries herself in the towels, rubbing her chestnut curls vigorously to remove all the water, then she twists her damp hair into a bun and pins it into place. She dresses and replaces her jewellery, turning her wedding and engagement rings over and over on her finger. They make her feel safer, when in the company of strangers. She then goes to find Rupert and Frankie.

The road outside the bathhouse is lined with all kinds of businesses, many are diamond related, but there's also an apothecary, a pawnbroker, a barber, the First National Bank, and what appears to be a brothel on her side of the roadway, and on the other side, she sees the Northern Cape Karoo Hotel, plus the butcher, the baker, a grocer, the Diggers Rest saloon, Wernher and Mege diamond merchants, and the general stores. In the opposite direction, she spots Rupert and Frankie sitting by the window of a luncheon bar and she crosses the carriageway and steps onto the boardwalk, before they see her.

Rupert jumps up and opens the door to let her inside.

"Do you feel better?"

"I do, thank you. It was well overdue." She smiles at him as he pulls out a seat for her. "After you've had your refreshments, I'll introduce you to Mr and Mrs Buthelezi who run the general store. I've an account there, which you can also use when you come into town for our household items."

Half an hour later they're being guided into the store, to be greeted by the owner. "Good morning, Mr Seymour. How are you this fine morning?"

"I'm well, thank you, Mr Buthelezi. I'd like to introduce you to Mrs Seymour, who's recently arrived from England with young Frankie, here."

"I'm very pleased to meet you at last. I know Mr Seymour has been eagerly awaiting your arrival."

She dips a small curtsey. "Likewise, Mr Buthelezi. I'm sure I'll be popping in here regularly to peruse your comprehensive stock. I'm particularly interested in some gardening tools today and some seeds."

"Then come this way, my dear. How about you, son? Are you also interested in helping your mama in the garden?"

"Yes, sir."

"Then I've a small wheelbarrow that's just your size." He pulls it out and demonstrates to Frankie, who's most impressed and looks appealingly at his mother.

Rupert then says to Lucy, "Just choose what you need, and I'll put it on my account."

She says, "What about the little wheelbarrow for Frankie?"

"I'm sure we can run to that."

In addition to the wheelbarrows, she selects a fork and spade, a hand fork and trowel, pruning cutters, and a variety of salad vegetable seeds, plus grass seeds for a lawn, a packet of multicoloured mesembryanthemum seeds, and packets of morning glory and nasturtiums seeds, for Frankie to plant and nurture.

The Khoisan lads assisting Mr Buthelezi help them load the items onto the cart, while Rupert settles their bill.

As they leave the shop, Mr Buthelezi, says, "Thank you for your custom, Mr and Mrs Seymour, and have a good day."

Lucy can't help but think that Rupert's deliberately implying they're a married couple and that Frankie's his son. She anxiously twists her rings. It may well be that she does agree to become his wife in time, but it's premature, and she's uncomfortable enabling this deception. However, she's delivered herself into his hands and she must make the best of it. He seems to believe she's here to stay and so in that case she'll make the place her home.

She turns to him. "Rupert, is there a draper here in Hopetown?"

"Yes, there is, at the end of the main street; why?"

"I'd like to make some curtains and also I was wondering, as we're so close to the river, if it might not be wise to have some mosquito nets."

"Well, we can have a look to see what Mrs Erasmus has in stock."

They move the mule cart along and pull up outside the drapers.

Lucy looks at Rupert. "Do we have enough money to purchase a sewing machine?"

"I suspect we'd have to order that from Port Elizabeth, but let's go and see what she has."

They all enter the premises and Lucy is pleased to see that there's an impressive display of bolts of cloth, stacked in rows and reaching as high as the wall plate, giving way to the vaulted roof. She spots a bright and colourful design she likes, with tropical birds and butterflies, ferns and flowers and she asks Mrs Erasmus if she could have a closer look.

"Yes, this is perfect, Mrs Erasmus. As it's a large pattern, I'd like twelve yards of this one, please, with two reels of thread to match? Also do you have any mosquito nets for hanging over the beds?"

"Yes, madam. I've some designed to hang from the ceiling."

"I'd like two of those please, to fit double beds."

Rupert watches on, his face impassive, and she hopes he's not worried by her spending. Frankie's exploring and Rupert goes to see what he's doing. He returns with a sewing machine. "This was over on the other side of the shop."

"Oh! How wonderful. Thank you, Rupert. Can we really have this too?"

"Well, it'll take you forever to hand stitch the curtains, and I'm sure it'll be useful for clothes for Frankie too."

Impulsively, she kisses him on his cheek, for his kindness, and notices his face flushing. This is really playing into his hands, giving the impression they're already a married couple, but he's been so good to them and to Ethan, and she's happy he's being so amenable.

CHAPTER SIX *(January 1873)*

THE SHEPHERD'S HEART

On New Year's Eve, Aurora is feeling bored. Her brother is busy learning from their father's law books and so she decides to go into town with her father, in order to pop in and see Luke at his work. She hasn't seen him since Christmas Eve, when he gave her a gift of perfume and she gave him a fountain pen and propelling pencil set. She's wearing the sweet-smelling apple blossom perfume today and wonders if he'll notice.

Joshua pulls up the gig in the borough. "I'm just popping in to see Bobby Tompkins and his brother to pick up half a pig for Flora. I also want to get something for Eli's fifteenth birthday on the nineteenth of January, so I might go along Princes Street to Whitby's the bookseller to see if they've anything suitable."

Aurora looks up at the clock tower, on the town hall. "Shall I meet you in Princes Street in about half an hour, then, Papa?"

"You'd better make it an hour. You know what it's like, folk always want to stop and chat and delay you."

"A quarter past eleven, then."

"Right, my dear. I'll watch out for you exiting Church Lane."

Aurora makes her way along Church Path to Mr Fairway's solicitor's office and then down the steps of Church Terrace. She knocks softly and enters the office, to find Luke and Clara in close conversation. Clara is seated with a ledger before her and Luke is leaning over her. They are totally unaware of her presence.

Luke's voice is persuasive. "Come on, Clara, you're a lovely woman and any man would be lucky to win you."

Aurora clears her throat, and at the sound, Luke jerks away from Clara.

"Am I interrupting something?" she asks, her green eyes glinting with jealousy.

"No, no of course not, Rora. I was just trying to convince Clara that Jacob would be lucky to have her on his arm."

Clara looks at her earnestly. "Please, Aurora, don't misunderstand. Your Luke is quite safe with me; he's more like a younger brother. Besides, he only has eyes for you."

Aurora smiles. "He's right. You and Jacob would make a good match and a fine couple."

She notes Luke sighing with relief, and thinks to herself, *I'm not yet done with you, young man.*

She asks Clara, "Have you heard from Lucy yet?"

Clara shakes her head. "No, I haven't. Has anyone?"

"She must still be travelling. It's a fearful way, both over land and sea. I know from experience, it takes forever."

Clara frowns with concern. "I hope they're both safe and well. There are so many possible hazards, with storms at sea, infectious diseases and poisonous creatures."

Luke reassures her. "I'm sure they'll both be fine, Clara. You worry far too much."

Clara changes the subject. "Would you like a cup of cocoa, Aurora? We usually have one at about this time."

"Yes please, Clara. That would be splendid."

Clara leaves the office area and disappears inside the cottage. Luke takes this opportunity to take Aurora's hand, pull her into his arms and kiss her and she allows this concession, enjoying the moment of passion, but they're interrupted when Mr Fairway enters and they both pull apart.

If he noticed, he doesn't comment. Instead he says, "Good morning, my dear. How nice to see you. How's your father?"

"He's quite well, thank you, Mr Fairway. He brought me into town earlier and I'm meeting him again in half an hour. He's been chatting about the wassailing ceremony on Sunday. Will you and Clara be joining us again this year?"

Clara enters, carrying a heavy tray, on which there are four mugs of steaming cocoa and a plate of biscuits.

"We'd love to. Wouldn't we, Clara?"

"What's that, Papa?"

"We'd love to go wassailing again this year, wouldn't we?"

"Of course, that would be lovely; but I think you mean next year, Papa," she says, smiling.

Until the appointed time to meet her father looms, Aurora enjoys the hot drink and homemade biscuits.

That evening Clara is thinking about Luke and Aurora's comments. *Is everyone talking about me and Jacob already? It's only been a couple of months, but there's no denying that I have feelings for him. He's so kind and handsome with his mop of dark brown hair and soulful blue eyes.* The thought of his lips on hers makes her blush and she gets up to clear away the dinner things, before her father notices.

While she's standing over the sink with her hands submerged in warm soapy water she continues to dream. *Is it possible that Jacob's genuinely in love with me, as he professes? Could this really be the love of my life? After suffering so much heartache at the hands of Rupert, it's hard to believe, but it would fulfil my dearest dreams to create a family with Jacob, before it's too late.*

Tears brim her eyes at the thought of it and she wipes them away with the back of her hand, in the process dripping soap suds down the front of her bodice and her apron.

Jacob has been courting Clara ever since Aurora and Lucy's party in September and he finds himself distracted, all over the Christmas and New Year celebrations, with delicious thoughts of her. He'd given up on love and a family of his own, contenting himself with being an uncle to Malachi and Rosa's children instead.

At first, he confides in Malachi, who seems delighted for his younger brother, advising him, "Don't dilly dally, Jacob. Time waits for no man and, if you want to have some nippers, you can't afford to wait any longer."

"But do you think we'll be compatible, Mal? I am but a poor shepherd and she'd set her sights a lot higher."

"What, with that arrogant prig, Rupert Seymour? You know what I thought of our Lucy marrying Ashleigh. Well he's just as bad, and Clara's a sweet girl who deserves better. She deserves someone caring and kind, like you, Jacob. Don't do yourself down, lad."

Buoyed by his brother's advice and, over the moon with happiness, he sets his plans in motion. After discussing his situation with his parents, he organises with Joshua to take over number four Camp Road, when the Porters eventually find a place nearer to their daughters and move away. His mother bursts into action collecting together linen and materials for cushions and curtains in readiness, even though he hasn't yet plucked up the courage to tell Clara his intentions.

He divides his time, over the festive season, between his family and the Fairways, and their Christmas gifts are all related to domesticity. Rosa and Malachi give them an attractive brass oil lamp, Bunny and Edwin, a fine walnut canteen of cutlery, and Clara's father purchases a washstand, decorated with floral ceramic tiles for Clara's bedroom. Which, she whispers to Jacob, will one day be perfect for their new home.

He's glad to be distracted by the celebrations, because they make the time pass by more quickly, and he can't wait to surprise her on twelfth night, at the wassailing fertility festival.

On the night in question, Clara arrives at Home Farm with her father. They're both muffled against the cold and Clara is wearing her fur wrap and matching hat. Jacob rushes outside to greet them and then together with the rest of the Warren family, they proceed to the Alvington Manor orchards. Clara's father and Bunny carry flaming torches. Isaac has his shotgun. Beth and Clara have pots and pans and Jacob has found an old broken shepherd's crook, which he can bang on a copper cauldron, like a drum.

They can hear the folk descending from Camp Road as Malachi, Rosa and the children join them. They merge with the kitchen staff and Joshua and his family. Joshua and Gabriel carry Flora's ornate silver wassail bowl between them, leading the way into the orchard, while everyone else makes as much noise as they can muster, with their improvised instruments.

They assemble under the oldest apple tree. The mouth-watering aroma of the spiced hot ale permeates the air around them. Jacob looks at Clara lovingly, her ice blue eyes sparkling in the cold, like the stars in the frosty, clear night sky overhead. He smiles at her warmly, as they each take a cup of the steaming brew to toast the most venerable tree in the orchard, and Joshua starts the traditional chant.

"Health to thee, good apple tree. Stand fast root, bear well top. Pray God send us a good howling crop. Every bough, apples endow. Every twig, apples big. Health to thee, good apple tree." Everyone drinks to the health of the tree, then they join in with the chorus. *"Hats full, caps full, full quarter sacks full. Holler, boys, holler!"*

Immediately the assembled folk shout, making as much noise as they can, beating the trees about the trunks and branches to begin the process of awakening the orchard and starting the sap flowing up the trunks. Both Isaac and John Boucher fire their shotguns up into the branches, to frighten away any evil spirits that might be lurking up there.

When all the noise and commotion is over, they all bow to the esteemed tree. Joshua lifts two-year-old Lydia May, the youngest person present, up into a low fork of the branches, where he can still hold her safely. She's passed offerings of bread, cheese and cider, to represent the spirit of the tree receiving the gifts.

Finally, the remainder of the wassail cup is sloshed over and around the trunk of the esteemed ancient tree and pieces of toasted bread, soaked in cider, are placed in the forks, branches or hollows of the other trees and left there as offerings.

Jacob can't help but see a correlation with his awakening love for Clara and he begins to tremble at the enormity of the decision he's made, but he's certain it's the right decision for him, and he hopes it will be for Clara too.

When he was just a young lad, he discovered a fossilised sea urchin, that he's kept in a drawer with his treasured possessions ever since. Now he has it secreted in his pocket. It's special to him, because it's known as a shepherd's heart, and he wants to give it to Clara.

He asks Joshua if he'd mind if he makes an announcement.

"Of course not, Jacob. Wait a moment." Joshua lifts Lydia May down from the tree and she runs to her mother. Then he borrows two pots from Ellie Proctor, the scullery maid, and bangs them together. "Excuse me, everyone. Jacob would like your attention please."

Jacob clears his throat and taking Clara's hand, he draws her out from the gathering to stand before him. "Clara, I have a small gift for you, and I hope that I can trust you to take good care of it." He hands her the heart-shaped fossil.

She studies it and to his delight she smiles and kisses him on his cheek. He's thrilled that she immediately understands. He then goes down on one knee and says to her, "I am herewith giving you my shepherd's heart to have and to hold with utmost care. My dearest Clara, will you do me the great honour of agreeing to become my wife?" Then he produces a small box, which, with shaking hands, he gives to her. He holds his breath in anticipation, as she opens the box to discover a gold engagement ring, with an elegant design of sapphires and diamonds.

Clara looks radiant as she says to him, "I will treasure your loving shepherd's heart and I am honoured to accept your offer of matrimony."

There's a huge cheer from their family and friends. Jacob takes Clara in his arms and kisses her passionately, accompanied by the squeals of delight from Louisa, Rosa, Lettie, Bunny, Ruby and Daisy.

Soon the wind gets up and folk are feeling the wintry chill of it. Louisa says to Joshua, "I'm afraid I must take Lydia May home to her bed now, she's feeling the cold." Joshua and his family say their farewells and the rest of the folk all return to the warmth of their firesides.

Ambrose Fairway returns to Home Farm with Clara, and Isaac says to them, "Please come inside with us, so we can all toast your happy betrothal."

He says, "Thank you, Isaac. That will be most appropriate and very acceptable."

He watches the giggling couple, standing arm in arm, as the drinks are handed around and Isaac makes the toast. He's in a fug of conflicting emotions, not wanting to lose her. His Lucy is taking flight, but he can see that she's already transformed from a sad, lonely and pining young girl into a radiant joyful woman, with the world at her feet. He couldn't be more delighted for her. He's only ever wanted the best for her and now he kisses her and shakes Jacob's hand, giving them his blessing. "I'm so pleased for both of you. It gladdens my heart to see such a happy couple on the brink of their lives together." He wipes the tears away from his eyes and Clara hugs him, her eyes also brimming with tears.

"I'll be near enough to see you all the time, Papa. I'd never desert you."

"I know that, lass, and I couldn't be happier." He lowers his voice. "I did fear that you might agree to emigrate to South Africa with your first love, Rupert Seymour, and I was never reconciled with it. I'm so relieved you didn't take such a huge, irreversible step. Now you have the love of a kind, genuine man who'll care for you for the rest of your life. I'm content you'll always be safe, whatever befalls me."

Bunny says, "So, when's the wedding and can I be maid of honour?"

Clara giggles. "Of course, and Ruby and Daisy can be flower girls too."

"We've a lot of decisions to make now, Bunny," says Jacob, looking a little overwhelmed.

Ambrose, sensing his anxiety, asks, "In what regard?"

"Well, our marriage ceremony has to be planned and I expect there'll be a great deal for Clara and her ladies in waiting to decide."

He says, "Well, I imagine you'll be married in St John's Church in the borough, as we live right on the doorstep."

Clara reassures him, "Don't worry, Jacob. I know the Rev Mathieson well, and when we've decided how soon we want the ceremony to take place, we can go to see him together."

Jacob looks at her. "How about August? Will that give you ladies enough time to prepare?"

Clara glances at her papa, and he immediately says, "Don't worry about the expense, that will be my concern and I want the best for my Clara. Please, you must choose whatever you need for you and your bridesmaids and I'll cover the cost."

Jacob's mother smiles. "I'm sure we can find some suitable materials in Ivell. Rosa, Bunny and I will all help with the sewing, so I'm quite confident we could do it by then."

Isaac removes his pipe and puffs out a cloud of Erinmore, adding, "And me and your ma will take care of the refreshments for the wedding breakfast."

Jacob gives a sigh of relief. "Well, that's settled, then. We'll go to the vicar, as soon as we can, and see if he can officiate at the ceremony for us, sometime during August." He hugs and kisses Clara, seemingly no longer being plagued with his shyness.

The following day, concerned because they've, as yet, heard nothing from her, Bunny decides to write a letter to her sister. She wants to be the first to tell her the good news, knowing how thrilled Lucy will be for her closest friend and her brother. She also wonders what Rupert's thoughts will be on the matter.

Mrs Lucy Seymour
C/O Hopetown Post Office
Hopetown
Pixley ka Seme
Thembelihle
Northern Cape Province
South Africa

Dearest Lucy and Frankie,

I am writing to tell you the wonderful news that Jacob and Clara are engaged to be married and their wedding is planned for Sunday 10ᵗʰ August this year. I am to be the maid of honour and Ruby and Daisy are flower girls again. Our Eli, Toby Boucher, Luke Proctor, Frank and Thomas Hawkins, and my Edwin will be ushers and of course Malachi is best man.

It would be wonderful if you could be here with us for this happy event, but I am sure they will both understand if it is not possible.

I have never seen our brother smitten before, but he is the happiest I have ever known him to be and Clara is so content with him, it is heart-warming. Ma and Pa are both thrilled that he has at last found happiness, and Clara's papa is happy to have Clara living close by on Camp Road.

We all hope that you and Frankie are both well and happy and we eagerly await your first letter, telling us all you have both arrived, safe and sound. Mama will not rest easy until she hears from you, so please write soon.

Your loving sister,
Bunny xx

She blots the ink and then wipes off her dipping pen, placing it back on its tray, then she puts her missive into an envelope and seals the letter with wax, ready for posting.

CHAPTER SEVEN *(January–February 1873)*

THE SEED OF SUSPICION

Lucy is quite content, turning their claim into a family home. Her relationship with Rupert is still at the affectionate stage, with the occasional kiss on the cheek from him, but nothing more and she's relieved that he's taking things slowly for now. There's an easy, relaxed atmosphere between them, although she still feels a frostiness from Tamela, which she tries to ignore. She tends to leave the girl to her duties inside the dwelling, while she enjoys the sunshine outside with Frankie.

When gardening, she's discounted her summer gowns as far too impractical and taken one of Rupert's old pairs of trousers and cut them down to her size. She wears these with string tied around her ankles, to ensure that no creatures can climb up her trouser leg. She does the same for Frankie and he's her shadow while they're outside working. Together they transfer the topsoil in their wheelbarrows to the garden behind the homestead and sift it for a seed bed. Frankie plants his flower seeds and in the process unearths some shiny stones that he believes to be diamonds. He collects them together and hides his treasure in an old tobacco tin that Jack Penberthy had discarded.

They work hard from early in the morning, then have a siesta when the sun's at its zenith. Frankie loves to be outside in the fresh air and his curls are even lighter, where the sunlight has bleached his hair. His mother keeps reminding him to wear his sun hat, but nevertheless, she often finds it hanging on the end of his wheelbarrow handles. His skin is as brown as a nut, as are Lucy's hands, where she hates working with gloves on. At night-time she massages cream into them to try to keep them supple.

One day, when they're outside working, Lucy whispers to Frankie, "Stand very still, Frankie, and look at the base of the house. There's a troop of mongooses there. Can you see them?"

"Yes, Mama, I can. Look, they're eating the bread we put down for the waxbills and the weaver birds."

"We ought to encourage them to visit, because they'll be good for keeping the snakes away."

A fly pitches on the back of Frankie's hand and he instinctively shakes it off. With the sudden movement, the dwarf mongooses take flight instantly. "Oh!" moans Frankie with disappointment.

"Don't worry, I expect they'll be back, now they know there's food here. We can put some fruit out for them tomorrow."

When they go inside for their luncheon, Frankie shows her his collection of gemstones. Lucy has also contributed, believing that this soil has already been checked by the men, but some of the gems look quite convincing. One definitely looks like a garnet. She decides to find an old piece of glass among the offcuts in the builders' waste pile, and check each of them, by seeing if they'll make a mark. Sure enough a few of the clear ones cut a mark in the glass and she believes they may be small diamonds, but she decides to keep it as their secret.

The dwarf mongooses become regular visitors, until one day after feeding, the pack leave, but Frankie finds they've left behind a small fellow with an injured back leg. He runs to his mother. "Mama, there's a baby mongoose who's hurt his leg and he can't keep up with the others."

Lucy goes to look, and finds the poor little creature is exhausted with the pain from his injured limb. She decides to make a splint for it. She finds a thin stick and cuts it to length and then ties it to his back leg with some tape. Frankie finds a small wooden fruit box and puts some of Tamela's dusters inside to make a comfy bed for him and they nurse him back to health together with gifts of grasshoppers and other bugs. Because he's so young, he accepts their administrations without complaint and after a few weeks of discomfort, he's ready to have the splint removed. He scampers around after Frankie, and thrilled to have a pet, the child names him Monty.

When he sees Frankie's adopted pet, Rupert also points out a resident chameleon. "Come and see what we have, living here on the *stoep*, Frankie."

He names her Camilla and he soon discovers that she's brilliant for demolishing all the bugs and flies. Frankie collects them from the windowsills and takes them outside to the *stoep* for her. Monty and Camilla seem to ignore each other; Monty has indoors, and she has the *stoep*.

One morning, she leaves Frankie with Rupert and accompanies Tamela to get the milk and eggs from the farm. It's a pleasant walk across this small part of the Karoo. The arid land extends to the far horizon, only being broken by the farm buildings in the distance, the occasional thorn tree, dots of sheep, termite mounds and the russet brown rosettes of the aloes.

Tamela carries the basket, the milk pail and the money that Rupert has given to her to pay for the produce. Although Tamela is usually monosyllabic, Lucy perseveres, trying to make friends with the young girl.

"How long have you worked for Mr Seymour, Tamela?"

"Long time, missus."

"What did you do before?"

"Work on farm, missus."

"Where do your family live?"

"On farm, missus."

She patiently dabs away some perspiration from the back of her neck with her handkerchief. "Do you have any brothers or sisters?"

"Brothers on farm, missus."

She studies the girl. She's of a sturdy build, with wiry black curly hair and deep brown sullen eyes. She pushes on with her questions. "Are you happy with Mr Seymour?"

"Yes, missus."

"Is there anything that you need for your room?"

"No, missus."

Lucy gives up. It's such hard work; she's sure the girl doesn't like her. Instead she stares ahead at the heat haze shimmering over the sandy terrain ahead and is pleased when they reach the shady confines of the farm.

Tamela makes straight for the dairy, but on her way, Lucy notices her glancing over to the servants' quarters. She sees an elderly black woman with a child in her lap, sitting in the doorway of the outbuildings; a flock of chickens busily peck around her feet. *I suppose that's Tamela's mother.*

She knocks on the front door. A young woman answers her knock, her fair hair, pinned up in a long braid, circling her head.

"Good morning. I'm Lucy Seymour and I was wondering if I might introduce myself to Mrs Van der Merwe?"

"Of course, please come. I am Anja, her daughter. Pleased to meet you."

"Tamela, our maid, has come to purchase our milk and eggs."

"My mother will be in the dairy, please follow me."

She follows Anja through the large kitchen and into the dairy attached, where they find Mrs Van der Merwe churning her cream to make butter. Tamela has already left.

"Mama, this is Mrs Seymour come to introduce herself."

"Ah, my dear. How nice to meet you." She turns to her daughter. "Please, Anja, replace me here for a while." Anja takes over the handle of the butter churn.

"Come and have a cup of tea with me. I don't often have visitors. It's a good surprise."

Lucy smiles at this warm welcome.

As Mrs Van der Merwe passes through their kitchen, she asks her maid to prepare some tea. She's shown into an attractive parlour. "Please make yourself at home."

"Thank you." She sits down in a comfortable armchair, immediately noticing a piano in the corner of the room and her fingers itch to play it.

"Now we're neighbours, you must call me Hilda."

"Thank you, Hilda. I'm Lucy."

Hilda sits down opposite her. "Do you have everything you need, on Rupert's claim, Lucy?"

"We're very fortunate, Hilda. Rupert prepared well for us and we're both settling in already. I've planted some lettuce, tomato, radish, cucumber and butternut seeds, which we are watering to bring on, but I'm a bit wary of the jackrabbits."

"I doubt they'll trouble you; they're far too shy."

"Oh, that's good. It's such hard work to do anything in this heat; it would be such a shame for it all to go to waste."

"Unfortunately, that's the trials and tribulations of agriculture in the Karoo, my dear. If it's not locusts, its drought. We're suffering from drought at the moment, not having had rain for several weeks now. We're praying it won't turn into months, as it has done in the past. You see, we're not far from the Kalahari Desert and so we get minimal rain from the north."

The maid enters with a tray, which she places on a small table, beside her host. "How do you like your tea, Lucy?"

"With milk and a teaspoonful of sugar, please."

There's a moment of quiet, while Hilda pours the tea. Then she passes a steaming cup to Lucy and sits back to enjoy her unexpected break. "How are you getting on with Tamela?"

Lucy screws up her face thinking and then answers, "I don't think she likes me."

"Well, that may be because she had to bring her child back to her mother to care for, here at the farm, just before you arrived."

She's stunned. "Really? Tamela has a child? But she's hardly more than a child herself. How old is she?"

"I believe she's about sixteen or seventeen, but she won't tell her mother who the father is, which has caused some bad feeling between her and her parents."

"Oh my! I'd no idea! I'll talk to Rupert and see if he'll change his mind."

"Maybe leave it a while and see if she settles down, only she won't be so useful to you with a small child to keep occupied."

"That's true."

"If you look out of the window now, you'll see she's with him and her mother. All our farm workers are members of the Xirikua or Griekwa clan, who were pastoral, nomadic, hunter-gatherers, until they settled here in Griqualand."

Lucy looks out at the servants' quarters and sees Tamela, sitting alongside her mother, with the child on her lap. The mother and daughter are a dark mahogany brown, but the child is coffee-coloured, and Lucy suspects she's been with a white man.

"She's named the child Berko, which she told Anja means 'firstborn son'."

Lucy sits back down and drinks some more of her tea, determined to switch the conversation. "You speak good English, Hilda."

"Yes, I've been learning for years, from some friends we've made on a neighbouring farm, who are English."

"Do they have a family?"

"Yes, a teenaged son and two daughters." Lucy relaxes a little. *Perhaps that's the answer to the question – the teenaged son.* But Hilda continues, "The lad's away at Oxford University back in England."

"Do you have a large family, Hilda?"

"Anja has a younger sister, Marta, and an older brother, Friedrich, whom we call Ricky. He works with his father on the farm."

Maybe he's the father? She changes the subject again. "Who plays the piano?"

"It was my mother's. I used to have lessons, but I'm not so good at it and very out of practice. We don't do much entertaining these days."

"It's one of the things I miss from home, in addition to my family, of course. I've left behind, in England, my parents, two older brothers and a younger sister. Plus, my eldest brother's married with three children. I miss them all, as you can imagine, but I have to admit this is an adventure and I'm quite enjoying it."

"Well, you know where we are if you need any help, or you have any problems, and you're welcome to come and play the piano whenever you wish."

"Thank you, Hilda. That's very kind. I'd better make tracks and leave you to get on with your butter making. Poor Anja will be glad of your return, I'm sure." She stands up to leave and Hilda shows her out into the hot sunshine. She replaces her sunhat and calls for Tamela to follow. She can't shake off the seed of suspicion that Rupert could possibly be the child's father and she feels homesick and uncertain of her situation. When she gets back to the homestead, she'll write to her family.

The weeks pass by uneventfully. Lucy has kept her unsettling suspicions in check and has said nothing. Instead she's busied herself completing the curtains, and making some cushion covers with the excess material. Obligingly, Rupert has helped her hang them on rods across the front and back windows.

Then one hot, dry day she enters their living room from the kitchen to discover, Frankie staring in horror at the arching neck and huge hood of a cobra, outside on the *stoep*, silhouetted in the doorway and staring inside, straight at her son.

She says shakily, "Stay absolutely still and close your eyes, Frankie. Trust me, they try to spit venom into your eyes." She moves bit by bit back towards the kitchen door to get the broom but, speedily, from the side of the front doorway flies Monty. His teeth clamp around the throat of the snake. They wrestle; the snake twisting and twirling around, trying to shake him off and poor Monty spinning and hanging on for dear life. Frankie screams, terrified for his tiny pal.

Then, out of nowhere, Moses is on the *stoep* and with one smooth strike, he decapitates the creature with his machete, just below Monty's tiny paws. Monty jumps out of the way and they all breathe a sigh of relief.

"Thank you, Moses. That was scary! You were very quick." She smiles at him with gratitude.

He picks up the snake's head and puts it into the rubbish sack. Then he holds up the remainder of the snake and points to himself."

She nods her head. "Oh yes, of course, take it."

He grins from ear to ear. "My woman cook," he says in explanation.

She says to him, "Do you have little ones?" and she holds her hand down at Frankie's height.

He nods his head and holds up five fingers.

"My goodness, five children. They must keep you busy."

He gives a toothy grin.

Lucy is conscious that she hasn't seen hardly any rain since her arrival. No wonder the ground is so dry and dusty. Her garden's being irrigated with piped water from the river, but because it's uphill, it has to be pumped out into buckets and then run through the small dykes she's created between the beds. Already the seeds have germinated, and tiny green shoots are peeping through the rich alluvial topsoil.

Today it's hot and heady. There'll be a thunderstorm judging by the thunder clouds on the horizon. Their seedlings are rather small to be beaten by a torrent of rain, but generally it will be a good thing and definitely good for the farm.

Soon the thunder crashes overhead, huge frozen balls of hail beat down, pounding the roof, and lightning flashes throughout the pewter-coloured sky all around them. Frankie sidles up to her for reassurance and she gives him a cuddle on the sofa. Monty hides under the sideboard. Rupert has told the men to take shelter with Tamela in the extension and he too takes refuge with her and Frankie. As darkness falls, the sky is illuminated by hundreds of electric strikes and the storm lasts for about another hour. When the rain ceases, she sees the flickering torchlight, as Moses and Solomon leave for their homes.

The following morning the diggers' trench is waterlogged. Moses and Solomon are back and busy pumping it out, while Rupert oversees their work. The sun is up, and all the hail has melted away. The land smells fresh and enlivened by the mineral-enriched rain. She inspects the garden and finds their seedlings are steadily recovering from being flattened by the downpour of hail. She wants to plant more flowers and also get some baking ingredients and so she asks Rupert if she can take the trap into Hopetown.

"Of course. And take Tamela with you. She can speak the local language if you need it. She'll be happy riding in the back of the cart. Here…" He pulls some money from his miner's belt and passes it to her. "Will that be enough to get everything you need?"

"Yes, I'm sure it will be. Thank you." She kisses his cheek, in gratitude.

She goes to find Tamela, but she must have gone off to the farm for some more milk. She doesn't want to wait around for her, so they set off without her.

Hopetown is busy with a variety of carts and wagons, but she manages to pull up outside the general stores. Inside, Mr Buthelezi stands behind the counter, with his large butcher's style apron covering his rotund physique. He says, "Good morning, Mrs Seymour. How are you this fine morning and how's young Frankie today? Have you been helping your mama in the garden?"

"He certainly has. We've planted all the seeds we purchased last time we were in here and they're all doing well, thanks to regular watering. But I wondered if you might have stock of some more mature plants or shrubs and if so, what would you recommend, Mr Buthelezi?"

"Well, in addition to our comprehensive selection of seeds, we also have some plants in the yard outside. If you'd like to take a look."

"Yes, please." She follows him outside, where they find his wife watering the pots that are for sale.

"Mrs Buthelezi will help you, Mrs Seymour. She's a better idea of things out here than I do."

"Thank you. I can see you have a good selection. I'm sure I'll find something appropriate." He leaves her and returns to his post behind the counter.

His wife is helpful, and talks her through the different plants, even though some are out of season and therefore not in flower. Lucy purchases what will be a flame-coloured bush lily, to go under the acacia tree, a blue and a white agapanthus, a peach-coloured protea, a pink and a purple bougainvillea, to go along the back fence, and some succulents. *This will make the garden more homely.*

She returns to the counter, with two young lads trolleying her purchases, and records what she's spent. "Thank you for your help, Mr Buthelezi."

"You're most welcome, Mrs Seymour. Please give my regards to your husband."

She's tongue-tied; should she correct him, or let it go? She watches him turn towards his next customer and the appropriate moment has passed. Rupert will be pleased his deception is working, but she wishes she'd spoken out immediately.

Standing, with Frankie, on the boardwalk outside the store, she's contemplating her difficult situation, while watching Mr Buthelezi's assistant loading all the pots into the cart, when a familiar voice says, "I do declare, it's Mrs Lucy Seymour and young Frankie!"

She spins around to find Ethan standing before them, wearing a brand-new, billy-cock hat. "Oh, Ethan! What a surprise! How lovely to see you!"

He raises his hat. "Good morning, Lucy. Do you have time to join me for a snack?"

"We'd be delighted. Wouldn't we, Frankie?"

"Yes please. I'd like a cake, please."

"Well, let's see what we can have at the luncheon bar, darling."

Ethan offers his arm and she takes it, to cross the carriageway with him, holding on to Frankie with her other hand. This would be decidedly improper were she really married to Rupert and she hopes that Mr Buthelezi isn't watching her.

They settle at a table and Ethan removes his hat and beckons to the waitress. He asks Lucy, "Shall we have a pot of tea, or would you prefer a cold drink?"

"I think I'd rather like some lemonade, please, Ethan."

"And me," cries Frankie, "and a cake."

He tells the waitress, "Could we please have lemonade all round and could we see your cake menu too, please."

The waitress, whom they learn is the daughter of the Dutch owners, called Benthe, brings the cake menu, which is written in Afrikaans, with English translations. She gives them a friendly smile. "I can recommend the *stroopwafels* and the *appelbeignet*, but the *stroopwafels* are nicer warmed over a cup of hot tea."

Lucy asks, "What's an *appelbeignet*?"

"It's like a doughnut with a slice of apple inside."

She smiles encouragingly at Frankie. "Mm that sounds nice, doesn't it, Frankie?"

He licks his lips. "Yes please, Mama."

Ethan orders the cakes.

"So, Ethan, how are you doing at Neville Frosdyke's claim?"

"Not too bad. The black fellows are hard-working, and we've unearthed some small diamonds, but I wanted to tell you what I've discovered from talking to the other miners. Simon McCallister's father is a wealthy rogue and a thoroughly nasty fellow, even worse than his son. Rumour has it that he exploits some of the natives by forcing them to steal for him from their bosses and yet he's vicious with his own workforce. He inspects them every time they leave his mines and if he discovers anyone trying to smuggle anything, they're beaten and thrown into prison. He keeps his ear to the ground and whenever a claim is abandoned anywhere in Dutoitspan, New Rush or Old De Beers, he buys it up and is building up a large portfolio of claims. So, I reckon we now know where my money went."

"Well, I doubt you can do anything about it, Ethan. It's virtually impossible to go up against an unprincipled, powerful man, because they have no rules of morality to hold them back. Whereas, of course, we do."

Benthe serves the tea and cakes and Frankie eagerly takes a big bite of his doughnut, shooting the piece of apple back out onto his plate. There's a pause of embarrassment, before Lucy, Ethan and Frankie all burst out laughing.

Lucy looks at Ethan's happy smiling face, with laughter lines etched into his tanned skin and she suddenly feels really happy. "We ought to meet here regularly on a Friday, Ethan. So you can keep me up to date with all your news."

"That's a good plan, Lucy. It's always so good to see you." He smiles. Then she sees the dark shadow of anger in his eyes and his face flushes red, his hands clench and he pushes back his chair in annoyance.

She follows his gaze, looks out of the window and sees Simon McCallister and an older man in a bowler hat, with a droopy moustache, walking along the opposite boardwalk. She grabs his hand to restrain him. "Don't go out there, Ethan. You must be clever and bide your time. These men have powerful people in their pockets, and you can't take them on alone. You need to have support from your fellow miners, and you need to be strong financially too."

She can see her logic registering in Ethan's facial expressions and the resigned shrug of his shoulders, as he sits back down.

"Turn your face away from the window, Ethan. It's better they don't notice us just now, until you're ready to take them on."

"I'll plan and fight to bring them both down, I promise you, Lucy. That Simon was so persuasive,

I can't imagine how many other unsuspecting folk will have fallen for his frauds, in addition to myself."

"Well, if you find others, maybe you could act jointly with them, to take him and his father to court, but I'm sure there will also be further ways you can contrive, to collapse their criminal enterprises, given time."

"You're right, Lucy. It's no use going off half-cocked. Let's forget about them and enjoy our tea and cake. How do you like your doughnut, Frankie?"

"It's yummy," he says, caster sugar and crumbs decorating his mouth and his hands.

CHAPTER EIGHT *(April–May 1873)*

A SNAKE IN THE GRASS

As the weeks pass by, Lucy sees no evidence of any impropriety with Rupert and Tamela and she begins to believe she was foolish to even have considered it. In April she receives a letter from her sister, Bunny. She breaks the seal and sits down on the sofa to read it.

Oh my! How wonderful, they're getting married! Thank goodness Clara has found happiness and with my darling brother too. I wonder what Rupert will think of this.

She sighs. She will miss the wedding. It's too soon to turn tail and set off back home. She hasn't yet given the place, or Rupert, a proper chance to convince her that their future belongs in South Africa.

When Rupert comes inside for a lunchtime snack, she waits while he washes his hands and eats his food, then she hands him the letter and watches his face with interest. Having read it, he hands the letter back to her and says, "Well, that's most unexpected. I'm pleased to hear that she's no longer pining for me. However, she's moved on much quicker than I thought she would."

Lucy lowers her voice so that Frankie won't hear her, from where he's drawing on the *stoep*. "I have to say I feel considerably less guilty about being here with you, now that Clara has found happiness with my brother."

He takes her hand and pulls her towards him, sitting her down onto his lap and kissing her, his hands straying and touching her thighs and her breasts. A shiver of delight runs through her body. She responds to his kisses. It's been such a long time since she was caressed by his younger brother, and her body aches with desire, as his arms tighten around her.

Suddenly Tamela is there clearing the table, noisily and clumsily, clanging the plates together. The moment lost, they part and Rupert gets up from the table and returns to his work outside.

Frustrated by Tamela, she resolves to plan a romantic meal, after Frankie has gone to bed, to celebrate the news from home and their freedom from guilt. Frankie is content doing his drawing and colouring of the *Syria*, outside with Monty and Camilla on the *stoep*, and so she spends the afternoon covered in flour, in the hot kitchen, preparing the food and fuelling up the small stove. There will be a steak and kidney pie with sweet potatoes, butternut squash and peas, followed by malva sponge pudding. She's pleased that she went to town yesterday and purchased all the necessary ingredients, including a bottle of Groot Constantia Merlot wine.

By the time the sun sets, all is ready. She has a quick wash and changes into a fresh gown. Frankie had a boerewors sandwich earlier and he's now preparing to go to bed. She sprays herself with perfume and kisses him goodnight.

Rupert is relaxing, reading the *Diamond News* in the lamp light, when she returns to the living room. "I hope you're hungry, Rupert. I've been working all afternoon to make us a special meal to celebrate Clara and Jacob's engagement and our freedom from guilt." She kisses the top of his head.

"You relax, while I put the finishing touches, before serving. I've given Tamela the night off."

She lights the tallow candles on the sideboard and the dresser and disappears into the kitchen, where she removes the steak and kidney pie from the oven and puts in the malva pudding. Then she mashes the sweet potatoes and the butternut squash with butter, and serves them up with the pie, and peas. "Come, Rupert. It's ready for you to help yourself."

"My word, Lucy. You've excelled yourself. This looks and smells delicious." He pours them each a glass of wine.

"Well, I hope the proof is in the pudding, as they say." She laughs, delighted with his reaction.

She's pleased that the meat is both tender and tasty and the pastry melts in the mouth. Although she wouldn't make any such claim, this is the tastiest meal she's eaten since leaving her parents' home, years earlier, and she's gratified that she hasn't lost her touch, thanks to her mother's expertise. As she eats, she's aware of the sound of them both chewing and swallowing, and she becomes self-conscious in the silence. Rupert is so quiet and thoughtful, she fears he's regretting his breakup with Clara.

She takes a sip of the wine, studying him covertly. "You're very quiet, Rupert. Is anything wrong?"

"No, nothing at all. I'm simply more content than I've been, since I arrived here. It's like I have a ready-made family and I couldn't be happier."

He takes up his wine. "To us!" he says, and they clink their glasses together in a toast to the future.

She smiles with relief and a feeling of hopefulness washes over her. Maybe this is the turning point? She reaches out and places her smaller hand in his and he squeezes it.

He chats companionably. "Have I ever told you how diamonds were first discovered in this area?"

"No, not really."

"Well, the first African diamond was found on De Kalk Farm near Hopetown by a fifteen-year-old lad called Erasmus Jacobs. The lad collected pretty stones along the south bank of the Orange River and he and his friends called them 'klippies' and used them to play games."

She smiles, reminded of Frankie's collection of stones, but says nothing.

Rupert continues, "One day his mother noticed a shiny pebble among them, and she showed it to a neighbouring farmer, who was so intrigued by its appearance he offered to buy it, but instead, thinking nothing of it, she gave it to him. The farmer thought it might be of some value and showed it to several folk in Hopetown, but found little interest, until a fellow called Lorenzo Boyes, the civil commissioner in Colesberg, examined the pebble and discovered it could scratch glass. He sent it to an amateur geologist in Grahamstown who pronounced it a diamond weighing twenty-one and a quarter carats. It became known as the *Eureka Diamond* and this surprise discovery led to Boer farmers along the rivers looking more methodically for these bright stones, or *blink klippe* as they were known."

She smiles. "Hence fate has led us to be here among them."

They continue to eat, while Rupert regales her with tales from his past experiences in South Africa and current events from the *Diamond News*.

She can smell the sweet malva pudding, tantalisingly ready to serve.

There's enough steak and kidney pie left for dinner tomorrow and she removes it and the other savoury dishes to the kitchen, where she covers them with upturned basins to cool. The malva pudding is cooked to perfection and she dishes up two bowlfuls and coats them both in custard.

"Mm delicious!" says Rupert. "Food for the Gods!"

When they've both eaten their desserts, Rupert takes the wine bottle and returns to the sofa with his newspaper, while she clears the table and, a little guiltily, piles the dishes up in the kitchen for Tamela to wash in the morning. She returns to the living room, picks up her copy of *Les Misérables* and sits beside him in the glow of the lamplight. Rupert refills her wineglass and they remain together, drinking the remainder of their wine, and reading. With their last sips of wine, Rupert puts down his paper, turns down the lamp, snuffs the candles and takes her hand, leading her into his bedroom.

Dawn breaks and she's still lying blissfully in Rupert's embrace. She's aware of his strong, manly arms and the masculine smell of him, but fears Frankie will wake up and discover her missing. So, she carefully extricates herself and, wearing Rupert's dressing gown, she quickly returns to her own room. In the process she disturbs Rupert and hears him getting washed and dressed, ready for work.

In the cold light of day, she's uneasy. Last night, she'd followed him willingly; after all, she was the one who'd instigated the situation with her romantic meal, but now she fears he could simply have been taking advantage of her compliance. He's a confident, experienced and considerate lover. He was gentle and tentative, cautiously exploring the contours of her body, aware of all her erogenous zones, kissing her urgently and passionately, before their bodies united as one and they both climaxed together. For Lucy it had been such a long time since the loss of her husband, and something her body hungered for, but was it love?

Tamela is in the kitchen washing up, when she and Frankie enter for their breakfast. Lucy immediately realises that the girl is in a bad humour, by her habit of clinking and clanging the crockery and scowling at them.

She ignores her ill temper and instead makes a point of laughing and joking with Frankie, while they eat their mielie-pap, trickled with acacia honey.

Now that she and Rupert have become closer she's more inclined to entertain, and after breakfast, she suggests that she and Frankie take a walk through the claims to see Jack Penberthy. He hasn't yet joined them for supper, and too much time has passed since she last mentioned it to him.

She calls to Rupert as they go, and he comes to see what she wants. "I was wondering if we might invite Jack to have supper with us, next Saturday evening? What do you think?"

"I think it's a grand idea. What are you planning to serve?"

"I was thinking of a roast of some kind, depending on what the butcher has that looks good, followed by a choice of banana pudding, or an apple, or plum crumble?"

"Mm! That sounds wonderful. I suppose you'll want the cart again on Friday?"

"Yes please. I need to make sure I have all the ingredients."

"That's not a problem."

She and Frankie take their leave and continue their walk towards Jack's claim. They reach his

120

property but can't see him around and so they continue to the wild area beyond to look at the weaver birds' nests and see what they can spot in the scrub. Lucy notices a long, slender green-coloured snake, moving rapidly through the bushes and she points it out to Frankie.

"We must look through your book to see what that snake is, when we get back home."

"I think it's a boomslang, Mama. They're green like that and they like it up in trees too. I can remember the picture and you reading me the funny name."

"Well remembered, Frankie. You can show me later and we'll check whether or not it's poisonous."

They turn to retrace their steps and catch Jack leaving his homestead, dressed in his scruffy working clothes. She calls out to him, "Jack!" He turns towards them.

"Hello, Jack, I was wondering if you might like to join us for an early supper on Saturday evening?"

He scratches his head. "I'd be delighted to, maid. Thank you for thinking of me."

"You're welcome, Jack. We should have invited you before now, but it's taken me a while to settle in and get used to the stove, but I should be able to produce something edible at least now." She laughs. "Shall we say six o'clock, to eat at half past?"

"That would be most acceptable. Thank you."

"See you then. Bye for now."

"Bye."

On their return home, as they approach the homestead, Lucy spots Rupert leaving Tamela's room. She immediately bristles. Her heart races and her stomach churns. *Whatever's he doing in there, as soon as my back's turned? How could he betray me, last night?* She

121

imagines Tamela giggling and Rupert touching her secretly… furtively. She takes a deep breath. *I mustn't jump to conclusions. As Malachi always says, I must roll with the punches and bide my time.* After all, Rupert has any number of excuses to enter part of his own property, which having only been recently completed is probably in need of finishing touches. As far as an explanation's concerned, she's not likely to catch him out.

She calls to him, "Jack has accepted our invitation for Saturday!"

Rupert replies, "Well done! I'll look forward to it."

She bites her tongue. The truth will out, it always does.

That evening Rupert tells her that he and Jack are going into town to let off steam. She's taken aback. This is unusual for them and she can't help wondering why he suddenly wants to go off with his buddy, leaving them alone and unprotected at night.

She doesn't want to be left, responsible for the safety of both Frankie and Tamela. *What if something bad happens, or there's some emergency, when we're all alone without any transport or anyone to help us.*

"I'm sorry, Rupert, but I'm not happy to be left here at night-time with no man to protect us. We saw a boomslang today in the trees at the end of the claims. It says it's extremely poisonous, in Frankie's book, *Venomous Creatures*, and it eats chameleons, so it could be attracted here by Camilla."

"Don't be silly, Lucy. It was probably just a harmless spotted bush snake. You've been quite safe here so far – why should that change because Jack and I are having a night in town? You worry too much. We won't be late, I promise you." He kisses her and smiles. "Just shut the door and have an early night, if you're worried. No one has any need to come this way; you'll all be quite safe, I assure you."

He's disregarding her worries, making her feel foolish, and so she gives in and says no more, despite the tight knot of anxiety in her stomach. She's disappointed that following so quickly after the events of last night, when they moved towards a closer relationship, he's not eager to spend more quality time with her and is cavalier about their safety, instead choosing his buddy Jack and abandoning them in this heartless way. Her gaiety has been quashed. *Will he kiss and tell and then have a good laugh over my naivety? Is it really Tamela who he wants? Have I made a dreadful mistake in trusting him with my heart?*

After Frankie is settled in bed, she sits in the lamplight composing a letter of congratulations to Clara and Jacob.

Miss Clara Fairway
Church Cottage
Stairs Hill
Ivell
Somerset
Great Britain

4th April 1873

Dearest Clara and Jacob,
I am so thrilled to hear the glad tidings of your betrothal and forthcoming marriage in August. I could not wish for a more perfect match for you both. My only regret is that we are so far from home, we will be unable to attend this wonderful family event.
Rupert is well and working hard on his own and his father's claims. He also is very pleased for

you. He has gone out with Jack this evening and hence I have the peace and quiet to put pen to paper.

We have had the most incredible journey to get here and seen the most amazing African flora and fauna, that most only ever see in picture books. It has been an enlightening experience for both me and Frankie and I don't regret my decision to bring him. But, although Frankie and I have settled well here with Rupert, and we are enjoying our African adventure, we both miss our family, and I, of course, truly miss you, Clara, my closest friend.

Please pass on my love to your papa, Clara, and all the rest of my family and please tell my mama I will write again when I have more news.

With much love from
Lucy (and Frankie)
xx

Then she tries to concentrate on the words of Victor Hugo, but in the end she does as Rupert suggested and turns in, to snuggle up with Frankie and give way to her dreams.

She awakes with a start, her heart thumping! She'd been dreaming about men singing, but now someone has entered their home! Shakily, she puts on her wrap and moves silently towards the bedroom door, opening it a crack to espy a dishevelled Rupert standing unsteadily in the doorway, silhouetted by the lantern that Jack is holding, on the *stoep*. She breathes a sigh of relief that there are no intruders. At least they're both home unscathed. Rupert's definitely drunk, and Jack doesn't appear to be much better. She shuts her bedroom door and leaves them to it.

On Friday, she and Frankie set off into town to get the things for Saturday's supper. She has timed it so they can use the bathhouse before meeting up with Ethan. Then shop later, so as not to be leaving the food in the mule cart, while they're enjoying nourishment in the luncheon bar.

Lucy is refreshed and smelling of soap, as they leave the bathhouse. She sees Ethan at the window table. He stands up with a wide grin, as they enter the café, and pulls back the seat for her to sit down. "Hello to you both. How are you?"

"We're both well, Ethan. Thank you. How are things going on the claim?"

"I've good news. The men have been working hard and on Wednesday Luan found a good quality diamond. It must be worth about £200. I gave him a bonus, which has motivated the boys to work harder, but it's going to take far too long for me to make a decent amount."

"But at least you're making some money and not starving." She smiles.

Benthe approaches and asks for their order.

Lucy looks at Frankie. "Shall we have the same as last time?"

"Yes please, Mama."

Ethan orders lemonade and *appelbeignets* all round. Then he turns back to Lucy. "Actually, I've telegraphed my parents to ask them to bankroll me £1,000 start-up money, because, rather than relying on diamond mining, I've decided to hedge my bets and invest in land to build some dwellings, for which I can charge rent and in that way pay back my parents and eventually I'll make some regular profit for myself."

"That's a wonderful idea, Ethan. I hope your parents agree. You must tell them how dire the diamond townships are and what a premium your nice buildings will rent for."

"Fingers crossed they'll see the long-term goal."

"I should think so. If they have that kind of money available, they'd be foolish not to invest in their son."

"How are things with you two?"

Frankie says, "I've bought a picture for you, Ethan." He gives him his picture of the *Syria*.

"Wow, Frankie, that's wonderful!"

"It kept him quiet for ages, while I was preparing a celebratory meal for myself and Rupert. He's even drawn tiny people, look."

"They are you, Mama, and Ethan."

"Oh my! I didn't realise that."

"What were you celebrating?"

"My brother's wedding to my friend Clara, who was once Rupert's fiancée."

Her mind returns to their romantic evening, which was then tainted by the following night when Rupert went off with Jack to get drunk, and by the moment she saw him leaving Tamela's room. Perversely, she makes a decision that she knows will annoy him.

"In fact, I'm cooking again tomorrow for Rupert's partner, Jack Penberthy. Would you care to join us, Ethan?"

Ethan beams with pleasure. "I'd love to. I can hire a horse from the ostler for the night."

"I'm so pleased, Ethan. If you've no objection, you can sleep on the sofa, like you did last time, and return on your horse the following day."

On Saturday morning Lucy is busy in the kitchen. She's given Frankie some pastry to play with and

126

he's covered in flour, but having a super time making jam tarts. The day is overcast and not quite as sweltering in the kitchen as the last time she cooked. Nevertheless, she still feels hot and bothered; there's so much to prepare and she wants it all to be perfect.

Just before darkness falls, all is ready and she and Frankie go to change into their evening attire, Lucy into her favourite jade-coloured gown and he into his nightshirt, ready for bed.

Rupert comes in from work, and rushes into his bedroom to get ready. Not long afterwards, Jack and Ethan arrive, both dressed smartly for the evening. Jack has brought whisky, and Ethan, wine and a big bunch of lilies and wax flowers. The different varieties of lily fill the room with their wonderful fragrance and Lucy is delighted. Rupert has no flower vases and so she uses a large water pitcher to display them and she places them on the sideboard.

She pours Jack and Ethan an aperitif and is about to return to the kitchen to put the finishing touches to her meal when Rupert comes out of his bedroom and sees Ethan there. She's satisfied by his thunderous expression.

She says, "Oh, Rupert, I'm sorry, I forgot to mention. Luckily, I saw Ethan yesterday and was able to invite him to join us, to make it more of a party."

Rupert presumably remembers his manners. "What a pleasant surprise. Good to see you, Ethan. How are things going on Neville's claim?"

"Not too bad at all, Rupert. I was telling Lucy that Luan had a lucky find in the week, with a good quality diamond worth about £200, in addition to the usual smaller stuff."

"That's good news indeed."

"I thought you'd be pleased. We're digging deeper through the diamondiferous yellow soil now and in places we've almost reached the blue ground rock beneath. I'm not sure whether this will also be productive, but I think it may need more elaborate equipment to extract it."

"Well, keep me informed of your progress and we can cross that bridge when we come to it."

Ethan asks him, "Have you dug that deep here?"

"No, we've not reached any blue rock yet, have we, Jack?"

Jack shakes his head. "I haven't on mine."

Ethan continues, "Some folk are giving up at New Rush, believing it to be only the yellow soil that contains any diamonds, but I'm not so sure, because the more astute business men, like Cecil Rhodes and Barney Barnato, are snapping up all the claims that become available, and they're no fools."

"That's true. Well, I'd suggest that once the yellow soil has been sieved through and we reach the blue ground rock, we don't sell up, but sit on our claims until we learn from the pioneers the easiest, most profitable way to extract it."

Lucy says to Rupert, "The food's nearly ready, Rupert. Would you please fetch Tamela? I'd like her to serve us."

"Of course."

She turns to her guests. "Please, gentlemen, come and take your seats. You're here, Jack, and Ethan next to you."

Rupert returns with Tamela. Lucy asks him to pour the wine, while she follows Tamela into the kitchen to explain to her what to do. Then she takes her seat at the table, opposite Ethan.

Ethan smiles at her. "The food smells wonderful, Lucy."

"Thank you. I hope you all enjoy it."

"I'm sure I will," says Jack. "It's a long time since I had any home cooking."

"Well, we have roast lamb with mint sauce, baked potatoes, peas, kale and cauliflower mornay."

Tamela serves everyone with plated meat and potatoes, so that they can then add the vegetables to their liking. There's a period when the serving dishes and sauces are being passed from one person to another, until everyone's plates are full and Lucy watches with satisfaction as the men hungrily tuck in.

Rupert is the first to speak. "I see in the *Diamond News* there's talk that New Rush is going to be renamed 'Kimberley', after John Wodehouse, the 1st Earl of Kimberley, and Secretary of State for the Colonies."

Jack scoffs, "Our British politicians like to have their names imposed in foreign places, to be recorded in perpetuity."

Ethan sighs. "I should be there, but for that swindler, Simon McCallister. The powers that be must realise that New Rush is a good investment. The diamond township's increasing in size daily. The original Colesberg Kopje's disappearing, as the land's being dug away. The De Beers family must be laughing all the way to the bank."

Jack shrugs. "I don't know about that. They'd have done better mining the land themselves."

"Many from the Hopetown workings left to try their luck there, before you arrived, Ethan," says Rupert. "Good news always travels fast."

Ethan shrugs. "Well, in my view, hard work pays off in the end. Look at you two. You've both managed to build your homes and you're doing well enough, due to your own hard graft."

"Yes, plus a bit of help from the natives," says Jack, wryly.

Lucy changes the subject. "Would anyone like some more roast lamb, or baked potatoes?"

Ethan says, "Yes please, Lucy."

Lucy beckons to the girl. "Tamela, would you please serve us with some more potatoes and meat."

She dips a curtsey. But with no eye contact, she says, "Yes, missus."

Tamela leaves the room and returns with a dish of roasted potatoes, which she serves to those who want more and repeats the process with the meat.

Lucy then leads the conversation. "Did you hear the sad news that David Livingstone, the Scottish Christian missionary, was found dead from malaria at Lake Bangweulu on the first of this month."

"No, I hadn't," says Ethan. "He's been in South Africa for years and travelled extensively, I understand, with his Zambesi expedition and his search for the source of the Nile."

Lucy continues, "I think he was an incredible man, campaigning as he did to bring about the abolition of slavery."

Ethan responds, "I agree, but in the end, he'd no choice but to become dependent upon the slave traders themselves."

Jack shakes his head. "Indubitably a sad loss. Malaria's a killer disease to be sure. We're lucky that this area here, so near to the Kalahari, isn't susceptible to it."

There's a lull in the conversation and Lucy can smell the fruit crumble is ready to be removed from the stove. "Please excuse me for a moment."

She goes into the kitchen. "Tamela, you're not paying attention! The crumble will burn if you leave it any longer."

"Sorry, missus."

She quickly snatches up the oven gloves and removes the perfectly browned crumble, just in time. "Right, go and clear away the savoury dishes, please, Tamela, and help yourself to anything you would like for your supper. I'll serve you up a portion of the dessert as well."

"Thank you, missus."

She calls to them from the kitchen, "What would you like, banana pudding, or plum crumble with cream?"

The three men all ask for the crumble and she serves it up into six dishes (to include a portion for Tamela and a small portion for Frankie for tomorrow). Then she pours over some of Hilda's cream. She returns with the tray of desserts and passes a steaming bowl to each of the three men. There are murmurs of appreciation all round.

"I thought you might like to have some banana cake with your coffee and brandy later."

"Mm, that sounds like a grand idea, maid," says Jack, tucking into the plum crumble.

When they're all sated, Rupert suggests they retire to the easy chairs for their coffee and cake, followed by Cape brandy and Cuban cigars. Lucy lingers with them until Tamela has finished washing the dishes.

"It's a shame you don't have a piano here. Lucy plays so beautifully."

"I do agree it would make a pleasant end to the evening, but at present I'm unable to justify the expense, I'm afraid," says Rupert, obviously irritated by the evidence of their friendship during their journey on board ship.

Once she hears Tamela leaving, Lucy goes to make the coffee, eventually returning with a tray of coffee cups and plates of cake, which she serves to the men. They have all taken different seats, leaving only a space on the small sofa next to Ethan. She is happy to sit down next to him, until she sees the annoyed expression on Rupert's face. *Well why didn't you sit here, then, if you are so determined to make a meal of our friendship?* She ignores his ill temper and enjoys her slice of banana cake instead.

Jack asks them, "Did Rupert tell you about the knife fight we witnessed on our night out in town?"

"No, he didn't. He didn't tell me anything at all about that night actually," says Lucy.

"Nor me. Why? What happened?" asks Ethan.

Rupert says, "Well, we started off in the Cape Karoo Hotel, but as it got later, we'd moved on to the Diggers Rest where we'd already downed a few drams, before things heated up. There was an argument between two diamond grubbers and the barman asked them and their mates to leave the premises. They were also three sheets to the wind, like us, but the drink had made them uppity. So, along with others, we followed 'em out to watch the fun."

Jack joins in the conversation. "We hadn't a clue as to what they were arguing about, but without any warning the one with the straggly beard pulled an African tribal dagger from his belt and commenced lunging at the other fellow. He dodged to and fro and then tripped up, falling on his backside. The bearded chap took the opportunity to thrust the knife at his throat. Rupert here yelled out in his upper-crust English accent, 'Hold fast, my man, or you'll be under arrest,' which was enough to make the fellow hesitate and his cronies dragged him off, thinking Rupert here was the authorities."

Ethan listens in awe. "Well done, Rupert, that was quick thinking. What did the fellow on the floor do? He must have been grateful."

"You must be joking. He let out a few expletives, his colleagues hauled him to his feet and off they all went together."

Lucy says, "Well, I'm impressed, Rupert. You obviously averted a serious assault, possibly murder, with no thought for your own safety."

Rupert grins. "That's the kind of upright, law-abiding fellow I am."

Lucy takes away their empty dishes and Rupert hands around his treasured cigars. Ethan takes one gratefully. "What a treat, thank you."

Jack declines. "I'll stick to my trusty pipe if you don't mind, Rupert; but a drop of your Cape smoke would finish off the evening nicely."

"Of course, forgive me." Rupert then pours them each a snifter of Cape brandy.

Lucy re-enters the room with a glass of water in her hand. She wishes to avoid the smoky atmosphere and retire. "Good night, all. I've enjoyed your company, gentlemen, but I am to my bed."

Ethan jumps up to kiss her cheek. "Thank you so much for that delicious meal, Lucy. It was very kind of you to invite me. I've had a lovely evening."

Jack follows suit. "Me too, maid. It's been most enjoyable."

Rupert remains seated but blows her a kiss. "Goodnight, my dear."

Lucy studies all three men, Rupert with his aristocratic air, good lean physique and handsome face, but too arrogant to stand up and kiss her goodnight; gentle kind Ethan with his smiling, twinkling blue eyes, thick black hair and happy disposition, who immediately jumped up to give her a kiss; and cheerful, amiable Jack with his thinning hair, and bushy sideburns, who followed Ethan's example.

She smiles. "I'm glad you enjoyed the meal; we must do it again sometime. Goodnight."

CHAPTER NINE *(May–September 1873)*

THE LANTERN OF THE WEST

In May, Beth Warren hears the flap on the letter box and goes to see if, at long last, there's a letter from Lucy, in the vain hope that they'll both be back home, in good time for the wedding. She picks up the envelope from the floor, where it's skidded under the heavy tapestry curtain, which Isaac put up to hold back the draughts in winter. Thank goodness she heard the flap, otherwise this letter could have hidden there until she next scrubbed the flagstones.

She takes the letter into the parlour, finds her spectacles and sits down in an easy chair, before impatiently breaking the seal, removing the letter and reading her daughter's words.

Mr and Mrs Isaac Warren
Home Farm
Alvington Manor
Ivell
Somerset
England
Great Britain

4th February 1873

My dearest Mama, Papa and all,
We are both settling in well on Rupert's claim, but the journey here seemed interminable. The

voyage was enjoyable enough and trouble free, but overland extremely tiring and a huge relief to arrive here unscathed. Rupert's working environment was simply a sea of dust and dirt and it has become my project to make it more pleasant for him and us.

I have been busy laying out a garden at the back of the homestead and I have planted salad vegetables and some plants. Frankie was thrilled to plant some nasturtiums, morning glory and mesembryanthemum seeds and we have these to look forward to. There was a lone acacia tree in the back garden when we arrived, which the birds love, but we have formed a lawn and some flower beds now, with flame-coloured bush lilies under the acacia, pink and purple bougainvillea along the back fence and some agapanthus, protea and succulents in the flower bed on the right-hand side of the lawn. It is looking more homely already and you would love to see the beautiful birds here, Mama. They are all so bright and colourful.

Frankie has befriended a young mongoose, whom he has named Monty, and he also has a pet chameleon who lives on the stoep (our veranda).

At the moment we are both enjoying the novelty of this lifestyle, even though it is quite primitive. The men had rigged up a shower for themselves outside, but of course that is not suitable for myself or Frankie and so Rupert has ordered a cast-iron bath and an ornamental folding screen from a company in Port Elizabeth, which I eagerly anticipate, as at the moment I am regularly obliged to visit the bathhouse in town.

How is everyone at home? Please pass on my regards to all our friends and of course our love to all in the family. I impatiently await all your news.

With fondest love,
Lucy and Frankie
xx

Oh my! A shiver of unease runs through her. *She seems to be planning for their future over there, rather than coming back home to us.* Bunny enters the room from upstairs.

"Bunny, look!" She holds out the missive. "A letter from your sister. Read it and let me know what you think."

"What do you mean, Mama? What I think?"

"Just read it first, darling, and you'll see what I mean."

Bunny reads the letter and then looks up at her mother. "You mean she seems to be settling down over there?"

"Exactly! I thought she was only visiting, not emigrating!"

Bunny sighs. "There's no mention of the wedding either, so Lucy's letter must have been written before she received mine. She didn't know about the wedding at the time she wrote to us. Regrettably, Mama, I think she probably received my letter too late to make arrangements to return to us in time for the wedding."

Bunny says, "I'll go and brew us some tea." She continues their conversation from the kitchen. "On a brighter note, she does seem to be happy over there. Happier than she has been in a long time."

Beth joins her and brings out some biscuits from the larder. "That's true. I suppose I'm being selfish, but I do worry so. I just wish they were both back here with us, safe and sound."

"She's a sensible girl, Mama. She'll not let any harm come to herself, or to Frankie, I'm certain."

The night before his wedding, Isaac and Malachi drag Jacob off to the Kings Arms in Montacute.

"You have to celebrate your last night of freedom, Jacob," says Malachi, grinning.

Jacob sighs. "But I don't want to be hung-over on my wedding day," he protests.

Isaac slaps him on the back. "You've no choice, son. We want to have a good night out and you're the perfect excuse. Come on, put on your best bib and tucker. Bunny's going to drop us off in the pony and trap and fetch us later."

He reluctantly dresses in his Sunday-best clothes and joins them in the yard. Bunny has the pony and trap ready and they clamber in. They're all squashed in together, but it isn't that far to Montacute.

It's a sultry summer evening, with light fluffy clouds drifting across the sky. As they pass the flax fields, worker bees are still searching for nectar in the mass of pale blue flowers wafting in the breeze. The birds are more relaxed now that their young have fledged and have become self-sufficient; their evening song is beautiful, with a song thrush the lead soloist. Jacob also relaxes a little. Like the birds, he too has the right to celebrate. Their cottage on Camp Road is scrubbed and freshly painted and he's been gradually building up their essential furniture. He's even constructed a new kennel for his sheepdogs, Fergus and Bess and he hopes they will settle well in their new environment. Clara has organised the linen with his mother's help, some even spun from their own homegrown flax. He can't wait to be united with his soulmate tomorrow, but for now he'll celebrate his good fortune with his family.

When they get there, Jacob is surprised to find Joshua at the bar, with John Boucher and his son, Toby; Jack Hawkins, Frank and Thomas and their cousin, Raymond; Robert and Harry Sandford;

Luke and his father, John Moore; and Edwin, all looking smart and eager to enjoy themselves. They simultaneously let up a hearty cheer as he walks into the room.

Jacob flushes and smiles self-consciously. "You bastard, Mal! You could've warned me!" he whispers to his brother.

"You won't regret it, I promise you. It will be a good laugh and something to remember in future times, when you're stuck at home with kiddies under your feet."

He has to admit the laughing and joking is great fun. He didn't realise that Robert and Harry Sandford were such comedians. Some time is spent playing arrows and then later, playing poker, and all the time drinking a fair share of ale and spirits. Joshua has generously put money behind the bar to ensure there's enough alcohol for all to be merry. His father, Jack Hawkins and John Boucher play cribbage, with some of their old farmer friends, smoking their pipes and keeping half an eye on the younger ones.

At the end of the night Jacob's ribs ache from laughing so much. They all leave the pub at around midnight. Joshua's new steward, Harvey Woodford, and the footman, Edgar Parish, collect them with the landau and the hay wagon, both filled to capacity, and there's boisterous singing all the way home.

Malachi was right, it was a night to remember; but will he be able to sleep? He's so anxious that all will go well tomorrow.

Clara awakes with the dawn chorus on the morning of her wedding day, to glorious August sunshine creeping beneath the curtains in her bedroom. She's invited Bunny to stay overnight to help her dress and prepare her hair. She's probably still sound asleep in their guest room, but Clara's eager to be making the most of this special day. She stretches herself awake and gets out of her warm bed to wash and put on her undergarments.

Her wedding ensemble is hanging up in the corner of her bedroom. Miss Budge, the draper in Princes Street, managed to procure some beautiful Honiton lace, in a design of orange blossom and roses, for her layered gown, veil and train. For dressing her hair, she has a garland of artificial orange blossom and white heather. Miss Budge has stitched her dress so neatly and professionally she'll be very proud to wear it.

Beth and Bunny have helped with the sewing of the handmaidens' gowns, which are all in ivory white satin, trimmed with the same pattern of Honiton lace. Ruby and Daisy will wear the artificial orange blossoms dotted among their curls. They'll also carry baskets of flowers, which Louisa has selected and arranged from the gardens at Alvington Manor.

As chief bridesmaid, Bunny will hold the bride's bouquet for her during the ceremony. Although she's grown close to Bunny, since she and Jacob have been walking out, her maid of honour should really have been Bunny's older sister and her old friend, Lucy, and she's suddenly downcast, missing her friend's warmth and familiarity. Then her thoughts return to dear Jacob, the man she's about to marry, and she pushes aside any sadness, again focusing on the day ahead.

She knows she can depend on Malachi, who promised to ensure Jacob arrives at the church on time and has also organised the carriages for the other guests from Alvington. John Moore is to take

Rosa and the children in the landau early, to enable the girls to perform their finishing touches at Church Cottage. He'll then return to the manor to fetch Joshua and his family in good time for the ceremony. The ushers, Edwin, Luke, Frank, Thomas and Toby, will all travel with the other guests in the hay wagon, driven by Edgar Parish.

Clara throws back the curtains to look out at the back of St John's Church. When lit up on winter nights their church is known as 'The Lantern of the West'. Now, the early morning sun is casting long shadows across the haphazard gravestones; butterflies flutter in the red valerian on the stone wall, and in her tummy. She wonders if Jacob is feeling nervous too this morning. She pulls on her robe and goes downstairs to prepare some breakfast.

Not long afterwards she's joined by Bunny and her father, who both hug and kiss her affectionately.

"We're soon to be sisters-in-law," says Bunny.

"And I'm soon to lose a daughter," says her father.

Clara feels for him. "But I'll be only a short distance from here, Papa."

He gives her a warm hug. "I know that, my darling, but it's still a wrench for me to lose you, after all these years together." He sighs. "I'm so happy for you, Clara, my dear, but there's no denying, I'll miss you too."

"I'm sure Miss Cavendish will be a blessing, once you get to know her better. According to her references, she's an excellent housekeeper and I believe she'll be good company for you too."

"I do hope so, my dear. What time will she be arriving tomorrow?"

"She said, in her letter, that she'd be leaving Sherborne on the steam train at nine o'clock, so if you're at Yeovil Junction before nine o'clock, you should be in good time to collect her."

She fills a saucepan with water from their newly plumbed tap. "Would you both like boiled eggs, toast and butter, with fruit preserve for your breakfasts?"

"That would be perfect. Thank you, Clara," says Bunny.

"And for me too, my dear. I'll brew the tea."

Bunny goes to the dresser. "In that case, I'll lay the table."

"After we've eaten, we'd better get organised, because Malachi is coming with the children at about ten o'clock, so we'll only have an hour before the ceremony's due to begin."

Bunny helps Clara to dress in her wedding gown, and using the hot tongs, she curls her golden hair into pretty ringlets and dresses it with the orange blossoms, ready for the Honiton lace veil. Finally, she leaves her alone to take stock, making sure she has all she needs for her honeymoon and that her going away outfit's ready for her to change into, after the ceremony.

There's a knock at the front door, and she hears her papa in the hallway, ushering the two girls upstairs and showing Rosa and Eli into their parlour.

Ruby and Daisy meet her at the top of the stairs. Young Daisy says, "My word, Clara, how beautiful you look!"

Clara smiles. "Thank you, Daisy. You're being kind, but everyone looks beautiful in their wedding clothes."

Ruby says, "Not everyone, Clara. Jacob will be most impressed when he sees you. I just know he will."

The two girls have their gowns with them and are soon undressing to change costumes. "Don't worry about us, Clara. We're quite used to dressing up for weddings. We've done it before for Lucy and Ashleigh."

"Well, I'm sure you can help each other with your gowns, but Bunny and I will help to decorate your hair for you."

Beth Warren holds back her tears as she pins the last white rose buttonhole on Malachi's morning jacket lapel, to match those worn by Jacob and their father. "I've never been more proud of my sons than I am today," she says, giving both their arms a squeeze and blinking away her tears. "I so wish our Lucy was here for this wonderful family celebration."

"Don't you worry your head about Lucy. She's well able to look after herself, Mama," says Malachi.

Her husband tries to hustle her out through the door. "Come on, let's get a move on, or we'll be late," says Isaac.

Beth adjusts her hat in the hall mirror before following her sons out into the yard.

Malachi has the pony harnessed in the trap, which he and Jacob have decorated with white ribbons and flowers ready for their arrival at the church. They clamber up, Malachi flicks the reins and off they go. On the way, they pass John Moore rushing back to the manor and they happily wave to each other.

Thankfully, it's a balmy summer's morning with little wind. Beth Warren's floral bonnet isn't even crooked by the time they reach Church Path and Malachi reins in the pony outside the churchyard. The bells are ringing as they disembark, and Isaac blocks the trap and gives the pony a nosebag to chomp on.

They make their way inside the church of St John the Baptiste to await the arrival of all their guests and finally the blushing bride on her father's arm with her handmaidens following.

For Jacob, the wedding ceremony takes place as if in a dream. The sun pours down on them through the stained-glass windows, covering Clara's gown of ivory white in a misty glow and making her appear to him like a heavenly angel. He adores her delicate high cheek bones, genuine smile, neat pearly white teeth, and ruby-red, kissable lips. He gazes into her tender blue eyes, as they recite their vows, and feels like the luckiest man alive. He's never been happier, nor more excited about his future with her. He repeats the vicar's words as if in a trance and before long he finds himself standing beside his new wife and signing the official register.

Then the campanologists commence their work and the bells are ringing. He and Clara walk, hand in hand, back down the aisle and out into the summer sunshine. Their family and friends pour out of the church behind them and they're soon enveloped in a haze of rice and white rose petals.

Mr Gosney takes a variety of photographs, as each group in the wedding party poses like statues in front of the church. Between the flashes and puffs of smoke he's in and out of his blackout cloth, backwards and forwards into his orange booth, before irrevocably everyone's preserved for posterity on thin slabs of Japanned iron. He's paid for his work and all are satisfied.

The wedding party then assembles to follow the bride and groom through the wrought-iron gates and down through the town to the ancient inn, where the reception is to be held.

Malachi catches Luke's attention. "Have you got keys to the Fairways' cottage?"

"Yes, of course, I need them for work."

"Good. I'd like you to do me a favour and go and collect Clara's travel chest and her vanity case from their cottage, load them onto our decorated pony and trap and then move it down the road, so that it's ready outside the George Inn for when Clara and Jacob leave for their honeymoon."

"Of course. Leave it to me. I'll try not to be too long."

Aurora notices Luke going in the opposite direction and she follows him. She steps inside the cottage, making him jump out of his skin when he sees her. "Rora, whatever are you doing here?"

She smiles her sweetest smile. "I thought it a good opportunity to get you alone again."

"But I have to do something for Malachi; we haven't time for messing around."

Her face drops. "Surely there's time for a tender kiss? We haven't had any opportunity to be together for weeks."

Luke finds her irresistible and she knows she can wrap him around her little finger, but they'll be missed if they dally too long. He takes her in his arms and kisses her gently and immediately feels the stirring in his loins. He can't afford to continue. Why does she tantalise him by picking the most inopportune moments to arouse him?

"Rora, we have to go. Malachi and the wedding

party will miss us and as chief usher, I have duties to perform."

"You're a killjoy, Luke Moore. I really don't know why I bother. It's always me who makes the first move and that's all wrong."

"Rora, you know very well that, on any other occasion, my greatest desire is to spend moments alone with you, but your parents wouldn't approve and now is not the time. Come on, we must make haste. Please, Rora, would you help me by taking the small toiletry case, then I can manage Clara's chest."

Aurora sniggers. "I bet you'd like to manage Clara's chest."

He knows Aurora is simply trying to annoy him, but he responds, nevertheless. "Don't be silly, Rora, that comment is beneath you, especially on her wedding day. She's a sweet, kind woman and I've loved working with her, but that's all – she's nearly forty, seventeen years older than me! How can you even think there's anything like that between us?"

"Sorry, I was only joking, but I guess I'm feeling as though my life has stalled. I'm feeling vexed and unfulfilled, Luke. Seeing other people making progress in their lives just brings it home to me that I'm a useless female, totally dependent on my adoptive parents. Gabriel is learning to be a JP just like Pa and I need to be doing something too. At the moment I'm no use nor ornament to anyone."

"We'll have a good talk later, at the reception, once all the ceremonials are over. Come on now. Let's get back to the wedding party."

On entering the Inn, Aurora goes to join her family, where she finds Louisa talking to Mr Fairway. "This is a beautiful old medieval inn; I love the upper story overhang at the front of the building."

"That's why I chose it for my daughter's wedding reception. I believe it's of a style more popular in the Weald of Kent and so unusual in these parts. The Mermaid also offered us a competitive price, but we thought this one's more intimate for our needs."

Malachi joins them with drinks, and they raise a glass to the newly-weds. "I was just chatting to the landlady and apparently, a couple of hundred years ago, back when this place was known as the Three Cups, a traveller stayed here who was suffering from the plague, which resulted in it spreading throughout Ivell and devastating the population."

Joshua looks up. "Perhaps he hailed from Wyke Regis, for when I was a nipper, I was told that that was the port where the foreign disease was first introduced into this country, when Dorset was famous for its wool and the ports were doing a roaring trade."

Louisa sighs. "It's hard to believe such dreadful decimation could result from a disease spread by tiny rats."

Aurora frowns. "Let's change the subject. This is a joyful celebration, so let's not cast a shadow over it."

Joshua grins at his daughter. "Sorry, Rora, it was Louisa who started it." Her mother is about to protest. "No… no, not your mama – Louisa Smith, the landlady."

Malachi picks up a spoon. "Right, back to the proceedings, no harm done. The happy couple are in a world of their own and didn't hear us." Malachi then taps the spoon against his tankard, to get the attention of the gathering. "Does everyone have something to drink for the toasts? If not, please go to the bar and

Louisa, our landlady, will attend to your needs. Then please find your seat at the table, ready for your victuals. Going by the delicious aroma coming from the hog roast, we'll soon be served our luncheon."

There are tears and laughter as the father of the bride, the groom and the best man make their speeches. The room fills with warmth and best wishes from everyone, for the young couple on the verge of their new lives together.

Aurora watches Luke being attentive to all the guests and still feels rather neglected herself. She longs to be in a truly loving relationship and married, just like Jacob and Clara. Clara looks stunning in her wedding gown, but it's not the beautiful outfit alone that makes the difference, it's the undeniable happiness radiating from her. Her eyes are sparkling with love for Jacob, making her look more attractive than she's ever seen her before.

Love is a powerful emotion and Aurora is now certain that it isn't her childhood sweetheart, Luke, who's uppermost in her mind, but passionate Rhys who's her soulmate, and she determines to be with him, come what may. She wants to be an asset to her family too, rather than being dependent on them. While observing the folk at the wedding feast, her mind wanders back to Australia and she wonders if she might persuade her father that she'd be an asset to the business in Bendigo, considering he has shares in it. She does, after all, have book-keeping skills from her schooling in Switzerland.

After the speeches, Jacob and Clara use one of the rooms in the inn to change into their travelling costumes. Alone at last, Jacob takes her in his arms and kisses her. He wants to make love to her there and then, but they have a steam train to catch. He observes her slender figure with longing and admiration as she stands before him in her underwear; then he comes to, and helps her don her olive-green carriage dress and paletot. While he puts on his own fine new suit of clothes he watches, as she expertly places a matching green bonnet, decorated with pheasant feathers, and pins it with a hat pin into her straw-coloured curls.

He tells her earnestly, "You look absolutely beautiful, Clara, my dear. I'm so proud to be your husband."

She smiles her happiest smile. "And I am truly honoured to be your wife, Jacob."

He kisses her once more, before gathering up their belongings and going back downstairs.

When they re-enter the room, they're bombarded with hugs and kisses, as they prepare to take their leave for their honeymoon.

Jacob takes his mother to one side. "You will take good care of Fergus and Bess for me, won't you Ma? Only I've never left them before."

"Of course I will, love. You just enjoy your honeymoon and don't worry about a thing. Your pa will keep an eye on the flock and we'll have Fergus and Bess indoors with us at night, until you return and move into your cottage."

"Thanks Ma, but don't spoil them too much, they are after all working dogs."

"Be off with you lad and stop your worrying, they will both be fine."

Clara is sharing a last farewell with her papa, before they both join hands to leave the reception together.

While the pony and trap has been tethered outside the inn, the ushers have decorated it, according to tradition, by tying tin cans, old boots and lucky horseshoes to the back of it. All turn out to wave them on their way as Malachi drives them off to Penn Mill Station to catch the steam train to their secret destination.

The following day Aurora decides she has to speak up about her desire to return to Australia. She's aware of Louisa's fear of the sea and so she decides to approach her father in his den. He's adamant that her mother will never allow it.

She stands before his desk. "Please talk to her, Papa. You know how I loved travelling with you, and my whole being is longing for some excitement. Besides, I really do want to try to see if the love between me and Rhys will stand the test of time. I believe he's my soulmate, Papa."

"I'm afraid I'm with your mother here, Rora. I couldn't condone you travelling all that way unaccompanied and I'm not prepared to leave Louisa again, after what happened last time."

"I'm not asking you to come too, Papa. I'm quite happy and confident to be travelling alone. Look how we made friends on board the *Delta*."

He appears thoughtful, as if his resolve is weakening, and she presses on. "I promise you I'll be desperately unhappy if you force me to stay here in Somerset, in this quiet backwater, when I could have an exciting and stimulating life with Rhys in Australia. I could help in the business that you've invested in, Papa. I have book-keeping skills to offer them. Please don't dismiss the idea out of hand. Please persuade Mama that I'm a grown up now. I'm twenty-two next month and if I was a man you'd be powerless to stop me."

He looks at her sympathetically. She's confident she's making sense. She goes around his desk and puts her arm around him, saying quietly, "I expect you to convince her, Papa. You know it will be the best path for me." She kisses his forehead and leaves the room.

That evening after supper, when they're alone, Joshua broaches the subject with Louisa. "Aurora came to me this afternoon, desperately trying to coax me to let her go back to Australia to be with Rhys."

"Oh no, not that again! What did you say?"

"Well of course I said no, but she did put up a good argument."

"No, Joshua, you can't let her go, not after what you yourself witnessed off Chesil only last year."

"You say that, my dear, but it was the captain's error and we did manage to save sixty souls."

"But seven perished in the most dreadful manner and I don't want that for Aurora."

"My dear, they'll be sailing for mile after mile without any obstacle, you know yourself that our particular coastline is more treacherous than most, and it's a risk many take for a better life."

"But how can she possibly have a better life than she has here in this beautiful home with us? Surely she'll be living in primitive conditions over there on the goldfields?"

"Not where Hugh and Bryn live, it's quite civilised really, but that's beside the point. She's longing to be with Rhys. She's in love and won't be influenced otherwise."

"I can certainly understand her wanting to be with the one she loves, but it's that dreadful three-month hazardous journey, suffering seasickness and God knows what, that I can't understand."

He gives her a reassuring hug. "She knows what to expect; unlike you, my little land lubber, she's done it before."

She turns to him, accusation in her eyes. "It sounds like you're on her side, Joshua? I may not have experienced it personally, but let's face it, the last time we were on Portland it wasn't only the *Royal Adelaide* that perished, it was also your father's friends in their small fishing vessel. We both know that the oceans are dangerous and the weather temperamental. I'll never forgive you, if you allow her to risk her life on this foolish whim."

He considers a moment. "What if we delay this discussion by suggesting she learns to swim? We can send her off to Portland and Ben can teach her. In the meantime, she may well fall in love again, or she may discover that she hates the sea up her nose and in her ears and decide she never wants to risk it, after all."

"I'm all in favour of anything that will put her off the sea."

"Well, let that be our plan. When she next mentions it, we'll send her off to Portland for the rest of the summer."

Aurora hopes that her father will have spoken to Louisa that night, after their chat, and she tentatively mentions it to her mother the following afternoon. But her mother still looks horrified. "No, no, no, Rora, you can't risk it, it's far too dangerous. I'll be worried sick about you; besides, I need you here to help me with Lydia May."

Her eyes fill with tears of frustration. "Mama, it's not fair to stop me from going for selfish reasons. I feel like I'm treading water here, that my life won't begin until I reach Rhys and Bendigo. He's begged me to join him and I'm beseeching you to let me go."

"Your father and I have discussed this many times, and we both agree, you can't possibly travel all that way unaccompanied."

She detects a seed of hope. "So, if I can find a travelling companion, will you then let me go?"

"That will depend on who this companion is, and on your father agreeing to fund the journey, and I think, before we even consider anything else, you should learn to swim."

Aurora smiles; these requirements are not entirely impossible to achieve.

"In that case I'd like to go and stay on Portland with Granny and Grandpa, so that Uncle Ben or Grandpa can teach me."

"I'm sure that can be arranged, Rora, but you'd better be quick and tell your papa, so you can enjoy the seaside in the August weather, before it gets too cold."

Aurora's delighted to be making slow progress towards her goal of emigrating, to begin a new life in the Antipodes. She'll miss her family to be sure, but she needs to make a family of her own and it's with Rhys that she sees her future evolving.

Her father sends a telegram to her grandparents to ask if she might stay with them for the rest of the summer and they reply quickly in the affirmative. She rushes upstairs to pack her bags ready for the following day, when she'll catch the train from Penn Mill Station to go on a short summer vacation, staying on Portland.

That evening she tells Grace her plans. Although Aurora and Gabriel no longer need tuition, Grace has been retained to help Gabriel with his law books, but now that Gabriel's seventeen years old, she believes that she's simply being kept on out of charity. When she hears that Aurora is looking for a chaperone to accompany her to Australia, she's tempted to offer her services. The only thing that's holding her back is her sister in Sherborne has been unwell of late and she'd feel guilty abandoning her.

The day after Aurora's arrival on Portland, Becky leaves Jessie with Violet and goes with Aurora to Henry Russell's drapery emporium in Fortuneswell, in order to purchase a ready-made bathing costume, but unfortunately, they've none in stock. Disappointed, they plan to go into Weymouth, the following morning, where they'll have more choice and they leave Jem and Jessie with Violet, while they take the omnibus into the seaside town to shop for both of them. They find what they're looking for in T H Williams and Sons, in Bond Street, and they have a fit of giggling in the fitting room while trying them on. They're so unflattering, but they'll do the job and that's all that matters.

That Sunday, the whole family, having rejected the idea of the small pebbly beach at Castletown and with the undertow off Chesil far too dangerous for beginners, decide to opt for the sandy beach and more facilities at Weymouth. And so together they catch the train from Victoria Square. The men carry the picnic hamper and towels and when they reach the esplanade, they hire four deckchairs. The beach is busy with day-trippers, but they find a good spot where their view of the sea is unhindered, and they've plenty of room to spread out the picnic blanket for Jem and Jessie. Matthew buys a bucket and spade from a kiosk, to amuse the children while the others are having their lessons.

Once settled in the sunshine, Ben and Matthew strip off their outer garments to reveal their bathing costumes underneath and run off down the smooth sandy beach and into the water. The girls go to the female changing booths. While Jem makes sandcastles for his little sister, Violet sits in comfort in her deckchair, keeping an eye on her grandchildren and watching the two women, as the swimming lessons begin, smiling at their squealing, and laughing at their slow progress.

Matthew and Ben begin by teaching them both to float. "You just have to lie on the water and relax, like lying on a bed and the water will buoy you," says Matthew, supporting Aurora by keeping his hand in the middle of her back. "There, now you're quite relaxed I can take my hand away and you're floating."

Aurora has complete trust in her grandfather and is delighted to find she's floating, until a small wave washes over her face and goes up her nose. She quickly finds her feet, spluttering and coughing, but isn't put off.

Matthew then demonstrates how to do the front crawl and she tries to copy him, holding her head up out of the water. "Well done, Aurora, that's very good, but you really need to let the water go over your head and take regular breaths, by lifting your head out of the water every other stroke."

She doesn't want to get her bathing cap or her hair wet, but she really wants to learn how to swim properly and her hair and cap will dry. She's soon successfully doing the front crawl and moving through the water, away from Matthew, Ben and Becky. It's a wonderful place to learn to swim; because it's such a broad, level, shallow beach, she can always stand up if she gets worried and there are no pebbles to stumble over, but smooth soft sand.

She turns and swims back to them, pleased to be making such good progress.

"Right, now I'll show you how to do the breaststroke." She wants to laugh as her grandfather swims along, rather like a frog, but he stands up and looks at her, saying, "Your turn."

She finds this stroke rather more difficult, because her body seems to be lifting and sinking as she goes and tension pulls in her tummy muscles, but she masters it and her grandfather is full of praise. "I'll say this for you, Aurora, you don't give up easily."

Becky has also made good progress, but now they're feeling tired and hungry, so they all go to their respective changing rooms to dry and dress themselves.

Aurora removes her wet costume and wraps herself in the large towel, rubbing herself dry. "That was such good fun, Becky. I hope we can do it again next Sunday."

"Well, I'm game and once we've learnt well enough, Ben's going to give Jem some lessons too. He wanted to learn today, but Ben thought they ought to concentrate on teaching us first."

"I'm really grateful to you all for doing this for me. I do so want to go to Australia to see if I can realise all my dreams with my Rhys, but Ma and Pa won't even consider it unless I can swim and even then, I have to find someone to accompany me. I'm hoping that Grace Tweedy will want to accept the challenge. I could see she was interested, but she's too worried about leaving her sister behind, at the moment."

Once dry, she puts on her normal clothes and removes her mob cap, shaking out her damp hair and rubbing it vigorously with the towel. "I haven't told Luke my plans yet, partly because I know he'll be really upset and partly because I have to be sure I'm going, before I break the news to him."

"He'll surely be devastated, Rora. He's loved you forever."

"I'm not so sure about that, Becky. Lately his ardour lacks enthusiasm. I think he's like a carriage stuck in a rut, but he's unwilling to risk the thought of anyone else loving him any better than I do."

"It's still sad. He'll be lost without you. After all, you've been childhood sweethearts since birth almost."

"Not really. It simply grew from our close friendship, but let's face it, he was the only lad I ever came close to knowing. Anyway, come on, Becky, I'm starving, aren't you?"

"I am. All that exercise certainly gives one a hearty appetite."

"Are you finished?"

"Yes, come on, let's go and enjoy the picnic."

Throughout August, they go regularly to Weymouth beach every Sunday with the whole family and sometimes, as Jem is off school, she and Becky also take the children in the week.

Aurora has noticed how artistic Jem is, by the way he carves amazing characters in the damp sand. He's done dolphins leaping from the sea, and on another day, horses or elephants, and they look so realistic, she thinks he has a real talent.

By the time he returns to school in September young Jem is an accomplished swimmer and they're close companions. He shows her his collection of stone carvings and tells her, "When my school friend's father, Mr Barnes, saw how interested I was in carving stone, he gave me an old set of chisels that used to belong to his grandfather and since then I've been chiselling away at any large piece of Portland stone I can manage to carry home."

Aurora is impressed. "Do you want to be a stonemason when you grow up, Jem?"

"Yes, I do, and Mr Barnes works for the Portland Stone Company in the sawmills by the station and he thinks I could be good at it too, and he should know."

"So do I, Jem. I think you're a talented lad and one day you'll be the best Portland can offer." She gives him a hug trying to picture him all grown up… and herself, millions of miles away.

On her return to Alvington, she tells her parents that she can now swim and is competent in both breaststroke and front crawl.

"Did you have a nice time with the relations?" asks Louisa.

"I really did, Mama. I learned a lot about Papa, when he was a boy. I knew he'd been a sailor in the past, but I didn't know that he ran away to sea when he was just sixteen!" she says pointedly.

Joshua grins. "Well, I was just a foolish boy, whereas you're a far more sensible twenty-two-year-old woman."

"This is true, Papa, and as Mama had no objection to me travelling to Australia before, I hope that you'll both accept my decision to go again."

Her mother sighs. "We don't want to stand in the way of your plans, Rora, but please find a travelling companion to at least allay some of my fears of you being accosted on the journey."

"I promise I'll try."

"I know it's unfair of me, to let my phobic fears of drowning prevent you from following your dreams, but as you know, your own poor mama, and my dearest sister, sadly drowned and I fear history has a habit of repeating itself. Besides, I've spent the better part of my life trying to protect you from harm and it's a habit hard to break."

"You've no need to fear, Mama. I'm well able to look after myself. Your advice to learn to swim has been very helpful, for I have no fears of the water now. My only concern is the unpredictable stormy weather conditions and my seasickness."

Elsie enters the room with the trolley and afternoon tea. Once they're all served and Elsie has left the room, her mother says to her, "We've had some bad news while you've been away; sadly, Grace's sister who lived in Sherborne has died."

Her face lights up. "That's wretched for poor Grace, Mama, but it may very well be fortuitous for me."

Louisa sits with her mouth open in shock.

Joshua looks from mother to daughter. "Aurora, how can you be so unfeeling?"

"Really, Papa, I'm truly forlorn for Grace, but she may well feel that now her sister's at peace, she too can follow her dreams and accompany me to Australia."

Her father says, "I'm lost for words, Aurora."

CHAPTER TEN *(September–October 1873)*

A WOMAN SCORNED

As soon as Ethan receives the money from his father, he sets about finding a suitable site to build his miners' huts. He finds what he's looking for, alongside the route leading from the shanty town towards Hopetown. Not far away is a large water pan and on the other side of the track is the Orange River. He believes he might even be able to sink a well to serve the properties. He purchases some corrugated galvanised iron and timber and sets about erecting a row of twelve huts, that can be used as homes, or preferably businesses, bordering the roadway. They are rudimentary, but the miners are soon queuing up to rent them and as each one's completed and the families move in, he begins to earn money, which he banks ready to pay back his father.

It's hard work supervising both the builders and Neville Frosdyke's claim, but it's paying off in spades. The end hut he decides to keep for himself to also use as his office, from where he now sells Frosdyke's diamonds. He begins dealing with the miners and buying and selling what they bring to him. The other diggers like his cheerful personality; he builds up a good reputation for trustworthiness and fairness and his trading goes from strength to strength. Among his properties, there are a few businesses, including a baker, a grocer, a barber, and a chandler.

Every Friday he goes into town to bank his takings at the First National Bank and to meet Lucy and Frankie. He really looks forward to seeing them, for otherwise he lives in a male dominated world and he misses female company.

As he rides into town, he thinks back to the girl with the golden hair he once had, back home in Salisbury, and how it had broken his heart seeing her with the pompous son of a local landowner, whom she chose to wed. She'd made him feel unworthy and he never wants to feel like that again. He's determined now to make a success of his life, come what may. The experience has made him cautious when it comes to women, but he likes Lucy and doesn't want to see her hurt like he was. He doesn't trust that Rupert, as far as she's concerned, and he's determined to keep an eye on her. She needs to know that she has choices; she doesn't have to be dependent on Rupert Seymour, not as long as he's around and can look out for her.

As the days grow warmer, so does Lucy's relationship with Rupert, and she begins to think that maybe they should get married and provide some stability for herself and Frankie. It will be autumn back home and the trees will be red and rust and gold in the gentle sunshine. She wonders what her parents would think if she told them she was marrying Ashleigh's brother, Rupert, and staying forever here in South Africa?

The Griqualand winter has been hot and dry, but now, as their spring approaches, they've had a few showers; the acacia tree's in bud and the weaverbirds are making their new nests, while the hot sun is dazzling off the Orange River. She and

Frankie regularly take a stroll across the veldt to visit Hilda, Anja and Marta and she values their feminine company, their gossip about the townsfolk and sometimes playing Hilda's piano.

However, she's been feeling nauseous over the last few days and has been keeping close to the homestead. She's been drinking peppermint tea, but it doesn't seem to be helping.

Tamela is still frosty with her and, no matter how hard she tries, she cannot warm to her. The girl is a law unto herself, but Lucy needs someone to help out and thankfully she keeps herself busy with her chores, cleaning and trimming the lamps, sweeping the house and *stoep*, scrubbing the floors when necessary, making the beds and tidying the rooms, cleaning the shoes, cleaning the fireplace and the stove, washing the dishes, washing, boiling, mangling and hanging out the clothes and walking to the farm to collect supplies. All Lucy has to worry about is the cooking, gardening, sewing and looking after and educating Frankie, all of which she very much enjoys.

A wave of nausea washes over her and she rushes to be sick in the chamber pot. A feeling of unease engulfs her. Surely, she can't be pregnant? The thought frightens her. If she's carrying Rupert's baby, it removes any choice she may have had, for propriety's sake, they must wed. She really doesn't want to have a baby here in this uncivilised place. She can't imagine Tamela as her midwife; maybe the girl's mother would oblige? Her heart races at the thought and she longs to confide in her own mother. Her eyes fill with tears. *I can't do this… I can't do this here!*

She pushes the thought away. It's too soon for her to be sure; she may just have a tummy bug.

Surreptitiously, she empties the chamber pot, continues with her daily routine and keeps her own counsel. Rupert leaves early to work and will have no idea, but she fears Tamela may have seen her with the chamber pot, or even heard her retching.

On Friday she goes, as usual, in the mule cart into Hopetown to meet Ethan, who's always reliably waiting for them in the luncheon room.

Frankie rushes inside to see him. "Hello, Ethan. We have a new bath."

"Do you now." He shakes his head to dispel the image of a naked Lucy bathing with the voyeuristic Rupert nearby.

Lucy smiles at her son's enthusiastic outburst. "Yes, Ethan, we no longer have to use the bathhouse, because the cast-iron bath and screen that Rupert ordered from Port Elizabeth has arrived and we're able to use that now, although Tamela takes ages to fill it with warm water for us."

Ethan grins. "Well, changing the subject, I'm pleased to be able to tell you that all of my premises are now being rented out."

Lucy smiles. "Well done, Ethan, you'll soon be able to pay back your papa."

"Lucy, you won't credit it, but my rental income is £1,760 a month, so by next Friday, I will be easily settling the debt."

"My goodness, that was an excellent plan, Ethan. I can't believe you can repay that loan so quickly."

"I have to say, I've surprised myself." He laughs, as Benthe comes to take their order.

While he chatters to her, Lucy wonders, should she confide in him about her fear of being pregnant?

He is after all her best friend in South Africa, but he's a man and maybe a woman would be more likely to understand; perhaps she should confide in Hilda instead. But there's no doubt she feels closer to Ethan. However, she doesn't want to discuss this in front of Frankie, and she's hardly ever without him by her side.

He asks her what she'd like to drink, and she asks for peppermint tea. He looks surprised, and then suspicious when she declines any cake.

Frankie has his favourite *appelbeignet* and a lemonade and Ethan tries a *stroopwafel*, which, as recommended, he warms over his cup of tea.

"I've kept one of my huts for myself to use as an office, Lucy, and I'm doing quite well dealing with the miners, buying and selling their diamonds."

"Gosh, Ethan, you don't let the grass grow under your feet, do you?"

"I'm eager to establish myself as a businessman, not just a diamond digger. One day in the future, I'd also like to be in a position to be able to help the various tribal natives, who are so thoroughly exploited by us foreigners taking over their amazing country."

"You're a good man, Ethan." She squeezes his hand across the table, longing to confide in him.

An elderly woman enters the luncheon bar with a small puppy in her arms. She sits at the other end of the room, but Frankie wants to go and pet the little creature. "Go on, then, but ask the lady if she minds, first."

She watches her son gingerly crossing the room and asking the lady if he can stroke her puppy. The lady allows him to stroke it and chats with him quite happily.

She returns to Ethan who's studying her. "What's wrong, Lucy?"

"I think I might be pregnant," she blurts out. "I've been feeling sick in the mornings."

"That explains the peppermint tea."

"I'm not ready for this, Ethan. I'm not sure about Rupert. Not sure I should commit to him for the rest of my life. Not sure for me, or for Frankie." She sighs. "I've made a stupid mistake. I should have been more careful."

"How long have you been feeling like this?"

"About three weeks."

"Perhaps you should go and see a doctor?"

She shakes her head. "No, not yet. I'm not ready for everyone to know just yet. You're the only person I've told."

"Well, it's early days, but you won't be able to hide it forever."

"No, I know. But I want to wait for as long as I can, before I'm forced to make a decision that will affect the rest of our lives."

Not many weeks pass before she's quite positive she's with child. She experiences tiny twitches and fine flutters of movement and her hands instinctively stroke her stomach. She can't help wondering if it will be a girl or a boy. It would be nice to have a brother for Frankie, but she'd also like a little girl. She's not sure what Rupert's reaction would be to the news and she is determined to keep it from him until he notices for himself.

By her calculations, she's about three months gone, when she's suddenly doubled up with severe pain in her stomach. It's a huge shock, as she's been feeling so much better now that her sickness has subsided. Her stomach muscles cramp in agony, as she grabs the edge of the table and works her way along the furniture, making towards her bedroom to collapse onto her bed.

Frankie is concerned. "What's wrong, Mama?"

"Don't worry, darling. I just have a bit of tummy ache. You carry on with your puzzle, while I have a lie down, 'til I feel better again."

She's frightened. She never had a pain like this when she was carrying Frankie. She fears she's about to miscarry. She wonders where Tamela is, in case she needs her, but the girl is nowhere to be seen. She takes deep breaths until the pain eases, but then the stabbing pains return, bringing tears to her eyes. She doesn't want to call out for Tamela and frighten Frankie, so she continues with the deep breaths, each time the pain returns and eventually it stops, and she falls asleep with exhaustion.

She wakes up with Tamela peering down at her. She rubs her eyes drowsily. "Where have you been, Tamela?" she asks, croakily.

"In my room, missus."

"I'm feeling under the weather today. Will you please keep an eye on Frankie for me?"

"Yes, missus."

She lies back down on the pillow but can't help feeling that the girl was aware all the time of her pains and is smirking with satisfaction.

Several days go by and Lucy has been free of pain. She's still aware of tiny movements and is reassured her baby's going to be fine. The previous cause remains a mystery, but she's more careful when gardening and helping Frankie plant his new seeds for the summer.

Then that afternoon the pain returns with a vengeance. She cries out and doubles over again, frightened for both her and her baby's life. She must have done too much, but she never had to be so careful when carrying Frankie. Once again, Tamela is nowhere to be seen. She struggles to reach her bedroom and collapses onto the sofa, groaning in agony and curling up into a foetal position with her legs up on the cushions.

Frankie is frightened and runs outside to fetch Rupert.

Rupert comes back with Frankie and when he sees her distress, he's shocked and concerned. "Whatever's wrong, Lucy?"

She whispers to him, "I think I'm losing our baby, Rupert."

He's stunned. "Baby! Why didn't you tell me? You haven't said a word!"

"I'm sorry, but I needed to be sure, before telling you. But I think I'm having a miscarriage." Again, she takes deep breaths through the pains and Rupert draws up a chair to sit with her. After about an hour the pains stop, and she feels better, just exhausted from her ordeal.

"The pain is easing now, Rupert. I'll stay here and rest; you go on back to work."

"All right, if you're sure." He turns to a worried Frankie, who's been sitting fondling Monty on the rug. "You come and get me if you're worried, all right, lad?"

"Yes, Uncle."

He strokes her hair off her face and plants a kiss on her forehead and then leaves the room.

Ten minutes later Tamela turns up with a basket of washing.

Lucy doesn't ask her where she's been all this time; it's obvious she was outside in the garden taking in the washing for a short period, but where was she for the first part of her suffering? She still suspects Tamela knew all along she was in distress and did nothing to help her.

That night when she undresses for bed, she notices with horror the blood in her underwear. During the night, the pains return in devastating wave after wave. Bathed in perspiration, she hangs on to the brass bars of the headboard and draws up her legs instinctively trying to protect the baby. She suffers hour after hour of agony. By sunrise, she knows she's miscarried. She's overwhelmed with sadness and distraught that all the time she was muffling her cries; Frankie was in the same room.

When he wakes up, she asks him to go and fetch Rupert who has to go and get the help of the local doctor and midwife to clean her up and make sure there's nothing left behind to poison her. She's an emotional weeping wreck, unable to hide her sadness from them all. Now she understands what poor Becky went through, losing Meakins' baby all those years ago. It's devastating.

During the period she's convalescing, Frankie is her errand boy. One morning he accidentally smashes a bowl. Tamela has gone to the Van der Merwe's to fetch their supplies and so he goes into her room to look for a dustpan and brush. He returns to show his mother what he's found.

"Look, Mama, Tamela has a little dolly." He puts it close under her nose on the pillow. and she stares at the grubby, well-worn, featureless cloth figure in puzzlement, then realisation dawns. Her Granny Warren had always been afeard of witchcraft and she recognises a voodoo doll, with sewing pins sticking out of its stomach.

Suddenly all her inertia disappears. She's furious. She always suspected Tamela was up to something, but this!

She gets out of bed and washes and dresses. She has to go and tell Rupert what his precious maid is really made of. She's on the *stoep*, about to go down to the claim, when Tamela returns. "What is the meaning of this?" she shouts at the girl, shoving the voodoo doll into her face.

The girl makes to grab it, but Lucy is too quick for her. She pushes past her and goes straight to Rupert, shouting over her shoulder to Tamela, "You can get inside and clear up the smashed bowl for Frankie."

Her blood is boiling as she stomps across the claim. She grabs Rupert by the arm and drags him away from Moses and Solomon. "Rupert, I'm sorry to have to tell you this, but your precious Tamela has been using black magic to abort our baby. Just look at what Frankie found in her room!"

Rupert stares open-mouthed at the voodoo doll. He stammers, "Surely you don't believe in that nonsense?"

"The evidence is here before your eyes, Rupert. Look at the pins piercing its stomach! She's cursed our baby and caused it to die. She's an evil monster and I want her gone."

She snatches the pins from the doll and tramples them in the mud, then she throws with all her might and watches with satisfaction as the doll flies through the air and lands in the swirling waters of the Orange River.

He shakes his head. "I can't turn her out. How will you manage without her?"

She puts her hands on her hips. "I'm a farmer's daughter. I can manage very well, thank you."

"But I have an arrangement with her mother."

She says, "Then you can terminate that arrangement. Either she goes, or Frankie and I go. It's as simple as that. I can no longer put up with her deceitful evil ways."

She storms off. *How can he defend her?*

When she returns to the homestead, Tamela confronts her, again on the *stoep*. "I not one who should leave, missus. I mother of firstborn son. I number one woman, not you." She tosses her head and goes back to her room.

Lucy is stunned! *So Berko is Rupert's son. Rupert and Tamela have an ongoing relationship, while he's also been romancing me! He was just using me for propriety's sake. That's why she wanted to hurt me and get rid of my baby! She saw it as a threat to her own son's security. I can't bear to look at either of them a moment longer. I'll have to use some of Malachi's money so that we can stay in The Cape Karoo Hotel in town for now, until I've formulated a plan.*

She checks the washing line and is packing all of their clothes in their trunks when Frankie comes to her, crying.

"Whatever's the matter, darling?"

He rubs his eyes with his little fists. "What about Monty and Camilla? We can't leave them behind."

She considers this. "Well, Camilla has lived here all her life and she has her home on the *stoep* now, so it would be unkind to move her, but we have had Monty since he was a baby so I think we could take him with us." He seems to understand and is pacified. "But we must hide him in my basket when we get to the hotel, because they'll not want him staying there with us. Go and put his bedding into my basket and we'll take a cloth to cover him."

He rushes off on his mission.

Once organised she loads up the mule cart, and after Frankie has said goodbye to Camilla and given her all the bugs he could find, they're off, before anyone can stop them. She leaves a note: 'Moses can pick up the mule and cart from the Karoo Hotel tomorrow.'

That night in the hotel, after Frankie has fallen asleep beside her, she listens to his regular breathing and is heartbroken that her second child never drew breath at all. She weeps silently into her pillow, longing for the comforting arms of her mother and the support and kind words of her steadfast father. They know nothing of what she'd planned, or how those plans have gone dreadfully awry. She'd dared to dream that she and Rupert might make a go of things and this is how she's rewarded. She should never have betrayed her best friend, Clara; this is the Lord's retribution.

On Friday for a change it is she and Frankie who are waiting in the luncheon room for Ethan.

"Well this is a nice surprise. You've beaten me to it today."

"I expect you've been busy, Ethan, but we don't have so far to come now."

The arrival of Benthe with her pad and pencil interrupts them, and Ethan orders for them all before they're able to continue their conversation.

"What do you mean, you don't have so far to come?"

"We're lodging in the Cape Karoo Hotel." Her voice breaks, the emotion bursting forth as she puts the situation into words. "I've walked out on Rupert."

He lowers his voice. "What's happened?"

"He's never wanted me and Frankie, Ethan." She sighs. "It was all a big charade to cover up the fact that all this time he's been sleeping with Tamela and is the father of her son."

"Oh no, Lucy. I can't believe it. What a swine!"

"It's not just him, Ethan. The girl has been against me all this time and she's been using black magic to abort my baby." Her eyes fill with tears. "I've had a miscarriage, Ethan."

"You poor thing! Are you sure you're completely recovered, Lucy?"

"I think so. I had the doctor visit, but Frankie found a voodoo doll with pins sticking out of its tummy."

"What an evil cow!"

She flushes with anger. "Precisely! I had no choice. We could stay there no longer. Since then, I've been looking for work in town, but without success."

"Well that's easily remedied," he says. "You can help me by running my office, if you'd like to."

She hesitates, a lump forming in her throat. "Are you sure you need someone, Ethan? I don't want you to feel obliged."

He bends forward earnestly. "You'll be doing me a great favour. At the moment I've my work cut out trying to run Frosdyke's claim and man the office."

Tears threaten at his kindness and a worried frown furrows her brow. "But you're the one who knows the value of the gems."

"Don't worry. I'll still be responsible for all the valuations, but there's legal paperwork that has to be completed and you'll soon pick that up. We can work it out together." He takes her hand across the table. "Lucy, you'll be a lifesaver, I promise you, and not for the first time."

Lucy sighs. "I'm afraid it won't be practical or economical for us to stay in the hotel and travel to your office each day, though."

"No, it won't. Can I suggest that you stay here in the hotel for another week and in the meantime, I'll transform my office into a home for you and Frankie."

"But what about you, Ethan?"

"I can stay in the shack on Frosdyke's claim for now, but I've plans to purchase a plot of land on which to build a smart homestead eventually. However, that will obviously take time. But I can manage quite well, as I did before."

"Thank you, Ethan, for coming to our rescue. We're very grateful, aren't we, Frankie?"

He glances up at her quizzically, not sure at all what's going on, but replies, "Yes, Mama."

She squeezes Ethan's big hand in hers. "What good fortune it was that we should meet on the *Syria* and make friends."

"We can certainly thank fate for that, Lucy. It's benefitted both of us."

The following week, Lucy and Frankie travel on the horse-drawn omnibus out of Hopetown to the mining township where Ethan is waiting for them outside his row of buildings, now named 'Eureka Row' after the first diamond discovered by Jacob Erasmus. Ethan hopes it will be a good omen.

He's standing under the awning on their boardwalk, leaning against the iron hitching rail. Two horses stand in the heat, further along the rail, flicking their tails against the flies, their flanks quivering.

He helps her and Frankie down from the carriage and the luggage is unloaded for them by a native man with large holes in both ears, which of course fascinates Frankie.

Lucy calls to him, "Frankie, you must look after Monty. He'll be frightened in these strange surroundings, so you must keep him inside, for a while until he gets used to it." She hands him the basket and they go into their new home, the first in the row, furthest away from the diamond fields. Frankie lifts Monty out and calms the little wriggling animal by stroking him gently.

Ethan apprehensively shows them around the building, but Lucy's delighted. "You've managed to make it homely for us, Ethan."

He shows her two small bedrooms and a toilet area at the back, with a living room, office and kitchen in the front. The living room has a fireplace, an upholstered sofa and two matching armchairs, a sideboard, a bookshelf and a low table in the centre of a large cowhide rug. In the kitchen is a black-leaded stove, a larder cabinet with a mesh door, a copper samovar, a Welsh-style dresser for the china and cutlery, and a cupboard containing water vessels and washing bowls, plus a mangle and a wooden table, for preparing and eating their meals, with four chairs. There are oil lamps in all the rooms. The office is equipped with an acacia blackwood desk and two chairs, and a wooden counter for serving customers, behind which is shelving and a lockable mahogany collector's cabinet for the gems and the money.

"I'm sorry it's so small and cluttered, but I promise that if you stick with me, things will soon improve."

"It's fine, Ethan. I'm sure Frankie and I will be very happy here." She stares at the front door with its heavy-duty bolts and the burglar bars on the front windows and her heart races at the thought of armed men breaking in, in the middle of the night, to thieve from them. She shudders and he picks up on it.

"What's wrong, Lucy? You don't look all together convinced."

She smiles at him. "The only thing I'm a bit worried about is that miners and dealers and all sorts of folk know that you have diamonds here. What if someone does manage to break in at night, when we're undefended?"

Ethan ponders. "I have to admit I hadn't thought about that. There's been no sign of anything like that since I've been here, but I do understand your concerns." He runs his hands through his hair and hesitates, then says, "You'd have to share with Frankie again, but would you prefer it if I stay here with you in the second bedroom, Lucy?"

"Well… it may be improper, but yes I would."

She smiles and he notes the wicked twinkle in her eyes. "In that case, I've made a decision. I'm going to tell your devious brother-in-law that I no longer wish to work for him. Instead I want to concentrate more on the buying and selling and become a travelling diamond buyer. What they call a 'kopje-walloper', covering here, Bultfontein, Dutoitspan, Klipdrift, Koffiefontein and Kimberley, as it's now known. In that way I'll build up a bigger reputation and also get a good idea of where the best stones are being found and who's finding them. You, my dear friend, being here and running the office for me is the perfect solution."

CHAPTER ELEVEN *(October–December 1873)*

RUMOUR AND DISAPPROVAL

In October, Grace Tweedy returns to the manor after her sister's funeral in Sherborne, dressed in her dour mourning weeds. She encounters Louisa in the passageway and dips a curtsey.

Louisa hugs her. "My dear Grace. I'm so sorry for your loss."

"Thank you, milady." She composes herself. "Alas, it wasn't unexpected. She'd been suffering from nervous fainting fits of late. The doctor informed me she died of apoplexy."

"Nevertheless, it's sad for you, for she was your only relative."

Grace dabs at her eyes with her handkerchief and continues. "My dear sister very thoughtfully has left me all her worldly goods, and I'm currently considering my options." She removes her mantle and folds it neatly over her arm, before continuing. "I know that, despite Lord Dryer kindly keeping me on, Master Gabriel no longer really needs my input with regard to his studies. Therefore, I could resign from my post here and go and reside in the Sherborne house, where I might make new friends and live a genteel life. Alternatively, I could put my sister's house and its contents on the market and take this golden opportunity to seek adventure. Thus, I'd like to discuss with you the possibility of accompanying Mistress Aurora to Australia. I've checked, and I'm told we can travel steerage on the Immigrants Assisted Passage Scheme. I can travel for £12 and Aurora can travel for £5, as she's younger. I know it's what she'd like, but I'm not so sure if you, milady, and Lord Dryer would be happy if I volunteered my services."

"I see. Well, come and sit with me in the oak and we can talk about it."

That evening Aurora is summoned to her father's study. As she enters, he indicates a small armchair. "Please sit down, my dear."

She looks from her mother to her father. "Is anything wrong, Papa?"

Joshua glances at Louisa for reassurance and she nods her head in final acceptance. He turns back to Aurora. "No nothing's wrong, in fact quite the contrary. I think you'll be pleased to hear that Grace has requested that she be allowed to accompany you on your quest to Australia and your mama and I have reluctantly agreed."

Her mouth drops open in surprise.

He continues, "Here are two first-class tickets for the voyage from Plymouth to Melbourne on the *Northumberland*. I won't have either of you travelling steerage. She's a well-appointed, auxiliary barque-rigged, screw-steamer."

She takes the envelope from him and looks inside. "Oh, my goodness! So soon. I can't believe it. Thank you." She hugs and kisses her mother, knowing she was the main obstacle and then goes behind his desk to embrace her father.

He continues, "We've no wish to lose you, child, but we're both aware that you're pining for your sweetheart and we realise we shouldn't stand in the way of your happiness."

Aurora wipes away a tear of pure elation. "You know, don't you, that I'll surely miss the family dreadfully and I'll always be grateful for all you've done for me? You took me in when I was a foundling, Papa, and I know I've been fortunate indeed to have had the privilege of two such loving parents."

Her father's voice breaks as he says, "My darling, you must know you've been a joy to us from the moment Rosa discovered you concealed beneath the clock tower on that misty September morning."

"You must promise to write to us all regularly with all your news," says her mother, dabbing away her tears. "Gabriel and Lydia May and the rest of the household will all want to know about your adventures."

"I promise." She kisses each of her parents in turn. "Talking of writing, I must let Rhys know that I'm coming at last." She turns to leave, then turns back, tears in her eyes. "I thank you both with all my heart, for permitting me to go." She brushes away her tears. "Please excuse me."

She runs upstairs to her bedroom and sits down to pen her letter to Rhys.

Rhys Thomas Esq
Brecon House
Waratah Street
C/O Bendigo Post Office
Sandhurst
Victoria
South Australia

5th October 1873

My Dearest Rhys,
Mama and Papa have finally given their consent to allow me to travel to Australia, with Grace as my

companion. *Papa has arranged the tickets and we leave on Wednesday the 15th October.*

It is a huge gamble for me, giving up my family home and venturing to start a new life in a foreign country, but I loved my time with you before and have not settled here, since my return home, because I believe my soulmate remains in Bendigo. I hope with all my heart that you still feel the same way about me, despite the time that has passed us by.

I am sure this is as big a surprise for you, as it is for me, but I can't wait to see you and start our new life together. I am hoping that I might be found a useful position as a scribe or record keeper within the Brecon Valley Mining Company. Grace is my old governess and will be looking for something similar, working with children. I would be grateful if you would arrange temporary accommodation for myself and Grace, until such time as we are able to make our own decisions.

This note is of necessity short, as I must make haste to sort out my wardrobe, ready to fill the steamer chests and everything else that I wish to bring with me. But be assured, I cannot wait to feel your arms around me once more.

Your loving sweetheart,
Aurora xx

Her head is filled with happiness and smiles, but then she sighs, for next she knows she must face her best friend, Luke.

The following day, she walks up Pound Lane to Camp Road, to meet him on his return home from work for the weekend. Her cheeks are rosy red, after striding up the hill in the autumn wind. They only have about an hour before darkness falls and she intends to get straight to the point. However, as soon as she sees him, she can tell by his expression he's already annoyed with her.

"I've heard a rumour that you're leaving us on Wednesday."

It's as she feared, the gossip has already reached him. She hangs her head, looking down at the roadway, trying to think of a kind way to respond. "I'm sorry, I wanted to be the first to tell you."

"So I should think!" He turns away from her, facing into the wind. "I suppose I should have been prepared; you've always derived pleasure from tantalising me – why should I be surprised?"

"I never set out to hurt you, Luke. I've always loved you and I always will."

"That may be so, but don't expect me to hang around waiting for you to return, because I've my own life to lead."

"I don't intend coming back, Luke. I can see, now that I've met Rhys, that I've always loved you in a brotherly way. I wish it was otherwise, but I have to be honest. I'm sorry."

He shrugs. "I suppose I have to accept that I've lost to a better man."

"Not better, Luke, just different. Maybe if you'd lived in Australia and I'd met you there, it would be new and exciting too, churning up my tummy and making my heart race, but we're like twins, you and me, and even though those millions of miles will separate us, there will always be a connection between us." She pulls him into her arms and whispers in his ear, "Please, I want you to write to me with all your news. Please don't forget me, Luke." Gradually his taut, unresponsive body yields and they kiss for the last time.

Aurora is also anxious about having to say farewell to her maternal grandparents. It's so hard knowing she'll never see them again, when they've both been so good to her. They'll be devastated. She decides to go with her mother's support, to break the news.

Arthur and Martha Bonfield are together, outside in the garden of Knapp Cottage, when they arrive at the garden gate. They're cutting back herbaceous plants and burning the dried stalks and foliage on a bonfire. There's a slight breeze and the smoke and the colourful leaves from the neighbour's maple tree are blowing around them as they toil. The smoke stings her eyes.

Her mother calls out, "Morning, Ma."

Her grandmother waves and smiles and then nudges her grandfather, who's a little hard of hearing. "Look, Arthur! Lou Lou and Rora are here." She turns back to them. "What a lovely surprise. Come on inside, we're both ready for a break."

Her grandparents remove their muddy boots and they follow them inside the familiar cottage. Martha removes her shawl and takes the ladies mantles, while her grandfather lays out some plates on the table and pours them each a glass of cider. Aurora watches her grandma opening their old Christmas cake tin (the colourful decorations on it having long peeled off) and cutting slices from a Victoria sponge for everyone, as she has done so many times before. Tears fill her eyes and she quickly wipes them away before anyone sees.

Her grandfather asks them, "To what do we owe this pleasure? Having you both here together is unusual?"

Aurora shuffles uncomfortably in her chair. "I've come to tell you both that next week I'm going away to live in Australia. Ma and Pa have finally given me permission to go with Grace as my companion."

Her grandmother's eyes open wide with shock, but then she rallies. "Oh my, Rora! I hope it works out well for you, my dear."

Her grandfather frowns. "What did she say, mother?"

Martha explains loudly, "Aurora's going to go to Australia after all, to stay for good."

"Oh." Arthur sighs, clears his throat and says huskily, "We both know you've been hankering after this Rhys chap. I just hope you've made the right decision and the lad will make you happy, love."

Her mother says in a voice loud enough for her grandfather to hear her, "It's not what I want at all, Pa, but she's been so determined, she's worn us down. She's even prepared to say goodbye to Luke."

Her grandpa shakes his head. "Well, lass, as the saying goes, 'you make your bed, you have to lie in it'. Let's hope it turns out not to be too lumpy." He flicks some cake crumbs from his jersey.

"I'm sure he'll make me happy, Grandpa. He assures me constantly that he loves me in his letters."

Her mother says, "He does write to her most weeks, so I do believe he must be sincere."

Her grandfather clears his throat again and continues, "The thing is, lass, you've been used to a cosseted lifestyle at Alvington Manor; it's going to be a different matter over there, I'm sure."

"I know that, Grandpa, but I'm prepared to work hard, save up and contribute to our lives together to create a home for our future family where we'll both be happy forever."

Her grandmother says, "Well, Aurora, you won't know if it's going to work, unless you take the plunge and give it a try, my dear." She wipes her eyes with her handkerchief and gives a little sniff. "We're behind you all the way. Aren't we, Arthur?"

He takes her hand. "Of course we are, child. We only want the best for you. But we'll both miss you dearly."

She tearfully kisses and hugs her grandparents in turn. It's so hard knowing that she'll never see them again.

On the fourteenth of October, Aurora and Grace say their farewells to the family, the staff and the manor and set off to the Junction Station at Stoford with John Moore in the landau, to catch the steam locomotive to Plymouth. Aurora's eyes are red from weeping. She hadn't expected it to be so hard to leave them all, but although torn, she's confident she's made the right choice.

Her companion, on the other hand, has no idea what to expect and looks anxious. Grace may hate the place; after all, the climate's totally different and they have poisonous spiders and snakes there. Has her old governess made a foolish decision, giving up her security to spend her inheritance on a huge risk, just for her sake?

Grace kindly pats her clasped gloved hands and smiles. "Don't fret, Aurora. As long as you keep in touch, they'll always be your family."

"I know, but it was so hard saying goodbye to them. Mama looked so crushed. I wanted to turn back just to comfort her." She dabs at her eyes with a crumpled handkerchief.

"She'll be fine again by now, my dear; it was just the wrench of saying goodbye to you, possibly forever."

There's silence between them at this thought, then Aurora takes Grace's hand. "We're both taking a massive gamble. You especially, Grace.

You don't have a clue what it's like over there, but I truly believe you'll enjoy the adventure and the challenge. You may even find yourself a husband. There are a lot of lonely men in Bendigo and on the goldfields."

Grace chuckles. "I don't know about that. I'm in my fifties; I suspect it may be too late for me, but whatever happens we'll face it together and support each other, both during the voyage and on our arrival."

Aurora squeezes her hand. "Of course we will."

"I hope Luke and Mr Fairway will be able to handle the sale of my house in Sherborne without any problems. I've given Mr Fairway power of attorney to act in this matter on my behalf and hopefully I'll soon have some more money in my bank account, which will help us when we arrive in Australia."

"I know they'll both do their best for you." At the thought of Luke, her lips tremble again, and she blinks away more tears.

In the meantime, back in Hopetown, Lucy is relieved to be under the protection of Ethan. He's always looked out for her and Frankie, since they first met on the *Syria*, and she knows she can trust him. Although Eureka Row is more primitive than Rupert's homestead, she's happier and feels safer with Ethan as their defender.

Sometimes, when the wind's in a certain direction, they get a whiff of the unsanitary middens on the diamond fields and she's relieved they're far enough away to be safe from contagion, but close enough for business, where they enjoy the clean air blowing off the veldt most of the time.

He's introduced her to their new neighbours: the grocers, Betsy and Norman Norris, are next door; then there's the chandler and his wife, Mr and Mrs Coffin; about three doors down from them is the bakery, 'Our Daily Bread', run by Mr and Mrs Bekker; and at the far end of the row is the Italian barber, Luigi Capello, who's flamboyant and artistic and lives alone. The other huts in between are rented by miners.

In way of thanks to Ethan, she stocks the larder cupboard with grocery items with the assistance of Mrs Norris, who is kind and helpful. She has an open, friendly face, is neat and tidy, with her fair hair plaited and wrapped around her head, and she appears to be only a little older than her. She's running her grocery store single-handedly, as her husband's working long hours on their claim. When they've finished filling her basket, Mrs Norris puts a hand on her arm. "Please call me 'Betsy', because I feel sure we're going to be good friends."

Lucy smiles. "I'm Lucy. It's wonderful to have a kindly neighbour, especially one who can provide us with all our essential foods."

Betsy laughs and generously gives Frankie a toffee apple, ensuring his eternal friendship.

When she's put all the groceries away, she sits down to pen a letter to her family back home, to Maisie in Cape Town and Ellen in Durban, to let them know her changed circumstances and her new address.

That afternoon Lucy bakes a malva pudding for their dessert, and when Ethan comes home after work, she cooks some sausages and mash with green beans and onion gravy. He appears to be so pleased to see them there in his home, it's heart-warming.

"Mm, I love the smell of onions cooking."

"Me too," says Frankie.

"Well, I hope you're both hungry, because there's malva pudding to follow."

"I'm actually starving, Lucy. I've been looking forward to coming home to see you both all day."

"Me too." She smiles. "On Friday we'll have to go with you into Hopetown on the omnibus, so that we can use the bathhouse, and also I want to purchase some fresh meat from the butcher."

He laughs. "Yes, it's a shame I didn't let one of the properties to a butcher; I seem to have covered everything else."

On Friday they set off in the horse-drawn omnibus into Hopetown. When they reach the stop, just down the road from the general store in the high street, they disembark.

Mr Buthelezi is outside his premises ordering his assistants around, as they reorganise the front-of-store display. He looks up and spots Lucy with Ethan. She's about to wave to him, when he frowns, and turns away from them. Lucy flushes crimson, knowing he's under the impression she's married to Rupert. Mr Buthelezi obviously disapproves of her being in the company of another man. She's too embarrassed to explain the situation to the man; after all, she's as much to blame as Rupert, because she failed to correct him that one time, when he referred to Rupert as her husband.

She and Frankie make their way to the bathhouse, while Ethan goes to the bank. They'll meet him in the luncheon bar after they've bathed.

The woman in the bathhouse hands her the soap and towels and she and Frankie quickly undress in their compartment. They share the bath and together they sink into the warm water. She soaps him all over and then washes herself, while he plays with the bubbles. He always hates having his hair washed and so she leaves this until last, ignoring his protests, rinsing off the soap and wrapping him in one of the towels. They're soon feeling clean and fresh once more. Lucy puts their discarded underwear in her basket to take home to wash. She takes Frankie's hand and they make their way to the luncheon bar, where Ethan's waiting for them.

Benthe serves them, as usual, and this time they have Dutch pancakes for their lunch, as it's later than normal. When Benthe has left them, Ethan asks her, "Was it my imagination or did the owner of the general store snub you earlier?"

Lucy says in a low voice, "You noticed that too. I'm afraid the townsfolk have the impression that Rupert and I are husband and wife. Rupert introduced me to them as 'Mrs Seymour' and they put two and two together and we never disillusioned them."

"I see."

"Mr Buthelezi did refer to Rupert as my husband on one occasion, but I hesitated before correcting him, and he'd turned away to another customer, so I said nothing. Besides, Rupert had invited us over here to see if we could start a new life together. He promised that, if we turned out to be compatible, we would marry, but I wasn't to know at the time he already had a son with Tamela!"

Ethan shakes his head. "He's as bad as McCallister. They both fed us bullshit, completely uncaring of the consequences."

She takes his hand and smiles. "This is true, Ethan, but there's a bright side. I wouldn't have met you, if we hadn't both taken the risk of trying our luck on the unpredictable and inhospitable diamond fields of South Africa."

He smiles back at her and a warm glow touches her heart.

Lucy and Ethan settle into a relaxed pattern of daily life. She's kept busy with office work and household chores, now that she has no maid, but as they go into summer, she and Frankie miss the *stoep* and the garden they had both worked so hard on.

Frankie is outside the back of their home on the open veldt, playing with Monty, when a small chubby native boy approaches him from the township. He's barefoot, wearing only a pair of grubby baggy trousers, but with the widest pearly smile and a cheerful friendly face. Frankie immediately warms to him and they play Jacks together with some *klippies* lying around. The little lad tells him his name is Roeli, and Roeli's as good and gentle with Monty as he is. His parents allow him to roam freely and he becomes a regular visitor. Even though initially Lucy was concerned about lice, he seems to be kept clean and well fed, despite his well-worn clothes, and she's glad that Frankie has at last found a young friend to play with and is happy to welcome the child into their home on many occasions.

One day, Roeli's still with them at around six of the clock, when darkness suddenly falls, as it does in Africa, and Ethan's required to escort him home. Before venturing into this violent and dangerous nocturnal world, he takes the precaution of arming himself with his pistol. The little lad knows exactly where he's going, but Ethan holds on to his hand, as he leads him through the maze of huts, following the flickering lights of the campfires, to his parent's squat in the Idayimane encampment on the eastern edge of the diamond fields. Ethan can smell the spicy food of all different nationalities emanating from the diggers' makeshift homes. He hears laughter and cross words, children's voices, the musical chanting of black voices, various dogs barking, mules braying and drunken, squabbling, cursing men outside the shebeens. All of humankind are here and mugging and thievery's not uncommon.

They reach Roeli's home and Ethan hands over the boy to his worried mother. "I'm sorry we're late, but Frankie wanted him to stay and share supper with us."

His mother nods and smiles the same pearly smile as her son, as she holds her boy to her. Ethan assumes she can't speak English; then his father steps forward and holds out his hand. "Thank you for bringing my boy back."

"You're most welcome. Roeli's a good friend to our Frankie."

Ethan shakes his hand, suntanned skin clasping dark mahogany.

"I am Khumo Tshwana. How d'you do?"

"I'm Ethan Hart. Pleased to meet you."

There's the noise of chattering offspring inside their dwelling and the mother and Roeli go inside, Roeli waving cheerfully.

"Goodbye, Roeli, see you tomorrow."

Khumo also puts up his hand in farewell and saying, "*Usale kakuhle.*" He too goes inside.

Ethan is turning to go back home, when he spots the shadowy forms of three men striding through the Idayimane encampment. Somehow, they look out of place. They are all white men for a start. One of the men is carrying a flaming torch and in that glow he sees he has a livid scar across his cheek, and that the man in the lead looks like a businessman, wearing European clothes and a bowler hat. Then in a moment of flickering firelight he spots the droopy moustache and recognises him as McCallister's father. It looks like the other two more thickset men are his minders. Ethan ducks between two shacks and stays in the shadows, watching with curiosity.

The two minders pull a small, terrified Khoisan man from one of the squats and commence punching, bullying and threatening him. The man frantically shakes his head from side to side, until he's thrown onto the dusty ground. One of the minders then drags out a young girl and the prone black man instantly prays and begs for mercy. McCallister senior then has his say and the man is soon nodding his head and submitting to whatever it is they're asking him to do. Ethan is appalled. He follows them from shadow to shadow, watching the trio going to more squats where either an exchange takes place or they bully the occupants with more threats. He resolves to return in daylight and see if he can find out exactly what's going on.

The next morning at first light the roosters commence their crowing and the diamond fields spring into life. Hadeda birds are calling out their welcome to the new day, as stray dogs root around for scraps of food. Ethan makes his way between the creaking horse whims, passing the water carriers and many workers with shovels over their shoulders, leather diamond belts slung around their waists and their billy-cock hats slanted against the early morning sun. He smells bacon sizzling and his mouth waters. Finally, he reaches the native

Idayimane encampment and catches Khumo before he leaves for his work.

"Khumo, can I talk to you? It's important."

"Of course, please enter." He stands to one side and Ethan enters his squat.

His wife says, "*Molo*," and continues pounding something with a pestle and mortar, while her smallest child plays with a rag doll.

Ethan speaks in a low voice. "Last night after I left you, I witnessed three men going from place to place and intimidating the folk who live here. Do you know what's going on?"

Khumo looks down at the floor and then eventually he lifts his head to look him in the eye. "I do, sir, but not want to tell."

"Please, Khumo, it will just be between you and me." He points to each of them to reinforce his words.

Khumo whispers, "There's important man not scared of police." He shakes his head as if worried for his neighbours. Then he continues, gesticulating to reinforce his words. "He forces our people to steal for him. If refuse they threaten harm to family. These brothers are frightened of him, but also of getting caught by bosses who inspect them when leave work; grubby hands poke in every place. If guilty they sent chained to very bad Breakwater Prison... family deserted, no food... very bad."

"I see. Can you possibly find out for me, quietly and over some time, who has been intimidated in this way, and who employs them? There may be a pattern here."

He nods his head. "For you, I try."

"Thank you, Khumo. Please make sure, for your family's safety, you do this secretly. Maybe with luck, we can find a way to put a stop to this for good."

"*Enkosi*. Err, thank you."
"I'll call on you after several days."
"*Usale kakuhle…* Goodbye, sir."

Having witnessed this intimidation, Ethan is even more determined to build up his own portfolio to give himself some standing in the area. He needs to identify the rich businessmen who are buying up abandoned claims and trying to amalgamate them into larger dominating companies. They have a great deal of power over all the smaller individual claim holders and he wants to be successful and respected in business just as they are and to have earned a say when it comes to the regulations imposed on the miners and their workers. Thus, he'll be better placed to weed out the rotten eggs, like McCallister, and he's prepared to play the long game.

Having transformed his office into a home for Lucy and Frankie, he then sets about looking for another larger plot of land on which to build a ranch-style homestead for them all.

With his second month's rental payment, he purchases a pony and trap and constructs a lean-to on the side of their home in which to house the trap and form a stable for the pony. The pony is called 'Reckless'.

In the meantime, he keeps close counsel with Khumo. Together building up a body of evidence to take to the authorities and nail McCallister once and for all.

As Christmas approaches Lucy receives a letter. She cracks the wax seal and opens the missive eagerly. Inside is a festive colourful Christmas card from her parents, with ivy, holly and golden bells decorating the border and the picture of a steepled church in the centre. She immediately feels homesick. Looking at her parents' beautiful Christmas card, she remembers the carol services held every year in the manor chapel and feels an overwhelming need to go to church. Also enclosed is a letter from Bunny. She sits down to read it.

Mrs Lucy Seymour
Eureka Row
C/O Hopetown Post Office
Hopetown
Pixley ka Seme
Thembelihle
Northern Cape Province
South Africa

18th September 1873

My Dearest Sister,
I hope that you and Frankie are both keeping well. I am writing this to send you Season's Greetings for Christmas, but also to ask you if, or when, you are planning to return home to us all. We miss you terribly and worry so much about you, so far away from us. It seems to us that you have no intention of returning to us any time soon. Please write to reassure us that all is well. Even Jacob and Malachi are becoming concerned now.
Jacob and Clara have settled well up on Camp Road and our brother is the happiest I have ever known him to be. I don't think it will be long before we hear the patter of tiny feet!
I have some news in that Edwin has finally asked me to marry him and of course I have said yes,

I love him so. We hope to marry in July next year, in the little chapel at the manor, but as yet we don't know the actual date, because we don't know where we will be living. It would be so wonderful if you were to return to us in time to be my maid of honour and for Frankie to be my page boy. Of course, I will try to understand if that is not possible.

I pray every day for your safety and long to see you again soon.

Ma and Pa both send hugs and kisses.

With fondest love,

From your hopeful sister, Bunny. xx

Lucy's ashamed she's not yet sent Christmas greetings to her family. She knows she must respond straight away to Bunny's letter, as it takes so long for post to get to England.

Mr & Mrs I Warren
Home Farm
Alvington Manor
Ivell
Somerset
England

12ᵗʰ December 1873

My Dear Family,

Thank you for your Christmas card and for Bunny's wonderful letter. It is so good to get news from home and I'm really happy to hear that you and Edwin are now engaged. Congratulations to both of you.

It's strange, but it doesn't actually feel like Christmas here, with it being so hot and dry, and that is my only excuse for not sending you our best wishes for the festival, as I know you won't be receiving this letter before March when Christmas will be a distant memory!

I'm kept really busy now, helping Ethan with his diamond dealings and running our little home. Frankie has befriended a young native child called Roeli and they play most days with Monty merrily joining in. We're both quite safe here, with Ethan as our protector, so please don't worry.

I'm sorry, but I'm afraid we won't be able to get back home in time for your wedding to Edwin, Bunny, but, needless to say, we wish you both a wonderful wedding day and a most successful union, blessed with beautiful children. I'm, of course, sad not to be there, as I was sad we missed Jacob and Clara's marriage, but it cannot be helped. It will take a lot of money and planning before we can return and at the moment I feel that we haven't given South Africa a proper chance yet.

Ethan plans to build a ranch here, when he has found a site for it and I would like to support him at least until he achieves this. Nevertheless, I do miss seeing you all and I miss the different English seasons. You'll be noticing the snowdrops and crocuses soon; I used to love looking out for their tips peeping tentatively from the soil, despite the frosts and snow.

In contrast it is extremely hot here at the moment, even in the shade and indoors. As I say, not like Christmas at all. Your lovely card brought back many happy memories of roaring fires and cold winter nights and it has stirred in me the desire to go to church to sing carols this year, which I plan to do.

Anyway, please be assured of my unceasing love for my family and friends and know that I have you in my thoughts constantly.

Your loving daughter and sister, Lucy, and of course, your sweet grandson and nephew, Frankie. xx

The only church in Hopetown is the recently built Dutch Reformed Church, and she persuades Ethan that it would be nice to attend their carol service.

On the Sunday morning before Christmas, when they're all dressing up in their finery, Lucy is frustrated because she can't find her mother's crocheted shawl, which goes so well with the blue and cream bonnet she's wearing, bringing her closer to the memories of the warmth of her family. Her searching proves fruitless and she shrugs with despair. "It's no use. I'll just have to go without it today!" Despondently, she climbs up into the trap next to Frankie. Ethan flicks the reins and Reckless sets off jauntily on the track into Hopetown.

There's a queue before they can cross the ford. "Do you think all these people are going to church?"

"I suppose so, Lucy. I don't know of anything else going on." But when they reach the town there's a Christmas market down the main street, with all kinds of bric-a-brac for sale. Lucy spots one stand selling painted china-clay models of the Madonna and baby Jesus and charming models of the nativity scene, with the crib and the animals within a wooden stable. Other stands are selling local food produce and biltong, but the stall that gets their attention is displaying sweetmeats like stollen, Christmas cakes and candies, cookie rings on ribbon for the tree, gingerbread men, mince pies, sugared mice, sugared almonds, dried fruit and nuts, etcetera.

They don't have long before the church service begins, but Ethan can't resist jumping down and buying three large slices of stollen and some sugared mice for Frankie. He climbs back up onto the trap and they continue to the church. He finds a hitching post free for Reckless and helps Lucy and Frankie down. The minister is standing outside the church, welcoming people on their arrival, and he shakes hands with each of them. Then they go inside and find a pew that has room enough for the three of them.

Lucy isn't sure if she's imagining it or not, but she believes people are tutting, as they pass by. She recognises the bald head and bushy sideburns of Mr Buthelezi, who's seated next to his wife, and Mrs Erasmus sitting in front of them. She's also familiar with some of the other shopkeepers, all wearing their best costumes and decorated bonnets, many looking in their direction.

She ignores the staring and whispering; after all, these are regular churchgoers and Lucy, Ethan and Frankie are newcomers. However, the service is long, with the only carol they actually recognise being 'Silent Night' or '*Stille Nacht*', as announced by the minister. Lucy is able to pick up the melodies of some of the other hymns and makes a brave attempt at singing along, but the boys are lost. Frankie is fidgety by the time it ends.

Despite not recognising the hymns, Lucy still feels uplifted by the wonderful acoustics of the church and the enthusiastic voices of the rest of the congregation.

As they file out, Frankie whispers, "Can we go to the market now?"

Ethan replies, "I'm not at all sure it will still be going by now, Frankie."

"Oh!" he says, disappointedly.

The noise of a man clearing his throat interrupts them, followed by a booming voice over and above the hum of muted conversation. "Good morning, Mrs Seymour. How's your good husband?"

Lucy spins around; standing right behind them is Mr Buthelezi peering down at her.

She draws herself up to her full height. "My husband unfortunately is dead, sir. Regrettably, I'm a widow." She pauses, then speaks clearly. "However, if you mean my brother-in-law, Rupert, I'm sure he's quite well. Although I haven't seen him for several months." She abruptly turns away from him, satisfied by his stunned expression. *How dare he try to humiliate me in front of everyone! I'll never set foot in this church again.*

Ethan takes her arm, unashamedly, and they walk out with their heads held high.

CHAPTER TWELVE *(December–February 1874)*

A NEW YEAR – A NEW LIFE

While in Hopetown, shopping for the Christmas Day celebrations, Lucy quickly nips across the roadway in front of an approaching mule cart. She looks up and is confronted with the sight of Tamela wearing her mother's cream lace shawl and sitting up front alongside Rupert. He catches her eye, but she turns away, too embarrassed to show her feelings of anger in public. *So that's where it went! The nerve of that little upstart wearing my shawl and sitting up front, bold as brass! Surely Rupert will pay for this, one way or another, with the judgemental citizens of Hopetown?* She will leave it to those disparaging folk to spurn them. But Rupert draws up alongside her, calling out, "Lucy, how are you?"

She forces herself to be courteous. "I'm fine, thank you, Rupert. How are you?" She avoids eye contact with Tamela.

"I'm quite well, thanks, but Jack isn't so good. He has a terrible cough and seems to be losing rather a lot of weight. I'm worried about him, but he's a stubborn old fool and refuses to see the doctor."

Concerned, she says, "I'm sorry to hear that. Please send him my regards."

"I will do. How's Ethan?" *So he knows we're with Ethan.*

"Ethan is fit and well and extremely busy. I'm helping him in his office."

"So I heard. Well, I wish you all a happy Christmas."

"Thank you. The same to you. Good day."

She carries her packages to their cart and, relieved to escape further scrutiny, she sets off back home. Her mind is full of Rupert's betrayal and Tamela's treachery. Now she knows what happened to her mother's shawl. Tamela must have deliberately hidden it from her! *She'll not get away with that. I'll get it back one way or another.* She tries to calm herself down, but because of her perplexity, she's sure she's forgotten something in her haste to leave town. *Oh well, hopefully Betsy will stock it, whatever it is.*

When she reaches Eureka Row, she remembers it was cornflour that she wanted, for thickening the meat sauces, and calls in to ask Betsy if she has some. Betsy finds some Maizena on the shelf behind the counter for her and she sighs, then attempts a grateful smile, but Betsy looks at her strangely.

She asks her, "Is something wrong, Betsy?"

"I was going to ask *you* that, my dear. You look like you've the weight of the world on your shoulders."

She can feel the tears welling up and there's nothing she can do to stop them. Luckily, there's no one else in the store and Betsy comes around the counter to comfort her. "Come, Lucy, I think you need a companion to confide in and I'm very discreet. You can trust me with your woes, my dear. I am your friend."

She shakes her head. "I'm so hurt… and confused… and angry, Betsy. I stupidly allowed myself to be duped by my brother-in-law and I'm so annoyed with myself that I was seduced by his charming promises, only to discover he was, all along, having a relationship with his Khoikhoi maid and not only that, unbeknown to me, they even had a child together!"

Her friend's blue eyes open wide with shock. "Dear me. You have been badly treated. Come, I'll close the shop early. I think you need someone to talk to." She turns the sign to 'closed' and leads her friend into their back parlour.

Lucy sits and dabs at her eyes with her handkerchief. "I feel betrayed and so full of anger. I've invested so much of my time on him and I'm already too old to find myself another man. What am I to do, Betsy? I don't have enough money, or energy, to journey back home to my family, dragging poor Frankie with me."

"But surely you're happy, now that you're with Ethan? He seems to be so kind and I'm sure he thinks the world of you."

"Do you think so?"

"I'm sure of it. Why else would he take you and Frankie in?"

"I'm afraid I've lost all my confidence, since being involved with the Seymour brothers; they were both so charismatic to begin with, but I eventually discovered their true colours. At first, we'd been so happy. My friend and I used to double date with them, and we had such fun together. Admittedly, there was usually drink involved, because my friend and I were both invited to attend their gentlemen's club. Women were allowed, as long as they had something to offer. Some offered more than we were prepared to, but I used to play the piano, so we were always welcomed and used to enjoy such merriment there. Then after we married, I became pregnant and was confined, so he'd go off on his own and come back paralytic, and in this state, he'd be violent towards me. I ended up being widowed, because he got involved with the wrong kind of folk. It'll take a long time before I'll be able to entrust my heart to any man ever again."

"Please don't let those brothers make you too cynical to make the most of your life. Besides, I don't know if you realise it, but you'd never have been able to legally wed his brother, Rupert. Because any union, between you and your deceased husband's brother, would have constituted a levirate marriage, which according to Leviticus is expressly forbidden."

She's shocked. "No, I didn't realise that!" *I wonder if Rupert already knew that?*

"Anyway, I'm convinced that you and Ethan belong together. He looks at you so lovingly and you make such a handsome couple. Take heart, my dear, and give the poor man a chance."

Betsy gives her a warm hug and she returns a watery smile, pushing all thoughts of Rupert and Tamela aside. She makes an impromptu decision. "Why don't you and Norman join us on Christmas Day, it will make it more of a party?"

"Are you sure?"

"Of course, I'm quite convinced that Ethan will be delighted." Saying this, she realises that Ethan would be happy whatever she arranged and that she already trusts him. She'd never have made the same assumptions about Ashleigh or Rupert.

"We'd both love to. Thank you. We'll bring some alcohol and my Christmas cake, which has already been well-doused."

"Thank you for listening to my woes, Betsy. You're a good friend to me, and I already feel much better and truly look forward to spending Christmas Day with you and Norman."

Betsy pats her hand. "Whenever you need a confidante you just have to pop next door."

"Bless you."

On Christmas Eve, she and Ethan decorate the small potted mountain cypress tree that Ethan has brought back from Kimberley, along with an angel for the top, some clip-on candles, and six hand-painted paper-mâché baubles – three with different scenes of the Nativity and three with Father Christmas with his elves and reindeer. Plus they have some cookie rings and iced gingerbread men that Lucy has made and tied with ribbon.

She stands back to work out where she should hang the delicate tinsel icicles and Ethan says, "Oh I forgot, I also bought some crepe paper to cover the pot and make a bow."

"That's a good idea, Ethan." She arranges the crepe paper around the pot and ties a large bow in the front. Then she places the icicles so that they hang prettily and evenly around the tree. She chats to Ethan as she works.

"That day I left you looking after Frankie and Roeli, I was lucky enough to find a pedlar in Hopetown selling wooden toys and I purchased two hobby horses, two hoops and two bags of marbles, for Frankie and Roeli. I also bought gifts for Betsy and Norman, but I can't tell you what, because I bought something similar for you. They're all wrapped and hidden under my bed. Would you please help me get them out and put them around the Christmas tree?"

"Of course, but we'll have to be quiet, so as not to wake Frankie."

"I think it will be all right. He's a deep sleeper."

They creep into the bedroom and Lucy holds her breath, as Ethan gets down on his knees and draws out the presents, before passing them to her. Monty stirs and watches them with interest but doesn't move from the comfort of his basket. She takes what she can carry and leaves the room, silently returning to search under the bed herself and collect another armful. Together they creep out and close the bedroom door. She then places the boys' gifts into two pillow cases and ties them with red ribbon. The gifts for Betsy, Norman and Ethan she puts in front of the two pillowcases.

"That looks very festive," says Ethan.

"Everything's prepared and ready for our Christmas dinner with Betsy and Norman. I also made an extra plum pudding for Roeli's family, which I sent back with him the other day."

"That's good of you, Lucy. I'm sure they were pleased with that."

She stands beside him admiring their handiwork. "Don't you think the nativity scene we bought from the market looks nice on the dresser? I've had to explain to Frankie it's for decoration only and not to be played with, but he loves the tiny baby Jesus."

Ethan doesn't seem to be listening; he's looking at her intently, his blue eyes sparkling in the candlelight. He moves slowly towards her as if he's going to kiss her. Her heart races, until he instead removes some fluff from her hair.

"You must have picked up a feather when delving under your bed."

"Oh dear, I'd better get out the feather duster on Boxing Day."

The next morning Frankie is out of bed as soon as the sun's up and he's peeping through his bedroom door to see the gifts arrayed under their Christmas tree. "He's been, Mama! He's been! Come quickly, Mama."

Lucy responds, rubbing the sleepy dust from her eyes and wrapping her dressing gown around herself as she enters. Ethan, hearing the commotion, joins them from his bedroom.

Ethan says, "Wow! Just look at those two sacks! One has your name on it, Frankie."

He shows Frankie which sack is for him and Frankie unties and discards the red ribbon. Excitedly he pulls out the hobby horse and immediately rides around the small room on it.

They watch him for a while, then his mother asks, "What else is in there, Frankie?"

He pulls out the hoop with its stick and tries to trundle it.

While he's playing, Lucy passes Ethan her gift to him and he unwraps the blue crepe paper to reveal a handsome buckskin waistcoat.

"Oh, Lucy, that's just the job! It'll go perfectly with my tan moleskin trousers. Thank you so much. How thoughtful of you."

"You're most welcome, Ethan. It's the least I could do, after you so kindly took us in. Besides, I thought you'd look very handsome wearing it." She smiles.

"What's in the other sack, Mama?"

"Well, it has Roeli's name on it. Santa Claus must have thought he also lives here because you're both always playing together."

"He'll be excited when he sees this, Mama."

"I'm sure he will be, sweetheart. I expect we'll see him later." She pauses thoughtfully. "Right, I'd better set out the table ready for our guests."

"Wait just a moment, Lucy. I've a gift for you too." He takes a small leather box from his breeches pocket and hands it to her.

Trembling, she opens the box to reveal a jade pendant necklace. "Oh, Ethan! It's beautiful!" She hugs him.

"I thought it would go perfectly with your jade gown."

He watches her closely, causing her heart to race. "It will. Thank you so much. You have a good eye for such things."

"I'm glad you like it."

She turns away before betraying her feelings. "Well, Frankie, I think you ought to help Ethan tidy up the ripped paper. Then, after I've served your breakfast, you can go outside to play with Monty, but stay within calling distance please. I'm sure Roeli will come soon."

While Lucy prepares their dinner, Roeli turns up and Frankie eagerly shows him the gifts.

Roeli goes wild with Frankie when he discovers that he too has a hobby horse, trundling hoop and marbles. They rush outside into the hot summer sun and cavort around the veldt playing cowboys and Indians.

At about twelve noon, Betsy and Norman arrive, wearing their Sunday-best clothes and bearing their gifts of iced Christmas cake, Madeira wine and a bottle of port.

"Oh, Betsy, that's beautifully decorated. I love the little frosted trees and the reindeer."

"We sell it all in the shop and I enjoy baking."

"Well thank you, and for the bottles of drink, Norman." She turns to Ethan. "Would you pour us some Madeira as an aperitif, please, Ethan?"

"Of course, allow me." He takes the bottles and places them on the sideboard. Soon they're all furnished with a glass. Ethan says, "Let us make a toast to our bond in friendship."

"Friendship!" they all cry in unison and then sup the wine.

"Can I do anything to help you, Lucy?" asks Betsy.

"No, my dear, everything's in hand, but please do come and join me in the kitchen while the men talk."

Betsy follows Lucy into the smaller room. Once out of earshot, Lucy confides, "I thought Ethan was going to kiss me last night, but he changed his mind at the last moment. I think I may have frightened him off, by my look of consternation."

"How did that make you feel, Lucy?"

"Well, in all honesty, I was a little disappointed in retrospect. It would have been rather romantic in the candlelight, but is it simply a little too convenient?"

"I despair of you, Lucy. What's the poor man got to do, to prove himself to you?"

She ponders. "He has been steadfastly my friend and protector, and we do have a lot in common. He likes to sing, and I like to play the piano. We had great fun on the passage here, but that was a long time ago."

"There's nothing to say that those pleasures can't be pursued in the future, my dear. You both work well together and if things go on, as they've begun, I see a promising prospect for both of you."

"Thank you for your counsel, Betsy. I'm beginning to think it might be possible. We'll just have to wait and see how things develop."

Although the kitchen is sweltering, Lucy manages to produce a roast lamb dinner with all the trimmings. Betsy and Norman are both pleased with their buckskin purses (each with a lucky Joey inside). When she was wrapping the presents the previous night, she remembered her mother telling her it was bad luck to give someone an empty purse and she'd hurriedly found some silver thrupenny bits in her reticule, among the ones she was saving for the pudding. Frankie nearly chokes on the one he discovers in his portion of plum pudding, but is thrilled to find a lucky Joey.

They have a relaxed day together, watching the two boys playing outside, eating nuts and dates and drinking, until Roeli leaves for home and it's time for Frankie to prepare for bed. Then the adults play cards, eating and drinking, late into the night.

Grace and Aurora arrive at Railway Pier, Port Phillip in Melbourne, on Friday, the ninth of January 1874. The sun is already hot at nine in the morning. Their ship is moored alongside whalers and seal boats and the dockside is busy with hawkers, sailors, fishermen, and passengers. Aborigine porters run to help them with their luggage, and Aurora directs them to the dock platform of Spencer Street Station where they'll catch the steam train to Sandhurst.

Her father told her, as soon as they hit landfall on the Australian coast, to ask the captain for a message to be telegraphed to Rhys, via the Bendigo Post and Telegraph Office, letting him know when the *Northumberland* was likely to dock. Now she watches out for him, not sure if he'd have been able to travel all this way to meet them but hoping so with all her heart.

They follow the porters towards the train station. Aurora suddenly spots an eager arm waving madly and recognises the tall figure of Rhys making his way towards them. She self-consciously pushes her hair out of her face as he approaches, but then he's lifting her off the ground and spinning her in an excited twirl. She screams, both with the excitement at seeing him and fear of them both falling onto the railway lines. "Put me down, Rhys. I'm too heavy."

"Nonsense you're as light as a feather." She's missed this soft, lyrical Welsh accent.

"Please, Rhys, people are looking at us."

"I'm so pleased to see you, Rora. I want the whole world to see you!"

"But I must introduce you to poor Grace. You're embarrassing her."

He places her feet on the ground carefully, as if reluctant to let go of her, and turns to Grace. "I'm sorry, madam. How d'you do? I am Rhys."

"Good morning, Rhys. I'm Grace Tweedy. Very pleased to meet you."

"The pleasure's all mine." He grins at them both. "Right then, follow me, ladies. Your carriage awaits."

The locomotive is belching out smoke and steam in readiness for the journey. Once he has supervised their luggage being securely placed in the guard's van, he leads them to their designated carriage. Aurora is pleased to have him take charge, after feeling slightly vulnerable, being two women travelling without the strength and authority of a man. Even though they managed quite well, it's nice to be looked after.

She's euphoric, unable to believe she's actually here with him, after all her begging and pleading and then the long sea voyage. She looks at him lovingly. He has the same flirty, twinkling, blue eyes she remembers so well and his brown wavy hair, curling about his ears, still looks wild and unruly, just as her own does. He has a fine shadow of a beard and moustache, which makes him appear manly and she approves entirely. He's extraordinarily handsome.

The train soon chugs out of the station. The three of them chat away as some passengers join the train, and others leave it at stations along the way. They come to an elegant stone-built viaduct and Rhys tells her they're passing over Jackson Creek. "Although some call it Kismet Creek, which is rather appropriate, don't you think?"

She smiles. "I do. For fate has brought us together again, against all the odds."

He kisses her.

She notices Grace tactfully looking out at the scenery, having given up trying to tame her passions long ago. Rather than a governess, she considers her a friend now, after their sea voyage together. Besides, she believes the English conventions are probably brushed aside here in the outback.

They stop at Woodend and then Kyneton, before crossing over another five-span, bluestone viaduct over the Coliban River at Malmsbury. Then ahead of Taradale they cross over Black Creek via the Taradale Viaduct, this time it's a five-span, iron structure, set on bluestone piers.

All the while the ladies are looking out at the heat haze, shimmering over the Australian salt bush, spotting the odd emu and several groups of kangaroo and wallaby. The sheep stations extend for miles and Aurora recognises the familiar flocks of Merino sheep dotted across the landscape.

She turns to Rhys. "Is Sam still working on the sheep station?"

"Yes, he is. He's the station manager now and loving it."

"And is Angelica still at the school?"

"Yes. It works out well for her, because she can go there with Camira and Connor."

"The mines are still doing well, as I understand it from my papa?"

"They are, but I'll let my father talk to you about that. He's the one with knowledge of the spreadsheets."

Suddenly they're plunged into darkness and Rhys is quick to take advantage. His hand gently turns her face to him to be kissed ardently. As the light appears at the end of the tunnel he draws away. He tells them, "That was the Elphinstone tunnel. The next stop is Castlemaine, then we stop at Ravenswood, before going through another long tunnel at Big Hill." He turns to Aurora, his eyes twinkling, she hopes a forewarning of kisses to come.

From his haversack he draws out a package wrapped in muslin. "Ma has made ham and mustard, or cheese and pickle sandwiches; which would you prefer?" He unwraps the muslin and offers it to Grace, who helps herself gratefully, and then she passes them back to Aurora.

Aurora chooses ham and mustard. "That was thoughtful of Nell. I'm actually quite hungry."

"Me too," says Rhys. "There are two for each of us."

"Mm, very tasty," says Aurora, munching away happily.

As the engine chugs along the tracks, Aurora sees the blue haze from the eucalyptus trees covering the distant mountains, beyond the miles of salt-scrub and pastureland. The nearer they get to their destination the more butterflies flutter in her stomach. How well is she going to fit in this time, now that she's here to be with Rhys? How's Gwyneth going to react, now that she's back?

She turns to Rhys and asks him, "How's Gwyneth?"

His face shows a slight flush, but he says, "She's fine, as far as I know. I haven't seen her much lately."

They're abruptly plunged once more into darkness and Rhys takes the opportunity to kiss her again. She responds enthusiastically, feeling exhilarated at the prospect of having this kind of loving attention for the rest of her life.

When they exit the tunnel, looking completely innocent of any impropriety, he says to her, "I'm sure you'll remember the next areas we come to of Kangaroo Flat and Golden Square, from your last visit."

"Yes, I do."

"Well, for Miss Tweedy's benefit, these are the last two stops before we reach our destination at Sandhurst, more commonly known locally as Bendigo, as the town grew up around Bendigo Creek from where the first gold was discovered. Kangaroo Flat and Golden Square are both gold prospecting areas."

"It's all quite fascinating and so different from the cosy hedged-in fields of England. I already love the vast vistas, the bright sunshine and the unfamiliar birds and animals."

"In that case you'll fit in well, Miss Tweedy."

"Please, you must call me Grace."

He grins at her friend, and Aurora can see from her coy blushes that Grace too is very taken with him.

They arrive at Bendigo station and the guardsman unloads their luggage onto the platform.

Rhys organises a growler to convey them and their steamer chests through the town to Waratah Street.

Travelling through the town, Grace is looking out of the window of the carriage, fascinated by the streets and businesses that are to be her new environment.

On route Rhys suggests, "Aurora, did you want us to stop at the post office so you can send a telegram to your father to let them know you've arrived safely?"

She nods her head. "Yes, good idea."

Rhys knocks on the roof of the carriage to signal the driver to stop, but as he draws the horses to a standstill alongside the boardwalk, Aurora spots Freyja through the shop window of the emporium. "Oh, Rhys, look, it's Freyja! Do I have time to go and see her?"

"Well, we'll be seeing her later, but if you're quick."

Grace suggests, "Look, while you're catching up with your friend, I can pop into the post office and send the telegram to your father?"

"Yes, please do, Grace. Thank you."

Rhys hands the ladies down from the carriage and Grace goes straight to the post office. The doorbell jangles as she enters the premises. A man dressed in an official black cap, and a uniform of black trousers, matching waistcoat and white shirt with silver sleeve garters, is behind the counter, processing some paperwork.

He looks up through wire-rimmed spectacles, "Good morning, ma'am. How may I help you?"

"I should like to send a telegram, please?"

"Of course, ma'am. If you wouldn't mind filling in this form, with what you wish to say, to whom you wish the message to be sent and what method of conveyance from the final post office."

She fills in Lord Dryer's address and writes their message: '*ARRIVED SAFELY. ALL GOOD. LOVE TO ALL AT ALVINGTON. AURORA AND GRACE.*' And she ticks the option 'by runner'.

She hands the form to the postmaster. He reads it back to her, to make sure he has the correct details.

She nods her head. "Yes, that's correct."

"That will be two shillings, then, please ma'am."

She passes him the coins and he rewards her with a smile. "Thank you, ma'am. Your message will go via the Overland Telegraph to Darwin and then through the submarine telegraph cable to the United Kingdom of Great Britain and on to the…" He checks her form. "To the Ivell Post Office from where their runner will deliver it to Lord Dryer."

"Thank you. I'm much obliged, sir."

"My pleasure, ma'am. Allow me to welcome you to our town. I hope you enjoy your stay."

On reaching the door she turns back. "Thank you. I'm sure I will do. Goodbye."

"Goodbye, ma'am."

Outside the post office, Rhys and Aurora are standing arm in arm, still talking to Freyja.

"Ah, here she is," says Rhys. "Come on, Aurora. There'll be plenty of time to chat with Freyja later."

Aurora, says, "See you this evening, then, Freyja. Bye for now."

They climb back into the carriage and set of once more towards Waratah Street.

When they arrive at Brecon House, Aurora remembers being impressed with the colonial style design of the two-storey building. It's surrounded by a white picket fence enclosing a variety of vivid flowering plants, shrubs and climbers. The house itself has a splendid wrap-around, balustraded, balcony on the top floor and matching veranda on the ground floor, which will be wonderful for sitting outside on balmy evenings. Alongside are the stable and outbuildings that Aurora remembers so well. It's where she and Rhys shared their last, memorable farewell kiss.

Rhys tips the porter and then helps them up the steps with their steamer trunks. Inside, they find the house deserted, apart from a young aborigine girl who's making up the beds in the guest room.

Rhys explains, "Pa will be working at the Eaglehawk mine, and Ma must still be at the school. But I'm here to show you both around. Please follow me, ladies. I'll bring up one of the steamer chests and fetch the other one later." They follow him up the wooden stairs. He leaves the trunk at the top. "You can unpack your trunks after we've had some refreshments," he says.

"This is Ma and Pa's bedroom." He opens the door for them to peep inside. "And this is my bedroom." He glances at Aurora and raises his eyebrows suggestively. Grace frowns in disapproval, and he continues hastily along the landing to the guest room, collecting the trunk on the way. They pass the maid, who dips a curtsey and continues downstairs. Rhys opens the door to the last room and says, "This was Owen's room, before he and Freyja married, but it's now our guest room, with twin beds for you to share. I do hope that's satisfactory?"

"Of course; we shared a cabin on the ship."

"Good. All the rooms have washing facilities and there's an earth closet outside for your toilet."

Aurora looks at the neat bedroom, with its colourful aboriginal art, designed curtains and bedding. She and Grace admire the view from the French window, which overlooks the back garden, and opens onto the balcony. "This is perfect for us. Isn't it, Grace?"

Grace nods and smiles. "I'm sure we'll both be very comfortable. Thank you."

They follow Rhys back downstairs. "Then on the ground floor we have the drawing room, living room, kitchen, dining room and Pa's study."

They both look inside all the rooms. "This is a beautiful home, Rhys. Much larger than I remember."

"Well our first house was next to Hugh and Sarah on Myrtle Street, but Pa decided we needed more room and so he designed this himself, incorporating ideas from buildings he admired and then he commissioned the same builders." He indicates the armchairs. "Please sit down and I'll ask Alinta to serve us our refreshments."

Later that day, after the ladies have unpacked their steamer chests and had a short siesta, the rest of the family return home from their work. There are hugs and kisses all round and both Grace and Aurora relax in the genuine warmth of their welcome. They tell their hosts all about their journey and both Rhys and Bryn are eager to hear how her father is faring.

It isn't long before Hugh, Sarah, Gwyneth, Lewys, Owen and Freyja arrive, all bearing contributions to the celebratory meal. Hugh and Sarah have brought a large cooked ham joint and some pickled pork, Freyja, a dish of brown trout gravadlax that she has made herself, Gwyneth, a homemade trifle, Lewys has brought a keg of

Victoria beer, and Bryn and Nell have supplied all the accompaniments. Gwyneth hands her trifle to Alinta, who takes it to the meshed marble shelf in the pantry, while Nell leads everyone into the dining room and they each add their contributions to the tableau. Once all the dishes are in place the table looks very colourful, with a variety of pork and cheese pies; red, yellow and green salads; mustard and pickles; and large bowls of rice and crushed potato mixes.

Aurora introduces Grace to the newcomers and Rhys comes to stand beside her, resting his arm around her shoulders. Gwyneth and Lewys hold back, as their parents move to the fore to embrace them both, then Aurora steps towards the siblings to embrace them each in turn, but there's no warmth returned from either of them. Her heart sinks, as she watches them both greeting Grace politely. Then there's a resurgence of conversation as folk help themselves to the banquet.

When everyone has finished eating and the ladies are clearing and washing the dishes, Hugh singles her out for a chat. "How's thy father, my dear?"

"He was quite well, thank you, the last time I saw him back in October. I was hoping there might be some letters from home for me when I arrived."

"Our mail service from England is unpredictable, and if letters were written after thou left, it's doubtful they'd beat thee here. But don't fret, I'm sure there'll be some mail soon. Bryn and I have been discussing how we might introduce thee into our business, because I know that's what thy father would wish. I want to suggest that thou work initially in the office with Bryn at Eaglehawk. Both Rhys and Owen work from there, Rhys in the Talliaris mine and Owen runs the Maerdy. Whilst I run Bryniau Gwyn in the White Hills with Lewys. Gwyneth helps me with the paperwork at the Bryniau Gwyn office, so it'll be good for thee to learn on the job with Bryn, if thou should agree?"

"I do, Mr Davies. That will suit me very well indeed, thank you." She couldn't be more thrilled to be able to work with Rhys and his family.

"Please, my dear, if we're going to be working colleagues, thou must call me Hugh."

She smiles. "I will do, Hugh. Thank you."

For the remainder of the evening she avoids Gwyneth and Lewys. Their parents both seem happy to welcome her, but she only senses animosity from Gwyneth, who held a torch for Rhys, and Lewys who was passed over for him. She hopes that Angelica and Sam Kelly don't feel the same, bearing in mind her father was Nathan Meakins, and Camira's her half-sister. She decides to visit them at her earliest opportunity.

A week later, she goes with Grace up the hill to the Kellys' house at Eaglehawk. The day's hot and sunny and, despite their parasols, they're both sweltering and exhausted by the time they reach the property. Aurora remembers promising to write to Camira and she wonders if the child will be happy to see her again.

She knocks on their front door. A young lady answers and it's a moment before Aurora realises it's Camira, four years older since she last saw her, now eleven and looking the image of her mother, with thick chestnut hair framing her face in attractive ringlets. Aurora is reminded of the last time she saw

Senga, now a young lady of fifteen, and sent away by her mother to finishing school in Switzerland.

"Hello, Camira. Do you remember me? It's your pen friend Aurora from England."

She smiles sweetly. "Mama told me you were here. I was hoping to see you. Thank you for all your letters."

Aurora and Grace close their parasols. "You're most welcome. Thank you for yours, too. This is my friend Grace, who has travelled here with me, to meet you all."

"How d'you do, Grace?" She gives a little curtsey.

"I'm well, thank you, and very pleased to meet you, Camira. Aurora showed me many of the pictures and letters she sent you, and those you sent to her, as I was her governess for some of the time."

Camira steps aside. "Please come in. Mammy is inside, but Pappy is off out with our grandpa and Connor."

They follow her through the hallway and into a large sitting room, with wide windows overlooking the whole of Sandhurst below them. "Wow!" exclaims Grace. "What an exceptional vista."

Aurora agrees. "It's quite a spectacle isn't it."

Camira calls, "Mammy!" and Angelica appears from a side door, her thick hair pinned up and escaping in tendrils around her face. "Well, hello there! This is a pleasant surprise! Did you have a good voyage?"

Grace and Aurora both dip a curtsey. Aurora says, "Good morning, Angelica. We did, thank you. This is my friend, Grace."

"Good to meet you, Grace. Please take a seat, and Camira will prepare us some refreshments. Would dandelion and burdock cordial be acceptable?"

Aurora says, "That would be splendid. We're both rather overheated from the walk up the hill."

Angelica asks Camira, "If you wouldn't mind bringing in four glasses of the cordial and a plate of date biscuits and some honey lattice as well. Thanks, love."

Camira goes off to the kitchen, eager to help.

"It must be around four years since you were last here, Aurora. How have you settled in?"

"We're both comfortable at Bryn and Nell's and they've made us feel welcome. I'm just a little concerned that Gwyneth and Lewys aren't so pleased to see me here, and I'm hoping that you and Sam won't be feeling the same."

"It's no business of ours what you do, Aurora. This is a country that embraces all kinds of waifs and strays, us included. Who are we to judge?"

Aurora doesn't like to think of herself as a waif or stray, more as a follower of destiny, but she overlooks the veiled insult. "We're both here to seek a new and exciting life, but we don't want to spoil the relationships you all have between you. I already feel that Hugh's family are now avoiding Bryn's family, because of my arrival here to be with Rhys, and it breaks my heart. I only want for everyone to be happy together."

"Well, I have to agree, you've set the cat among the pigeons rather, but they'll all get over it eventually and if you and Rhys are meant to be together, then Gwyneth and Lewys will just have to get over it."

"But you don't feel I'm a threat at all, because of who I am?"

At that moment Camira returns with the refreshments, but her mother continues with her response. "As far as I'm concerned that's all ancient history and best forgotten. We should let bygones be bygones."

"Good, I'm so relieved and really pleased we can all be friends."

Camira passes round the drinks and tea-plates and then the large plate of home-baked biscuits and they each help themselves. "So, Camira said that Sam and Connor are out with her grandfather. Does that mean that Sam and his father have finally made contact after all those years?"

"Yes. As you know, Sean Kelly was in America working on the Union Pacific Railroad until 1869, when it was completed ahead of schedule. He arrived here last year, after travelling home to Ireland first to visit his brother's family, and then on to emigrate here to be with Sam."

"That must be wonderful for Sam, after all those years on his own, worrying about his father."

"Yes, he and Sam get along like a house on fire. During the week, they're working together now, out on the Ravenswood Sheep Run with Ray Clark. They're off together in town today."

Grace says, "These biscuits are delicious, Angelica."

"Thank you, Grace. Please call me Angel, everyone else does."

Aurora relaxes and they enjoy a pleasant afternoon chatting and making plans to meet in town the following week.

CHAPTER THIRTEEN *(March 1874)*

THE DIGGERS REST

Ethan gradually reinforces his reputation as a reasonable and honest trader among the hard-working miners. He soon gets to know the genuine claim holders and always gives them a good price. He then takes the rough uncut diamonds to Julius Wernher and Charles Mege who have set up a branch of the firm J Porgés and Co, owned by the wealthy and renowned French diamond dealer. After regularly getting fair exchanges from this company, he builds up a good business relationship with both Julius and Charles.

He is, however, astute enough to develop an eye for some of the illicit diamond hawkers. These are invariably foreign fortune seekers, who are unable to speak English, and it is easy to get the best of the bargain, because they don't really understand the true value of what they're selling, many believing the Cape diamond to be of an inferior quality to those already established from other parts of the world. He always questions his customers about where they've found their gems, and is able to pick up on their anxiety, when they make up fictitious stories. Nevertheless, he trades with these ignoble men, despite believing in his heart they deserve nothing for their jewels; he simply takes this into account when valuing them, and quietly monitors their activities.

While Lucy's busy preparing their supper one evening, Ethan leans against the dresser, sips his brandy and explains to her a little of what he's learnt of the history of the diamond fields.

"When the 'Star of Africa' diamond was first discovered near the Vaal River in 1869 the local Griquas were the 'Cape-coloured' people inhabiting the region. Living in settlements nearby, they were the first diggers to prospect along the banks of the river for alluvial stones. At that time, the Griqua chiefs held sovereignty over this area and white men had to seek permission from them to prospect here. Then the Orange Free State took control of governing the mining of diamonds and they prohibited the granting of licences to black prospectors."

She sighs, impatiently brushing a stray tendril of hair behind her ear. "That's blatantly unfair. It was their land after all."

Ethan grins at her indignant reaction. "I know, but it seems that because it played into the white man's hands, no one did anything to protest against it. On the contrary, the many Europeans who came to seek their fortunes were quite happy to keep African black and coloured people in a position of subservience. However, in 1871, with the annexation of Griqualand West, the British administration reversed the prohibition of black licence holders and thus, once more, claims were again in the hands of black proprietors."

"Quite right too. I'm actually surprised our British leaders did the right thing for a change!" She drains the water from the butternut.

"That may be so, but there were still many white men who were against claim ownership by black diggers, who were busy casting aspersions that they were dishonest. According to these white men, claim ownership entitled the black men to sell diamonds, and this therefore, provided an opportunity for servants to rob their masters. Thus, there was racial tension in some areas."

Lucy says, "Please sit down; supper won't be long now."

Ethan sits, but still persists with his story. "Then, I'm told that in July 1872 the British commissioners were forced by these discontented white men to take action against the black claim holders and they suspended the licences of some black diggers at Dutoitspan and Bultfontein. However, the Cape Governor at that time refused to sanction this discrimination and instead compromised, announcing that black diggers should hold a 'certificate of good character' from a resident magistrate, or a Justice of the Peace. Even with this added measure in place, the black diggers still increased in number on the poorer sites, like Hopetown, Dutoitspan and Bultfontein, as the white man gravitated towards New Rush."

Lucy calls for Frankie to come for supper and pulls out the chair for him to sit down.

Ethan continues, "Even now the white man is getting the upper hand with ownership, and I'm told that in many cases the native digger is still being conned, by being paid with a shiny gilt medal of little intrinsic value or, as I myself have witnessed, he's often coerced to thieve by unscrupulous white bullies, like McCallister."

"He's a hateful man and so's his self-important son." Lucy plonks the plates down on the table. "My sympathies are all with Roeli and Kofi's family."

"What's wrong with Roeli's family, Mama?"

"Nothing for you to worry about, my dear. Here, pass your plate and let me serve you some sweet potato."

"Well, as you know, I too hate to see the native diggers being exploited and threatened by the white men and I've decided to do something about it. I'm going to form a paramilitary group."

Lucy stops in her tracks. "Oh, Ethan! That's admirable, but please be careful who you antagonise."

"I will, I promise you, Lucy. I've developed many friendships through my business associations, and I believe there's safety in numbers, so please have no fear."

Over the following few days, Ethan informs those of the miners he's found to be true to their words and honest that a meeting is to take place at the Diggers Rest Saloon Bar in town where they might discuss the lawlessness of the diamond fields and make a plan to police it.

Charles and Julius have their office right next door to the Diggers Rest and Ethan has invited them both to attend and bring along any of their trusted friends, including John O'Reilly, another diamond dealer, and Barney Barnato, who supplies Jamaican rum to Stefan Rensburg, the landlord, plus several other concerned diggers, miners, and traders on the Hopetown diamond fields.

Having discussed the issue next door, Norman agrees to join them, and they set off together. When they arrive, they find an excited cacophony of voices, laughter and chinking of tankards. Charles and Julius beckon to Ethan from the bar and they work their way through the gathering, Ethan receiving pats on the back as he goes.

There are foreign adventurers here from all classes and all nationalities: Irish dissidents, cockney traders, aristocratic fortune hunters, German speculators (like Julius Wernher), French businessmen (like Charles Mege), seasoned diggers from the Australian goldfields and forty-niners from the Californian gold rush.

Ethan is elected to chair the meeting and he uses Stefan's bell to bring the crowd to order. "Good evening, gentleman. I've been elected to chair this meeting, where we might discuss the criminal activities going on undeterred, under the noses of the authorities such as they are. It's become necessary to bring you all together here this evening, because our current police force, of nine officers and twenty-four men, is wholly inadequate to police our diamond field with upwards of 20,000 men, increasing daily. I respectfully suggest it's down to us to take responsibility and help them to keep law and order."

There are cries of "Here! Here!" from various corners of the building, which gives Ethan the confidence to continue.

"Do any of you have any information relating to criminal activities that we might act on?"

A fellow, further along the bar, puts up his hand.

Ethan encourages him. "Go ahead, my friend."

The man spits out his tobacco into the spittoon, wipes his hand across his mouth and then stands up to speak. "Good evening to you all. My name is Bruce Robinson and I know for a fact my native workers have in the past been coerced into stealing from me, but because I know their families have been threatened if they should refuse to do so, I've done nothing about it." He takes a swig of his Cape brandy and continues in his Australian drawl, "I've a young family of my own and I couldn't bring myself to be the one to expose them; to have them sent in chains to the Breakwater Prison, when they were given no option, having been beaten and bullied, and their woman-folk, even a young pubescent girl, threatened with rape. But, of course, I'm losing money over it. This situation can't continue; we need to find a way to put a stop to it."

Ethan says, "Thank you for your contribution, Bruce. Does anyone else have any suggestions as to how we might accomplish this?"

Another man puts up his hand to speak.

"Please go ahead, sir."

The man scratches his head, then speaks with an Irish accent. "I've also witnessed certain groups of ruffians, armed with revolvers and shillelaghs... or *knobkerries*, terrorising the folk in the Idayimane encampment. Perhaps if we formed our own well-armed defence force, they'd be persuaded to quit their lawless activities?"

Ethan is relieved. "I think that's a grand idea. Let's have a show of hands. All in favour of forming a paramilitary group, designed to dissuade thieving, patrol the native encampment and deter the and intimidation of the Griqua peoples."

It appeared that everyone's hands went up, but Ethan, to be sure, asks, "All against?"

Half a dozen men raise their hands. "In that case the motion is carried, but I should like to know the reason for the objections, if anyone would care to volunteer?"

A small elderly bearded man puts up his hand. "As far as I'm concerned you can't trust 'em. Every black person born's a potential thief, or participant in the flourishing illicit diamond market. You don't just want to watch out for the white rogues; the blacks be far worse, as far as I'm concerned."

Ethan responds, "I think that's what we'll be trying to do, sir. To develop a system enabling us to protect the weaker element in our society, whether they be black, white, or coloured."

A second man puts up his hand. "My name's Frederick Badenhorst. Forgive me, but I'm concerned that any armed group could be just as dangerous as the men they're formed to deter."

"Well, I understand your concerns, Mr Badenhorst, but we'll provide armbands stating membership of the Miners' Defence Unit, and the men wearing these bands will be vetted and will be asked to swear on the Holy Bible to uphold the British laws of the land and abide by our Victorian ethics and morals. Besides, most of the men here present have been vouched for by myself, or my esteemed colleagues, Julius Wernher and Charles Mege. Of course, there are also some regulars who are not known to us, but who have every right to be here."

Julius then stands up at the bar. "Thank you, Ethan. I think we've made some progress here this evening. To further our project, do we have anyone present with policing or military experience, who might wish to lead our Miners' Defence Unit?"

A young man, obviously in his prime, stands up and clears his voice. "I hesitate to put myself forward, but I'm an army officer, currently on a twelve-month furlough, of which there's still ten months outstanding, and I'd be happy to set up a system of shifts with units of men, to patrol for a period from 6pm to twelve midnight, initially. Then if our quarries get used to that and alter their activities to later, we can match them by extending our shift patterns until daybreak. Then in time, natural leaders will become evident I'm sure, before I have to return to my regiment."

"Thank you, Mr…?"

"Lieutenant Greaves. Andrew Greaves. You're welcome. I want this problem solved as much as anyone."

"We're much obliged to you. Please take the chair."

"Right, let's get down to business. If all volunteers would be good enough to give me their names and what arms they hold, I can make a list of manpower and then break it down into units."

Ethan and Norman head the queue and behind them a line forms, of eager young, fit, stalwart men. The landlord passes Lieutenant Greaves a dipping pen, inkwell and pad of paper and he compiles his list of names.

Ethan returns to the bar grinning with satisfaction. "This is a great start. We can see how we get on here and if it works for us, we can maybe extend the system to Klipdrift and Kimberley."

The remainder of the evening is spent discussing all the criminal activities that various people present are aware of on the Hopetown fields and all the known villains they fear they'll have to take to task.

Once they've been issued with their paramilitary armbands, Ethan decides to go with Lieutenant Greaves and Bruce Robinson on the first foot patrol, to get a feeling of what they might encounter. As he puts on his official band, he shivers more with nerves than the cold, although the temperature has dropped considerably since the sun set. They've been structured into five units of three men to patrol each evening. Each unit has at least one man armed with a rifle. They set off moving silently between the tents and shacks, listening to the sounds of life within them, but avoiding campfires and dogs who might betray their presence and destroy the element of surprise. It's not long before his group stumble across two men beating up a native fellow outside of his tent.

The lieutenant holds high his lantern and they see the poor fellow's covered in blood and no longer able to stand unsupported. Ethan hears whimpering from inside the tent.

The bullies look around, alarmed by the light glinting on Bruce's cocked rifle. The lieutenant barks at them, "What's going on here?"

The bearded muscleman holding the fellow up drops him into the dirt and his partner in crime drops his cudgel, replying, "The *kaffir* was sassing us, so we taught him a lesson."

The lieutenant speaks in his clipped English. "Well, *we're* here to teach you two fellows a lesson. You no longer visit this encampment at night, intimidating these folk. There's no edict that would defend two men beating another to a pulp. We're members of the Miners' Defence Unit' — he points at his armband — 'and we're here now to maintain law and order, which doesn't involve any white man using his fists, bullying and taking advantage of the natives. Do I make myself quite clear, gentlemen?"

One of the thugs shrugs his shoulders. "How else are we going to keep 'em in their place?"

Ethan is incensed. "That's your problem, but how about this for a concept? I'm sure that if you treat your diggers fairly, you'd get far more work out of them in the long run. But, whichever way you look at it, we're not going to stand by and condone any more intimidation or violence under any circumstances. Do you understand?"

Greaves picks up the blood-smeared cudgel. "Let this be a warning to you. We're all armed and ready to act, should anyone decide to ignore our counsel in the future. On this occasion you're both free to go, but if we should come across you in these circumstances again, it'll be a different story, I promise you."

The hard man steps forward to retrieve his weapon, but the lieutenant says, "Your weapon is impounded." They both scowl, as they slink off into the night.

Bruce helps the man back into his tent and his woman bathes his wounds and settles him into his bedroll.

Ethan regrets they were too late to save the poor fellow from a beating, but at least they've got their message across to the villains. Hopefully, the other units have managed to deter other criminals this evening and if they continue in the same vein, it will surely make the formation of the MDU totally justified. At the end of his shift he thanks Andrew and Bruce and they split up to return to their billets.

Ethan lights a lamp as he enters his home and is amazed to find Lucy has fallen asleep by the fading light of the fire. She looks so beautiful with the waning firelight flickering softly in her chestnut curls. He stands and stares, before waking her gently.

"Why are you not snuggled up in bed with Frankie?" he whispers.

She blinks in the light of the lamp. "I was so worried about you, Ethan. I was tossing and turning so much, I was concerned I'd wake Frankie up, so I came out here to wait for you, but I must have dropped off."

He's pleased that she cares for his safety and can see in her expression that she's relieved to have him home. "Well, bless you for worrying about me, but I'm absolutely fine and you can't do this every time I'm on duty."

He holds out his hand to help her up and she takes it slowly. He wants to pull her into his arms and kiss her passionately, but she's half asleep and it would be taking advantage.

The following day Lucy pops next door for some groceries and Betsy asks her, "How did the MDU men get on last night, with their first shift?"

"I think it went well. Ethan told me this morning that they caught two fellows beating up a poor native man, but they were too late to prevent him from being hurt; nevertheless, they confiscated their cudgel and prevented further harm from being done to him. I'm sure the other units must have come across similar incidents, but Ethan didn't know last night. I fell asleep beside the fire and he woke me up when he returned."

Betsy continues packing her shelves with jars of pickled foods. "Norman wasn't on duty last night, but I think it's his turn this evening, and I'm so worried about him. My Norman isn't a fighter, you know, but he really does want to help."

"I'm sure he'll be fine. I believe Lieutenant Greaves will be making sure each unit has a strong brawny digger and a rifleman, so he'll feel more confident when he's with his unit. They'll all get to know each other and work as a team, after a short while."

Betsy sighs. "I just hope it isn't bravado, that's making him volunteer."

"Well, I suspect there's an element of that with all of the men, but I'm sure that if Norman has second thoughts, no one will think any less of him if he drops out."

"Oh, I don't think he'd do that. My Norman isn't a coward."

She puts her arm around her. "Please, Betsy, I'm not suggesting any such thing, just that there are horses for courses and soldiering doesn't suit everyone. You haven't seen Luigi volunteering, have you?" They both laugh. "I must admit, I was relieved when Ethan returned safe and well last night. I don't know what I'd do now without him."

Betsy studies her carefully. "Do I detect progress, and maybe a romantic attachment developing?"

She smiles. "I don't think he considers me in that way. Nothing has happened since I thought he was going to kiss me on Christmas Eve."

Betsy raises her eyebrows. "But do you think of him in that way?" she asks her.

The bell rings as a customer enters the shop. Betsy winks at her and goes to the counter to serve the man.

Lucy continues to fill her basket with preserves, fresh fruit, root vegetables and some biltong for the boys to snack on. Then, as the other customer leaves, she goes to pay.

Betsy looks at her and she responds quietly, "In answer to your question, I really don't know. I've been on my own so long now. As I told you, Frankie's father was a drunken gambler who bullied me, until he met his match and was murdered. Then his brother let me down by fathering a child with another woman, so I've rather lost faith in men."

Betsy frowns.

"I admit I do have feelings for him, but I can't let him know. He's younger than me and I've been married before. I'm aware that he's handsome and

233

kind and very good with Frankie, but he'll be looking for a young virginal bride, not an old widow-woman like me."

Betsy looks at her compassionately. "Oh, Lucy, you can't be serious! You're perfect for him. There can't be that many years between you, and you obviously both get on so well; don't be so hard on yourself. Let him in, my dear, I'm convinced you won't be disappointed."

"I'll see."

CHAPTER FOURTEEN *(May–June 1874)*

'SIMON SAYS'

After several meetings with Ethan, Khumo confides in him that he's worried about his eldest son, Kofi, being a target for McCallister. Ethan understands his concern and offers to employ Kofi to look after Reckless and the stable and to run errands for him and Lucy, or escort Lucy into town occasionally, when he's away on business.

He reassures Khumo, "He'll be safer staying with us. We can make him a comfy place to sleep above the stable."

Khumo is relieved and grateful to him.

When Khumo introduces his son to him, Ethan can see why he's worried, because the fourteen-year-old lad is shy and deferential, holding his hands meekly before him and keeping his head lowered. Ethan encourages him, "Come on, lad, we'll get on fine together and you'll love Lucy, as much as Roeli loves our Frankie."

The lad answers, "Yessir," and follows Ethan back to Eureka Row.

Ethan shows him round and explains his duties, including revealing to him where he keeps his Enfield revolver hidden, in case of any trouble when he's away. They have supper together and he settles the lad on a straw pallet in the space above the stable for the night, before he takes Roeli back home to his parents.

After about a week of working for them and eating with them, Kofi begins to open up and relax. He even laughs at Monty's antics with the two boys, and Ethan feels he's ready to be left to his own devices.

The following day, Ethan demonstrates to Kofi how to create a wattle, fenced off area of garden for Lucy, so the boys are retained within her sightline, and once Kofi's in the swing of it, Ethan decides he can leave Lucy in charge of the office, with Frankie, Monty, Roeli and Kofi content at the back of the house, and he sets off on Reckless to go to Kimberley on business.

In his absence, Lucy is kept busy with paperwork and the occasional diamond seller, and she deals with them by using a template that Ethan has made for her, kept behind the counter. Using tweezers, she places the rough diamonds on the scales and by referring to the template guide on colour, clarity, size and shape, she knows how much to give the seller.

She's learnt that most of the local diamonds have a slightly yellow tinge and these are designated Cape Diamonds and are thought to be inferior to those from Brazil and India. However, the abundant yield from the Kimberley mine suggests it will one day be the richest mine in the world. The De Beers mine produces the largest stones, but those from Dutoitspan are of the finest quality. She's had three customers during the morning and has paid out a total of £84. She's just about to go and prepare some luncheon for the children and Kofi when the door opens and the bell chimes for a fourth time. She turns around, smiling, to greet her next customer, but her body freezes in mid movement, as Simon McCallister stands before her.

"Ah! Here's a surprise! I was looking for Ethan Hart and who do I find but Mistress Seymour! I thought you were intending to wed some mining fellow?"

He peers at her in that lascivious way of his and she's wrong-footed. The counter no longer between them, she's vulnerable, but she finds her voice. "It didn't work out."

"I see. Well, I must admit it's a pleasure to find you here." He smiles, but it doesn't quite reach his eyes. "Where is Ethan, pray?"

"He's out and about, doing his business on the diamond field." She's not going to let him know he's miles away.

"I've heard on the grapevine that he's doing well for himself. That he's also the key person who's instigated the formation of the farcical Miners' Defence Unit."

"Yes, Ethan's the sort of man who'll do well anywhere. He's so fair and friendly with the diggers, they all love him, and they agree with him that someone has to stand up for law and order around here."

"My father has instructed me to seek out his competitors and I believe Ethan to be one of them. I trust he'll confine his diamond dealings and his defence force to the Hopetown fields and not wander towards Kimberley, or Klipdrift, for my father will not be pleased if he should."

Lucy is indignant. "I'll tell him of your visit, but I can't for the life of me see why it should be any of your father's concern where Ethan does his business. Surely the MDU's no threat to him, as long as he's an honest diamond merchant."

"Is that right, Mistress Seymour?" He steps forward and grabs her wrist, yanking her towards him, breathing into her face. "Well, you can tell your man that 'Simon says', if he decides to disregard my warning, there will be dire consequences."

She wipes his spittle from her cheek. She mustn't show her fear; she faces him off defiantly. "Is that right, mister high and mighty? Who made your family the dictators around here?"

She realises her resistance hasn't helped when he shoves her violently against the desk, sweeping the paperwork, inkwell and tray of dipping pens onto the floor. He straddles her, pinning her down across it, proving his superior strength. "Not so sassy now, are we?"

She kicks her legs against his and slaps and scratches at his face. She'll not let him have his lustful way with her. But he's stronger than her and she struggles to stop him. There's nothing left on the desk to use as a weapon. If only she had the letter knife, or the inkwell.

He puts his face close to her ear and says, "'Simon says', spread your legs apart, my dear, and you'll enjoy this."

Fear runs through her. *He has no shame, no conscience. He's playing a game with me!*

She hears the mechanical sound of a revolver being cocked and McCallister turns his head. She can just make out the bright colours of Kofi's shirt as he says, "Get off her, or I shoot you in the arse."

McCallister quickly slips off her, but she fears Kofi will follow through with his threat, looking more dangerous waving the gun around wildly than if he was well practised with it. She pulls herself up from the desk and gently takes the gun from the lad. If she were to shoot the bastard herself, then it would be reasonable to claim self-defence, but if Kofi did so, he wouldn't stand a chance in a white man's world.

She points the gun at him, menacingly. "You and your father are both low lives and the world would be a better place without you. Get out and don't come back. If you show up here again, I promise you, I'll be more than happy to shoot you in the arse."

Frankie and Roeli appear, peeping around the door to see where Kofi's gone and McCallister laughs. "Am I supposed to be concerned about a female *kaffir* lover and a bunch of kids?" He moves towards her and Lucy fires at his feet. He jumps with shock as she prepares to fire again.

"Get out of our home and don't let me catch you here again. I know you swindled Ethan out of £150 for a false claim at New Rush, and I promise you our Miners' Defence Unit will take you and your father to task over all your other shady dealings, if you continue to intimidate the diggers at the Idayimane settlement."

"This isn't over…"

"It is now!"

Lucy shoots once more and the lead skims his calf as he turns to run. "Ow! You've hit me!" He limps out of the door and Lucy follows to make sure she sees the back of him. She watches him clamber up onto a large grey horse. He cracks his riding crop angrily and sets off towards Hopetown.

Lucy gives a sigh of relief and turns to go back inside but is shocked to see several customers coming out of the baker's looking concerned, and Betsy standing on the *stoep* outside her shop, staring at her in awe.

"Whatever happened? I heard gunshots!"

"Don't be alarmed, Betsy. I was forced to defend myself. It was Simon McCallister, Mervyn McCallister's son; he was trying to assault me and, thank the Lord, young Kofi came to my assistance and we saw him off."

"*You* should join the Miners' Defence Unit! I'll shut the shop."

"No, no. Don't you worry, my dear. He's gone now. I must go and thank Kofi for saving me and calm the boys down. I'll tell you all about it later."

Once back inside, she can't stop trembling. Her body is roaring with adrenalin. She goes through the house to the back and finds Kofi, again working on the fencing.

"Come here, Kofi." She hugs him. "Thank you for saving me. You did so well. Mister Ethan will be really impressed when I tell him how brave you were."

"He bad man, deserved to be shot at."

"Yes, he did."

As soon as Ethan returns home, she recounts to him what happened. He is furious. "Thank goodness for Kofi!" He studies her with concern and takes her hand in his. "Are you sure you're quite recovered, Lucy?"

"Yes, I'm calmer again now. I have to say it was a good decision to employ Kofi though, Ethan. And his actions today clearly demonstrated how loyal and valuable he is to us."

"I intend to give him a bit extra whenever he goes above and beyond his duties, as he did today."

"I did learn that the McCallisters know about the MDU already and he'd the nerve to warn you away from Klipdrift and Kimberley."

"That's not such a bad thing. It means the word's getting around that we'll not tolerate their criminal activities here."

"There's another thing, Ethan. I'm sorry, but I was so angry, I let him know that you're onto them with regard to the intimidation of the folk in the Idayimane encampment."

"Well, we were hoping to get the upper hand with the element of surprise, but it might also put them off altogether and send them elsewhere."

"But rather than divert them, I thought you were hoping to catch them red-handed."

"Yes, well that would have been ideal, but from Khumo's perspective, if we can frighten them off at least, he might feel his family's safer."

"I suppose we'll just have to wait and see."

Weeks later, Lieutenant Greaves enters the office, when Lucy's again left in charge.

He removes his hat. "Good morning, ma'am. Is Ethan about?"

She smiles and shakes her head. "No. I'm afraid he isn't. Can I be of any assistance?"

"I don't know. I believe I've discovered quite a nice-sized stone and I was hoping for a valuation." He hands her a large marble-sized piece of blue kimberlite, within which she can see clear edges of a blue/white diamond. She's impressed with its shape.

"Well, it does look to be a good size, shape and colour." She takes up Ethan's eyeglass and studies it, then takes out the template. "I hesitate to give you a price, as this is larger than the other diamonds I've valued, and I believe it's a stone of the first water. I think you ought to speak to Ethan. Would you like to join us for supper this evening, Lieutenant?"

"I'd be delighted, ma'am."

She holds out her hand to him, expecting him to shake it. "Please, if we're going to dine together, you must call me Lucy."

He takes up her hand, bows and kisses it.

Despite feeling quite calm, she finds herself blushing.

"Shall we say six of the clock? I'm sure Ethan will have returned by then."

He regards her, his eyes steady, and says, "Perfect."

Ethan arrives back home at lunchtime and is pleased to hear that Lucy has invited Andrew Greaves to join them for supper that evening. "I think you'll be impressed with his diamond, Ethan. It looked to be a good size, but it was still imbedded in kimberlite, so it was hard to tell from simply weighing it."

"I'm quite excited to see it, Lucy. Andrew has only ten months left in which to be able to discover something that will make all his hard graft worthwhile."

Lieutenant Greaves arrives a little before six that evening and the two men huddle over his discovery with an eyeglass, alternately peering at a small window in the volcanic kimberlite, while Lucy puts the finishing touches to their supper.

When they're finally all seated around the table, Ethan says, "You were right, Lucy. I'm quite sure Andrew has a fine quality blue diamond and I've recommended he takes it to Charles and Julius tomorrow. I know they'll give him a fair price."

"Well done, Andrew. I'm so pleased for you."

They all enjoy the meal and then, once Frankie's abed, they sit and chatter over a few Cape brandies.

At the end of the evening, as the lieutenant is leaving, he shakes Ethan by the hand. "Thank you, Ethan, for your help and advice. I've had a lovely evening. Lucy is a fabulous person." Ethan smiles, and the lieutenant continues, "I wonder… would you mind me asking you, if you're in a relationship with her?"

Ethan looks at the floor, hesitating, but is forced to admit, "No, I'm not…"

"In that case I presume you've no objection to me coming to court her."

He looks him in the eye and says, "No, none at all." Ethan was about to admit that he wished there were one, but it's too late now.

The following day the lieutenant turns up with a bunch of colourful proteas. The bell chimes and Lucy's heart races, in the fear that McCallister has returned, but she smiles with relief when she sees Andrew standing before her with a beautiful array of fynbos. She loves the sugarbushes and smiles when he gives them to her.

"In thanks for the wonderful meal yesterday."

"Oh! How kind. You were very welcome. I'm so pleased Ethan believes you've found yourself a worthy diamond."

"I was wondering if you might care to spend an afternoon with me, Lucy?"

She's shocked and then she thinks about Mr Buthelezi's reaction if he should see her with yet another man. "Well, it's kind of you for thinking of me, but I've Frankie and the office to oversee, so I can't think of a moment when I'd be free."

"Don't you worry about that. I'll devise a plan with Ethan to release you for a few hours." He smiles encouragingly and so she concedes.

"Well, it would be helpful if you could accompany me on a visit to Rupert's claim, so that I might retrieve my silk shawl from the maid, Tamela."

"It would be my pleasure. Then we'll get to know each other further on the way."

He bows and leaves her pondering the wisdom of this decision.

A week later, Ethan has agreed to stay behind and be babysitter and office clerk for the afternoon. He's also offered their pony and trap for the excursion.

Lucy is wearing her Sunday-best sky-blue outfit with her blue and cream bonnet and she's hoping that Tamela will be absent when they call, but she knows that's unlikely. There's a chilly wind, as they're now in the South African winter, and she's glad of her mantle.

After they've forded the Orange River, Andrew chats to her about his adventures in India and then he asks if she has any hobbies.

"My main interest is music and my piano playing, but I also love to spin and sew, cook and read books. I've just finished a book that my friend gave to me before leaving England called *Les Misérables* by Victor Hugo and I loved it. I'm always so sad when I finish reading a good book. The characters become like friends and I feel the loss of them."

"I only have books that are instructive. I've no time to immerse myself in fiction. There's a manuscript I've left behind in India called the *Kamasutra*. It's an old Hindu text on erotic love, written as a guide to the art of living well and lovemaking, attributed to a number of Indian philosophers. It's a mixture of prose and poetry about finding a life partner and maintaining a pleasurable love life, but it also includes a large number of intimate sexual positions and it served me very well with the exotic Indian maidens, I have to say." He laughs at her embarrassed blushes.

She wonders if he thinks this kind of talk will impress her. She's never heard of anything like it before, but it makes him sound like a philanderer, and she's not impressed at all, rather the opposite. Maybe if he hadn't mentioned his success with the exotic Indian maidens it wouldn't have been so bad, but she now imagines him as a dashing officer in India with all the beautiful Indian women at his beck and call and wonders how many women he's seduced with his *Kamasutra*. She now sees him in a different light and feels uncomfortable in his presence. He presumably wishes to make her another conquest and she hopes to disillusion him as soon as the opportunity arises. But, for now, she has another fish to fry.

They pull up outside Rupert's place and he hands her down from the trap. She can see Rupert working on his claim with Moses and Solomon and she waves to them. He strolls back up to the house. She's walking around the *stoep* looking for Camilla when she notices Frankie's little wheelbarrow abandoned at the edge of the barren vegetable garden, tipped on its side in the mud.

Rupert reaches them and she smiles politely. "Hello, Rupert. This is Lieutenant Andrew Greaves."

"How d'you do." They shake hands.

"Andrew has kindly offered to accompany me over here to collect my silk shawl and anything else we may have left behind."

"Of course. I'm pleased to see you, Lucy."

"In that case, Rupert, would you mind very much if I take the little wheelbarrow you bought for Frankie back with us?"

"Not at all. I'll put it in the back of your cart now." He does so and she thanks him. "Come on in. I can offer you a cup of cocoa. It's chilly today."

She's relieved that Rupert is being cooperative and affable, and they follow him inside the place she used to call home. Rupert tells Tamela to go and make the cocoa and the girl tosses her head and marches off to the kitchen. She sees that Tamela is living here with the child, Berko, and she inwardly bristles. The child's in a cot in her old bedroom.

Her mother's silk shawl is draped across the back of an armchair and she quickly repossesses it. Rupert must realise that Tamela has been using it and so, looking straight at him, she says, "Ah here it is, I'm so pleased, because my mother took hours crocheting it for my twenty-first birthday and I was upset to have mislaid it."

"I think you may have left behind some of Frankie's books as well. I'll go and get them for you." While he's gone, Lucy scans the room and spots her sewing machine. Again, Rupert bought it, but she's sure that Tamela won't be using it and so she decides to ask him if she can take that too.

He returns from the bedroom with a couple of Frankie's toy books, plus his copy of *Alice's Adventures in Wonderland* by Lewis Carroll, which his grandmother, Helen Seymour, had given him the Christmas before they left England; book one of the seventh edition of *Grimms' Fairy Tales*, that used to belong to his auntie Becky; and his copy of *Venomous Creatures*, all of which they'd forgotten about.

"Oh, thank you, Rupert. We've all been so busy we haven't had much time for reading and I forgot all about them. Where were they?"

"Under his bed."

"Ah, that explains it."

They sit politely chatting over their cocoa and Lucy plucks up the courage to ask him about the sewing machine. "Rupert, I notice my sewing machine over in the corner. If no one's using it, would you mind dreadfully if I took that too?"

"No, not at all. We've all the furnishings we need, thanks to you, Lucy. Please take it with you. I'm sure you have more use for it than we do."

Andrew carries it out to the trap leaving Lucy alone with Rupert. She asks him if there's any news from family in England, but Rupert admits to not having been in contact for a while.

Lucy is thankful when Andrew returns, because he's keen to talk with Rupert about their fossicking and the time goes by relatively quickly. Tamela keeps out of the way and the baby continues to nap.

She asks after Jack, and Rupert tells her he's completely recovered from his bronchitis and she says, "Please pass on my kind regards to him for me."

"I can send Tamela to fetch him for you, if you like?"

"No please don't disturb him, I'm sure he's busy, and we don't wish to delay you any further. Besides, we ought to be making tracks ourselves, if we want to be back home before darkness falls." She's no wish to prolong the visit, all the time feeling sick with anxiety, aware that Tamela is out of sight somewhere and concerned the little witch may have found herself another voodoo doll with which to torment her.

Rupert says, "Of course. Well, it's been nice to see you again, Lucy." She stands up and puts down her empty cocoa cup, and the men follow suit. Rupert continues, "You look like the world's treating you well, and it's good to meet you too, Lieutenant. I was interested to hear that Ethan's the instigator of forming the Miners' Defence Unit." They shake hands.

She's relieved it's time to leave. She steps out onto the *stoep* and surveys the land and the river, seeing the tents and huts on the opposite shore and remembering throwing the black-magic effigy into the swirling waters. She has a surge of adrenalin reliving the moment, then, the next instant, Rupert is handing her up into the carriage.

On the way home Andrew comments, "What a pleasant fellow your brother-in-law is."

Lucy doesn't disillusion him.

She's lost all interest in any possible connection developing between herself and the lieutenant by the time they arrive back at Eureka Row. She smiles at him as he hands her down from the trap. She picks up the books and her shawl. "Thank you for accompanying me today, Andrew. It was most kind of you. I must go check on Frankie now and sort out some food. If you linger here a moment with the pony and trap, I'll send Kofi out to unload the sewing machine and wheelbarrow and unshackle and stable Reckless. Then would you care to come in to see Ethan?"

The lieutenant apparently doesn't feel the warmth of her invitation and he declines politely. "I expect you've seen enough of me for one day and I'll be seeing Ethan on our next MDU shift, so I fear I must decline your invitation and return to my digs. Farewell for now, my dear." He takes up her hand

and kisses her palm in a seductive way. She leaves him on the boardwalk and as soon as she's inside her home, she wipes her hand in her skirt, before wholeheartedly greeting Ethan and calling out for Kofi, who goes to deal with the pony and trap.

Ethan's relieved to have her back home with him. He's been so jealous, while she was in the company of the dashing lieutenant. He packs away his bags of alluvial diamonds and watches Lucy making a start on their supper.

She says over her shoulder, "This won't take long to cook. It's just bratwurst, beans and eggs, so you could help by laying the table, if you're hungry."

He's itching to ask her about her afternoon, but he selects the plates and cutlery for the table and lays out the rush mats. Finally, he can wait no longer. "How did you enjoy your day out with Andrew, Lucy?"

"Well, I've retrieved Frankie's little wheelbarrow. I'm sure the boys will have great fun with that, pushing each other around in it. Also, Rupert said I could keep the sewing machine he bought for me, and I recovered several of Frankie's books, which we'd forgotten about, and my mama's shawl, which is a great relief. So, it was time well spent."

"I actually meant, how did you get on with your admirer?"

"Oh! Not so well, really. I preferred him before he set his cap at me."

Ethan laughs. "I thought you ladies were supposed to keep us men guessing."

"I'm afraid I don't go in for guessing games, Ethan." She pauses and then continues, her eyes averted, "Actually, there's someone else, who I already feel genuine affection for, but I confess I fear he'd be looking for a younger lady, not one who's been married before." She glances back at him.

Ethan's heart races. If she's referring to him, now's the moment to show her how he feels. He slowly and deliberately moves around the table towards her. Gently, he places his hands either side of her face and pulls her towards him for a kiss. Although she seems taken aback, in seconds she's responding, returning his kisses ardently.

Then he smells burning and feels her pulling away from him. "Stop, Ethan, or I'll burn the sausages!" He allows her to return to the stove, but sneaks up behind her, caressing her neck until she turns back to him for more kisses. When their lips meet, a small electric shock makes her draw back and laugh. "Wow! Did you feel that?"

"I certainly did; there's definitely chemistry between us. Come here." He pulls her towards him again and kisses her neck lovingly, until she's tingling with desire.

That night, lying in his arms, she realises the delight of all her past pleasures put together doesn't amount to the overwhelming joy of her feelings of love being returned in equal measure by her Ethan. She's glad that the pep talk from Betsy gave her the courage to trust her instincts and risk placing her heart in possible jeopardy once more.

CHAPTER FIFTEEN *(June–August 1874)*

HOME FIRES

In June, Ethan receives a long-awaited letter from his father. He shows Lucy the letter and she reads it with interest.

> *Mr Ethan Hart*
> *Eureka Row*
> *C/O Hopetown Post Office*
> *Hopetown*
> *Pixley ka Seme*
> *Thembelihle*
> *Northern Cape Province*
> *South Africa*

25th March 1874

Dear Ethan,

How are things going with your hunt for a plot of land for your ranch?

I have recently discovered a manufacture of prefabricated homes in Manchester. Mr Bellhouse constructs small houses made of cast and wrought iron, wood and glass, and sends them out, flat-packed, to all corners of the world, especially to areas where prospectors need a roof over their heads and materials are at a premium. They even produce a tin tabernacle.

I remember you saying that building timber is scarce where you are, and I was wondering if you would like me to organise the purchase of several of these kit homes from Mr Bellhouse? Eureka Row worked out well for you; what do you think? I can fund the original purchase and when you have constructed them, rented or sold them, you can then pay me back, when you have recouped the funds.

Your mama has encouraged me to suggest this to you and she sends you her love.

Please give our kind regards to Lucy and Frankie.

With much love from Mama and Papa.

"What a brilliant idea, Ethan! It seems to me that your father's a generous man. He obviously loves and trusts you very much." She folds the letter and returns it to him.

Ethan is thoughtful. "I think these homes will sell at a premium, especially for the Kimberley mine, which is expanding rapidly every day."

Lucy cautions, "As long as you don't step on McCallister's toes."

"I don't see why we should; it is, after all, a completely different business."

"Will it make you lots of money, Ethan?"

"Lucy, I think it'll be a Godsend. We'll be needing a good income to make up for what we're spending on the ranch." He hugs her. "I'm truly motivated by this. I think I ought to send a telegram back to Papa immediately to suggest he starts by sending us ten flat packs for Kimberley and a tin tabernacle for Khumo and the Idayimane encampment. They can use it for worship and for a school. What do you think?"

"I think it's a grand idea."

About a fortnight later, Ethan finds the perfect plot of land for their homestead on the outskirts of Hopetown. He and Lucy settle down that evening beside a flickering fire to sketch out their ideas. Lucy's excited, feeling secure in their relationship and involved with the planning process.

"I'm so pleased we've decided to move to the other side of the river, nearer to the businesses. It will be much better for Frankie to be attending school in town."

"Well, I did get a move on when I realised his fifth birthday's next month."

"I know. Thank you… My only concern is he'll miss Roeli."

"But we can't let that get in the way of his education. Lucy, please don't worry about Roeli. I can always take Frankie with me to the office so they can see each other when they're not in school. We both know he needs to mix with other Europeans and there's a decent dame school in Hopetown, where he'll be able to study the Cape Dutch language, as well as English, which will hold him in good stead in later life."

"You're right, Ethan. And like you say, they can see each other at the office." She smiles. "I'm so looking forward to designing our own place, away from all the interruptions from your customers. How long do you think it'll take to build?"

"I can't say, until we find a good builder. The men who built Eureka Row have since moved on. Can you remember the name of the builders who built Rupert's place?"

"I think it was a Dutchman, called Johan Meyer. I know Rupert said he'd some Tswana boys working with him and he was pleased with their teamwork."

"I'll make some enquiries and try to get the same fellow. I was impressed with the workmanship on Rupert's place."

When Ethan first takes Lucy and Frankie to see the site, the day is clear but cold. Lucy is dressed smartly in her travelling costume, to protect her from the winter chill, and the deep blue colour is reflected in her eyes. Ethan feels butterflies dancing in his stomach, as he witnesses her pleasure and enthusiasm. They'll soon all be living here together, like a proper family, and he makes a momentous decision. "Come here, Lucy, my dear. I want to ask you something important."

He takes her hand in his and draws her closer. "Lucy, you may not realise this, but I've been besotted by you, since the first day I set eyes on you, on the ship." He smiles at her surprised expression. "I really would like to make an honest woman of you, before we officially move in here. Since we've been living together, you've given every hour of every day new meaning. I'm the happiest I've ever been in my whole life. I want to look after you and Frankie and keep you both safe from harm and I don't want folk like Buthelezi to turn his nose up at you ever again."

Frankie looks on intrigued, as Ethan gets down on one knee. "My dearest Lucy, will you do me the great honour of accepting my hand in marriage?"

Lucy's stunned, and thrilled and for a moment speechless. She thought she might be a widow for the rest of her life and now the vivid sun has emerged from behind a grey cloud. She smiles with tears in her eyes. "I'd be delighted to accept your hand in marriage, my darling Ethan. I couldn't be happier! You're a perfect match for me and Frankie. I love you, Ethan, with all my heart."

Ethan draws himself back up. "In that case we must celebrate our betrothal by finding you an engagement ring. Come, let's go and see Charles and Julius. They may have the perfect ring for you. In any event, I've some decent-sized diamonds back at the office and they can recommend a jeweller for us. Come on, Frankie. We're off into town."

Charles and Julius are full of congratulations for their friend Ethan and charming towards both Lucy and Frankie. They show Ethan a velvet-lined drawer containing a variety of diamond rings, all in different designs, shapes and sizes. There are no prices marked and Lucy's reticent about choosing. "Please, you select one that you like, Ethan. Then I can try it on and see if it fits me."

To her surprise he selects a prominent diamond with a cluster of smaller diamonds encircling it. She tries it on, but it's too loose. Julius tells her, "Don't worry, I've a similar one here, which is a little smaller."

She tries that one on and it's a perfect fit. Emotional tears fill her eyes. "It's beautiful, Ethan. I love it, but can we afford it?"

"Cash flow's a bit tight at the moment, only because of the upcoming cost of building our own house, but Charles and Julius have agreed to include some of my own stock in this deal and we'll soon recoup our money, with Papa's kit homes. So, it's all settled," he says.

"Here, my dear Lucy, please put it back on." He kisses her lovingly as he places the ring on the third finger of her left hand.

On the fifth of July, Frankie has a birthday celebration tea. He dresses in the new clothes that Ethan bought for him in Kimberley, with soft leather shoes his mother had specially made for him in Hopetown, in readiness for him starting school.

Roeli is the guest of honour. He turns up with a gift wrapped in cloth and proudly hands it over to Frankie. "For you – present."

Frankie eagerly unwraps the gift to reveal a carved wooden figure in the image of a standing mongoose. "It's Monty!" he cries, and he shows it to Monty, who sniffs it with interest, which turns into confusion when it doesn't move.

Lucy admires the workmanship. "Wherever did you get it, Roeli?"

"My *tata* make it for Frankie."

"That's very kind of him. Please tell him we're all really impressed."

Roeli nods his head and she's sure he understood her.

Betsy, Norman and Kofi join them for a typical English afternoon tea. Betsy hands Frankie their present, which turns out to be the game 'draughts' and Ethan ends up teaching the three boys how to play it, along with other children's games like blind man's buff. During the parlour games, Betsy notices Lucy's ring and exclaims with delight at the good news. "You kept that quiet, you two," she says, grinning.

Lucy grins back. "Well, it was probably a bit overdue, considering we've been living in sin for the last few months, but we'd little choice, thanks to my brother-in-law and his concubine."

Finally, when the two young lads are flagging, Lucy settles Frankie for bed and the adults continue to socialise, playing a few hands of whist, while Kofi takes Roeli back home, returning just before dark.

That night, Kofi's disturbed from his sleep by Reckless snorting and prancing. He hears a strange crackling sound and smells paraffin and the acrid tang of burning. In panic, he clambers down his loft steps and discovers fire rapidly developing in the straw, Reckless stamping and whinnying, with his eyes rolling and nostrils flaring. His heart races, as he speedily opens the stable door and leads the frantic Reckless out into the open and around to the front *stoep*, to tether him on the rail. He hammers on Ethan and Lucy's front door shouting, "*Uncedo! Uncedo!*" in his alarm, using his native language.

Ethan's roused by the noise and soon realises the emergency. Together they manage to douse the flames with buckets of sand and water from the well. Lucy and Frankie sleep on in oblivion.

Norman and Mr Coffin both come outside in their nightshirts to see what the commotion's about, but by this time, with the help of Ethan, Kofi's saved the day.

"Thank goodness for your quick response, lad," says Norman, clapping Kofi on the back.

Mr Coffin stands before them scratching his head and looking horrified. Finally, he says, "It's lucky the boy's such a light sleeper, or he and the pony, and perhaps even the whole of Eureka Row, would have been engulfed in flames. We could have lost everything, including our lives."

They hear footsteps and turn to see some units of the MDU returning home after their shift. "What's wrong?" asks Bruce Robinson.

"Someone tried to set fire to the stable, with young Kofi and my pony in there. Luckily, the lad woke up, or they'd surely both have been burnt to death. I'd like to get my hands on the villain, I can tell you!"

"We saw a rider galloping past us on a large grey horse, heading towards the camp. He was riding like the devil was after him."

Kofi gasps and looks at Ethan. "That bad man!"

"You mean McCallister?"

He nods his head.

"Don't worry, Kofi, he's tried and failed. You take Reckless back into the stable and get some sleep. You can help me fix it up tomorrow." Kofi does as he's bid.

Ethan glances towards Bruce. "Right, men, I know you've only just finished your shifts, but we need to go back to check all's well. This could have been a diversionary tactic. If it had been successful and the whole of Eureka Row had gone up in flames, your MDU units returning to Hopetown would have been totally preoccupied with saving lives. As it is, we've an opportunity to catch them red-handed. If possible, we need to cut off the head of the snake, by catching Simon McCallister in the act. He'll carry the incriminating aroma of paraffin." He looks at the men in turn and cries, "Who's with me?"

The twelve men all hold up their hands. "Right, let me just go and dress and fetch my pistol and I'll be ready."

Norman suggests, "Let them go on ahead, Ethan. I'll accompany you."

"All right, men, you set off and we'll catch you up." He turns back to Norman. "But we don't make up a unit."

Mr Coffin interjects, "I'll join you, if that helps."

"Are you sure, Mr Coffin? It could be dangerous."

He nods. "We have to do what's necessary to protect our families, and I too own a firearm. Incidentally, my name's Jasper."

"Good man, Jasper. You'd better get some clothes on. I'll meet you back here in five minutes."

Moments later Ethan and Norman are back outside, waiting for Jasper. When he emerges from his store with a blunderbuss under his arm they're both shocked. "Wow, I hope you're safe with that, Jasper," says Norman.

"It was my father's, but I look after it well. It's our only form of defence for ourselves and our store."

Ethan grins. "Come on, then, let's go." They set off at a trot, hoping to catch up with Bruce and the other MDU men, but they're too late.

As they approach the diamond settlement there's the sound of gunfire. They duck down cautiously, making towards the noise. A brawl is taking place in the middle of the Idayimane encampment, with some of the MDU in hand-to-hand combat with the intruders. In the moonlight, Ethan notes some bruised and battered black fellows with their hands and feet tied and then he recognises Simon McCallister, in the thick of it.

He whispers to Norman and Jasper, "We must concentrate on McCallister. Let's try to separate

259

him from his bullyboys and the rest of the rogues, then arrest him before he gets away to his home and washes away the evidence of the paraffin. If we wait until he's on the outer edge of the brawl, we can do a pincer movement from behind and separate him from the others. Make sure he gets a good look at the blunderbuss."

As the affray moves away from the captive natives and McCallister, Norman takes the left hand and Ethan the right, with Jasper stepping immediately behind the man, with the blunderbuss pointing at his back.

When Ethan is close enough, he points his pistol at McCallister's head and says, "Turn slowly around and you'll see we're well armed. Then walk over there." He points towards the shadows, away from the affray. McCallister does as he's instructed, and Norman ties his arms behind his back.

McCallister laughs. "You don't think you're going to get away with this, do you?"

Ethan scoffs, "Why not? You've been caught red-handed?"

He sniggers. "You've no idea who you're dealing with. My father has powerful friends."

Ethan says, "Gag him." Norman stuffs his handkerchief into McCallister's mouth and then ties his neckerchief tightly to prevent any sound escaping. Ethan then says, "You were seen riding from the scene of the crime on your grey horse and you reek of paraffin, you bastard! You're under arrest for arson and intimidation. You'll be taken to the lock-up in Hopetown and held there to await trial in the next magistrates' court." He shoves him. "Move!" But the villain makes a run for it; moving swiftly among the tents and shacks, he disappears from view. Ethan doesn't want to shoot and draw attention.

"Damn!" He's furious! How stupid is he? He should have tethered the creep to one of them at least. They set off after him, taking different routes through the tents and shacks, but following in the same direction, but he's disappeared. How could they have let him go?

"We can't give up; he may simply be hiding somewhere. Keep searching. I can't go back to Lucy and tell her we've failed."

Then they stumble upon him lying face down on the ground with Khumo standing guard over him. "Well done, Khumo. You've saved the day. Thank you. We won't let him escape again."

Khumo grins with the praise. "I saw him before on horse and keep look."

"Where's his horse?"

Khumo says, "I fetch him and take him to Kofi for you."

"Thank you, Khumo, but first, if you can do it safely, please release the two men tied up; find out their names and why they were detained by the gang."

"Yessir." He rushes off, disappearing from view.

They rope McCallister to Norman. Then Ethan and Jasper walk behind him with their guns trained on his back. Ethan's eager to make ground in separating McCallister from his cronies and they push and shove the man until they're back at Eureka Row. Khumo, who joined them en route, tethers the grey to the boardwalk rail and goes to check on Kofi.

By now the cocks are crowing, the sun's a red glow on the eastern horizon and the hadeda birds are calling. Ethan leaves the prisoner momentarily in the hands of Jasper and Norman while he goes to put Reckless into the traces and bring out the pony and trap. They unceremoniously push McCallister into the back of the trap and rope him to the side. Finally, Ethan ties the grey to the back of the cart.

Norman says, "You go on inside, Jasper. I'll go with Ethan."

"No, Norman. I'm seeing this through with you. You sit up front with Ethan. I'll go in the back with old Bessie here. We don't want him thinking he can escape, do we?"

They set off with their prisoner restrained in the back, staring miserably into the flared muzzle of the blunderbuss. Jasper guards him diligently.

When they reach the lock-up, Ethan hands him over to the constable in charge. He explains what's occurred and fills in an official MDU arrest form. He also tells the man the horse belongs to the prisoner and will need stabling. When he hands it over to the officer, he notes McCallister's initials 'S J McC' etched into the polished leather saddle.

Bruce and another unit arrive with some more of the bullyboys under arrest. He explains to Ethan, "These men were planning to hold captive two of the native fellows, so that even though they'd paid for their licences, their land couldn't be worked for the stipulated seven days and would therefore be forfeited, classed as abandoned and available to be re-licensed in McCallister's name. Apparently it's one of his favourite methods of taking over more and more claims."

Ethan asks him, "Do you have the names and statements of the two men?"

Bruce nods. "Yes, Khumo was able to translate for us."

"Good. That means we've even more evidence against McCallister and his rotten father. Well done, men – a good night's work. We're off home now.

I'm actually shattered, and I've got fire damage to repair."

On his return home, Lucy throws herself at him in a recklessly warm embrace, thankful to have him back home unscathed, as well as their neighbours and the MDU soldiers. She kisses him. "Well done, Ethan. Kofi told me what happened last night. I was so worried about you all." She sighs. "We've got him at last."

He savours the feel of her in his arms, but he's not as assured as she is. "Hm!" he says thoughtfully. "I just hope his rogue of a father can't subvert the rule of law."

After Lucy's made him a big English-style breakfast and he's changed into his moleskin trousers, a cool white calico shirt and the buckskin waistcoat Lucy gave him for Christmas, he goes outside to inspect the damage.

The outer wall of the stable is blackened and the wood charred. He now has to go into Kimberley to the timber merchant to buy some expensive replacement struts, before they can commence the repair work. He leaves Kofi scrubbing the soot off the galvanised iron.

CHAPTER SIXTEEN *(August–October 1874)*

ACACIA LODGE
AND STRAWBERRY FIELDS

By August work is well underway on their plot. They've chosen a single-storey building with slate flooring obtained from the bluestone quarry on Robben Island. Johan and his men are making good progress. They've already created the six rooms and the Dutch-style ornate, rounded brick gable structures at either end and over the central front gable and entrance area. They'll soon be constructing the roof, in readiness for the thatchers.

Lucy calls in from time to time, after she's dropped Frankie at school. She's impatient for their new home to be ready for her to choose the furnishings.

Towards the end of the month she's amazed to receive a letter from Aurora and she eagerly breaks the seal to learn all about her young friend.

Mrs Lucy Seymour
Eureka Row
C/O Hopetown Post Office
Hopetown
Pixley ka Seme
Thembelihle
Northern Cape Province
South Africa

Dear Lucy,

I hope this letter finds you well. I wanted to write to you, as we are both now living in the Southern Hemisphere.

My old governess, Grace, was my companion on the passage from England and it was a terrific adventure for her on the ship. (I am, of course, an old hand.) I was initially worried about Grace settling here before we set off, but she has surprised me by finding herself a job in the Bendigo Post Office and I do believe she has a soft spot for the postmaster there.

Thus, we are now living with Rhys and his family and I am happily working at their office in Eaglehawk.

My only worry is that I believe I've forced a wedge between the two families who have always been so close before. Hugh's family seem to be keeping their distance from Bryn and Nell since we arrived. I'm sure I am responsible for this, as before I came on the scene and stole his heart, Gwyneth had set her cap at my Rhys, and also because I chose Rhys over Lewys who also was keen on me. It is casting a shadow over our otherwise idyllic life here and I don't know what I can do to salvage the situation.

I'm sorry, Lucy, but I just need to vent my feelings at the moment. Please don't concern yourself with my problems; I am sure you have plenty of your own.

I would love to hear all your news. Have you made your fortune yet? How are Frankie and Rupert? Please do write soon. Despite being the happiest I could possibly be with my dear Rhys, I do miss my

old girlfriends and their wise counsel. Please give
Frankie a big kiss from me.
  With fondest regards,
  Aurora x

She decides to write back immediately; letters take a long time to travel such a distance and Aurora has written her return address on the back of the envelope.

Miss Aurora Dryer
Brecon House
Waratah Street
C/O Bendigo Post Office
Sandhurst
Victoria
South Australia

28ᵗʰ August 1874

Dear Aurora,
  How nice to hear from you. What a lot has happened to both of us since we were last back home in Ivell. I am no longer with Rupert. Although, I admit, we did grow close, he betrayed me with a native girl and so I left him. I recently became betrothed to my good friend Ethan. We met on the voyage over here and immediately there was a rapport between us. We share a love of music and singing, and he has always been totally reliable and helpful towards both me and Frankie. Ethan is a very hard worker; his business is dealing in diamonds. We are building our own homestead in Hopetown and the builders are currently working on the roof structure. It is so exciting.
  I last heard from home, when Bunny wrote, back in December, to tell me she was engaged to

Edwin and they planned to marry in June, but they were looking for somewhere to live. I hope all went as expected. I'm sure I'll soon be getting the thrilling news that I have another niece or nephew, either from Bunny, or from Jacob's union with Clara.

Anyway, enough about me. I'm so pleased to hear from you. Letters are few and far between here. I understand your frustration with the two families, but I'm sure all your problems will be resolved when Lewys and Gwyneth find themselves new partners. It is a shame their jealousy has cast a shadow over your happiness, but you and Rhys have the right to seek your own happiness too. I can only suggest that you encourage them to socialise more with other people to facilitate the opportunities of meeting someone new.

Do keep in touch and let me know how things progress.

With best wishes,
Your friend and confidante,
Lucy x

Having written to Aurora, she realises she's been neglecting her own family. She's been busy, but she hasn't written to them since Christmas and still doesn't know if Bunny and Edwin did tie the knot as arranged. If she writes to them now, she can then post the two letters together.

Miss Beatrice Warren
Home Farm
Alvington Manor
Ivell
Somerset
England

Dearest Bunny,

I imagine you are now Mrs Edwin Proctor, but I don't know, and I don't have your new address, so I sent this to Home Farm? I hope your nuptials went ahead as expected and you and Edwin are now happily married.

Please let me know how you both are and where you are now living, and please give my love and best wishes to Ma and Pa and our brothers and their families. I miss you all very much and feel guilty for not being in touch for so long, but we've been really busy here. Ethan found a plot of land and we've been building a homestead.

I'm thrilled to announce that I too am now betrothed to my dear Ethan and things are going really well for us. He's a good father to Frankie, who loves him, as I do, and we're a proper family at last. Ethan's parents live in Salisbury and his father is organising the purchase and delivery of some flat-pack homes, from a fellow in Manchester, which will sell, or rent, easily in the area of the Kimberley diamond mine. His father is very supportive of Ethan and is quite happy to invest in him for a small return. Ethan is really excited about this project and we hope to have these kit homes by October. It should help to recoup the cost of us building our own home.

We've not yet set a date for our marriage, but it will be a small affair, with just a few friends attending. I'm not sure if we will invite Rupert even, as he now seems to be living openly with his Khoikhoi maid and their son, Berko, and I don't want to have to say she's not welcome. I'm not being intolerant here; she's a thoroughly evil and untrustworthy person and the reason we moved away from Rupert.

Anyway, enough about that. It only saddens me to think of the two weddings I have missed, although I'm sure you must have some beautiful photographs which we will be able to see someday.

Frankie is now attending a dame school in Hopetown and is making new friends and seems to be very happy. When we move, he will still keep in contact with his little mate Roeli when not in school.

I'm afraid that is all our news for now. Please write soon, I miss you all so.

Your loving sister, Lucy. X

She could have told Bunny all about their problems with the McCallisters, but she didn't want to worry her family on that score.

The next time Lucy calls in to view their new homestead, the thatchers have nearly finished their work. Johan has his men whitewashing the exterior and interior walls and fixing the wooden shutters on the outside of all the windows. They still have to construct the larder and fix the shelving, install the range with a mantelshelf over it, and build a separate stable for Reckless to the left of the main building, but she and Ethan can at last begin ordering their furniture now. With spring in the air, she can't wait to start nesting.

In the meantime, Ethan has found a large plot of land, south of the Kimberley mine, where he can site his kit homes. He organises a bank loan using Eureka Row as collateral, completes the purchase and goes into town to sign all the legal forms in the estate offices.

While there, he visits the ironmongers and orders a cast-iron bath from Port Elizabeth, which he knows will please Lucy enormously, before shopping for a four-poster bed, complete with muslin curtaining. He also purchases a large matching black and yellowwood wardrobe, chest of drawers and a slender cheval mirror and asks the shop owner to organise delivery to Acacia Lodge, the name of their new homestead, for Monday the twentieth of November.

On his return home he gives Lucy some money so she can choose the soft furnishings. She goes into Hopetown the following day to organise this, and to select bedding, curtain material and rods from Mrs Erasmus, who's most conciliatory and eager to be of assistance. She's glad her sharp retort to Mr Buthelezi at the carol service must have made a favourable impression on Mrs Erasmus. She chooses similar material to that which she chose for Rupert's home, because she loves the exotic birds and flowers of South Africa; they're so colourful to hang against the fresh white walls. She also purchases some buckskin rugs from the same roadside trader she used for her Christmas gifts, which she believes to be a bargain. She hopes Ethan will be pleased.

During September, Simon McCallister is up before the bench at the Michaelmas quarter session for fraud, arson and kidnap. Ethan attends the court in Cathcart Street and recognises a couple of the jurors from the Diggers Rest. Ethan, Norman, Jasper and Bruce are all called as witnesses and their statements tally. Ethan also explains how he was duped out of £150 by McCallister when he sold him fraudulent claim papers. These he'd kept all this time as evidence. No mention's made of the previous assaults against Lucy; Ethan doesn't want to bring her name into the proceedings. Ethan is relieved when the jury find Simon McCallister guilty, despite McCallister senior engaging an experienced defence lawyer, and he is given a sentence of three years in prison. It only remains to be seen how his father will react.

In October the flat packs arrive at his site near Kimberley, which Ethan has called Salisbury Fields, after his father's generous contribution. Ethan sets about finding manpower for these and starts off by going to the market square, early in the morning when the labour touts arrive with their native workforce. He watches deals being struck, the labour contractor wanting a percentage of any diamonds discovered through their labour, and the various tribesmen are snatched up. He leaves empty-handed.

He decides to ask Johan if he can spare some of his Tswana boys for a short spell, promising to pay them the same rate as he does. Johan, who's become a pal to Ethan, surprises him by replying, testily, "What? You're setting up now in competition with me?"

He hadn't given that a thought and immediately tries to pacify his friend. "No, of course not, Johan. There's no comparison between my kit homes and your substantial buildings!"

Johan laughs. "I'm teasing you, my friend. As it won't take long to put those flat packs together, I'm happy to let you take my two apprentices."

"Thank you, Johan. I'm much obliged. I'd also be grateful if you could source ten small cast-iron stoves. You have better contacts than me and I'll settle with you, when you bill me."

"I can do that. No problems. Changing the subject – did you, by any chance, see any signs of trouble while you were in Kimberley?"

"No, why?"

"Because it was reported in the *Diamond News* that an Irish Fenian and revolutionary protestor, called Alfred Aylward, along with a number of other disaffected white fellows, has formed what they're calling, 'The Committee of Public Safety', with the intention of agitating against the government for reform. They're upset with the governor, Sir Richard Southey, about high taxation, increased rent and unrest among the coloured workers."

"Well, I didn't see anything amiss. The streets were crowded with tradesmen and mule and oxcarts; there were Mpondo men herding cattle and some South Sotho men selling grain, but all was good natured."

He slaps him on the back. "Good. Unrest is bad for business. I'll send my men to meet you at Eureka Row tomorrow morning. Then you can take them with you to the site and perhaps help them on their way with the instructions. Do you mind if they squat in the first hut raised, while the work's ongoing?"

"Not at all, that'd be good for me, because they'll then be onsite and can also act as security."

"Then that's agreed. Glad to be of help, Ethan. You take care now."

"Thanks, Johan. Goodbye."

Having got the kit homes organised, Ethan asks Khumo if he can gather some men together to help erect the tin tabernacle. There's a wide swathe of grassland separating the Hopetown diamond fields and the Idayimane encampment and he decides to site the tabernacle so that it faces onto this expanse of grass, allowing the children somewhere safe to play and exercise during school hours and also giving plenty of room for the arrival of worshipers on Sundays. Khumo quickly puts together a work gang and, with Ethan overseeing, the tabernacle is soon erected. Now Ethan has to find a priest and a schoolteacher.

It's a hot, dry day in November when Ethan, Lucy and Frankie finally pack for the move into Acacia Lodge. The cast-iron range has been fitted by Johan, the bath has arrived from Port Elizabeth and the four-poster bed has been delivered from Kimberley and re-constructed in the master bedroom, along with the matching wardrobe, chest of drawers and cheval mirror. Although much of their furniture will be left behind for Ethan to use in the office, there's sufficient to employ a wagoner.

Frankie's thrilled to have Roeli travelling with them in the trap. He fidgets with uncontained elation on the journey, excited to be showing his friend their new home. Monty's in his basket, on Lucy's lap. The wagoner follows behind them, packed to the gunnels with the bookshelf, the Welsh dresser, the sofa and armchairs, the mangle, a single wrought-iron bed for Frankie, and several tea chests of cutlery, crockery and pans, plus a couple of oil lamps and their steamer chests full of their clothes. Kofi and Khumo travel with the wagoner, to help unload the furniture at the other end.

Lucy is bursting with eager expectation. There's so much to do before nightfall and she can't wait to get there. She watches the waves of water caused by the two vehicles crossing the Orange River at the ford, the spray cooling her. Not long now.

They pull off the carriageway and onto their land. Ethan draws in the reins and Reckless halts outside his new stable. The wagoner pulls up in front of the house and the men disembark. Lucy, Frankie, Roeli and Ethan all clamber down and Ethan calls to Kofi. "Kofi, I want you to unharness Reckless and settle him in the left-hand stall, introduce him to his new environment and give him some oats."

"Yessir."

Ethan opens up the house to allow Khumo and the wagoner to unload the furniture. Then he helps Lucy with the steamer chests, taking them into the bedrooms. Lucy fetches the bed linen and makes up the beds.

Frankie's wildly running around with Roeli and Monty, exploring every room and then the large area of uncultivated land around the house.

Once Lucy's made up the beds, she displays the finest crockery on the Welsh dresser, the cutlery in its drawers, and places the remainder of the crockery, cooking pots and pans, the samovar and their dry foods, preserves, and stuff like biltong in the larder. She's hot and tired by the time she's finished and suffering from back ache. It's too hot to light the range and so Ethan offers some lemonade to everyone.

The wagoner is returning to Hopetown once they've finished and so Khumo plans to set off on foot back to the camp with Roeli. Ethan's arranged with Bruce Robinson to stay overnight at Eureka Row for the sake of future security. It's not far from his claim, more room and comfort for him, and it will also be company for Ethan on the odd occasion that he stays over himself.

Ethan pulls Kofi to one side. "Kofi, now that we've moved here, some distance away from your family, I want you to decide whether you'd like to continue to work for us and live above the new stable, or go back to be with your parents?"

Kofi thinks for just a moment and replies. "I like to stay here, boss, with Reckless."

"I'm pleased, Kofi. You're like one of our family now. When I can afford it, I'm also thinking of getting another horse, so Lucy has Reckless and the trap, and I'll have my own horse for the *kopje-walloping*, so with two animals you'll be kept busy."

So, it's settled. Kofi makes himself comfortable in the stable loft and Khumo and Roeli happily set off back home together, with some silver coins jingling in Khumo's pocket.

At the end of the month, Lieutenant Greaves joins them for supper for the last time, as he will be travelling back to India, his furlough at an end.

The two men relax on the back *stoep*, after the hearty meal prepared and served by Lucy. Ethan pours the Cape brandy and Andrew offers him one of his cigars. They can hear the night-time song of the cicadas from the bushes surrounding their garden.

Ethan is sad to be losing his companion. "It's been a pleasure to meet you, Andrew, and thanks for all your valuable help with the formation of the MDU."

"I've enjoyed it, my friend. It's been an interesting year and that good quality gemstone I brought to you has since been valued by Charles and Julius at around £400, so it's not been a waste of my time and more than covered my adventure."

He asks him, "Have you sold it already?"

"I have. The cash will come in handy on my journey home."

Ethan sighs. "I could do with a lucky find myself now, considering the size of the bond on this place, but it's worth it just to see how happy it's made Lucy and Frankie."

Ethan hears Lucy crossing the *stoep* and she joins in the conversation. "Well, this has been a very pleasant evening, Lieutenant."

Andrew Greaves stands up at the sound of her voice. "Thank you, Lucy. I'm grateful for your kind hospitality. Your meal was delicious and the company excellent." He smiles his roguish smile.

"I'm gratified you enjoyed it, but please excuse me, I'm ready for my bed and I know you two gentlemen will continue to enjoy your cigars and brandy, whilst discussing politics and other complicated matters, not suitable for my delicate feminine ears." She smiles innocently, dips a curtsey to the lieutenant and kisses Ethan on the top of his head.

"It was nice to get to know you, Lucy."

"You too. I found it most illuminating, Andrew. Now, I wish you both goodnight and to you, Andrew, bon voyage."

Andrew watches her go back inside. "So, my friend, you were holding back on me when you said there was nothing between you? That betrothal ring must have cost you a pretty penny!"

"Well, I have to admit to a secret passion developing between us, but nothing had been put into words at that point. Neither of us knew how the other was feeling and both of us were too scared to pursue it. But I have to say, I felt so jealous when she went off with you, that day, that it was the impetus needed for me to come clean."

"I'm pleased for you, Ethan. She's a lovely person and will, I'm sure, make you a good wife."

They sit and chat for a while, until the brandy bottle's empty, when Andrew says his final farewell, returning to his digs on horseback, in readiness for his long journey over land and sea back to his regiment the following day.

In Ivell, Jacob and Malachi are sparring together in the barn at Home Farm in preparation for the St Leonard's Day Fayre when Bunny calls in to see her family. She goes straight inside the farmhouse, as it's bitingly cold outside in the October wind. She can't understand how her brothers can bear to be out in the barn on such a day.

Inside, her mother is surrounded by freshly filled jars of damson jam and the sugary smell of the preserves permeates the warm kitchen. She's pleased to see her, as always, and puts the kettle on to make some cocoa.

Bunny asks, "Where's Pa?"

"He's gone to see Bill at Lease Farm about putting their ram to Jacob's sheep."

"Oh good. Not too far, then; I'll see him when he gets back."

Her mother says, "I'm glad you've popped in, Bunny, because there's a letter here for you from Lucy and I've been itching to open it, but it's addressed to you."

"I wouldn't have minded, Ma. Let's have a look."

Her mother picks up the letter from the dresser, hands it to her, then continues setting out the mugs. Bunny reads it quickly. She's shocked by its contents regarding Rupert, but makes no comment, curiously waiting to see her mother's reaction. She passes it back for her mother to read.

After a while Bunny says, "It looks like our Lucy's going to get married again. I hope this Ethan's as nice as she thinks he is."

Her mother sighs and looks up from the letter. "I'm sure he is. He sounds like a gentleman, hardworking into the bargain, and best of all, he gets on well with young Frankie. But I can't believe she's marrying all those hundreds of miles away, where it's impossible for us to attend. I do worry about her. She can't really do worse than last time, can she?"

"No, Ma, he sounds perfect for her, as long as she isn't looking through rose-coloured spectacles."

Her mother reads on. "What's this about Rupert having a child with his black maid?"

"Hm! It seems like shocking behaviour to me, but it sounds like he's continuing true to form," says Bunny with a shrug.

Her mother pours out the cocoa from a large jug into four mugs and sits wearily down at the kitchen table. "I wouldn't want to be in the vicinity when his parents find out about that!"

Bunny says, "I'll take the two mugs outside and say hello to my brothers."

She picks up the mugs and takes Lucy's letter to show them out in the barn. "Hello, you two. Time for a rest." At the sound of her voice, they both put their woolly jerseys back on, while they take a break, drink the hot cocoa and listen to her reading the letter to them.

Malachi's pleased with the news. "Wow! I'm glad she's getting married again. It was worrying, her being over there without anyone, apart from that prick, Seymour."

Bunny grins. "You haven't heard the best bit yet, Mal."

"What do you mean?"

"Just listen." She reads on to the end of the letter and her brothers listen in silence.

Jacob sighs. "I hope Clara doesn't get to hear about that."

"Don't be daft, Jake. She won't be worried about what that idiot gets up to anymore. She's got you now and I've never seen her looking so happy. Especially now you've got a nipper on the way."

Jacob grins at Malachi. "I'll get her to write to Lucy with the news. I know she'll be thrilled for us."

Bunny looks at her brother lovingly. "Would you like a boy or a girl, Jacob?"

"I really don't mind either way, as long as Clara and the baby are both fit and well at the end of it."

That evening, sitting with Clara on the sofa, before a roaring fire, in their cosy cottage on Camp Road, Jacob tells her about Lucy's letter. "Bunny's had a letter from our Lucy, telling us she's now betrothed to marry that Ethan she met on the ship. He seems to be a nice enough fellow and, like Mal, I'm relieved that she's someone to look out for her."

"Oh, that's wonderful, I'm pleased for her. She's far too young to be on her own."

"I knew you would be, but maybe we should let her know about our good news? I thought you might like to write back to her? She sends us her love in Bunny's letter, which was mainly congratulating Bunny on her marriage to Edwin."

Clara sighs. "I should have done so already but, as the birth's now imminent, maybe it's better to wait until we know if it's a boy or a girl and write then?"

"Good idea… She says they're busy building a house for themselves, out of the proceeds they hope to make from constructing prefabricated flat-packed homes that her future father-in-law is sending out from Britain."

"My goodness that sounds very entrepreneurial."

"It does, doesn't it? But good for them." He wonders if he should tell her more. Perhaps it's preferable for it to come from him, rather than another. "There's something else, Clara. I wasn't going to mention it, but Malachi seems to think it won't bother you… In her letter she also mentions that Rupert has a child with his Khoikhoi maid, and they're openly living together, even though it's frowned upon. Lucy says she doesn't want to invite Rupert to their wedding, because she'd be obliged to invite his maid and she dislikes her. In fact, she said the maid's 'evil and untrustworthy'."

Clara turns to face him. "Oh my! I didn't expect that!"

"Does it upset you, Clara?"

She shakes her head. "No! Of course not, darling! I have you now and couldn't be happier. When we have our little baby, I'll be making my papa the happiest man alive. Just imagine how he'd be feeling now, if I was pregnant in South Africa and he'd never get to see the baby."

"You'll be making me the happiest man alive too." He kisses the top of her head.

CHAPTER SEVENTEEN *(January 1875)*

THE YEAR OF THE WOOD PIG

Aurora and Grace have been in Australia for a year and Grace enjoys her job in the post office and is walking out with the postmaster, Archie Woodbury. Relationships between the Davies and Thomas siblings are still frosty and both Bryn and Hugh are troubled by the ongoing situation.

"You'd think they'd have buried the hatchet by now!" says Bryn.

"Well, thou must understand that Gwyneth carried a torch for thy Rhys and when Aurora came along, all her hopes were dashed. Lewys similarly was attracted to the girl, only to be thwarted by his best mate. They're both feeling offended and the only way I can see it will be resolved is for them to move on and find someone else to set their caps at."

Bryn looks concerned. "I can see they're both hurt, Hugh." He thinks awhile. "Why don't we all go together to the spring festivities in the Lotus Gardens, this year? The Chinese Lunar New Year celebrations are always well supported and great fun for the young at heart. The Chinese diggers near to us, in White Hills, will be going in force with their contributions to the procession and all of the hundreds of Orientals from Kangaroo Flat, Back Creek, the two gullies, and Peg Leg will be there. It's fun and colourful, attracting crowds of all nationalities and Aurora and Grace will be seeing it for the first time."

"I think that's a grand idea. They might all make some new friends and widen their social circle."

On the afternoon of Saturday the sixth of February, the weather is hot and sunny. Lewys dresses in a cool, clean, white calico shirt, moleskin waistcoat and his coolest trousers. It's been a long time since both households have joined together for a social event and he's a little uneasy.

His father has arranged for everyone to meet early, outside the Joss House Temple, in order to get a good position in the Lotus Gardens from where they can view the festivities. He and his parents, Gwyneth, Freyja and Archie are all waiting there, when Aurora, Grace and Bryn's family arrive. They arrange themselves on rugs laid out on the drought-shrivelled grass, which will be their base, or meeting place. The ladies each have parasols and fans with which to cool themselves and, all in all, they make a colourful scene. When the processions commence, the younger ones can stroll alongside if they wish, but prior to this, some young Chinese men suddenly spring into action from behind the bushes with an impressive display of martial arts, accompanied with the sound of kettle drums.

"This must be the *kung fu kuosha*," says Owen. "I've been looking forward to this."

"Me too," says Rhys.

Lewys isn't that interested, but during the demonstration, he spies, standing in the wings, a group of chattering young girls, giggling behind their hands and all dressed in matching red and gold silk hanfus with their raven black hair pinned up with bamboo pins and decorated with red and gold artificial flowers. He's mesmerised by the tableau of youthful beauty. The tallest one of the girls catches him staring. She smiles and flutters her fan in a coquettish way; his heart leaps and he is smitten.

When the *kung fu* display is over, some tinkling oriental music starts up with Chinese lutes, *erhu* wind instruments, moon guitars, gongs and bamboo flutes, and the Chinese maidens commence their peony feather dance. Lewys is spellbound by their poise and gracefulness. They hold their large feathered fans in each hand, forming the most beautiful patterns and shapes, opening and closing the fans in fluttering movements, throughout the dance. He's never seen anything so wonderful. The others on the picnic rug are also enthralled, but he needs to find out more about the one who caught his eye.

When their dancing is concluded and the enthusiastic applause has died down, Lewys hears the gongs and drums of the dragon dancers, approaching along Bridge Street from the Ironbark camp. The young girls stand in line ready to follow the lads carrying the colourful head and long body of the *Sun Loong* imperial dragon, fixed to tall bamboo poles, as they twist and weave along Pall Mall towards the town centre, accompanied by strings of noisy firecrackers and squeals from pedestrians who get too close. Lewys is eager to follow them, but doesn't want to be rude, so he suggests to the others, "Shall we follow the dragon?"

Freyja, Owen, Aurora and Rhys all jump up to join him, but Gwyneth stays behind with the others.

Gwyneth says, "I'm too hot to move. Besides, the lion dancers will be along in a minute."

Lewys calls back, "We can catch them on our return."

Lewys keeps his eyes on his prize, as he follows the girls and is soon leaving the others behind. He can hear them chattering in their own strange language and wonders if she'll understand him. He catches up with them and bows to her respectfully. Tongue-tied, he grins inanely but eventually manages to ask her, "Do you speak English?"

She nods her head.

"What's your name?"

She smiles shyly and says, "Zhang Qinyang. What's your name?"

"Lewys Davies."

He points to the girls. "Are these your sisters?"

"No, I have brothers, these are girlfriends. My brothers were doing *kung fu kuosha xiǎnshì*."

Lewys plucks up the courage to ask her, "Will you walk with me?"

She looks horrified. "No, no, my brothers will not like."

Firecrackers snap at his feet and he jumps aside. The dragon sways close to them and he sees the layers of colour and the turquois fringing, as he's nudged out of the way. The Chinese operators are dressed in the same multicoloured silk material as the dragon they carry aloft.

Lewys wonders if the nudge was accidental. He frowns but persists in his quest to get to know Qinyang. "But I'd like to talk with you."

She is firm. "We talk now."

He concedes. "Where do you live?"

"We have house on Bridge Street, in the Chinese quarter, not far from here."

"I live on Myrtle Street with my sister and our parents and we have our goldmine, Bryniau Gwyn, in the White Hills. There are a lot of your countrymen working up there too. We also have two shafts in Eaglehawk, but Pa's partner runs those."

Suddenly the girls grab Qinyang's hand and excitedly pull her along Pall Mall; she looks apologetically at Lewys and he decides not to pursue them.

Aurora, Rhys, Owen and Freyja catch him up. "What have you been up to, boyo?" asks Owen. "We lost sight of you."

Lewys looks at Aurora. "I've just seen the most beautiful girl. She's Chinese."

Rhys asks him, "Did you speak to her?"

"I did. She even speaks English."

Aurora asks, "Do you think she likes you?"

"I thinks she does. It was her who was looking at me first, when she caught my eye, but she's young and innocent."

Owen sighs. "This won't work my friend. Not only are you too old for her, there's a huge cultural difference."

Freyja frowns at her husband and turns back to Lewys. "Did she tell you her name?"

"Yes, it sounded like 'Jong Cheen-yong'."

Freyja is horrified. "Oh no, Lewys! She's Zhang Wei's granddaughter! The apple of his eye. He'll never let you get anywhere near her."

Lewys sighs. "Zhang Wei, the opium king?"

Freyja nods her head. "Yes! Well he was, back in the day. He's more upstanding in society, now his family's growing, and he wants to protect them from criticism. But I'm sure his granddaughter will be expected to marry well among their own people."

Owen tells him, "She's probably betrothed to one of those *kung fu* fellows. You don't stand a chance, mate. Forget about her."

"I can't, Owen. She's bewitched me. I must try to see if she's interested. I can't just give up at the first hurdle."

As they wander back along Pall Mall, the five lions appear, and Freyja tells them, "They symbolise power, wisdom and superiority." They are in Chinese New Year colours for good luck, with traditional gold faces and red and green shaggy fur. They cavort among the crowds to the sound of the beating drums, clashing cymbals and melodic gongs. Lewys walks with a new spring in his step. *Nothing ventured, nothing gained. After all we're surrounded by symbols of good luck everywhere; surely it's not only intended for the Chinese?*

Freyja catches up with him. "Lewys, I've a few friends among the Chinese community, and I know the New Year celebrations continue for several days, with many celebratory meals shared, and traditions such as incense burned at the ancestors graves on the second day and dumplings eaten on the fifth day. It's also common to again shoot off firecrackers, to get Guan Yu's attention, thus ensuring favour and fortune for the year to come. But most significantly, on the fifteenth day, marking the end of the festivities, there'll be the Lantern Festival, where families walk along Pall Mall carrying lighted lanterns and candles are lit outside people's homes. It's similar to your Valentine's Day in that women are promenading in order to find a romantic partner."

"You think she might be among them?"

"She may well be. It's worth going along to find out. Although be prepared, Lewys. She might also be accompanied by her intended. At least you will possibly find out a little more about her."

"Thank you, Freyja, for not dismissing the idea out of hand."

"Well, I do feel it'll settle it one way or another, if she's already with someone else."

"Maybe… The way I look at it, you're Norwegian and Owen is Welsh, those are different cultures, but you married him and you both get along famously. Why should it not work out well for me?"

Owen overhears, as he draws up alongside them. "I'm not saying it won't, Lewys, but it's not only your cultures that are different, it's also your morals. Zhang Wei's known for his criminal activities. I don't think *your* parents will be happy with this union, let alone hers."

He sighs. He hadn't thought of that.

The following days drag, but Lewys is distracted from his daydreams on the thirteenth of February by a tremendous thunderstorm, breaking the long months of drought, but also flooding Bryniau Gwyn and giving him problems with pumping out the mine. Kangaroo Flat and all the lowlands around Bendigo are flooded, but at least the Myers Flat Reservoir's again at full capacity. A contributor of the *Bendigo Advertiser* was bemoaning the loss of this valuable commodity, as it soon drains away and is lost, for the want of more storage facilities. But Lewys is glad the floods have dissipated quickly, because he's looking forward to the Lantern Festival.

On the Monday in question, Lewys persuades his sister to go with him to witness the lantern procession through the town. It begins late afternoon so that the lantern lights will look most effective. They both dress in their Sunday-best outfits and make an attractive couple. Lewys feels that, with Gwyneth by his side, he'll appear no threat to Qinyang, or her brothers.

They join the milling crowds of Europeans, Chinese and indigenous people, strolling along Pall Mall, nodding to their acquaintances and admiring a troupe of acrobats and two men walking on stilts. They pass a handcart and a pigtailed man selling tasselled red lanterns. Lewys stops to buy one each for himself and Gwyneth. There's something rather romantic about the flickering lights of the lanterns and Lewys feels a shiver of excited anticipation run through him, as his eyes scan the crowds searching for her.

They must have been strolling along, back and forth, for about an hour before he espies her with an older woman. He says to Gwyneth, "She's here! Look, Gwyn, she's the lovely young girl in the gold hanfu with the red flowers in her hair. I think she may be here with her mother. There's no suitor, Gwyn!"

He makes towards her with Gwyneth in tow. He bows to both women saying, "Good day to you both. Happy *Shangyuan*."

Qinyang giggles at his pronunciation of the Chinese name for the festival.

He says, "This is my sister, Gwyneth." Gwyneth dips a curtsey and the two ladies respond.

Qinyang says, "How do you do? This is Ling, my mama."

Both Lewys and Gwyneth say, "Hello."

Lewys asks her, "Would you like a lantern, Qinyang?"

She smiles. "It nice for man to carry lantern. It get heavy."

"In that case, may we escort you?" He looks respectfully at her mama, when he asks this, and she nods her head in agreement.

"Does your mama not speak English?"

Qinyang smiles. "She may not speak it, but she understands most of it."

He smiles back. "I see."

As they stroll past the stores and homes along Pall Mall and back towards Bridge Street, they pass a China teahouse. Lewys suggests they stop for some refreshments. He's thrilled when Zhang Ling agrees. They hand their lanterns to the proprietor who takes them aside and they all sit together in the small Chinese teahouse and enjoy the jasmine tea and the tea-making ceremony.

The teahouse is strung, inside and out, with its own attractive red paper lanterns, decorated with gold trimmings and black Chinese writing. The table's laid with four, blue and white, tall, narrow porcelain cups, upturned inside four matching drinking cups, Chinese bowls (like ginger jars) of different teas, a kettle suspended over an oil burner to boil the water, a small clay teapot and a jar containing bamboo scoops and chopsticks.

Qinyang is pleased, because she knows Ying Yue, the young girl who's serving them, who uses her fan at the start of the ceremony and seems to do everything in slow motion.

Qinyang explains to them as the ceremony commences, "The porcelain cups are arranged in circle, and Ying Yue pours all four in one go, filling tall cups only halfway up, because believed remainder of cup filled with affection and friendship. Then Ying Yue passes cup to each of us, but you only smell it. That's right. Then you tap on table with finger, three times to thank her. Next she pours tea from tall cups into drinking cups and Ying Yue will ask you to smell empty tall cup. Finally, it is custom to drink tea in three swallows."

The tea is refreshing. Lewys watches Qinyang all the while she's explaining. The more he sees of her the more she bewitches him. During the ceremony he feels unable to chat, but after the ceremony's concluded, he begins to question her.

"Last time we met, I told you about the family business. Can I ask you, what's your family business?"

"We have market garden near Back Creek. Ma and I sell flowers, plants and vegetables. My papa also own brick kiln. My brothers make bricks and we trade locally and with Yee Hing Company."

Gwyneth also joins in the conversation with Qinyang, complimenting her on her costume and asking if it was difficult to get such exquisite material in Bendigo.

Qinyang replies, "We can order through Yee Hing Company, who trade directly with China."

Gwyneth smiles. "It's really beautiful."

"Thank you."

As they leave the teahouse, dusk is falling and they hear the sound of the lantern procession approaching; many Chinese adults and children parade past, with their lucky red lanterns held aloft. Lewys is pleased that they too have lanterns to show they're joining in.

They watch the parade pass by, then Lewys offers to walk the ladies home. To his delight Zhang Ling seems happy to agree to this. All the buildings along Bridge Street are displaying either red lanterns or candles for good luck. Lewys observes Qinyang's gold hanfu shimmering in the light cast from them, thinking she looks like a royal princess.

The sun finally sets and darkness falls. They say their goodbyes outside the Zhang family home and Lewys, not wanting to linger there, bows to the ladies and takes Gwyneth's arm.

Once they're out of hearing, he asks Gwyneth, "Do you think I might be allowed to see her again?"

She smiles. "Perhaps you should visit their market garden, next week in the pretext of purchasing some vegetables."

He asks, "What do you think of her?"

"She's charming, Lewys; but she's such a pearl, her father will be wanting a high price for her hand in marriage."

"Hmm… That gives me something to aspire to."

They stroll back home to Myrtle Street, in the ambient glow of numerous lanterns, having both enjoyed a new experience of Chinese culture and a pleasant afternoon.

It's the end of February when Lewys finally finds the time to visit the market gardens. He finds Qinyang with a large trug, harvesting vegetables and partially hidden between a trellised row of dangling Chinese cucumbers and a row of oriental pumpkins. She's dressed plainly in a simple, long, cream-coloured cotton tunic and matching slender underskirt, with her raven hair in a long thick braid down her back and topped with a straw paddy hat.

He reaches the place where she toils and bows to her. She holds her hands together at her waist and bows back in their traditional greeting. She seems pleased to see him, a dainty smile lighting up her face, although she modestly avoids eye contact. "Can I help you, Mr Davies?"

He holds out his wicker basket. "Yes please, I've come for some vegetables."

She puts down her trug. "We have good selection. What would you like?"

He observes the neat rows and chooses some rounded colourful vegetables. "I'll have one of each of these, and one of these."

She holds up her hand to hide her giggles. "You know not what you buying, do you?"

He grins. "Not really, but I'm sure my mama and Gwyneth will be able to find an appropriate receipt for them."

"They're gourds, good in stew, and eggplant can be fried, baked or roasted."

"I'd also like a watermelon, please, and what greens do you suggest?"

"Amaranth good, like spinach."

"That too, then."

Qinyang fills his basket with the items Lewys has chosen.

"Anything else?" she asks him.

"No, I think that will be all for now. Thank you."

They stroll back through a mass of orange daylilies. Qinyang strokes them as she passes. "These are to eat. We slice plump buds and cook in fry-pan, can also be dried and called 'golden needles'. Flowers and tubers also good."

"I'll take a bunch of those too. My mama will love them." He's not sure if she'll cook them, or admire them in a vase, but either way she'll be pleased. He watches Qinyang cut the stems of the lilies and hold the bunch out to him. She could be the subject of a painting; it makes such a pretty picture and he can contain himself no longer. "You know, Qinyang, I'd like to be able to walk out with you; do you think your parents will agree?"

Her quandary shows in her beautiful almond-shaped, deep brown eyes, which she lowers modestly. "I know not... Maybe?"

"Will you ask your papa, please?"

"I think better to wait, Mr Davies."

"Please call me Lewys."

"I not want them to prevent it, but I don't think Papa will allow. Better not to wake dragon, you understand. For my brothers will be vigilant."

"Perhaps we could meet in secret?"

She giggles nervously then lowers her eyes again. "I good girl, Mr Davies."

"No, no! I only wish to pay court to you, Qinyang. I'd never disrespect you. You'd be quite safe. Would you meet me this evening for a stroll around the lake?"

"Maybe… I try."

"Good. I'll be waiting for you at the southern end of Lake Weeroona at five of the clock. Please come, it will make me so happy."

"I try. Now please I take you to pay my mama."

On his arrival home he takes his purchases into the kitchen where he finds his mother preparing their supper. She gazes at him in amazement, not surprisingly as it's the first time he's ever bought her flowers. "These are for you, Mama. I'm told you can enjoy their beauty as they are, or if you wish, you can snip off the buds and stir fry them, with other vegetables."

"Oh my, Lewys, they bring the sunshine into the house; it would be a shame to desecrate them. I'll put them in a vase on the sideboard, where we can all enjoy them. Thank thee. To what do I owe this honour?"

"Can't I surprise my mother on occasion?"

"Well yes, of course, and I'm thrilled, but thou have never done it before."

"Well to be perfectly honest with you, I've met a girl who works in the market garden and it was an excuse to go and see her."

"Ah! That explains it!" His mother is studying him carefully. "What's she like, this girl, and when did thou meet her?"

"She's exquisite, Mama. I met her at the Lunar New Year Festival."

"Really! Thou haven't mentioned it."

"No, well it's early days." He strolls out of the kitchen as if the conversation's over, but he bumps into Gwyneth on the stairs.

"Pa was asking for you and I mentioned you were meeting a girl. I didn't think he'd be so interested, but he quizzed me. I told him I didn't know her name, but I'm sure he'll be asking you about her, as soon as he sees you."

"Why did you have to tell him anything, Gwyn? Now I'll have to come clean!"

Over supper, Lewys feels his father's eyes on him and it's not long before he asks him, "I hear thou have met a young lady, Lewys?"

He glances at Gwyneth. "Yes, Pa."

"Are thou not going to tell us all about her?"

He busies himself cutting up his meat. "It's early days yet, Pa."

"When did thou meet her?"

"At the New Year Festival."

His father looks at his mother. "We never saw her."

"No, she was with her girlfriends."

"Where does she live?"

"On Bridge Street."

His mother adds, "She works at the market gardens near there."

His father looks suspicious. "What's her name?"

Lewys inwardly sighs, bracing himself for the protests. "She's Zhang Qinyang."

His mother exclaims, "She's Chinese!"

"Yes, Mama. Gwyneth and I took tea with her and her mother during the Lantern Festival."

His father gives Gwyneth a dirty look and goes quiet. After a pregnant pause, he asks Lewys, "Am I to understand that thou are walking out with Zhang Wei's granddaughter?"

"Yes, Pa, but as yet, we hardly know each other."

His normally calm father raises his voice. "Well, everyone hereabouts knows Zhang Wei by his notorious reputation. Thou can't seriously be contemplating a romantic relationship with his granddaughter?"

He reasons with him, "You haven't met her, Pa. She's strikingly handsome with wonderful almond-shaped brown eyes and raven black hair, and she's clever and funny. I must be honest with you, Pa. I'm smitten, and I know you couldn't fail to love her, but she's also shy and I'm taking things slowly to start with."

"Saints be praised for that! Thou are too old in the tooth for me to tell thee what thou should or shouldn't do, but I advise thee to proceed with caution and, if thou can, to extricate thyself before too much harm's done."

"Surely you don't want to tar her with the sins of her father, or grandfather in this case? It's just not fair to judge her, when you don't know her."

"I know it's not only Zhang Wei who's dreaded, but all the men in his family – sons, uncles and nephews – they all belong to those Chinese secret societies that are so feared and revered in China. Thou really needs to give them all a wide berth."

"I'll think about your wise counsel, Pa, but currently we've only met a couple of times, so I'm sure you're worried about nothing."

"I'll simply say this, before we change the subject. I believe thou needs to consider that many lives were ruined in the past, due to her grandfather's opium dealings. I also suspect it was through Zhang Wei's dubious connection with Nathan Meakins that the Hanging Rock Gang were informed of the day our gold consignment was being taken into Melbourne. I'm sure thou will remember that the Hanging Rock Gang ambushed the troopers. Many were killed, and Nathan Meakins cold-heartedly finished off the survivors, making off with our community's gold."

"Well, there you have it in a nutshell, Pa. You've not blamed Aurora for the sins of her father, so why should you blame Qinyang? It seems to me, in that case, Nathan Meakins was even more dastardly than Zhang Wei!"

His father sighs in defeat but still has to have the last word. "Nevertheless, Lewys, regardless of her innocence, we don't want our family to be involved with those people. They've prospered on the backs of others. I can only warn thee, but if thou goes ahead, I'm sure there'll be trouble and unforeseen repercussions."

That evening, as planned, regardless of his father's warnings, Lewys decides to go to meet Qinyang. He pays good attention to his toilette; Freyja has told him that the Chinese people do not like perfumes or colognes and so he uses simple soap and dresses in his cleanest and best clothes.

He anxiously waits, fearful she'll not be able to come, but then he spies her walking through the trees, along the footpath, chaperoned by three of her girlfriends. His disappointment at not being able to see her alone is overwhelmed by his feeling of pleasure that she's turned up, wanted to see him and arranged this with her girlfriends.

He bows and they all respond politely. Then they set off, with her friends walking at some discreet distance behind them.

Freyja has tutored him in Chinese courtship, and he knows he mustn't even hold hands with her in public, so they stroll side by side, enjoying the tranquillity of the lakeside and the sounds of birdsong. With the background incidental music of a twittering fairywren, he tells her of their turbulent and terrifying passage from Wales to join their father and of how they built up their mining company.

He asks her more about her own family and she volunteers that her grandfather's a powerful man with influential connections, being a founding member of the Chee Kung Tong Society in Bendigo, who meet at the Golden Dragon Lodge, and her father's the Lodge Worshipful Master.

"He's kind to me, but strict, and I can't go against his wishes. My brothers also my minders. They members of Yi Ho Chuan Society; you may have heard of 'Fists of Harmonious Righteousness'. Emblem is clenched fist." She holds up her arm and clenches her fist to demonstrate.

Despite this information reinforcing what his father has warned him, he smiles. The gesture's supposed to represent force, but her slender limbs are far too feminine and inadequate for the task.

Lewys points out a sleeping koala huddled high up, in the cleft branch of a eucalyptus tree. As she looks up to see it, he wants to caress her slender neck, hold her hand, even kiss her, but he holds back, knowing it'll scare her off and scandalise her friends.

A pair of black swans glide across the waters of Lake Weeroona, making small wakes through the red and gold reflections of the sky and the setting sun.

The hour passes by too quickly and, despite his misgivings, he wants to enjoy her company again. He gazes at her with love pouring from his heart and asks her, "Will you meet me here again... Please, Qinyang?"

She lowers her eyes. "Maybe."

"Will you try to be here next Saturday at the same time?"

"I try."

He watches as she joins her friends and they link arms and go off chattering and giggling.

She's such good company. *What harm can it do?*

CHAPTER EIGHTEEN *(March–July 1875)*

THE BLACK FLAG REVOLT

Ethan, Lucy, Frankie, Kofi and Monty have settled well into Acacia Lodge. Ethan's only hidden worry is where he'll find the ready cash to pay for their wedding ceremony and a memorable wedding gift for Lucy. Hence he works long hours, trying to recoup some capital in order to fund another venture and invest in some more flat packs. It would be even better if he could repay their bond on the homestead. He's determined not to worry Lucy over these financial matters.

Frankie has made friends at his school and today has invited his best pal back to play. They've been crazily chasing around in the paddock, until Lucy suggests they calm down for a while before tea, so they're now playing Jacks on the lawn.

When Ethan comes home from work, after warmly greeting Lucy, he goes outside to meet their young visitor. Frankie introduces them. "This is Maghiel, my friend from school, Papa."

He's overwhelmed with emotion. This is the first time Frankie has called him 'Papa'.

He smiles. "Hello, Maghiel. I'm pleased to meet you."

The lad responds, "Hello, sir."

"So, who's winning?"

"I am so far," says Frankie.

He glances down at the heap of *klippies* piled up

near the old tobacco tin, beside Frankie. Could that be a glint of light in one of the larger stones? He picks it up for a closer look. He can hardly contain his elation. He looks through the other bright stones and one looks to be a garnet. He'll examine the remainder at some other time, but for now he asks Frankie, "Do you remember where you found this one, Frankie?"

"It was on the veldt at the back of Eureka Row. It's my favourite one."

"Well, can I tell you a secret?"

"Yes, Papa."

"I think you've found a special stone here. It may even be a diamond. If it is, do you think, if I replace it with another stone, we could use this one to buy your mama a special, secret wedding present?"

"Of course. What will we buy her?"

"I'll think of something very special and tell you, but we must keep it a big secret from your mama, so it will be a lovely surprise for her."

Ethan takes the stone and the boys continue with their game. On further inspection he's convinced it's a fine blue diamond, and heaven-sent. With this stone he should be able to buy a suitable wedding gift, a golden wedding band for Lucy and hopefully reduce their bond.

The following day he takes his melee pouch and his diamond belt along to Charles and Julius and he also shows them the stone. They calculate it weighs two point five grams in the rough and could produce, when cut, a five-carat diamond, which would be worth anything between £250 and £500, depending on clarity.

Ethan tells them, "I've studied the window with my eyeglass, and I believe it to be a good quality blue diamond beneath the kimberlite."

Julius looks at Charles and back at Ethan. "We don't know what we'll find, until we cut through its coating. How about we give you £350, allowing £50 per carat plus a further £100 because we're friends."

He grins. "We may be friends, Julius, but this is business and you know, as well as I do, £50 per carat is for the most basic quality diamond and this promises to be of the finest water. Plus, it's a good shape, and in the hands of an expert diamontologist, could be cut to a decent-sized gemstone. I think you can do much better. After all, you said yourselves that this size could be worth anything between £250 and £500. You're offering £350 and I believe it will easily make £500, so I think you need to up your bid?"

Charles says, "I can see where you're coming from, Ethan. How about £400?"

Ethan shakes his head. "I wanted £480… so how about we split the difference and call it £450?"

Charles looks at his partner with raised eyebrows and he responds by nodding his head. He holds out his hand. "As a friend, you drive a hard bargain, but seeing as you do a lot of business with us, we have a deal." They each shake hands to seal the agreement.

Ethan has since paid off his bond, secretly ordered the wedding gift for Lucy from Port Elizabeth, bought himself a fine gelding he's named Butch, and purchased for Lucy a cockerel called Poppycock and some hens. He's also fenced off a paddock for the horses, with a smaller area for the chickens, and has dug out vegetable and flower gardens for Lucy.

Lucy is preoccupied with planning their wedding, hopefully to take place sometime in August. It was unfortunately delayed, partly due to

McCallister setting the fire at Eureka Row and the ensuing court case, but also because Ethan's been so busy combining his *kopje-walloping* with his building projects. Now they can relax a little and concentrate on the ceremony. It's to be a small affair with only the residents of Eureka Row, Khumo's family, Hilda, Anja and Marta, and some of the MDU men attending.

Lucy discusses with Ethan where the ceremony should take place. "I know I swore I'd never enter that Dutch Reform Church again, but it's clear that only a church wedding will satisfy our neighbours in Hopetown, so I don't know what to do. There are no other churches in Hopetown."

"Well, there's a small, wood and iron church in Jones Street, in Kimberley. We could go there?"

"It seems a long way to travel for everyone." She imagines the perfect simplicity of it and then she has a brainwave. "How about your tin tabernacle, Ethan?"

He grins at her. "Why didn't I think of that? I think that's a grand idea and it'll be good for public relations too. I'll set the wheels in motion and speak to the reverend tomorrow."

A few days later, Ethan reads a report in the April edition of the *Diamond News* about Alfred Aylward and his followers. '*Upset about increased rent, high taxes, and unrest among the coloured workers, Aylward has encouraged the men to take up arms and form a paramilitary "Combined Diggers Protection Association". Comprising seven armed companies, totalling one thousand men, under the command of a war council, they've begun patrolling the streets of Kimberley; a black flag being the signal for his supporters to rebel. Aylward declared, "If I erect the English ensign with a black flag under it, I expect to see you with your rifles and your revolvers ready in the name of heaven and your country, to protect yourselves from injustice.'"*

He tells Lucy the news. "Apparently a hotel owner, William Cowie, has been arrested without bail for selling guns to Aylward without a permit, which has led to Aylward mounting their 'black flag' on a debris mound called Mount Ararat, the signal to revolt, in response to Cowie's arrest." He reads on, "*The rebels have blocked the prison, with a wall of three hundred men, to prevent the imprisonment of Cowie. Governor Southey's been forced to enrol two hundred extra white volunteers to help regain control. He's had all public offices sand-bagged, along with the powder magazine, police barracks, magistrates' court and legislative council room.'* Thus, it says, the governor's been forced to proclaim that '*Certain evil disposed persons to be in rebellion against Her Majesty the Queen'*."

"Oh dear. That sounds serious!"

"It does. I suspect they'll have to send for military reinforcements from Cape Town, before they can regain control, because the government forces are completely outnumbered."

Lucy sighs. "I'm glad we're not living in Kimberley, Ethan. People must be afraid to go about their lawful business, at the moment, especially the women."

"Well, I'm afraid I've no choice. I have to go there to oversee the final stages at Salisbury Fields."

"Oh dear. Do be careful, Ethan. I don't want you to get caught up in it."

"Me neither. But, having said that, I do believe Henry Tucker, one of the followers of Aylward, has already shown an interest in buying the last of the flat-pack homes."

"Well, I suggest you don't conclude an agreement, until you know what the outcome of all this will be."

By the end of April, just in time for winter's approach, all the stoves have been installed in the homes at Salisbury Fields. Ethan and Lucy are enjoying a candlelit supper, after Frankie's been put to bed. He tells her, "I'm glad to report that the last place has been handed over to someone who wasn't involved in the revolt."

"Thank goodness. It could have proved problematic otherwise."

"I agree, but now I can settle up with Johan and repay my father back with the proceeds. They've sold so easily, I've sent Papa a telegram to order a further ten flat packs from Mr Bellhouse, which means I now have three months to find another suitable site on which to build them, whether it be Kimberley, or one of the other diamond fields."

"I think that's an excellent idea, Ethan. It certainly seems to be working out well for you. Do you think Johan will lend you his apprentices again?"

"I'm sure he will, for a small inducement, but if not, I expect Khumo will know of some fellows who could do with the work; now I've helped with the first ten, I'm sure I can oversee the work of some uninitiated men."

By the time Ethan's in receipt of his second order of flat packs and has purchased land closer to them, on the outskirts of the Koffiefontein mine, the rebels have held control of the streets in Kimberley for ten weeks. Ethan's proved right; Governor Southey organises British troops from Cape Town to come to his aid and the redcoats arrive on the thirtieth of June.

They're a sorry, dusty, dishevelled sight, nearing the end of their 700-mile journey, as they march through Hopetown on their way north to Kimberley. Lucy stands to one side on the boardwalk, tightly holding Frankie's hand as they pass by, and one of the soldiers winks at Frankie. He waves back shyly.

The following morning seven of the rebel leaders are arrested and put on trial. Ethan informs Lucy, "It's reported in the *Diamond News* that '*the three ringleaders face charges of sedition, conspiracy and riot.*' However, after three days of hearing evidence, '*a jury of local men takes only twenty-three minutes to return a verdict of not guilty*'. The other four accused men are also acquitted."

Lucy looks over his shoulder and puts an arm around him. "Well, I suppose there are a lot of folk who don't agree with Governor Southey. He's very unpopular. Folk hate the power of his legislative council, especially as he has the casting vote and the right to veto anything he disagrees with."

"You're right, my dear, folk will always rebel at what they see as injustice, but we can't have such lawlessness here on the diamond fields; too many people are armed, and things would be sure to get out of hand. I'm actually quite relieved the troops are here to maintain law and order."

She sighs. "Hopefully, that's an end to it."

On a crisp morning in July, Lucy is inside busy polishing the dining room table when there's a knock on their front door. She's surprised because they don't often have visitors, especially early in the morning. It's the runner from the post office who hands her a telegram.

She delves into her reticule to find a sixpenny tip for him and then sits down, her heart racing. *Is it good news or bad?* Her hands shake as she opens the envelope and anxiously reads the words: *HENRIETTA ELIZABETH WARREN. BORN 10.30AM ON 9TH JULY. WEIGHING 8LBS 2OZ. MOTHER AND BABY FINE. LOVE CLARA AND JACOB.*

She breathes a sigh of relief. *What wonderful news. I've a new baby niece, named Henrietta after Clara's mother and Elizabeth after our own mother. They must all be so pleased.* She'd love to be there with them and see the little one. She's missing out on all the family celebrations. *Bunny will be next. Maybe one day, when we've made our fortune, Ethan will be happy to return to England once more.*

She sits down at her desk and writes a letter of congratulations to her friend and her brother.

As Lucy's loving thoughts travel the thousands of miles back home to Somerset, Clara nurses her sleeping baby and Jacob watches her adoringly. "It makes me so happy to see you with our baby in your arms, Clara. We're so blessed to be so happy."

"I've just got her off, after winding her for ages. Would you mind gently taking her and putting her in the cradle for me?"

"Of course."

She carefully transfers the little one into his arms. "There's so much to be done and so little time, but it's tempting to simply sit and nurse her."

"You don't have to worry, sweetheart. You need to recuperate, and you know I'll help you with any of the chores. Besides, Bunny will be here soon to do the washing for us, and Flora promised to send Toby up with some of her baking from the manor."

"I don't know how I'll manage when you're back at work."

"You'll be fine, my darling. Luke's mama is just along the lane, if you're at all worried. Louisa and Rosa will also be popping in to see you with all their news. All you have to do is care for Hettie. I can always prepare us a ploughman's, or cold meat and some of our own salad vegetables."

"You're a wonderful husband, Jacob. Would you mind if I was to go and have a stroll outside in the garden, to get some fresh air, while Hettie's sleeping? It's such a beautiful sunny day today."

"Not at all. If you wander near the vegetables make a noise and scare away those blooming rabbits, before they devour all our lettuce."

"I was thinking of picking some flowers to brighten up the place before Lou Lou and Rosa visit us."

"Good idea. I'll wash up the breakfast things, while you enjoy the sunshine."

Preoccupied, picking snapdragons, Clara hears someone walking along the lane. She looks up to see Luke peering through the hedge.

He says, "I thought I saw someone. May I come in? I want to show you something."

"Of course! How nice to see you, Luke. Come on round." She continues to pick more flowers, finding a few carnations and sweet williams; then Luke approaches and she leads him to their garden bench, set under Jacob's archway of honeysuckle.

"What's wrong, Luke? You look unsettled."

"I've written a letter to Aurora and I wondered if you'd mind looking at it for me; only I don't want it to sound bitter at all."

"Here, let me have a look." He passes her the sheet of paper and she reads it to herself, while he watches for her reaction.

> *Miss Aurora Dryer*
> *Brecon House*
> *Waratah Street*
> *C/O Bendigo Post Office*
> *Sandhurst*
> *Victoria*
> *Southern Australia*

> *14ᵗʰ July 1875*

Dear Aurora,

I am glad that you and Grace have arrived safely in Australia and that you are happy with your decision to emigrate. I am still very content working with Ambrose, although, of course, we miss Clara's proficient clerical contribution, now that she has married Jacob and is at home, looking after their little girl, Henrietta. Nevertheless, Miss Cavendish is enthusiastic and has settled in well as housekeeper and we are a cheerful team.

However, my main purpose in writing to you is to let you know that you no longer need to worry about my broken heart, because I have found a new sweetheart and I am no longer pining for you. I am walking out with Ruby Warren and she's a delight to me. She is loyal, thoughtful and kind and we have grown up together (just like we did, really). She does not know it yet, but I wish to spend the rest of my life with her, and when I am ready I will propose.

I hope that we will stay good friends and I wish you all the best of good fortune with Rhys and your life down under.

With fondest wishes,
Luke xx

"My goodness, Luke! I'm so pleased for you."

He smiles, his hazel eyes twinkling. "Well, just keep it between us for now. I don't want to jinx it, and no one else knows besides us. But what do you think of the letter?"

"I think it's fine. It won't do Aurora any harm to feel a little guilty, but now you've cast aside her guilt and freed her to be with Rhys, while you can feel free to enjoy your budding relationship with Ruby. I'm truly thrilled you've found happiness at last, just as I have with my Jacob."

"I knew you'd understand, because you too have had a previous love that didn't work out." He smiles. "We're a right pair, aren't we?"

She smiles back. "I just hope it turns out as well for you and Ruby as it has for us. I'd better go back inside and see how Jacob's doing with Hettie." She stands up. "You take care now and post off that letter to Aurora. I'm sure she'll be thrilled for you." She kisses Luke on his cheek and they part.

The following day, Louisa and Rosa arrive bearing flowers cut from the herbaceous border at the manor for Clara, and gifts for the baby.

The bouquet is huge. "Oh my, Lou Lou! Those put my snapdragons to shame!"

"I had Percy pick them for you. He's chosen well."

"Thank you. They're magnificent."

Jacob takes them from her, saying, "I'll put them in water."

Rosa rushes inside to see her new niece. "Oh, Clara! She's gorgeous, and I do believe my present will fit her perfectly." She passes her gift to Clara, admitting, "I've secretly been knitting this for you over the last nine months."

Clara unwraps the package, revealing a fine white woollen matinee jacket. She holds it against her cheek and feels its softness against her skin. "Thank you, Rosa. It's just what we needed. Isn't it, Jacob?"

"It's smashing, Rosa. Thank you."

Louisa steps forward. "And this is from me, Joshua and our family." Louisa hands her another beautifully wrapped gift and Clara carefully unties it, to reveal a silver-handled teething ring in the design of a lamb. Jacob smiles with pleasure at seeing they've chosen a lamb.

"Thank you, Lou Lou." She gives her friend a hug. "That's so generous. I'm sure that'll be a comfort to her in the near future."

While Clara tells the ladies all about the birth, still fresh in her mind, Jacob disappears and eventually returns with a tea tray and some refreshments.

Rosa assures her, "It gets easier with every child, Clara. It won't be so exhausting next time."

Clara pours the tea. "That's good to know. I have to admit to being frightened beforehand, because of losing my own mama when I was born. It didn't help either, appreciating how my papa was so terribly worried."

Rosa looks at her brother-in-law. "I hope Jacob was supportive. Considering his mama has had four babies, I hope he wasn't too dismissive?"

Jacob defends himself. "No, actually my experience as a shepherd means I know only too well how things can go wrong, but the majority of births are a joyous experience and Hettie was no exception. I know Clara was wonderful, because I was there helping the midwife, much to her vexation."

"You weren't?"

"Really, I was. I was far too concerned to be told to wait outside the door."

Clara holds out her hand to him. "I was so glad he was there. I was totally reassured by his presence."

Louisa is shocked. "Well, I never did! I can't imagine Joshua wanting to be present at such a time."

Rosa smiles. "Nor Malachi!"

CHAPTER NINETEEN *(August 1875)*

THE TIN TABERNACLE

One of the events Malachi would have wished to attend is his sister's wedding in South Africa. She's written to tell them all of her plans, but she herself will be missing them dreadfully on this most important day in her life. Her first marriage fades to insignificance, set against her overwhelming love for Ethan and her elation and delight to be promising herself to him for evermore.

On the cold, crisp spring morning of Sunday the fifteenth of August, she wakes up to Poppycock's morning alarm, followed by a chorus of hadeda birds, as they fly across the clear blue skies. She stretches languidly, savouring her anticipation of the day ahead. The house is quiet. Ethan has stayed overnight at Eureka Row with Bruce Robinson, and Frankie and Monty are still asleep.

Hilda Van der Merwe and her daughters, Anja and Marta, will be here shortly to help her to dress and braid her hair, before they travel together to the church. She looks with satisfaction at her wedding outfit hanging against the wardrobe; a sky-blue walking skirt, with a cream overskirt, printed with forget-me-nots and trimmed with lace, and a matching fitted jacket, with nipped-in waist and sixteen tiny pearl buttons to the neck. On her dressing table is a neat sky-blue, Marie Stuart styled bonnet, decorated with an artificial hummingbird and fine cream ostrich feathers, which Mrs Erasmus managed to order from Port Elizabeth.

She bathes and washes her hair, feeling refreshed and ready for anything. She dons her dressing gown and goes to wake Frankie who's sleeping still, with Monty lying on his feet.

"Come on Frankie. Today's the day you're to be our page boy. You must hurry and get washed, before Hilda arrives to do my hair."

She goes downstairs to prepare some crumpets for their breakfast, and by the time they're ready, Frankie is washed and dressed and downstairs with Monty.

Hilda, Anja and Marta arrive at around ten o'clock with a golden bouquet of Barberton daisies and gazanias that they'd promised from their well-established garden.

"They're wonderful, Hilda. They'll contrast beautifully with the blue in my gown."

"That's what I thought."

They go upstairs to complete her toilette. Hilda helps her by lacing her corset, and assisting her with her underskirt, while Anja prepares to do her hair.

After Anja has performed her magic and her hair hangs prettily in looped braids, they help her with her skirt, her printed overskirt, and with buttoning her jacket. She checks herself in the cheval mirror and although having been married before, and not feeling it appropriate to wear the traditional white gown, she still feels like a bride should in her cream costume with its pretty blue flowers and her fancy bonnet.

She helps Frankie change into his long white socks and white ruffled shirt, then his navy-blue, bloomer-style trousers and bracers and finally his smart navy-blue waistcoat.

"Oh my, Frankie! You look such a smart fellow," says Hilda.

Frankie looks embarrassed, but he can't help but grin.

Lucy says, "Come on, it's half past eleven; if everyone's ready, we should be making tracks." They all follow her. Anja picking up the bride's bouquet on the way.

Kofi has decorated Reckless and the cart, now pulled up outside the front door in front of Hilda's gig.

To her utter amazement Rupert stands beside it. She gasps. "What are you doing here?"

"I couldn't let you marry Ethan without being here to give my blessing. I'm sure my brother would want me to be his proxy and give you away, if you'll have me?"

She looks up at him in utter amazement, but only sees tenderness and kindness in his eyes.

"I never meant to hurt you, Lucy. Please forgive me?"

She takes his hand, allowing him to help her up into the gig. Anja passes her the bouquet. She smiles and thanks her.

Rupert says, "We're here to celebrate with you." Her heart sinks and she turns around anxiously, dreading the thought of her nemesis being there. Only to see Jack Penberthy waving merrily in Rupert's carriage and Hilda and her daughters climbing up beside him. She gives a thankful sigh. To her great relief there's no sign of Tamela.

Luigi has given him his closest shave ever and Ethan now confidently waits outside the tin tabernacle with his best man, Norman, and Jasper, Bruce and his other friends from the MDU. Some of the

MDU men are sharing a twist of tobacco among themselves. Ethan and Norman are identifiable as groom and best man, by their artificial, blue and white, bird of paradise buttonholes that Mrs Erasmus procured for Lucy.

Inside the tabernacle is a hive of activity where Khumo and his wife and children are helping Betsy and the other women put the final touches to the floral decorations. Roeli jumps and runs around with excitement at the thought of seeing his friend Frankie again.

Before Lucy's appearance the men all step inside the tabernacle, leaving the reverend, Mayhew, waiting outside to receive her.

On their arrival, Hilda, Anja, Marta, Jack and Kofi all file into the tin church. Lucy then makes her entry on Rupert's arm following Frankie and Reverend Mayhew down the aisle of the tabernacle, smiling at her friends seated on either side.

She notes Ethan looking back at her with love in his eyes and astonishment at seeing Rupert there ready to give her away. She's reminded of her last wedding ceremony at Sutton Bingham Church when Rupert was standing alongside Ashleigh, as his best man. *Strange that he should be playing a part in both events, considering what's happened between them since then. After the ceremony, the churchyard was a sea of snowdrops, and snowflakes fell all around them – truly a white wedding. Then, back at the house, Rupert announced his intention to travel to the diamond fields, and it was his absence that inadvertently led to Ashleigh's downfall.*

Although glad she found out the truth about Rupert and the child, she's still angry with Tamela for causing her to lose her baby. She prays, for

Ethan's sake, it's not too late to have a child with him. After all, she's not yet forty and it would be the perfect seal on their union.

The tabernacle is warm in the midday sunshine, but the reverend is droning on endlessly about all aspects of love, unnecessarily tiring for those expected to stand for so long. In between the prayers, they sing 'All Things Bright and Beautiful' and 'Give Me Joy in My Heart'.

Once the marriage ceremony is concluded, with the main members of the wedding party signing the register, Lucy is relieved and exhilarated to be able to file outside on the arm of her husband, into the fresh breezy air once more. Rice is thrown and there are congratulations all around. Frankie and Roeli run about in an unruly manner, but she's far too happy to reprimand them.

They gather in the pole tent, for the toasts and refreshments already supplied, prepared and laid out by Betsy and Mr and Mrs Bekker. Folk passing call out their felicitations and with plenty of beer, wine and Cape brandy, there's laughter and jollity for the rest of the afternoon.

Although circulating separately among their guests, Ethan, attentive and affectionate, looks after Lucy all afternoon, supplying her with plates of food and wine.

Hilda tells her, "You've got yourself a good man there, Lucy, and handsome into the bargain."

"I know, Hilda, I couldn't be happier. He's my soulmate. We've so much in common and get on so well together. I thank the Lord we both travelled to South Africa on the *Syria*, for, but for the grace of God, we may never have met."

The afternoon passes in a whirlwind of laughter, chatter and merriment, until it's time for the bride and groom to leave for their honeymoon. Ethan and Lucy are simply going home to christen their four-poster bed. Betsy and Norman have offered to let Frankie and Monty stay with them for a couple of days. It gives the lovebirds some special time together and Frankie's happy with that, because he can spend time with Roeli.

They say their farewells and prepare to leave. Kofi brings the carriage around for them, only to discover the native children have conspired with Frankie and Roeli to tie all sorts of things on to the back of it. Lucy and Ethan playfully scold them but, as they drive off, they throw pennies behind, for them to chase after. They leave with a racket of tin cans and squeals of delight from the squabbling competitive youngsters.

When they reach home, Ethan hands her down from the carriage and they leave Kofi to deal with Reckless. Once inside, she removes her hat and unpins her hair, while he goes into the kitchen and picks up a bottle of bubbly to toast their wedding day. Then he takes her hand and leads her into their drawing room. There, in the light from the window, stands an ebony parlour grand piano with a matching stool.

Lucy can't believe her eyes. "Oh, my goodness, Ethan! How did you do that? When did it arrive? It's wonderful!"

Ethan grins. "Well, you actually have Frankie to thank for it. We've been keeping it a secret, but he found a rather good diamond on the veldt and I noticed it among his *klippies* a while ago."

"Really? Some of those were from Rupert's land. I did think some of them might be gems, but it had completely slipped my mind."

"Well, this one was his favourite and he assured me he found it at the back of Eureka Row on the veldt. Anyway, I managed to squeeze £450 out of Charles and Julius for it, so the Steinway's as much from Frankie as it is from me. He was excited to be planning a surprise for you. I'm amazed he's managed to keep it a secret. Johan's been looking after it for us and he and his men delivered it this afternoon."

She goes to cuddle him. "Oh, Ethan, what an amazing present!"

He strokes her arm. "Well, it's travelled rather unceremoniously overland across the veldt from Port Elizabeth and so I expect it'll need tuning, but it looks to have weathered the journey well."

She plays a few bars, loving the depth of tone, compared to her little old spinet at Home Farm. She kisses him. "It's magnificent, my darling. What a wonderful wedding present. Thank you so much." He returns her kisses, enfolding her in his arms, kissing her neck, her hair and her lips once more. Then he carries her along the passage to the master bedroom and the inviting four-poster bed, where two glasses are waiting in readiness, and he pops the cork on the champagne.

A few days later, when Frankie returns with Betsy and Norman, she shows off her wedding gift with an impromptu recital. She gives Frankie a special cuddle and kiss to say thank you for the surprise. In return, they've bought him a pregnant nanny goat, which he discovers outside with their chickens. He names her Heidi. From then onwards, Lucy involves Frankie in looking after the livestock. Frankie loves feeding Heidi and the chickens, and especially enjoys searching for the eggs each morning.

As the days go by, Ethan has organised the men with the flat packs and is also busy with his diamond dealing, but he does like to relax with his copy of the *Diamond News* and here he learns that *'Governor Southey has been severely criticised for his handling of the Black Flag incident. Military intervention has cost the imperial government in London £20,000. The Cape Governor, Sir Henry Barkly, has commented that he does not consider morality and justice to be worth such a high price and Governor Southey has since been relieved of his post'.*

He sits back and takes another sip of his Cape brandy. *Unforeseen repercussions!* He feels like someone has just walked over his grave, as a shiver runs through him. *It's nearly a year since Simon McCallister's court case and we still haven't had any response from McCallister senior; I wonder what devilment he might be planning?* However, he keeps his own counsel.

Back in Somerset on Camp Road, Clara now has a confident regular routine with Henrietta, a happy baby who feeds well and sleeps well, only disturbing them, on average, once during the night for her feed. No longer so fragile she now looks bonny and chubby.

Towards the end of September, Henrietta's asleep in her perambulator in the garden, with a fine mesh protecting her from bugs and flies and surrounded by Jacob's chrysanthemum blooms, when Louisa and Rosa visit again; this time bearing the ongoing news of the death of a man staying at the Three Choughs Hotel in Ivell.

They've hardly had time to sit down, before Louisa tells her about the sad tale. "Clara, do you remember when we were all sharing the book *Lorna Doone*, by RD Blackmore?"

She remembers it well. She'd found the story quite engrossing. "Yes, you mean the story set on Exmoor."

"That's the one. Well the man who died in the Three Choughs the other day, Henry Turberville, was using a pseudonym and he was actually the famous author's brother."

She's surprised and curious. "Well, I never did! What was he doing in Ivell?"

"He used to use the Three Choughs Hotel regularly on his travels to and from North Devon and he'd befriended Thomas Maggs, the local pharmacist and dentist. Apparently, Mr Turberville had had dinner with the Maggs family on the evening before he died, and when he returned to the hotel, he was in considerable pain. His condition caused concern and so the next day the hotel boots was sent to fetch the chemist from the Medical Hall, who gave him several remedies, but Henry grew worse. He told Mr and Mrs Sharland, the proprietors, that he'd been poisoned, so they called in Dr Aldridge, but despite all efforts he didn't improve. Mr Turberville seemingly also confided in the boots, saying, *'People are plotting against me. They want to benefit from my will.'* Then in the early hours of the morning, he was dead!"

She stares at both her friends. "Oh my! That does sound suspicious!"

Louisa continues, "Exactly! The post-mortem has since revealed traces of cyanide in his mouth and stomach. The inquest was held at the Three Choughs and having heard testimony from Mr and Mrs Sharland, the hotel staff, the doctor and the chemist, the coroner concluded that Mr Turberville was of unsound mind and had taken the cyanide of potassium with a view to taking his own life."

"What? Even though the boots had told them that Mr Turberville thought people were plotting against him?"

Rosa reasons, "They must have thought his illness had made him paranoid, but it's definitely suspicious. Anyway, since the inquest has resumed, it turns out that he'd not only fallen for the daughter, Elizabeth Maggs, but he'd actually proposed to her and made out a new will leaving around £19,000 to her and her family and naming Thomas Maggs as the sole executor."

She's flabbergasted. "My goodness, that's a fortune! But Lizzie never said anything to me about being engaged. I thought he was in his fifties and Lizzie's only twenty-three."

Rosa asks her, "Do you think that large sum's worth murdering for?"

She frowns. "What do you mean?"

"Guess who the pharmacist was, who prescribed the medicine for the victim?"

Her eyebrows raise. "Not Mr Maggs?"

"Yes!"

She shakes her head in disbelief. "Gosh, it does sound most irregular!"

"To say the least of it."

Louisa hands the copy of the *Western Daily Press* to Clara. "Look, with RD Blackmore being the famous author, it's even been sensationalised in the newspapers."

Louisa points to the comments. "Apparently, Mr Blackmore remains unconvinced, saying '*there were too many unhappy coincidences*' and that '*this was no clear case of suicide*'. He's since written, '*They say he poisoned himself. I say they poisoned him. Under his will he leaves all to the chemist in Ivell, whose daughter he fell in love with and who'd every motive to poison him.*'"

Rosa gives a deep sigh and a shrug. "Well, I must say that all of us Ivellians will be interested in the outcome of that dispute!"

Louisa responds, "Indeed… It's a sad story, though. For it must be dreadful for Mr Maggs and his family if he is, in fact, innocent."

Rosa adds, "And even more dreadful for Mr Turberville, if he was not!"

Clara refolds the newspaper and pushes back a loose strand of her hair, pushing those dreadful thoughts out of her mind. "It really is very unsettling!" *Maybe Lizzie turned him down and he did truly try to kill himself?* Then she pulls herself together. "Forgive me, I'm a dreadful hostess. I'll go and organise our tea and cakes."

Her hands are shaking as she places the teacups and plates on the tea tray. How could someone, living just across the borough from them, who's always in the past been so helpful to her and her papa, when they've needed medicine or dentistry, do something so horrific? She can't help but feel sorry for his poor wife, his daughter Lizzie and her seven other brothers and sisters who'll all be affected by this dreadful accusation.

She re-joins her guests and lays the table with the refreshments.

Louisa says, "This looks lovely, Clara. How did you ever find time to make the Victoria sponge?"

"Oh, it's much easier now that Hettie and I have a regular routine. I can get loads done while she's napping."

Rosa takes a sip of her tea. "Well, we actually have some more news, Clara. With all the excitement of the murder case, we forgot to tell you that Bunny and Edwin are expecting their first happy event."

She's thrilled. "Oh that's wonderful! A little one who'll be a playmate for Hettie. When's the baby due?"

"It'll be in the spring, around the middle of March next year."

Considerably cheered, she says, "That's definitely something to look forward to."

That night she tells Jacob the salacious tale. Shocked, like her, he says, "I'll order a regular delivery of the *Western Gazette* so we can keep a track of how the case progresses."

As the weeks pass by, they read the coverage, revealing that Henry Turberville was an eccentric personality, in the habit of making wills in favour of people or projects that interested him on a whim. His first will was to a shoemaker in Barnstable, called Henry Essery. The second was to create a statue honouring Shakespeare and the third left a considerable sum to the free thinker Charles Bradlaugh.

Jacob says, "What's a 'free thinker' when he's at home?"

Clara's thoughtful. "I understand the expression refers to someone who questions everything he's told by authoritarians and only believes what he knows to be true. In Mr Bradlaugh's case I think he's an atheist and isn't afraid to say so in parliament, which has led him into trouble in the past."

"So, do you think that Mr Turberville was an atheist?"

"I don't know, Jacob, but I suppose he knows the truth about the afterlife now!"

"Yes, I suppose he does." Jacob shakes his head sadly then continues to read, "It goes on to say that *'his last will and testament was made on the twenty-first of July 1875, leaving everything to the chemist, Thomas Maggs. Thus, the victim's brother, Richard Blackmore, Charles Bradlaugh and the other interested parties argue that it's invalid, being made only within days of his untimely death. They also dispute the coroner's verdict, believing Thomas Maggs murdered Henry Turberville, by administering drugs.'"*

"Oh dear, Jacob. I can't believe our friendly neighbour would have stooped so low as to murder a man in cold blood for money."

"I know; it doesn't bear thinking of. I don't know the family like you do, but I'm afraid many people reading these newspaper reports will believe there's no smoke without fire."

CHAPTER TWENTY *(January 1876)*

THE YEAR OF THE FIRE RAT

In January, Aurora receives a letter and a pretty Christmas card from her parents wishing all down under season's greetings and best wishes for 1876. She goes outside to sit in the shade of the macadamia tree to read the letter.

> *Miss Aurora Dryer*
> *Brecon House*
> *Waratah Street*
> *C/O Bendigo Post Office*
> *Sandhurst*
> *Victoria*
> *Southern Australia*

> *25th November 1875*

My dearest Aurora,

This is a short missive from me and your mama to wish you and Grace a merry Christmas, along with Hugh's, Bryn's, and Sam's families. I hope you are all well and happy and wish you all good fortune, prosperity and excellent health for the coming year, 1876.

Our family are thriving back here; Lydia May is growing up fast and a real chatterbox and Gabriel is doing exceedingly well with his law studies. Your grandparents are both in good health. Ambrose,

Clara and Jacob are the happiest I've known them, being blessed with their little baby, Hettie; and to Beth and Isaac's delight, Bunny and Edwin are also expecting a happy event in the spring.

I'm sure you've read the amazing news that His Highness the Khedive has sold his shares in the Suez Canal to Disraeli, instead of to the French, funded by the Rothschilds; our government agreeing to pay them two and a half percent commission. Disraeli has always been concerned with foreign policy and has done a grand deal and I thought you would find this particularly interesting, my dear, as we were in the very first convoy of ships to pass through it.

I hope all is going as planned with your sweetheart Rhys, and Australia is offering all you hoped for. We miss you dreadfully and pray every night for your continued safety and happiness.

Your loving Mama and Papa,
Gabriel and Lydia May.
xxxx

Their letter makes her feel homesick, reminding her of her first trip to Australia, when she felt so special to be travelling alone with her father. She misses the company of her siblings and the hugs from her mama. She recalls all the wonderful Christmases they shared over the years, the enormous tree they always decorated in the main hall, Flora's delicious sweetmeats and the fun of the huge Christmas dinners they traditionally shared with all the staff.

However, her joy of living with Rhys and seeing him daily overrides all these things. She sighs at the memories, but smiles at the promise of her future happiness, making a family with the love of her life. She folds up her letter and fans herself with it, thinking about their news of baby Henrietta, and Bunny's new arrival on the way, and she knows it would be her dearest wish to have a child with Rhys. They ought to be making wedding plans by now. Then a thought comes to her. *This year is a leap year! Maybe I'll propose to him on the twenty-ninth of February, according to tradition!*

Lewys has been meeting Qinyang regularly beside Lake Weeroona, respectfully chaperoned by her giggling girlfriends, but his whole being longs to hold her in his arms and show her how much she really means to him.

"When will I be allowed to see you alone, my treasure?"

"It not possible, *tián xīn*. My father never allow. We have to keep secret."

"But I want to tell the world. I want to marry you, Qinyang. I love you; don't you understand?"

"I do… I feel same, but my family never permit. We must make most of now, before they find out."

"But this isn't enough for me, Qinyang. Can you not persuade them?"

She hangs her head. "Maybe… Someday."

He grabs her hand and draws her out of sight of her friends, behind a large flowering Christmas bush. "Come, my *Qíng rén*, I want to kiss you. Please don't say no?"

He pulls her close to him, before she has a chance to duck away, and he kisses her full on her sweet rosebud lips. Although startled, she responds with desire and a fire is kindled between them. He's been so patient, but now it's settled in his mind;

he has to speak to her father before the New Year celebrations, then hopefully they may be seen together in public.

Three curious faces appear around the red bracts of the Christmas bush and he casually picks a sprig and tucks it into her hair. "See how beautiful she is," he says to her friends. The girls giggle and blush before continuing on their perambulation around the lake.

The following evening, having gone over his decision all day, he boldly walks up to Qinyang's front door and knocks. Zhang Ling answers. At the sight of her mother, his boldness dissipates. He clears his throat, nervously. "Good evening, madam. May I please speak with your husband?"

She nods and steps aside for him to enter their clean and uncluttered living room. He finds Qinyang clearing away their supper things. She looks horrified to see him. Her three older brothers are seated around their table, taking snuff and setting up a game of mahjong. Her father stands, as he enters, and waves a dismissive hand for Qinyang to leave the room. She glances back at him with fear in her eyes.

The men all wear traditional Chinese robes, with jade or ivory toggles, and have plaited pigtails. The father also wears a skull cap and has a straggly beard growing from under his chin, with two long strands of hair growing from either side of his upper lip.

He trembles, as adrenalin surges through him, but manages to pluck up the courage to speak. "Good evening, sir. Thank you for seeing me. I have a gift for you." He holds out a bottle of red wine and her father looks down his nose at it, suspiciously taking it and passing it on to his wife.

He says, "Thank you. How can I help you?"

"Well, I assure you I have the most honourable intentions, sir." He pauses, glancing at her mother. *The best way is to just spit it out!* "I wish to respectfully request your permission to walk out with your beautiful daughter, Qinyang?"

The father looks shocked and angry. "What you mean, 'walk out wi' my daughter'?"

His sons stand up behind him.

"I should like to be her escort at the New Year festivities?"

"Is not permitted! She destined to marry business colleague, not some *Gweilo*!"

One of her brothers steps forward menacingly. Her father continues to shout at him. "Get out my house. Don't go near daughter. Leave now, or sons thro' you out!"

"Please, sir, you must understand that I love and respect her. I'd never dishonour her, or your family. I wish to be betrothed to her and I believe she loves me too."

"This not true. You insult her with your lies. Get out! You never cast eyes on her again."

He steps back towards the door, his heart and mind racing. *What have I done? She warned me to keep it just between them! I'm an arrogant fool! I should have been satisfied just to spend time with her, now they'll be determined to come between us!*

The father slams the door behind him.

He wanders disconsolately in the direction of home, passing a grog shop on route and deciding to enter. He's hit by the aroma of beer and tobacco smoke, with miners and diggers of all nationalities laughing and joking and playing cards and dominoes.

A fat pot-bellied pig wanders around among them, snuffling and looking for snacks, but he sits alone in the corner drowning his sorrows. Finally, after several hours, he drags himself home.

Gwyneth has been concerned about her brother and his relationship with the Zhang family. Thus, when all retire to bed and he's still not home, she lies awake worrying and listening out for his return. She hears him enter just before midnight and goes downstairs to find him sitting with his head in his hands.

"Where've you been, Lewys? I've been so worried."

He hangs his head. "Oh, Gwyn, I've made a dreadful mistake!"

She can smell the alcohol and tobacco smoke on him. "You've been drinking to excess and Pa will not be pleased."

"That's the least of my worries."

"What do you mean… What've you done?"

"I've ruined everything!"

"Why?" She asks, exasperated with him getting into this state.

"I went to see Qinyang's father and he told me in no uncertain terms to get out and never to see his daughter again!"

"You really are a fool, Lewys! Whatever did you expect!"

"Don't rub it in, Gwyn. I know I've made an almighty mistake and I don't know what to do."

"Well, getting blind drunk isn't the answer."

"He told me she's destined to marry one of his business partners. He's probably an old goat and I can't bear to think of Qinyang being forced to marry someone against her will. They might even bring the marriage forward, because of my stupidity!"

"There's no point agonising over it, Lewys, especially when you're under the influence of alcohol. You need to sleep it off and sober up. You'll see it all in a new light in the morning."

The New Year celebrations on the twenty-sixth of January come and go by, but no one suggests attending. Lewys is lovesick, moody and bad tempered at work and Gwyneth has disclosed to her father that his relationship has ended. Hugh decides to confide in his buddy, Bryn.

"I don't know what to do with the boy. Every time I open my mouth he snaps my head off!"

"I guess we need to find him another woman," says Bryn.

"I doubt he's ready for that, Bryn. His heart is broken, and he needs to recover."

"How about I get my lads to take him out, so they can let their hair down?"

"That might help, my friend. At least it might take his mind off it."

Aurora's disappointed to hear of the planned 'lads' night out', but, a typical man, Rhys couldn't be happier to have an evening of drinking, joking and carousing, to encourage lovelorn Lewys to think of other things. He decides to ride into town and stable his horse at the Rifle Brigade Hotel; it being conveniently situated not far from their homes in the south of Bendigo, he can meet his brother and Lewys there. He plans to stay overnight with Owen and Freyja on Wattle Street.

He settles his horse in the hotel stable, looking forward to enjoying a few jars of alcohol with his brother and Lewys, and soon he spots them striding along the tree-lined Rowan Street.

When they enter, he buys the first round of ale.

They each have a couple of pints at the hotel and, leaving his horse behind to be collected in the morning, they set off to visit several grog shops on their way into the centre of Sandhurst. They end up in the splendid, regency-styled, Shamrock Hotel. The impressive interior stucco archways, and the rich carved oak wainscoted bar, give the whole place a grand palatial appearance. Here the upper echelons of Bendigo society are eating and drinking with their friends and thus the three men are on their best behaviour.

As they take their seats, he notices a large family group celebrating some important occasion. He hesitates. "I think we ought to move on elsewhere, before we order and get too settled; that's William Vahland, and his nearest and dearest. He's the fellow who designed this place and most of the important buildings in Bendigo. There are also a lot of other members of the Golden Lodge here too, who know our parents well. I think we ought to go somewhere else, less salubrious, to let our hair down. I don't think our fathers would be pleased if we besmirched our family names."

Owen suggests, "How about the Eureka? Jethro always makes us welcome."

Lewys laughs. "You mean the beady-eyed old fellow?"

He nods. "Yes, he's good friends with our pa and Angelica."

Lewys sniggers.

He stares at him. "What's that about?"

"Well, my pa let it slip, after a couple of brandies, that Jethro let Angelica have a room at the Eureka, before she got with Sam, and she used to pay her way by having gentleman callers."

"What!" he exclaims, with Owen echoing him.

"I don't believe it. He was having you on!" says Owen, aghast.

Lewys' eyebrows raise. "No, really. When she first arrived here, times were hard for a lone woman; I bet there's some truth in it. Pa would never have implied it, if it wasn't true."

Owen says, "Ah! Implied it, that's different. What exactly did he say?"

"I can't remember. It was ages ago and I'd had a few jugs too."

Owen is indignant. "Well, you shouldn't be spreading gossip, especially if you don't know the truth of it, Lewys."

"All right, all right, are we going, or what?"

They leave the building and wander along the boardwalk, down the gaslit street towards the Eureka Hotel, where they find a rowdy singsong in full swing and the noise reaches a crescendo as they open the saloon-style door to enter. They happily spend the next couple of hours there, chatting to the other miners and workers, and sinking a great number of ales between them, but this is no place to seek a woman. Not that anyone mentions that.

Finally, they are well inebriated, and the conversation dries up. Rhys suggests, "I think it's time we hit the road, lads."

They say their farewells to their drinking pals and exit via a meandering route. The stars are shining in a clear sky and Lewys seems in a better frame of mind. Owen decides they'll accompany Lewys to his house on Myrtle Street, before turning homeward themselves. They follow Pall Mall, until they can cut through to Bath Lane, then turn in to

Creek Lane. As they go, Rhys keeps turning back, thinking he can hear a footfall behind them, but he sees no one.

He can hear the trickle of water in the creek and smells the vanilla scent of the silver wattle growing in places beside it. He loves the smell of the fresh outdoors and is thinking of Aurora when suddenly two men leap out of the bushes ahead of them. They both take up *kung fu* poses and look menacing in the moonlight. He gasps with fright, knowing immediately who they are. They mean business and adrenalin surges through him.

He looks to Owen for inspiration, but they're all too inebriated to be in any fit state to fight. Creek Lane is narrow and deserted. Then he hears a noise behind them. They're trapped! He turns to defend them from behind, with his fists up in a pugilist's pose, and his opponent follows suit; but approaching him speedily, the Chinaman surprises him by stomping with his foot against his knee. He ducks down in pain but takes the opportunity of grabbing a rock for self-defence.

At the same time, he sees the two men in front of them spring into acrobatic action. The tallest one leaps forward, with a high whipping leg kick that hits Owen on the side of his head, knocking him off balance, towards the edge of the creek. Horrified, he sees the glint of moonlight on a silver blade, as the third Chinaman does an athletic leap towards Lewys and plunges the knife deep into his chest. Rhys springs up, lashing out desperately with the rock with all his strength, hitting the man senseless. He looks behind him ready for the other fellow to attack him, but somehow his brother regains his faculties, realises the urgency and remembers his pistol. He draws it from its shoulder holster, shouting angrily, "Stand still or I'll shoot the lot of you!"

The Chinamen freeze.

Owen continues, "You've wounded our friend and your man is down. I suggest we take care of our own, and call it quits." No one reacts, so he asks them. "Do you understand me?"

They nod their heads. They take that for agreement and he and Owen help Lewys to his feet. Supporting him between themselves, they struggle to carry him home. When they're out of sight of the Chinamen, they lower Lewys to the ground and plug the wound with Owen's clean handkerchief. He groans with pain and struggles to catch his breath.

"Do you think it's safe to move him, Owen?"

"I don't know. Maybe you should leave me with him and run and get his pa?"

"No. I'm not leaving you out here with him on your own. We must continue and hurry; he's losing a lot of blood and finding it difficult to breathe. If we don't get him home soon, I fear he'll die."

They try to lift him gently between them, but he cries out in agony, then goes limp. Rhys apologises, "Sorry, mate, but we've no choice; we have to get you away from here."

They struggle on until they reach the bridge and the slope up towards Myrtle Street. It's hard work trying to drag an unconscious man uphill, but they manage it. He's a dead weight and they fear the worst. Finally, they reach his home and they carefully lower him down onto the porch step. Rhys bangs on the door and they wait in breathless silence, until they hear footsteps approaching.

"Who is it?"

"It's us, Uncle Hugh. Quickly open the door. Lewys has been stabbed."

The door opens and a white-faced Hugh helps them inside. "Whatever's happened? Who did this? Would one of thou go for the doctor?"

Owen says, "I'll go. Where's the nearest one?"

Hugh makes an effort to focus. "On the corner of Londonderry Lane… Dr Thornberry. I think it's number two, but he has his plaque outside his house."

Owen sets off speedily.

Rhys then tells Hugh, "We were ambushed by some Chinese youths and one of them knifed poor Lewys. I hit the fellow over the head with a rock and we were able to leave them to try to get Lewys home safely, because they were tending to their own fellow." He looks at Lewys slumped on the sofa, making a gurgling noise as he tries to breathe and looking as white as a ghost.

His heart races. "Do you think he's going to make it, Uncle Hugh?"

"I don't know, lad." He strokes his beard. "It seems a harsh price to pay for falling in love!"

Lewys groans as he comes round. His father asks him if he'd like some water.

He shakes his head. "I think I've wet myself, Pa."

"Don't worry, son. Owen has gone to fetch the doctor."

Lewys whispers, "Am I going to die?"

His father shakes his head. "Of course not! Just keep talking to me. Try to keep awake until the doctor gets here."

With a huge effort he manages to say, "Please tell Qinyang I truly loved her, Pa."

"Thou must forget about her, Lewys. She's the reason thou are wounded!"

He stutters, "Not her fault, Pa… Her brothers to blame." Then he passes out again.

Rhys tries to suppress a sob. Then, to his horror, Gwyneth and her mother come downstairs.

Sarah exclaims, "Whatever's happened?"

Hugh replies, "Our boy's been stabbed. Owen's gone for the doctor, but I warn thee, it's serious."

Moments later the front door opens, and Dr Thornberry and Owen arrive, both out of breath from running. The doctor immediately takes charge.

Hugh takes Rhys and Owen to one side. "Thank thee for bringing our son home to us. We're grateful thou were both there to help him."

Owen wipes his eyes with the back of his hand. "We'll all pray for him, Uncle Hugh. Please wish him well when he comes round."

"I will. Thou take care now and hurry home." He gives them both a bear hug. "Please let your ma and pa know what's happened, for we won't be in to work tomorrow."

"I will, Uncle Hugh. I'm not going to stay with Owen now, I'm going to go straight back home tonight."

Owen looks at him. "No, you're not, we're sticking together. You'll be safer heading home in daylight."

He thinks about the lonely walk back to the Rifle Brigade Hotel and rethinks his plan. He turns to Hugh. "I suppose Owen's right. I'll tell them first thing tomorrow morning, Uncle Hugh."

They leave and walk home hurriedly and in shocked silence.

The following morning, after a terrible night's sleep, constantly interrupted with fearful nightmares, Rhys dresses and goes downstairs to find Owen telling

Freyja what had occurred. He can't bear to hear it all over again and excuses himself.

"I must go immediately and tell Ma and Pa what's happened."

"Won't you stop for some breakfast, Rhys?"

"No thanks, Freyja. I really couldn't manage to eat a thing at the moment."

Owen gives his brother a hug. "Take care, Rhys. We don't know how the Chinamen will react to the events of last night."

"I will, Owen. I won't be hanging around; I can tell you. I plan to run all the way to the Rifle Brigade, get my horse and be home in minutes. I promise you."

On reaching home, he stables Meredith and rushes inside nervously to see his ma and pa. They're having their breakfast. Grace and Aurora are yet to join them. His mother looks up, pleased to see him home. "Ah, you're back! Did you have a good night?"

He sighs deeply. "I'd so much like to say 'yes' to that, Ma. It started off well, but I'm afraid it all ended badly."

"Here, sit down. I'll get you some coffee."

"No, Ma. I need to tell you what happened. It's important. Please, you sit down."

His mother sits back in her chair, looking concerned.

His father takes over. "What's happened, lad?"

"Lewys has been stabbed by one of Qinyang's brothers and he's in a real bad way. We managed to carry him home between us, but he was bleeding badly and finding it hard to breathe. Uncle Hugh asked me to tell you that none of them will be in work today. We got the doctor to come out to see him last night, but it didn't look good, Pa." He runs his fingers through his hair in agitation. "I went home with Owen last night, to leave them in peace, but I'm so worried about him. I was too cowardly to call in this morning to see how he is, because I fear the worst, Pa." He breaks down.

"Come on, lad, don't let on so. It's not your fault they took against him. He was warned by his pa to leave well alone, but he was stubborn and that was his choice."

He takes a deep breath. "There's something else, Pa." He shakes his head and swallows the lump in his throat. "When the fellow stabbed Lewys, I was afraid he'd keep on attacking him, so I wacked him over the head with a rock... but I didn't see him get up again... I fear I may have killed him!" He puts his head in his hands, mumbling, "Although the *Chink* bastard deserved it. It could mean they'll be coming after me now."

Unbeknown to Rhys, Aurora stands in the doorway behind him, listening in horror to his ordeal.

"Hang on, lad. Don't jump the gun. I'll go now to Hugh's and see how Lewys is, first. Then we need to somehow find out how Qinyang's brother is. Maybe Freyja can help us there? After I've seen Hugh, I'll go to Owen's and see if Freyja has a contact who'll know the situation. You stay here with your ma, Grace and Aurora."

"It was so terrifying, Pa. It reminded me of when the bushrangers stopped our carriage when we first arrived here, and you handed over your great-grandfather's gold watch to save me! If Owen hadn't remembered he had his revolver with him, who knows what might have happened? They were like a well-oiled killing machine. Whereas our reactions were slowed, well-doused in liquor as we were! I had nightmares all last night. My mind going over and over what happened."

"You poor thing!" cries Aurora, before kissing the top of his head.

He spins around. "I didn't know you were there, Rora. Did you hear everything?"

"I heard enough, my love. It must have been a terrible experience for you."

"I'm so sorry." He shakes his head. "I'm afraid of what will happen next!"

Bryn gets up and puts on his boots. "Everyone stay indoors. I'll be back as soon as I know how Lewys and the Chinamen fare."

CHAPTER TWENTY-ONE *(January 1876)*

THE CHINESE VENDETTA

When Bryn returns, it's apparent to all that he bears sad tidings. His eyes are red and swollen and his expression solemn. Nell embraces him.

He clears his throat. "I'm sorry to have to tell you that Lewys didn't make it. He died during the night and his family are all in shock and devastated, as you can imagine."

His mother's eyes fill with tears. "Oh no, how terribly sad. I feel so bad for them all!"

His father continues, "I went afterwards to see Owen and Freyja. I'm afraid her Chinese friend has told her that the Chinaman also never regained consciousness."

Nell bursts into tears.

Aurora collapses into a nearby chair. "Oh my God, Rhys! How dreadful! Whatever are we going to do?"

He shakes his head in confusion. "I don't know… I can't get it out of my mind… poor Lewys… I can't come to terms with it… I know we have to get away, but I can't think straight… Perhaps we could go north, Aurora, to Queensland, to the Eromanga mineral fields? I could join the opal miners there."

His father shakes his head. "I realise the villains might be reluctant to follow you there, son, but you can't expect Aurora, nor the horses, to ride that far into the interior. It's too hot and dry there, that's why the miners and their families live underground. You'd need camels for that journey." He rubs his beard thoughtfully. "No, Rhys, Chinese secret societies are like a spider's web; one small disturbance can send rippling vibrations across the whole web, alerting all their members." He shakes his head. "To be sure of your safety, my son, I hate to say it, but you'll both have to leave the country and with haste, before Zhang Longwei and his sons are recovered from what's occurred and before the territory police investigate."

His mother protests, "Oh, no, Bryn! Surely there's another way?"

"I'm afraid not, Nell." He turns back to Rhys. "They'll never forgive you, son. You have to leave as soon as possible and avoid going through the town. You and Aurora must take the horses north to Epsom station and catch the steam train from there, back down to Melbourne. Her brothers will probably be checking Bendigo station, so you must keep out of sight, as the train passes through there. Go quickly and prepare yourselves for the journey. Owen will be arriving at any moment on Rhiannon and plans to go with you up to Epsom and then return with the horses."

Aurora looks horrified. "But where shall we go and what about all our things?"

Bryn tries to pacify her. "Don't worry. We'll send your personal possessions on to you, once you're settled. Where would you like to go?"

"Well, I don't want to go all the way back home. Besides Rhys would hate it there. As he said before, he needs to find prospecting work, don't you think?" She looks at Rhys.

He shrugs. "It's all I know."

Nell says, "I don't want either of you to go, but I want you both to be safe and so I have to agree with your pa."

Bryn says, "Aurora, I'm afraid you're as much at risk as Rhys, for once they focus on us, they'll surely discover you're related to Nathan Meakins."

Nell suggests, "How about going to your friend in South Africa, Aurora? To the diamond mines. It's in the middle of nowhere, so it'll be safe to hide there, but Rhys may well be able to find work there too."

Bryn agrees. "I think that's a grand idea, Nell. South Africa is a huge country and its vast mineral wealth is ripe for development. You'd be in the right place, my boy, and Aurora would have a friend to welcome her."

Aurora relaxes a little. "That's a good idea, Nell. Well done. It'll be another adventure for us; and Lucy, I'm sure, would welcome us both. I know she'd love to meet you, Rhys. What do you think?"

"I don't think we have any other choice." He turns to his father. "If you and Hugh agree to fund us through the company, Pa, we could widen the horizons of Brecon Valley Mines to another continent."

Bryn nods his head. "Don't look so worried, son. It'll all turn out fine. Fill the duffle bags with the bare minimum you can carry and make sure you pack your revolver. Aurora, leave your friend's address for us and we'll forward your things on, as soon as Grace and Alinta have packed them up, so they won't be far behind you."

He observes his son's stricken face, and adds, "Rhys, when you get to Port Phillip, try to get passage on a steamship. There's bound to be one travelling to the east coast of South Africa, most likely Algoa Bay, Port Elizabeth, from where we import our tobacco, cotton and sugar."

"I will, Pa." He sobs. "I'm so sorry about all this. I'd do anything to turn back the clock."

"It can't be helped. You were trying to defend poor Lewys. What's done can't be undone. You go and make haste, and in the meantime, I'll get some money from the safe for you."

Owen arrives and his father asks him, "While they're both getting prepared, would you mind saddling the other two horses?"

Although worried, he says, "Of course not, Pa," and goes straight back out to the stables.

Upstairs, while getting organised, Aurora explains to Grace what's happened. "If I hastily write a letter to my parents, would you post it for me?"

"Of course I will. I'll miss you though, Rora; we've become such good friends. I have to admit, though, I've been keeping a secret from you, which I must tell you now, before you leave. Archie's asked me to marry him and I've said yes. I was going to ask you to be my maid of honour at our wedding next summer."

"Oh, Grace, how wonderful! I'm so pleased for you both. It's a shame I won't be here for the wedding, but I know you'll be happy together. It actually makes it easier for me to say goodbye to you, knowing I'm leaving you in safe hands with Archie. I told you we'd find you a husband over here."

"I must admit, I'm really content working with him in the post office. You meet everyone in Sandhurst over the counter there and Archie has loads of friends, so I'll have an interesting life, thanks to you, my dear."

Aurora looks at her old governess affectionately and sees there are tears in her eyes. She hugs her.

Grace explains, "They're tears of happiness for my own future, but sadness at losing you and dear Rhys to another continent."

"Don't worry about us, Grace. It'll be such an adventure, and although we're running for our lives, as long as the damned Chinamen don't catch up with us, we'll both be fine."

She hurriedly packs a change of clothes, her washbag and her official paperwork, then she writes a quick note to her parents telling them they're planning to go to the diamond fields in South Africa to expand the business. She doesn't mention the Chinese vendetta. She'll send a telegram to Lucy when they reach the South African shore. "Would you seal it for me, please, Grace?"

"Of course."

Rhys calls, "Aurora, are you ready yet?"

"Yes, I'm just coming."

She goes downstairs wearing her leaf-green riding costume, with the duffle bag slung over her shoulder. "I'm ready."

"Here you'd better borrow this." Nell hands her a lightweight, circular cape, and fixes the hood with a hatpin, to hide her easily identifiable mass of copper-coloured hair. "That's better; we don't want to take any chances, and don't forget, you can use that hatpin as a weapon."

"Thank you, Nell. I hope I'll have no occasion to need that!"

"You just stay safe and take great care," says Nell, kissing her fondly. Then she sobs as she nearly hugs all the breath from her son.

"Don't worry, I'll look after him." She reassures her.

Bryn hands Rhys their wages up to date, plus a leather moneybag jingling with gold guineas taken from the company money in the safe. "Keep it secure, son. You'll need it to set up a business over there and to pay for your travels."

"I will, Pa. I'll miss you and Ma, and Owen, so much."

"We will miss you too, boyo. You can have no idea how much, but your safety is paramount."

"Please make sure to let Uncle Hugh, Aunt Sarah and Gwyn know how sorry we are to be leaving them at this terrible time and how devastated we both feel at losing our good friend Lewys."

"I'm sure they'll understand the position you're in, lad, but I'll give them your message."

There are tears and hugs all round as Rhys and Aurora make their farewells. Then they go outside to the stable, where Owen has the horses saddled and ready to go.

Mounted and prepared to flee, they wave goodbye and are soon galloping overland towards Jackass Flats and the Epsom railway station. They arrive breathless, wary and exhilarated. Rhys helps her dismount and Owen emotionally hugs them both in turn, making a hurried goodbye lest they should be seen, before they watch him riding away, leading Meredith and Rhiannon back home. Then Rhys and Aurora set off with their duffle bags to get tickets to Port Phillip, Melbourne, and another adventure of freedom and discovery.

Rhys is vigilant as they enter the station, checking the passengers for any Chinese faces and keeping close to Aurora. He's relieved to see there are few passengers waiting and all have European features.

The train approaches and trundles to a halt, and he and Aurora board and find an empty carriage. He sits in the corner in the shadows, beside the small window, and Aurora sits beside him. "Keep your hood up for now, Rora," he says, "At least until we pass through Bendigo, and look away from the window, so they can only see the back of your hood from the platform. I'll sit back in the corner here and keep watch, just in case they're checking out the station."

Aurora whispers, "I suppose that will be the most dangerous point on the journey. If they're there and spot anything suspicious, they may board the train and we're done for."

"Don't worry, I'm sure they're not yet organised. They've lost one of their brothers and will have to organise his funeral. I'm sure that will be their priority at the moment, but just to be on the safe side, we must remain vigilant."

As the train pulls into Bendigo Station, Rhys takes hold of Aurora's hand and squeezes it. Aurora finds it hard to turn her head away from the danger, but she knows Rhys keeps watch from the shadows. He tenses, as a Chinaman walks along the platform and peers into the carriages. He resembles the brother who stomped on his knee and Rhys feels for his revolver. Then he observes the man leaning back against the station wall, having not seen the fugitives, and the train continues on its journey.

"You can relax now, Rora. We're on our way. The Chinaman didn't see us. I expect he was looking for a lone man anyway and your presence beside me was enough to put him off the scent."

"Oh, Rhys, we've such a risky unprepared journey ahead of us, with no passage booked and no place to stay overnight. I must admit I'm rather anxious about it all, but mostly about the Chinese vendetta against you. What if they catch up with us?"

"Please don't worry, darling. We've acted swiftly. They'll still be in shock at the loss of one of their men. Much like poor Gwyn, Hugh and Sarah are, over their boy and our good friend, Lewys." He pauses, thinking sadly of his partner in business and his lifetime friend… He clears his throat and continues, "It'll take time for them to get organised and by that stage we should hopefully have escaped from Australia and be at sea."

The journey seems interminable and this time there are no kisses in the tunnels, because Rhys wants to keep his wits about him. Finally, they reach Port Phillip and he checks the station platform before they emerge cautiously. He's worried when he spots a group of young Chinamen huddled around the P&O booking office. Are they looking for them? They could be staking out the place. They're too far away to be able to identify them.

He diverts Aurora away from them, walking with a prominent limp in the hope that they'll resemble an older couple from behind.

"Don't look back, Rora. There are Chinamen there."

"Why are you limping? Are you hurt?"

"No, it's my disguise! I want them to think we're older."

She giggles and he's glad she's not as anxious as he is. Then salvation. He points. "Look, there's a steamship unloading passengers further along in Hobsons Bay. Maybe we can at least escape along the coast, rather than hang around here and be caught."

"Good idea, but don't forget your limp in your haste."

Rhys hobbles along the beach road beside her towards the jetty. "It's the Adelaide Steamship Company. They'll take us west to Adelaide then we can get another ship from there. At least we'll be away from here." He looks back and sees with relief that the Chinamen haven't moved. "We're not being followed."

"Thank the Lord!" says Aurora.

They go to the ticket office and purchase one-way tickets to Adelaide on the *Flinders* then wait patiently before joining the queue of folk being ushered on board by the stewards. They find themselves a comfortable seat.

Rhys says, "You can relax now. We're much safer and I'll find us somewhere to stay when we get to Adelaide, until we find a ship to take us to the Cape Colony and a new and exciting life together." Calmer now, he cuddles and kisses her, whispering, "I don't know what I'd do without you, Rora. You mean the whole world to me."

She kisses him back. "Me too," she says.

Just before sunset, Aurora and Rhys arrive at North Parade Wharf in the Inner Harbour, Port Adelaide, two days later. It's been an interesting journey, sharing the *Flinders* with another ninety-odd travellers, and Rhys has questioned the helpful townsfolk of Adelaide about their next destination. It seems the best place to stay is the Port Admiral Hotel on Black Diamond Corner and as soon as they disembark they make their way to that establishment. Aurora walks arm in arm with Rhys, as they cross a rickety wooden bridge over the Port Adelaide River, towards the settlement. She's relieved the tension's unwinding at last, away from the threat of the Chinamen.

Rhys says, "We'll sleep well tonight in the comfort of the hotel and make enquiries tomorrow morning, about a date for our possible passage to the Cape Colony."

She whispers to him, "I'm looking forward to sinking into a soft feather mattress, after the disarray of our escape."

He responds equally quietly. "I think we're going to have to pretend to be a married couple, Rora, and share a bedroom. Otherwise you'll be considered a loose woman."

"But I don't have a wedding ring."

"Then you'd better keep your gloves on."

She giggles. "Well you'd better keep your breeches on!"

He looks at her and they both laugh out loud. "I'm not going to take advantage of the situation, you may rest assured, but I'm not saying it will be easy for me."

"My darling, don't think it will be easy for me, but there'll be plenty of time for lovemaking, once we're settled, and for you to make an honest woman of me. It wouldn't do for me to arrive at Lucy's house in an interesting condition." She goes on tiptoe and kisses his cheek.

They reach the corner entrance of the hotel, where a carriage is just departing and several horseman are going about their business. Rhys opens the door for her, and they enter into the hotel foyer. Aurora removes the hatpin and her cloak and looks around at the other guests milling around the reception desk and the bar area.

Rhys registers them as Mr and Mrs Thomas and the porter shows them to their room.

He hands Rhys the key. "Supper's between six and eight o'clock, sir."

"Thank you." Rhys tips the man and closes the door on the world outside. He looks at Aurora, needing reassurance. "The room is sparsely furnished and functional, but at least it's not moving."

"It's perfectly fine, sweetheart," she replies, kissing him lightly on his lips. "It's just wonderful to have you all to myself."

After they've both washed and changed out of their dusty outfits, into the rather creased alternatives they draw from their duffle bags. Aurora's delighted to discover she can step outside onto the wrap-around balcony and look out to sea. "When we've eaten our supper, how about we bring our drinks up here and watch the world go by?"

"Sounds good to me. Although I don't think it'll be long before my bed's calling for me. Nightmares robbed me of sleep on the night Lewys was killed and since then we've been travelling."

They are served *wonga-wonga* pigeon with bread sauce, roasted potatoes and *warrigal* greens, followed by treacle pudding. They're both hungry and eat the platters clean. Rhys orders some ginger beer to take up to their room and they're soon back upstairs, settled on the balcony and enjoying the fresh sea breeze.

"How long do you think it'll take us to get to Hopetown, Rhys?"

"I don't know, darling. Once we get our passage booked it will be easier to estimate, but I'd guess it'll be about two months by sea, depending on the conditions and then the journey overland, which also might take several days, if we have to go by stagecoach."

"Well then, let's raise our glasses to a successful voyage and a propitious arrival, in good time, at Hopetown."

They raise their glasses of ginger beer, clink them together and drink to their impending journey.

The breeze gets up and the damp chill of night settles on them. "I'm beginning to feel a little shivery, and I think I'm ready now for a good night's sleep. How about you, darling?"

"Yes, me too. Come, let us snuggle up together. I'll soon warm you up." He has that wicked grin that's so attractive and as much as she longs to be held in his manly arms all night, she doubts her own self-control and her ability to subdue his ardour.

The following day they stroll along the river, from North Parade, smelling the seaweed and the mangrove swamp, further inland, as they pass by the different wharfs, now a hive of industry. Seabirds swoop and cry overhead, as they observe the large number of vessels, moored all along the river, being loaded with a variety of produce such as wheat, wool, wattle bark, seal skins, tallow, etc., all with their own distinctive smells.

In the distance, Rhys sees three tall chimneys. He hopes they're those of the copper smelting works and that the traveller on the *Flinders* was right when he told him they export to South Africa and they should be able to get passage on one of their vessels. The man on the boat told him that the English and Australian Copper Company's Wharf is along Gawler Reach and they make towards the chimneys.

They pass the sooty Coal Quay, Port Wharf and Prince's Dock. There's a tidal creek between the busy McLaren Wharf and Queen's Quayside (which has a faded sign for 'Fox Ltd & Co' painted on its warehouse). They cross the bridge on the other side, which links the McLaren to the Levi Wharf, and they pass Fletchers boatyard and slipway. They come to the Corporation Quay, sited opposite the Colonial Sugar Refinery Jetty, and hopefully, on the other side of the bridge, they'll find the Copper Company.

They pass under the bridge and, relieved, he cries, "Look, Rora! We've found it. Let's go and see if we can arrange our passage."

They follow the wall around the smelting site, until they discover a small office building at the back. They enter and request to speak to the manager.

A clerk asks them to take a seat. They wait for about ten minutes before the man materialises.

Rhys stands up. "Good day to you, sir."

They shake hands. "Sorry to keep you waiting. How can I help you?"

"We've been told that you export copper ore to the Cape Colony and we're hoping to get passage on one of your freight ships. We do have the guineas to pay for this service."

"I see. Well, you're correct, but our next consignment to Port Elizabeth isn't due to leave until next Wednesday. If you're happy to wait, I can reserve a cabin for you, but these are spare crew quarters and are pretty basic. For two of you sharing a cabin, I can do it for forty guineas all in, but I'd need a deposit of ten guineas up front."

"We accept, thank you. When do we need to be here?"

"We up anchor and embark at high tide around seven thirty, so please be sure to be here well before that."

"We will be, sir. Here's the deposit." He's sensibly separated his spending money from their main capital, and he hands the ten guineas to the manager, who gives them a receipt.

They shake hands and Rhys says, "See you on Wednesday at seven of the clock."

They wander back to the Port Admiral Hotel, knowing they have to book for a further eight nights, both thinking of the temptations they must resist.

CHAPTER TWENTY-TWO *(February 1876)*

THE COVERED WAGON

Towards the end of February, Khumo bursts into the office in Eureka Row, stressed and in a panic, looking for Ethan.

Ethan immediately says, "Khumo, my friend, whatever's wrong?"

"Roeli's gone, and six other *inkwenkwi* also missing."

"What?" Ethan jumps up and goes around his desk to give him his undivided attention. "When did you last see them?"

Khumo gesticulates madly towards the direction of the tabernacle. "They were in small group when *isifundo*s over and man seen to give them biltong."

He grabs his arm. "Come with me. We must go to the school and see if anyone has any information."

They rush through the busy noisy diamond field, with its myriad of smells good and bad, across the wide swathe of grassland, disturbing the crickets, until they reach the Idayimane encampment and the tin tabernacle that's been acting as the school.

The building's deserted. Ethan asks Khumo, "Where does the teacher live?"

"I take you to *Umfundisi*."

They go back towards the diamond fields and Khumo points out the brown, tented home of the teacher. After they call for her, she emerges from the tent. She appears to be middle-aged, upright and wearing a high-necked, navy-blue gown.

Ethan asks her, "Are you aware that seven of your charges didn't return to their families after school today?"

She looks horrified. "No, I'm not! I'm so sorry! Who's missing?"

Khumo names the children and she frowns. "I remember them all leaving together. They were taking it in turns with Roeli's hoop."

"Did you see anything out of the ordinary?"

She squints in the bright sunlight, concentrating. "Well, there was one thing that was different. There was a covered wagon, pulled up opposite the school, and a man was offering some of the children biltong. But I heard no shouts, nor cries for help. I didn't see any harm in it, but now you tell me some are missing… I suppose they could have unwittingly climbed into the wagon for a ride and then been taken, but who would do such a terrible thing?"

Ethan feels anger rising. "I think I've a likely candidate!"

Khumo looks at him, worried. "Who do this bad thing?"

"I think it may well be down to Mervyn McCallister's revenge." He puts his arm around his shoulder. "Don't worry, Khumo. I'm not going to let the bastard get away with it. We'll find Roeli and his friends. I'm summoning the MDU to help us."

Word soon spreads that children are missing and the MDU members need to meet at the Diggers Rest.

As soon as a dozen men have arrived, Ethan clangs Stefan's bell and starts the meeting. "I've called this extraordinary meeting because seven native children have gone missing and a thorough search has not resolved the situation." Silence reigns throughout the saloon, as Ethan gains their full attention. "I fear they may have been taken, either for ransom, or more probably for the illegal slave trade, by the likes of Mervyn McCallister." There's a rumble of mutterings among the men and when it grows quiet again, Ethan continues. "I understand there was a covered wagon pulled up opposite the school at the time, and a man giving out biltong to the kids. If this is the case, we need to track this wagon to work out its possible destination. They could have been taken to the coast to be shipped abroad for slavery."

There's a gasp of disbelief around the bar.

More men arrive as Stefan, the landlord, clears his throat and says, "I know the capture and exportation of slaves has been illegal for many years now, but I believe the trade with Cuba and Brazil still continues furtively."

Ethan says, "Well, time is of the essence; we need to get a posse together and chase after these villains. Which would be the most likely port they'd be heading for?"

Stefan shrugs. "It's hard to say. The Guineamen slave ships no longer operate along the Gold Coast, so the barracoons are all closed up, but now the prohibited trade has moved south to smaller inlets. They'll likely be travelling to Rio de Janeiro, or possibly Havana. The only possible ports I can think of are Port Nolloth or, further south, Saldanha Bay. If you can track the wagon's initial direction, it will tell you which port they're headed towards, but both places are about three days away."

Ethan scratches his head. "Does anyone know of a San bushman who could be our tracker?"

Khumo says, "I do, boss."

"Good, Khumo. Would you please hurry and find him? Tell him of the urgency and say he'll be well paid to help us."

"Yes, boss."

"In the meantime, all those with horses and firearms meet us outside the school at four of the clock. Wear your MDU armbands and bring your bedrolls, because we may have to sleep under the stars."

As the ragtag bunch of men assemble, Khumo arrives with the bushman. He calls him Mpho. Small of stature and dressed in his native attire, he seems honoured to be asked to help. Khumo and he share the same language and so he acts as interpreter.

Mpho studies the ground where the wagon was seen and picks up the wheel tracks. He tells Khumo it was pulled by four horses with no outriders and sets off on foot at a fast trot, with the mounted men following. Bruce and Ethan are both leading mules behind them for Khumo and Mpho to ride, once they establish their intended destination.

As they leave the settlement behind them, the trail seems to be leading them south across the Great Karoo and the thorn-veldt. Under different circumstances, Ethan would be admiring the view of the stripy zebra, elegant eland and red hartebeest scattered across the plains, but now he's only one thing on his mind: to get to the children before they reach the coast.

Mpho and Khumo are now astride the mules, Mpho believing they're headed towards Brits Farm, which suggests their ultimate aim is Saldanha Bay. A cloud of dust follows their trail as they hurtle across the veldt and the hot afternoon sun beats down on them. The track divides at Brits Farm, either heading towards Beaufort West or Carnarvon, and Mpho dismounts and studies the junction with care.

In the meantime, Ethan purchases some refreshments for the men at the farm, before Mpho decides the rogues are making for Carnarvon.

"Is he sure, Khumo? This is important."

"Yes, boss, he sure."

They all mount up and set off once more, passing some Khoikhoi tribesmen, herding goats and karakul sheep with their characteristic long flat ears and fat tails. Ethan acknowledges them as they pass.

They ride hard to reach Carnarvon before dark, because one of the posse told him the trail again divides there and Mpho needs to decipher the vehicle tracks, before they're obliterated by other wagons. They finally see the white church, surrounded by small round corbelled buildings and mountain karee trees, in the distance. Ethan sighs, relieved to make it just as the sun's setting. Bruce organises a flaming torch to study the ground at the junction. Mpho explains to Khumo that one of the larger back wagon wheels has a nick in its iron-banded tyre, which means he can distinguish it from other cartwheel imprints. He concludes their quarry have taken the westerly route towards Calvinia.

Ethan decides they should all bed down for the night and set off again at dawn. "I believe we're only about three hours behind them and will make up that distance tomorrow. Hopefully, their horses, between the traces of the wagon, will be finding it heavy going over this rough terrain, compared to our mounts galloping freely. Anyway, get some sleep and the first awake rouse the rest of us. I want to leave at sun-up."

While trying in vain to fall asleep, he thinks of Lucy and feels guilty. He should have organised someone to let her know what's happened, but he was in such haste to get the posse on the trail he didn't think. He's let her down and she'll be worried.

In the darkness, miles ahead of the posse, Roeli silently weeps. Huddled up against his friends, he tries to keep warm, but nevertheless he still shivers. His damp breeches are not helping. The lurching of the wagon was exhausting; at least his bony bum is no longer being jolted. Their guards are groaning, wheezing and snorting away, lying beneath him under the carriage. If he weren't chained with his friends to the side of the wagon, they could sneak away in the night. But it's no use; he'll never see his *umama*, *tata*, *usisi*, or *ubhutis* ever again and he's terrified. Where are they taking them? What horrors await them at the end of the journey? He doesn't want to go on a ship, especially without his *usapho*! They'd thought the men were being friendly, now he wishes he'd never touched the biltong. He didn't like it when the men shouted at them and started waving guns around when he and his friends were all thirsty. His hoop was chucked, by the nasty man, into the corner of the wagon. He thinks of Frankie and wonders what his friend would do if he were with them. Maybe he'd be brave like his *tata*, Ethan, but he'd surely miss his *umama* and Monty. Maybe he'd cry too, just like him. With that thought, the tears run freely down his salt and mucus-stained face.

Ethan has a restless night, listening to the background sound of the cicadas, the MDU men snoring, tossing and turning. When dawn breaks, he gladly gets up off the cold, damp ground, ready to go. They ride hard again that day, across the vast expanse of veldt, only broken by smatterings of aloes and termite mounds, but there's no sign of them. Doubts tear through him. *What if they've taken the wrong route and the kidnappers are, after all, on their way to Port Nolloth, further north?* They plough on regardless, on through the Hantam mountains, divided by deep river gorges, and across plateaus of colourful wildflowers, until they reach the settlement of Calvinia, built up beside the Oorlogskloof river. Again, they purchase refreshments from a farmer before setting off once more.

Ethan aches today, his body stiff from spending so long in the saddle and a night lying on the hard, cold ground. Although he and Butch are great pals, they're not used to riding so hard. They pass through small gorges of rocky terrain, from where baboons, defensive of their home territory, peer down at them curiously from on high. Then they reach a deep ravine, with granite slabs either side of them, the horses hooves echoing as they thunder through it. They emerge into the bright sunlight and ahead of them Ethan can see, above the heat haze, a vehicle moving across the plateau. He holds up his hand and the men halt behind him, still merging into the shadow of the gorge.

Bruce says, "Could that be them do you think?"

He replies, "We can't tell from this distance and we need to approach with caution, if it is. I think it'll be wise to wait until they're out of sight, before we break from the shadows."

They watch and wait until the vehicle is a speck in the distance, then set off again at full pelt across the plain. Buck and other game divide and scatter as they pass, until they reach another rocky outcrop and they rein in and proceed with caution. Ethan indicates to the men to draw their firearms.

Emerging from the gorge, they see their quarry less than a mile ahead of them, following the course of the Olifants River towards Clanwilliam. The river forms a wide ribbon of blue, meandering through the veldt. Ethan waves the men onwards, with their rifles and muskets at the ready. They surround the heavy wagon and, seeing the firearms and the MDU armbands, the driver pulls the six horses to a halt.

The man looks belligerent. "What the hell's going on here?"

Ethan speaks clearly. "I want your men to come out of the wagon with their hands up and no monkey business."

A woman cautiously puts her head through the front canvas opening and says, "It's only me and my children inside."

Ethan eases Butch forward and can see inside their travelling family home, three youngsters cowering in the back. He sighs. "I'm sorry to disturb you, and for frightening your family. You see, some of our lads have been taken for slavery and time's running out. Have you seen any other wagons on this route?"

The bearded man calms down and looks at his wife. "We did have a prairie schooner overtake us back on the plateau, didn't we, Sarah? Pulled by four horses."

Ethan looks at Bruce and Norman. "That must be them. How far ahead do you think they'd be by now?"

Again, he looks at his wife. "Maybe two miles? Being lighter they can travel faster than our Conestoga wagon."

Sarah replies, "Yes, I'd say so."

"Thank you. I'm sorry if we caused you any consternation, but I'm sure you understand there are innocent children's lives at stake."

"Of course. Don't concern yourself. May God go with you."

"Thank you." He turns back to his posse. "Come on then, men. Let's make haste." He flicks his reins and Butch is off at speed, with the rest of the group tearing along behind him.

Back home in Acacia Lodge, Lucy is concerned by the prolonged absence of her husband. She knows he sometimes stays over at Eureka Row, but she thought they'd agreed he'd come home last night, and it's unlike him to let her down without any word.

She decides to go with Kofi to the office to check all's well. They set off as soon as Frankie's gone to school. It's hot and sunny and Lucy has no reason to be downhearted.

They arrive at the office and Kofi jumps down to help her. She sees immediately that the office is shut up and a shiver of fear runs through her at the thought of the unspoken threat from Mervyn McCallister. She goes straight to see Betsy next door, leaving Kofi minding Reckless.

"Oh, my dear, Lucy, what a dreadful state of affairs."

"Why? Whatever's happened?"

"Has no one told you?"

Lucy shakes her head.

"Young Roeli and his schoolfriends have been abducted."

She's stunned. "What?" Her heart sinks and her head spins. "Where's Ethan?"

Betsy comes around the counter and takes her arm. "He's formed a posse and they've gone chasing after the kidnappers. My Norman and the boy's father have gone along. They left mid-afternoon yesterday."

"How did they know which way to go?"

"Khumo has a bushman friend, who offered to be their tracker."

"Oh God, Betsy, what will happen when they catch up with them? There'll most likely be some kind of gunfight and someone's sure to get hurt."

"Come on, Lucy. I'm sure the good Lord will not preside over you being widowed a second time. The important thing is they catch up with the villains and bring the children back home. None of the men gave a second thought to the danger, not even my Norman! Besides, they say there was only track marks for a wagon. There were no outriders, so their opposition will be outnumbered. I'm sure you should have no fear. Ethan isn't stupid. Anyway, now that you're here, come inside and have a lemonade with me, before you go back home. I'm afraid it'll be some time before we know the outcome."

"I would do, but I need to tell Kofi about his little brother. Can you spare some lemonade for him too? It will be a dreadful shock for him."

"Of course, please go and ask him to join us."

Finally, the prairie schooner's spotted up ahead and all follow the same instructions as before, approaching the wagon with caution, but swiftly surrounding it.

The kidnapper has a henchman riding shotgun and as soon as they realise they're surrounded, this fellow starts shooting randomly at them, but the carriage lurches over the rough ground and his shots go awry. Bruce yells, "Lay down your weapon or I'll shoot you." The man disregards him, continuing to fire, so Bruce carefully takes aim and takes him out. Ethan breathes a sigh of relief. Jasper and Norman ride alongside the horses in the traces, pulling them to a standstill, while the other members of the MDU all aim their rifles at the driver and wagon.

Ethan yells, "Come out with your hands up!" and he watches warily, as white, heavily tattooed hands appear to be untying the tapes of the back canvas. He rides around to face the back of the wagon and trains his revolver at the man. Then a rifle shows through the split. Ethan cautions, "Your pal didn't heed our warnings and now he's dead, so I suggest you don't try anything."

The rifle lands on the ground and the swarthy fellow's head emerges, hands in the air, he clambers down. The man, who sports a livid scar across his right cheek, is quickly searched for any other weapons by Tobacco Joe (one of the MDU diggers who constantly chews), then roped, with his arms behind his back. The fellow looks familiar, but Ethan's more concerned about the children.

He calls out, "Roeli, are you in there?" and he hears a small voice calling back, "Yessir."

"Are there any more men in there?"

"No, sir."

Ethan looks at Khumo with sheer relief in his eyes. "Your papa is here with us. Can you and your friends come out now, please?"

"We can't, Mister Ethan. We chained together."

Ethan gets the keys from the belt of the swarthy overseer, climbs into the wagon and unlocks the neck braces on each of the boys. They all in turn rub their necks, trying to ease the chafing.

Roeli's lifted down into the arms of his father and the two cling together. The six other children all are lifted, one by one, from the wagon so they can stretch their legs and have some water. Their faces, stained with tears and mucus, soon break into thankful smiles.

"We scared, Mr Ethan. They nice and friendly and give us biltong. They say, 'would we like ride?' And we say 'yes'. Then, when we inside, they drive off fast, not stopping until we gone far. They chain us... tell us we going in ship across sea. We scared and want *umama* and *tata*."

"Well, all's well again now, Roeli. We're going to take you home. You're all quite safe."

With relief and gratitude, in his eyes, Khumo says to him, "Thank you, boss. I never forget you save my Roeli's life."

The two kidnappers soon have their hands tied behind their backs and are shackled like slaves with the neck braces inside, towards the back of the wagon. Their dead colleague is draped over one of the mules with his feet and hands tied together under its girth, to keep him from falling off. Both mules are tethered to the back of the vehicle.

Khumo and Mpho take it in turns to sit up front and drive the wagon with the boys peering out over their shoulders. Safe in the knowledge that the tables have turned, and their captors are now unable to move, or harm them, they begin the long journey home.

Ethan wonders how they'll be able to connect this incident with Mervyn McCallister. The driver he doesn't remember, but he tries to think where he's seen the fellow with the scar and the tattoos before. Then it comes to him. *He was with McCallister that first night in the Idayimane encampment when they were intimidating the indigenous diggers. He's one of his enforcers. Maybe the police will be able to persuade him to talk and incriminate his boss, rather than take all the blame himself? I'll make sure the custody sergeant knows of the connection.*

CHAPTER TWENTY-THREE *(March–May 1876)*

RUPERT IS SUMMONED HOME

On the morning of the eighteenth of March 1876, Edwin sits downstairs in Stable Cottage with his head in his hands, exhausted from listening to the moans and groans emanating from their bedroom. The midwife has been up there throughout the night with Bunny for eight hours now; surely the baby can't be any longer travelling that short distance?

He contemplates going up and interrupting the proceedings to ask what's wrong. Then he hears the indignant wailing of his firstborn. He sighs. *Thank the good Lord for that!*

He rushes upstairs, calling through the bedroom door, "Is everything all right?"

"Everything's just fine, Mister Edwin. You have a handsome son."

He hears Bunny's voice. "Let him come in, Mary."

"Just give me a moment, child. I have to swaddle the little fellow and clear away the afterbirth first."

Finally, Bunny is tidied up sufficiently to satisfy the midwife and Edwin's allowed to step into the bedroom and see his baby son. Bunny sits up in bed, propped up against the feather pillows, cradling him in her arms. She's thrilled to see the look of wonder in her husband's eyes at his first sight of their tiny boy.

She smiles at him. "So, it looks like our baby's name will be Wilfred Lloyd Proctor."

Edwin grins. "Well yes, he doesn't look like a Millicent!"

Bunny giggles. "So, it will be Willie and not Millie after all!"

Edwin nods. "When he's little, but Will Proctor sounds good for when he's older, or he may choose to go with Lloyd."

"Don't you think he's beautiful?"

"I do. Look at his perfect little fingers, and he has some dark hair too. He's a handsome little fellow, no mistake."

"Would you like to hold him?"

"I don't know about that! I might drop the little man."

The midwife says, "The sooner you get over your fears, the easier it will be to bond with him. Here, you sit down in the nursing chair and I'll pass him to you."

Bunny watches Mary passing her treasured baby to Edwin and tears spring unbidden into her eyes, at the sight of him lovingly cherishing their boy. She knows it's hard work caring for a young baby, but she couldn't be happier that she's successfully delivered, hopefully, the first of many.

"We've produced your mum's first, and my parents' sixth grandchild, after Malachi's Ruby, Daisy and Eli; Lucy's Frankie; Jacob's Hettie, and now we have our Wilfred." She says proudly, "There's going to be a fabulous family celebration at his christening on Easter Sunday, because it'll be a joint one with Hettie."

Edwin can't take his eyes off his tiny baby, nestling in his arms, but eventually he says, "I suppose I ought to go and tell our parents the good news, but

I don't want to leave you by yourself, especially now the midwife's leaving."

"We'll be fine. He's been swaddled and suckled and if you carefully lay him in the Moses basket, while he contentedly sleeps, I'm totally exhausted and will be soon be sleeping too. Just don't be too long, love."

After settling Wilfred, Edwin sees the midwife out, muffled against the wind, and crosses the yard to the manor to find his mother and sisters. He enters the warm kitchen, smelling eggs and bacon, and the staff all cease clearing away the breakfast things and look at him expectantly.

Ellie nudges Hattie, who says, "Well, go on, then. Tell us what she's had?"

He scans the kitchen. "Where's Ma? I can't tell you all without Ma hearing it first."

Ellie says, "She's in her office." She calls out, "Ma, Edwin's here."

He hears footsteps on the flagstones and his mother appears in the doorway, an anxious look on her face. Then she sees Edwin smiling. "Well, is it a boy or a girl?"

"A little lad, Ma. He's gorgeous!"

There's a chorus of "Congratulations!" Edwin hugs his mother and sisters and then everyone else wants a hug.

Flora says, "What's 'ee weigh, and what's 'is name to be?"

"He was eight pounds and five ounces, and we're calling him Wilfred Lloyd Proctor. Wilfred after my pa, and Bunny and I both like the name Lloyd."

"Sounds like a name for someone important, lad," says the steward, Harvey Woodford.

Edwin grins. "Well, let's hope it stands him in good stead."

His mother asks, "How's Bunny?"

"She's fine, Ma. The whole process seemed to take forever, and she's exhausted, but she wanted me to come and tell you all. I'd better go now, as I don't want to be gone too long and I obviously want to go to Home Farm and tell Bunny's family too."

"Well done, Edwin. Please give Bunny our congratulations and best wishes."

"I will do, Ma. Thank you."

He rushes off, happy to be the bearer of glad tidings. The trees are swaying in the wind and the beautiful magnolia has a puddle of white petals at its feet, but at least it's dry.

When he arrives, he realises Clara must be there with Hettie, because he can hear a baby cooing and giggling as he enters the outhouse. Glad to be able to tell both families at the same time, he knocks on the back door.

Beth Warren answers the knock. "Ah! Edwin. What's the news?"

"You have another grandson, Mrs Warren."

"That's wonderful. Come on through. Jacob's here with Clara and Hettie."

He follows her into their parlour where he finds Hettie playing on the rug and Jacob and Clara drinking tea. She asks him, "Would you like a cup of tea, Edwin?"

"No thanks, Mrs Warren. I've only just popped round to tell you the news, then I must hurry back. I don't want to leave Bunny for too long."

Beth Warren looks at Jacob and Clara. "He's come to tell us that Bunny's had a little lad."

Jacob jumps up to shake his hand. "Congratulations, mate. How are they?"

"They're both doing well. He was eight pounds and five ounces, and we're calling him Wilfred Lloyd."

Clara stands up to kiss him. "Congratulations, Edwin. Please give Bunny our love."

"Of course, I will." He smiles. "Your Hettie's looking bonny. She's even crawling now. I bet she keeps you on your toes."

Clara nods her head. "Yes, she certainly does. We were just talking to Ma about the joint christening. Apparently, according to Rosa, Joshua has said we can use St Andrew's Church and then have the reception in the orangery. It should be a wonderful Easter celebration for us all."

Beth Warren suddenly says, "Oh, Clara! I forgot to say. Rosa mentioned that Colonel Seymour has been gravely ill since Christmas and they've sent urgently for Rupert to come home to see him before it's too late."

Clara looks concerned. "What's wrong with him?"

Beth replies, "Apparently he has heart disease, which is causing dropsy."

"Poor man. He and Helen have both found it hard since Ashleigh was murdered. I expect it's the trauma and anxiety that's caused it."

"Well, I don't wish the man misfortune, but it's because of that family that our Lucy settled in that God forsaken place, thousands of miles away, missing both your weddings and Hettie and Wilfred's births, and now we've missed her wedding too!" She finds her handkerchief and dabs at her eyes.

Jacob says, "Don't let on so, Ma. I doubt she'll be gone forever."

"But I miss her so, Jake. We were such good companions."

"You mark my words, Ma. She'll be back, sooner than you think."

Helen Seymour has had to ease off the laudanum to be able to cope with her husband's illness. His legs are so swollen it's too painful for him to walk and she's been forced to employ a nurse to care for his personal requirements.

Presently she waits on tenterhooks for Rupert to arrive. His telegram said that he'd be arriving on the twenty-fourth of March, thus she sits beside the front window, her eyes focused on the driveway. Finally, she hears the sound of the brougham rattling through the gravel and returning from the station, bearing her eldest son. She jumps up to go and greet him.

She watches Rupert leap down from the carriage before Robson has a chance to lower the step. Then, astonished, she sees him lift a small, tanned, wiry-haired child to stand beside him. Robson lowers the step for someone else to disembark and she's further astounded to see he has a black woman travelling with him! They stroll towards the entrance porch, as Robson begins to unload their trunks.

She opens the door and stands in the front doorway, stepping aside to allow the black woman to enter, with Rupert following behind her, leading the boy by the hand.

She finds her voice. "Well, this is a surprise, Rupert. I'd no idea you were bringing guests. Where's Lucy and Frankie?"

"Lucy's married a fellow called Ethan Hart. Has she not written?"

"Not for ages."

"Well, I believe they're both quite well and happy. Although I haven't had a chance to tell her about Papa. Anyway…" Rupert waves his arms flamboyantly. "Allow me to introduce you. This is my son, Berko, Mama, and this is Tamela, his mother."

The hallway spins. She gasps. "I need my smelling salts, Rupert. Quickly!"

Rupert flushes with annoyance. "Where are they?"

Robson says, "They're in the top drawer of the side table, beside her armchair in the drawing room, sir."

"Thank you, Robson."

She leans dramatically on his arm, and he leads her into the drawing room and sits her down in her favourite chair, carefully placed to catch the sunlight from the bow window, where she usually does her tapestry. She fans herself frantically and watches him searching through the drawer for the hartshorn.

"Here, Mama, take this." He holds the salts under her nose.

She snatches the bottle from him and sniffs at it haughtily. Recovering her composure, she says, "Well, this is a huge shock! Why've you sent no word to prepare us for such a revelation?"

He lowers his voice. "It didn't seem appropriate for me to tell you in a letter. Besides, I wanted you to meet Berko. You'll love him, Mama; he's such a clever little chap, considering he's only four years old."

She exclaims, "Berko! You've named the poor child Berko! What kind of name is that?"

"It means 'firstborn son'."

"Does it indeed. Well, I dread to think what your father's going to say about that. You'd better go straight up and prepare him. He's been looking forward to seeing you. I'm sure that's all that's kept him going these last few weeks. He's been terribly poorly. It's been such a dreadful strain."

She watches him leave the room and then she rings the bell for Gladys. Moments later Gladys enters. "Would you take this child and its mother down to the kitchen and ask cook to feed them, please, Gladys. Then go and make up beds for them in the servants' quarter."

She watches them, sheepishly following Gladys from the room, and sighs. *Whatever's the world coming to? Surely Rupert can't think his father's going to be happy that their hard-won estate will end up in the hands of a picaninny?*

Easter Sunday falls on the sixteenth of April, and the family celebration promises to be a memorable occasion for all. It's a beautiful spring morning with cherry blossom petals falling like snow, as Edwin and Bunny carry young Wilfred across the manor driveway towards St Andrew's Church.

The small holy building is filled with their friends and families and the main participants in the ceremony are gathered around the font. Jacob's brother, Malachi, and Clara's friends, Louisa and Rosa, are honoured to be chosen as godparents for Hettie. Edwin's sister, Harriett, and his friends, Toby Boucher and Bobby Tompkins, are pleased to bear witness for Wilfred.

The two babies, dressed in their traditional christening gowns, are both well-behaved during the ceremony, only reacting with shock when the Rev Phelps trickles water in the sign of the cross over their foreheads. The older children watch as the babies are baptised. Dressed in their Sunday-best clothes, they heartily join in the singing of 'All Things Bright and Beautiful'. Then they listen to the Rev Phelps Easter sermon, before finally singing Charles Wesley's hymn 'Christ the Lord Is Risen Today'.

Everyone seems animated as they file from the church to the orangery. Malachi has asked Mr Gosney to attend there, to take his tintype photographs, and Beth and Isaac are eager to be pictured together with all their children and grandchildren in a multi-generational tableau. Beth bemoans the absence of their Lucy and Frankie.

After the photographs, Louisa makes sure everyone's served drinks and Joshua invites Malachi to toast his brother's and sister's babies.

"Good afternoon, ladies and gentlemen. It's fallen to me, as uncle to both babies, to raise a toast to their future health and happiness. Thank you, Lord Dryer, for allowing our celebration to be held here, and Rev Phelps for his moving and inspiring service. I want to thank you all for joining us here today and call on, not only their parents, grandparents and godparents, but all those here present to watch over these children and help guide them on their journey throughout their lives. To teach them to know right from wrong and to grow up to be helpful and kind adults, following in the path of our Lord Jesus Christ." He raises his own glass. "Ladies and gentlemen, please be upstanding and raise your glasses to toast both precious babies, Henrietta Elizabeth Warren and Wilfred Lloyd Proctor."

There's a chorus of responses, then a hubbub of general chatter follows. The godparents hand over gifts for the babies, and there are hugs and kisses in return and cuddles for Henrietta and Wilfred. The whole room fills with merriment, as the other children run around excitedly dodging the adults in their haste.

Clara, Louisa and Rosa are sitting together looking out through the glass of the orangery onto the garden. Baby Henrietta's with her papa. Emily has served them some sandwiches and they're happily catching up on their news.

Clara asks, "Have you heard from Aurora lately, Lou Lou?"

"No, not since Christmas. But I believe all's well and she's settled into her work in the mine office. I think the relationship with Gwyneth and Lewys has also improved of late. How about you? Have you heard from Lucy at all?"

"We had a card at Christmas, but no letter, not since last year when she wrote to congratulate us on Hettie's birth, but she seemed happy, settling into their new home and planning her wedding to Ethan."

Rosa comments, "Perhaps we worry too much about our loved ones when they emigrate to foreign lands; they all seem to prosper, after all."

Louisa frowns and snaps, "It's all right for you, Rosa, you don't have a daughter living a million miles away."

Clara notices Rosa's chastened look and feels sorry for her.

Rosa apologises. "I'm sorry, milady, I didn't mean to upset you."

Louisa changes the subject, turning back to Clara. "Have you read any more about Mr Maggs' court case?"

She nods her head. "Yes, the verdict was suicide and I'm glad to say, for Lizzie's sake, her father was exonerated. Although Mr Blackmore's not at all happy about it and is pursuing the matter of the will in court. I don't think it goes to probate until August."

Louisa responds, "I'm glad for your friend's sake that her father got off, but I still think it highly suspicious, nevertheless. Especially considering the amount of money they'll gain from his will." She then turns to her lady's maid. "Rosa, I must say that all your children look very grown up and beautifully turned out."

Clara hopes Rosa realises that Louisa's attempting to make amends. She knows Louisa wouldn't normally bite Rosa's head off like that.

Rosa smiles. "Thank you, milady. Ruby will be twenty-one next year and looking at them together now, I think she's taken a shine to Master Luke."

They turn in unison towards the young couple, who are looking relaxed, chatting away together. Clara smiles, knowingly.

Louisa comments, "Luke does seem to be enjoying the attention. Maybe there's a new match in the making!"

Aurora's letter arrives at Alvington Manor in May. Emily delivers it to the oak on a silver platter, recognising Aurora's handwriting and knowing her master and mistress will be eager for any news from her.

Louisa sits down in an easy chair to read it.

Lord and Lady Dryer
Alvington Manor
Ivell
Somerset
Great Britain

Dear Mama and Papa,

I am writing to let you know that Rhys and I are leaving Australia to travel to the Cape Colony. Hugh and Bryn want Brecon Valley Mines to expand their horizons and Rhys wishes to prospect in the diamond fields for a change; thus, we will be diversifying. I hope that Papa agrees it will be good for the business. We should arrive in Algoa Bay, Port Elizabeth, by April or early May, but there will be no further news from us, until we reach the diamond fields around Kimberley. I wish to reconnect with Lucy and Frankie and hope to stay with them until we establish ourselves and are settled there.

Grace is happy to stay on here, as she's betrothed to her Archie now (the Bendigo postmaster) and is looking forward to being married next year. She sends you all her fond regards.

I hope you are all well and Hettie is thriving. She must be sitting up by now and taking notice of everything. Please give my love to Clara and Jacob and let me know as soon as Bunny has her little one too. In the meantime, kindly send any correspondence to Lucy's Acacia Lodge address.

Please send my love to Gabriel and Lydia May and to everyone else (including Luke). I love and miss you all so much, but life down under with Rhys is a revelation and the stimulation is unending.

I must close now as I have to pack for our journey. Please don't worry about us, Mama, we will be fine.

With fondest wishes,
From Aurora and Rhys.
Xxxxx

Horrified, she goes to find Joshua to tell him. She finds him outside talking with the gardeners. She calls to him, "Joshua, we've a letter from Aurora."

He finishes his conversation with Percy and Thomas and joins her on the terrace, where they sit down in the spring sunshine, with the scent of the wisteria and mock orange blossom wafting around them.

She somehow manages to remain silent while he reads the letter, until he gives a deep sigh. "Whatever are Bryn and Hugh thinking of, sending Rhys and Aurora to a strange and dangerous place like that, without consulting us, her parents? I'd never have agreed, had I known."

Louisa laments. "It was hard enough for us to agree to her to travelling all the way to Australia! When will it ever end?"

"It was slightly different her going to Australia, though, my love. At least I'd already invested in Brecon Valley Mines and I knew there were two kind families to look out for her welfare and a good civilised town had already developed around the gold fields, but to send two youngsters off prospecting with no family support like this is completely ridiculous!"

She shakes her head. "But I'm afraid it's a fait accompli, darling… It's too late to stop them now… The letter's dated the thirteenth of February… They must already be there… At least they know Lucy and Rupert."

He snaps, "For all the good that will do them, when they're trying to make a home and start a business in a foreign land!"

Louisa puts her hand on his arm. "I'm going to write to her now, offering our support, should they need it."

Joshua jumps up. "Well, I'm going to write to Hugh and Bryn asking them what they damn well think they're playing at!"

Back in his study Joshua picks up his dipping pen and writes:

Hugh Davies Esq
Brecon Valley Mining Company
C/O Bendigo Post Office
Sandhurst
Victoria
South Australia

8ᵗʰ May 1876

Dear Hugh and Bryn,
I have received a letter from Aurora telling me that she and Rhys are now in the Cape Colony prospecting for diamonds.
I am extremely disappointed that I was not consulted on this matter, as I would not have condoned such a dangerous mission for a young lady and her beau.
I trust there is a worthy business reason for this decision, and I await your explanation with interest.
Yours sincerely,
Joshua

He puts down his pen and heats the wax for the seal, sighing heavily. *What the devil were Bryn and Hugh thinking of, condoning such a reckless venture!*

CHAPTER TWENTY-FOUR *(February–May 1876)*

PORT ADELAIDE TO PORT ELIZABETH

Considering they're crossing the Indian Ocean, the voyage from Port Adelaide to Port Elizabeth is tedious and uneventful, apart from one memorable evening when Aurora and Rhys are standing at the prow of the ship, with the wind streaming through their hair, watching the sun going down ahead of them. Aurora asks Rhys, "Is it the first of March today?"

"No, you silly, it's the twenty-ninth of February, because it's leap year."

"Oh of course. I was forgetting." She smiles. "In that case, Rhys Thomas, you know the tradition, don't you?"

"What do you mean?" He looks down at her suspiciously.

She takes his hand. "I have a very important question for you, Rhys." She drops to one knee. "Having given up my homeland and travelling the globe to live the rest of my life with you, and loving you more than life itself, will you do me the honour of marrying me?"

He pulls her up into his arms and kisses her with a tender passion. Her eyes close as she enjoys the love flowing from him. They draw apart, and he says, "There's no question that I want to make you my wife, but I was hoping to prospect for our own special diamond to set in your engagement ring, before asking you."

"What a lovely idea, Rhys. That sounds just perfect."

"However, now that you've pre-empted me, I'm delighted to accept your proposal and will be truly honoured to take you as my beautiful and adored bride."

They kiss and cuddle together, standing arm in arm, looking ahead towards a sunset of pink and purple stratums of colour, dotted with small fluffy clouds edged in gold.

Weeks later, Aurora finally glimpses land ahead, with the soft curve of Algoa Bay drawing them closer to the safe haven of the harbour. Along the waterside and up the sloping hill beyond it, she can see a prospering town with church spires, dwelling houses and buildings of every design and architecture.

The westerly wind caresses her face as they approach the harbour. Once anchored, Rhys thanks the captain for their safe delivery and pays the remainder of their fares, and they descend from the deck down into the lighter, which will deliver them to the jetty. Rhys drops his duffle bag and holds out his hands to help her into the smaller boat. She jumps down into his arms and he kisses her.

The lighter takes them to one of two landing jetties where Rhys assists her onto the dry land of the Cape Colony. Here they find warehouses, stores, factories, shops and offices. Aurora is especially excited to see this well-established, busy town and eager to spend her wages on some fashionable clothes to take with them across the Karoo and into the hinterland. She doesn't want to meet Lucy and Ethan still wearing the clothes she's travelled in.

On Jetty Street they spot the Eastern District Railway Station and Rhys goes to enquire if there's a train travelling to Kimberley or thereabouts.

The man says, "I'm sorry, sir, the train only goes as far as Addo, currently, only a fraction of the journey. I'm afraid the railway construction's been slowed considerably by the Cape Fold Mountains."

"Never mind. Thank you for your help." He turns to Aurora. "I think we ought to get a Cobb Stagecoach instead, Rora. There's not much point going on the train to Addo, only to find there are no coach companies there to carry us onward to Hopetown."

"I agree, darling, but may we not stay here overnight, so we can purchase some more outfits and a trunk? I really want to have a hot bath and I need some clean garments to put on afterwards."

"All right, look, let's wander around the market square. I've already noticed the telegraph and post offices over there. I think we ought to send a telegram reassuring my parents that we've arrived safely, and another one warning your friend, Lucy, we're coming."

"Of course, and there's an impressive coaching hotel. We can see if they've a room for us."

"Where?"

"There, look. The Phoenix." She points. "It looks to be quite respectable and we can get the stagecoach from there too." She puts her arm through his. "Come on, let's send the telegrams first." They enter the post office building and Rhys finds a pen and paper for Aurora to write down their messages, before going to queue at the desk.

That done, they go around the edge of the market square to the hotel. The square itself is a sea of wagons and fearsome wide-horned bullocks.

The carts are heavily laden with a variety of goods and produce, such as bales of white, washed wool, animal skins and ivory.

They skirt around it, until they reach the hotel, and Rhys books them a double room, again in the name of Mr and Mrs Thomas. Aurora would prefer to immediately bathe and wash her clothes, but she must first find some alternative outfits to change into, so they go back out into the town to shop instead.

After being confined to the ship for so long, they enjoy a leisurely stroll. They pass the impressive town hall with its beautiful portico of Corinthian columns and wander along Main Street, noting the Guardian Insurance Buildings, the warehouses of Dunell, Ebden and Co, and Mosenthal's Wool Merchants, until they find, next door to the London and South African Bank, Kettle's Emporium with some attractive costumes in its window and they step inside to choose some stylish outfits that will be suitable for their onward journey.

Back at Acacia Lodge, Lucy's suffering from a sickness bug and is still in her dressing gown when there's a knock on the front door. The post office runner stands before her, holding out an envelope, and she hurriedly goes to find him a sixpenny tip. She closes the door and backs into the nearest chair. Concerned for her family back home, her nausea intensifies. She anxiously breaks the seal and rips open the envelope to see the words: *ARRIVED PORT ELIZABETH 5*TH *MAY. COBB COACH TO HOPETOWN 7*TH *MAY. HOPE TO STAY WITH YOU? EXPLANATION WHEN WE SEE YOU. AURORA AND RHYS.*

She's stunned. *Oh my goodness! What will Ethan make of this? I hope he doesn't mind my friends descending on us. But what a lovely surprise! To see Aurora after all this time and to meet her Rhys. It's wonderful! I'll have to prepare the guestroom for them. They're leaving Port Elizabeth on the seventh of May and it took us around four days to get here, so they should be with us by the eleventh.*

She goes down to her old room and makes up the bed for them, hoping they'll be happy to share. She assumes they must be married by now, otherwise why would they be travelling together? The room looks out onto their back garden where Lucy has planted a central bed of hibiscus, birds of paradise plants and several varieties of roses and grasses, which look wonderful in the summer, but are bare of foliage currently.

Beyond the flower bed is the fenced off area for the chickens and in the paddock, at the south of the plot, she can see Heidi, their long-eared nanny goat, and her two angora kids named Hansell and Gretel, who are at this moment jumping on and off an upturned empty bucket. She smiles at their antics, knowing that Heidi needs milking and they all need feeding, but then the awful nausea again. *I wish I could get rid of this annoying tummy bug.*

She dresses lethargically. Luckily, Kofi has taken Frankie to school for her. *He'll be back soon, maybe I could ask him to milk Heidi and feed the chickens instead?*

She goes along to the kitchen and makes herself a cup of ginger tea; she can't face anything to eat. She actually feels quite lonely when Ethan's at work; she also misses popping next door to see Betsy. It's fine when she's busy, but when unwell she misses her family around her. *It'll be so good to have Aurora here and we can reminisce together over old times. As long as I can get rid of this blasted sickness bug!*

She hears Kofi and goes out to ask him to feed her livestock and milk Heidi. He's happy to oblige, and she goes back to her bedroom to lie down for a while.

She wakes to find Ethan and Frankie looking down at her with concern. Ethan rests his hand on her forehead. "Are you still feeling unwell, my love?"

"Oh no, please don't fuss. I'm fine, Ethan." She gets up. "I was just feeling rather exhausted, after making up the spare room earlier, and I must have dosed off. I'd no idea of the time. I'm so sorry I haven't even prepared the supper."

"Why have you made up the guestroom?"

"Because, my dear, we're going to have some visitors." She finds the telegram and shows it to him.

"Well, that's very interesting, but who are these people?"

"Surely you remember me talking about my friend Aurora, who's Lord and Lady Dryer's adopted daughter, and how she emigrated to Australia to be with her sweetheart, Rhys, whose family own a gold mine over there?"

"Ah yes, I remember you receiving a letter from her."

"That's right. Well, I don't know any more than you, as to why they're coming, but I'm sure you'll like them both, so I hope you don't mind them staying with us for a short while."

"Of course not, darling." He ponders for a moment. "They must be planning to set up here. After all, you don't travel all this way simply to visit."

"Well, perhaps they're diversifying and want to prospect for diamonds, as well as their gold... Maybe their gold reefs in Australia are dwindling?"

"Maybe. But, my dear, I'm more concerned about you at present and I think I ought to take you to see Dr Forbes tomorrow."

"No, really, darling, I'm sure it's just a silly tummy bug. It will pass soon enough."

"All right, but in the meantime, you rest, and I'll prepare our supper."

She knows she can look forward to bratwurst, with their own hens' eggs, and bacon, followed by pancakes, which are his favourites and the only things she believes he can cook. She actually feels starving again now and that will perfectly fit the bill.

Rhys and Aurora finally descend from the stagecoach outside the Cape Karoo Hotel in Hopetown. Travel weary, Aurora looks around her, noting the difference between the well-established gold mining town of Bendigo and this small, quaint prospectors' town, with its dusty carriage way, wooden boardwalks and corrugated shop buildings, sporting different coloured shutters and awnings. A man approaches them and introduces himself.

"Good day to you both. I'm Ethan Hart, Lucy's husband." He and Rhys shake hands and then he takes up Aurora's hand and kisses it, before saying, "Welcome to Hopetown. I understand you're to be staying with us at Acacia Lodge."

Aurora feels embarrassed and a little uncomfortable. "Thank you, Ethan. We'd both be grateful if you could put us up for a few days until we find our feet here. I know it's a cheek to arrive practically unannounced. I hope you don't mind?"

"Not at all. Any friend of Lucy's is a friend of mine. You're both welcome, I assure you. I have to say, Aurora, I've not seen Lucy so excited since we received your telegram."

She smiles at him. "We're also thrilled to be here and eager to see Lucy and Frankie again."

She continues to elucidate as Ethan helps Rhys load their new trunk and duffle bags onto the carriage. "We've so much to explain about the unforeseen circumstances that led us to travel to the diamond fields and try our luck in a completely new venture. It was a momentous decision, but we were unfortunately forced to leave Australia and our choice of destination was obviously influenced by the fact that my friend Lucy's here."

"Please don't worry about a thing. You're here now, and Lucy and I aim to do our best to help you to settle here with us until you're ready to move on."

Rhys climbs aloft and helps her up into the seat beside him. They set off at a trot and she remains quiet, busy taking in their new surroundings.

Lucy's in the front garden tidying a flower border when they arrive. The carriage pulls to a halt, and she sees the familiar mass of red hair and freckled smiling face. She drops the trowel into her trug, removes her gardening gloves and crosses the driveway, eager to greet her friend.

"Oh, Rora, how wonderful to see you." They embrace and then she turns to Rhys. "And you must be her legendary sweetheart I've heard so much about. It's marvellous to meet you and have you both staying with us." She picks up one of the duffle bags. "Come inside and let me show you around, so you can get your bearings. Then we'll have supper and you can enlighten us as to what's brought you here."

Aurora carries her own duffle bag and Rhys and Ethan carry the trunk between them.

Inside, Frankie's lying with Monty on the rug, doing a dissected map puzzle of Africa. He looks up shyly as Aurora and Rhys walk in.

His mother tells him, "Frankie, this is Aurora, my friend from Ivell, and this is Rhys, her…"

Aurora helps her out, "My fiancé. Actually, as it's leap year, I proposed to Rhys on the ship and we hope to find our own diamond here, for an engagement ring."

Ethan says, "Congratulations! This is a further good reason for us to celebrate in addition to your arrival. I'll look out another bottle of bubbly for later."

Lucy says, "Congratulations indeed," and kisses her friend again. "I'm so pleased you're here. We've so much to talk about."

Aurora wearily pushes her hair back off her face. "You've no idea, Lucy. It'll take all night!"

"First, I'll show you to your bedroom." She glances back at Aurora. "I hope you're both happy to share?"

"Of course, we are. We'd little choice on the journey here." She whispers, "We pretended we were married, but even so, Rhys has been the perfect gentleman."

"Well, Ethan and I have been in a similar position; things are definitely less formal on the diamond fields, but I warn you Hopetown is far more judgemental."

Aurora says, "Thank you for helping with the trunk, Ethan. We bought it and filled it with some new clothes while we were in Port Elizabeth. We'd only the contents of the two duffle bags up until that moment. Grace and Nell are organising some more of our things to be sent on here; only we left in rather a panic."

Although concerned, Lucy calmly says, "I suggest you both unpack your things, while I give Frankie his tea and put on our supper. Then you can finally relax and tell us all."

Rhys says, "Thank you, Lucy. This is a wonderful place you've built here, and we're truly grateful to both of you for letting us stay for a few days. You've no idea how much it means to us." She immediately sees the attraction for Aurora in this handsome young man with the warm sparkle in his eyes.

"You're most welcome, I assure you," says Ethan, gently patting Rhys on his back.

Aurora looks at her fiancé. "We have your ma to thank for it, Rhys; it was her idea."

Rhys smiles sadly, maybe remembering all he's left behind. "That's true, but I never thought it would work out so well."

Later they're sitting around the dining table enjoying Lancashire hot pot, and a variety of green vegetables from the garden. Frankie ate earlier and is now tucked up in bed and so the adults talk freely.

Rhys begins to explain, "Our situation began when our friend Lewys fell in love with a young Chinese girl. They started meeting secretly, because she told him her family would not approve. But he was so besotted that he decided to go and see her father and declare his undying love for her. The thing is, she had three older brothers who were present at the time and all experts in *kung fu*. After her father angrily threw Lewys out of his house, unbeknown to Lewys, the brothers decided to take things further. Lewys was obviously heartbroken, Qinyang refused to see him anymore, probably for his own safety, and he fell into a deep depression. My brother, Owen, and I decided to try to cheer him up and arranged a night out, but, to cut a long story short, we were ambushed by the brothers on our way home. There was three of them and three of us, but they were athletic and leaping all over the place and we were the worst for drink." His voice breaks. "Poor Lewys was stabbed in the chest by one of them."

Lucy gasps with shock. "Oh no, how savage! Did he survive such an attack?"

Rhys shakes his head, wretchedly. "I'm afraid not, no. But at the time we didn't know that, and his assailant was preparing to strike again, so I panicked and hit him as hard as I could with a rock. I admit I was scared, defensive and full of adrenalin, but also full of beer. Tragically, we learnt the following day that Lewys died during the night and the Chinaman never regained consciousness." Rhys rubs his eyes and then takes a large slug of the wine.

Aurora, although also tearful, takes up the tale. "Unfortunately, the Chinese are an unforgiving race and even though it was perhaps an eye for an eye, and in Rhys' case, obviously self-defence, we were terrified of a vendetta against us. Qinyang's grandfather is Zhang Wei, the old opium king, and if he'd discovered that Nathan Meakins was my father, they might also seek revenge against me, for what he did to them all those years ago, so Nell and Bryn felt we'd no choice but to leave. In our panic, we thought about going up to the opal mines in the outback, where Rhys at least might find work, but decided it would be safer to leave Australia altogether, for our own peace of mind. That's when Nell suggested we come to you."

"Thank goodness for that!" says Lucy.

Aurora continues, "Well, she obviously felt reassured for us to be staying with people we knew, and because it's quite inaccessible here, we all thought the Chinese wouldn't consider our escape route. So, we fled for our lives, leaving our Australian friends and family behind us."

Lucy exclaims, "Wow! You poor things. Well, hopefully, you've found a safe haven here with us."

Rhys says, "We intend to pay you for our keep. We also have some company money and I'd like to buy some land, where we could fossick for gemstones. If you know of any claims available."

"I'll certainly put my ear to the ground on your behalf, Rhys. But in the meantime, you can help me with the *kopje-walloping*, if you like?"

He frowns. "What's that?"

"Buying and selling diamonds."

"Thank you, Ethan. That'll be grand."

Lucy gets up to clear away the empty plates and Aurora helps her.

In the kitchen Aurora looks at Lucy. "So, what's your news, Lucy? How come you fell out with Rupert? If you don't mind me asking."

"It didn't work out with us, I'm afraid. He enticed me and Frankie out here with secret promises of marriage and security and I was hopeful of an agreeable relationship, but he let me down. Actually, he's back home in Somerset, at the moment. He had a message that his father's seriously ill, and he was summoned home."

"Poor Colonel Seymour, that's a shame. But does this mean you're still friends then?"

"Well, he's still my brother-in-law and he didn't set out to hurt me, but he was selfish and thoughtless. You see, even before I arrived here, he had a child with his black maid and kept the fact hidden from me."

"Oh! My goodness. I'd no idea."

"Then, when I myself was expecting his child, the conniving maid set out to destroy it with black magic. I've pretty much forgiven Rupert and have no problems with being civil to him, but I can't stand Tamela, his evil maid, who caused me to have a miscarriage, by using a voodoo doll." Tears fill her eyes and she rubs them away with the back of her hand.

Aurora puts her arm around her friend. "Oh dear. You poor thing. I'm so sorry. I've brought it all back to you."

"It's not your fault, Aurora, but at the time the only person I had to confide in was Ethan and he's been absolutely wonderful to both me and Frankie. I don't know what I'd have done without him."

She smiles. "Well, you have us here now and we'll all help and support each other from now on. But I have to say your husband is quite charming."

"Well, looking at your Rhys, we've both done well for ourselves and each found the best kind of man, hard-working, supportive, loving and loyal."

Aurora grins. "And handsome into the bargain."

CHAPTER TWENTY-FIVE *(June 1876)*

LEGAL MATTERS

The tattooed man and his burly colleague are in court, before the honourable District Judge Metcalfe during the winter quarter session in June. Ethan attends with the other members of the MDU, Khumo and the parents of the other stolen children. The small court is packed. He remembers speaking to the gaoler, telling him of his suspicions that they were working under the authority of McCallister and suggesting that the men's defence lawyer might offer them leniency, if they reveal their boss to him. He wonders if they made any progress with that.

He watches the men being marched into the courtroom and their names and the charges are read out. The man with the tattoos is Axel Hoffman and his companion is Marius Brandt.

After the district judge has entered and taken his seat, the trial commences with the prosecution opening its case. "Good morning, Your Honour. I am Charles Voss, the prosecutor in this case, and I wish to prove to the court that not only are the two men charged, guilty of kidnapping seven young native boys, with a view to selling them into slavery. Further, that they did not act alone in this endeavour."

"Firstly, I'd like Mr Axel Hoffman to take the stand."

The man does so, looking around at the faces in the gallery.

"Mr Hoffman, you've pleaded 'guilty' to this offence. Do you now confirm this plea?"

"I do, sir."

"Do you have anything to say in your defence?"

He shrugs. "Not really, sir. I've admitted to the charge, being caught red-handed, but I've also explained, I was simply following orders."

"This in no way excuses you from blame, Mr Hoffman. Do you not realise those young boys were terrified at the thought of never seeing their families again? Where exactly was their destination?"

"We were delivering them to the quay at Saldanha Bay."

"And thence?"

"I believe they were being shipped out to Valong Wharf, Rio de Janeiro, sir."

"Hmm. Well, it's fortunate that the MDU posse were able to discover they'd been snatched, and overtake you before the boys reached the coast, for they'd otherwise have been lost to their families forever. However, the man behind the orders still has to take responsibility for what's occurred. Will you please tell the court the name of your employer, Mr Hoffman?"

The man hangs his head and mumbles, "I'll give you his name if the court will bear this in mind when deciding on my sentence."

"That remains to be seen, Mr Hoffman. Please… the man's name?"

He raises his head and looks his prosecutor in the eye. "It was Mervyn McCallister, sir. I've been employed as his minder for about five years now."

"Thank you, Mr Hoffman, you may step down."

Hoffman leaves the stand, as the clerk calls,

"Will Marius Brandt please step forward and take the stand?"

Brandt, having heard his partner in crime's testimony, also confirms his guilty plea and corroborates his colleague's statements. The chief magistrate tells him, "You've pleaded guilty to a joint charge of kidnapping seven young boys. You may now step down to await sentencing."

To Ethan's surprise and satisfaction, Mervyn McCallister is called next. He's interested to see how this self-important gold magnate handles himself in court. The man is dressed smartly with a thick gold pocket watch chain dangling from his waistcoat. Today he's wearing wire-rimmed spectacles, which Ethan doesn't remember him wearing the last time he saw him at Idayimane. He appears to be a respectable businessman, but Ethan knows better. *He's a bully and a rogue.*

The clerk of the court tells him, "Mr McCallister, you've been called as a character witness for two men in your employ. Would you please remain standing and raise your right hand whilst you repeat the oath after me?" McCallister does so. "I swear by almighty God that the evidence I shall give shall be the truth, the whole truth and nothing but the truth."

The prosecutor says, "Good morning, Mr McCallister."

"Good morning, sir." The man doesn't smile.

"Do you recognise the two men seated before you, beside the police officers."

He nods his head. "I do. They're both my diggers."

"Your diggers, you say?"

"Yes, they work on my claims at Kimberley."

"You'll not have heard their previous testimony that they were employed as your minders?"

"No, sir. They're both my gold sifters and diggers."

"As you well know, Mr McCallister, these men were caught red-handed, kidnapping seven young boys to be sold illegally as slaves, under your orders."

McCallister snaps, "I can't be held responsible for their actions. I tell you, I'm an honourable man."

"I dispute that, Mr McCallister. It may come as a shock to you, but we have evidence that you and your son are responsible for selling fraudulent claims to travellers en route to the diamond fields, so that when they arrive here, full of ambition, they're often practically destitute, as they've spent all their money on non-existent claims."

"Objection, Your Honour! Mr McCallister's here as a character witness, and this is not relevant to the case!"

Mr Voss responds, "It may seem unconnected, Your Honour, but I intend to prove that the McCallisters have perpetrated a long-term vendetta against the organisers of the MDU and their previous misdemeanours are quite relevant."

"Objection denied. Please make your point quickly, Mr Voss."

"Thank you, Your Honour." He turns back to the witness box. "Do you deny that you and your son sold these fraudulent claims, Mr McCallister?"

"Of course I do. I tell you, I'm a respectable businessman."

Mr Voss passes some paperwork to the judge. "I have here, my lord, several examples of certificates for claims that are indeed fraudulent, signed by McCallister junior, and the victims of his deception are present in court today and prepared to testify to that end."

Ethan looks around the folk gathered in the

court and suddenly spots David and Roger Moss. They must have suffered the same experience as him and he's glad they've come forward with their evidence, along with the others.

McCallister is belligerent. "Then you must prove it, Mr Voss."

"Oh, indeed I will, Mr McCallister. To further illustrate to the court that you're guilty of using unprincipled methods to get what you want, I also have statements from black diggers, some of whom have been intimidated until they steal for you, and others who've been forcibly prevented from attending and working their claims for the regulated seven-day period, thus have been forced to forfeit those claims, classified as abandoned. These claims have then been taken up by your company, Mr McCallister. Do you have any comment?"

"I do not."

"I also contend that your son's feud with Ethan Hart, whereby he tried to burn his stable down with the poor horse and stable boy still inside, leading to your son's imprisonment, has led you to perpetrate this revengeful act against the young brother of his stable boy, in order to punish Hart and his friends for successfully prosecuting your criminal son."

McCallister pushes his spectacles back up the bridge of his nose. Ethan wonders whether they're fake and only for effect.

Mr Voss suddenly turns towards the defendant dramatically. "Mr McCallister, I believe you have dealings with a blacksmith, who goes by the name of Joss Blake?" He studies McCallister, waiting for a response.

The man looks down and fiddles with his watch chain. Then he admits, "Yes. I know the fellow."

"Well, Mr Blake has informed us that he fitted

out your prairie schooner with chains and coffles. This was ordered by you, with the sole purpose of detaining the young boys who were kidnapped. We have his sworn testimony. What do you say to that, Mr McCallister?"

The man looks stunned. "I've nothing to say," he mumbles.

"I've no further questions for this witness. That is the case for the prosecution, Your Honour."

Ethan is jubilant. *They've got him!* He looks across at David and Roger and they respond with the thumbs-up sign.

The judge says, "This court is adjourned until tomorrow morning."

"All rise!"

As they stand, the judge leaves the courtroom. Ethan makes his way over to speak to Roger and David. They shake hands and greet each other like old friends, even though their previous acquaintance was short-lived.

"Where are you both living now?" asks Ethan.

David answers, "We're still at Klipdrift, but we had to work for someone else for a pittance, before we could save up enough earnings to be able to afford to license our own claim. Now we finally have one each, but that scoundrel really took us all for fools, didn't he, Rog? I have to say it's been a struggle that we certainly didn't bargain on."

Roger agrees. "That pair of rogues deserve everything they throw at 'em. I hope McCallister senior rots in hell. The arrogant bastard has ridden roughshod over us all."

Ethan companionably slaps them on their backs. "Well, it's good to see you here, hopefully getting retribution."

"I hope so, Ethan. Let's just pray the Honourable Judge Metcalfe sees it the same way as we do."

"Quite."

"Where are you living now, Ethan?"

"Well, you remember Lucy Seymour, who was travelling with the young lad, Frankie?"

"Yes, of course."

"Well, it may come as a surprise to you to hear that Lucy and I are now married."

David gasps. "No! Wow! Congratulations!"

Roger says, "Well I never did! I'm not surprised though; you both looked so animated when you used to sing together, and Lucy accompanied you on the piano."

"I assume you'll be here tomorrow for the summation?"

"Definitely!"

"Well, why don't you come back with me afterwards, to Acacia Lodge to see Lucy and hopefully celebrate the verdict? The ranch is on the outskirts of Hopetown, between it and the ford across the Orange River, not far off the beaten track."

Roger and David nod to each other in agreement and David says, "We'd both like that very much, Ethan. Thank you."

The following morning, Ethan's keen to attend court on Cathcart Street, to hear the closing arguments of the case and to know the sentences handed out by the judge, but he finds Lucy's again feeling sick, and rather than delay any further, she's pleased when he decides to forgo his attendance at the court. They have his signed statement and so he doesn't envisage a problem.

He puts his arm around her. "I plan to sort this out, once and for all. You've been feeling under the weather for a few weeks now and it needs to be dealt with."

She smiles, loving the way he takes care of her, but also trying to hide her anxiety. "All right, darling, I'll not put up any resistance, this time."

Thus, they drop Frankie off at his school in Hopetown and then go to Dr Forbes' surgery along the main street. After waiting their turn, the doctor finally calls them into his consulting room. He questions her about her symptoms and then he asks her to go behind the screen and lie down on the examination bed, while he examines her. Afterwards she readjusts her clothing and re-joins Ethan. She watches the doctor wash his hands thoroughly and return to his desk, asking as he takes his seat, "Mrs Hart, when did you last have a monthly period?"

She tries to remember and realises with shock that it's been over two months. "But I can't possibly be pregnant. I'm too old; besides, I lost my last baby." Tears sting her eyes at the memory that still haunts her.

"How old are you, Mrs Hart?"

"I'll be forty in September!"

"Well, my dear lady, you're definitely not too old, and I'm happy to confirm you're with child."

"Oh my! Ethan. What about that!"

Tears now stream down her face and she sees Ethan is overwhelmed with emotion as he says huskily, "It's wonderful news. I'm so relieved you're not ill and absolutely thrilled we're going to have a baby together. I must say I thought it was too much to hope for when we married, but I'm over the moon. Thank you, Dr Forbes. Allow me to settle your account, while Lucy sits awhile and gets used to the idea."

"Of course. That will be two guineas, please."

Ethan hands over the coins, then he takes her arm and they say their goodbyes and leave the surgery.

He studies her carefully. "How about you, darling? You've gone rather quiet. Are you content to be going through it all again, after what happened last time?"

"Of course I am! I couldn't be happier for all of us." She grins. "Just keep me away from that witch, Tamela."

As Ethan hands Lucy up into the carriage, she sees Rupert coming out of the First National Bank. He waves to them and approaches smiling. "Good morning to you both."

"Good morning, Rupert. How are you?"

"We've just got back here, after going home to see my father and sadly attend his funeral."

"Oh, I'm so sorry, Rupert. I'd no idea it was so serious."

"He had heart failure and I was lucky to see him, before it was too late."

"How's your mama holding up?"

"Well, she's the same judgemental old bat you'll remember. She took an immediate dislike to Tamela and turned her nose up at Berko. She said to me, 'He may be the firstborn son, but he's not the firstborn grandson.' Then she went on to persuade my father to change his will, leaving his claim over here to me, but Bingham Manor and the estate back home to your Frankie. In effect disinheriting me, because she couldn't contemplate the local gossip and disapproval, if the estate was to end up in Berko's hands."

"Oh, I'm so sorry, Rupert."

"It's no skin off my nose, Lucy. I'd no intentions of ever returning to live there anyway. I was only annoyed for the sake of Tamela and my son. I wish I'd never taken them there and put them through it. They were both frozen with the March weather and were obliged to sleep in the servants' quarters. Anyway, I have to get on; we need to re-stock our supplies of food."

"Well, we're both sorry for your loss, Rupert," says Ethan, thinking, *In both respects.*

Lucy says, "I'll write to your mama with our condolences."

"She'll probably be back into her fog of laudanum by now."

She responds, "It will be lonely for her, though, Rupert. Not at all the life she'd have envisaged, ten years ago. She always hoped you'd return."

"I know, but she's burned her bridges now." He waves and strides off towards the butchers.

Ethan flicks the reins and they set off towards home.

"Well, that's a turn up for the books."

Lucy is thoughtful. "Hmm. If it's true, then it's rather reassuring to know that Frankie's future is secured, and that we might have a bolt hole, if things should turn sour here."

"What do you mean 'turn sour'?"

"Well, you know that I'm extremely happy making our family home here, but we've settled in a foreign country and politically there always seems to be factions fighting against each other. Hopefully, we'll continue to prosper, but things could go wrong, and if they do, Frankie will always be able to return home. I'm sure, after this, Helen would make him and us welcome, should the need arise, but I'll definitely write to her. I do feel I've neglected her rather."

On returning home they go straight inside to tell Rhys and Aurora their glad tidings.

Rhys shakes Ethan's hand and Aurora kisses her friend warmly. "That's wonderful news, Lucy. You must both be so thrilled!"

"We are, and I can't wait to tell Frankie." She looks up at Ethan. "Do you suppose he'll be pleased?"

"I'm sure he will; a little brother or sister will complete our family. I also think Betsy and Norman, and our old neighbours at Eureka Row, will be delighted for us too."

Lucy ponders on that. "Hmm, I think we ought to keep it between ourselves for a while longer, darling. Can we please keep it as our secret, until I begin to show, and I'm confined?"

"Whatever you wish, my love. I just can't believe it's happening. It's such wonderful news. I'm to be a father! I love being a papa to Frankie, but it must be magical to see your own traits developing in your child."

"It is, Ethan. You'll love it." She kisses him.

At around midday they hear a knock on their front door. Ethan finds David and Roger Moss standing on the threshold and he recalls inviting them back to his ranch after the trial.

David says, "Good day, Ethan, we missed you at the court and decided to look out for Acacia Lodge on our way back home to Klipdrift, to call in to make sure that nothing's wrong."

"No, nothing's wrong at all; I just had to take Lucy to see the doctor."

"Oh dear, I'm sorry to hear that. Is she unwell?"

"No, thankfully, not at all." He lowers his voice. "Don't tell her I told you, but we're expecting a happy event."

"Oh, my dear fellow, that's grand news." The brothers each shake his hand.

"Thank you. Changing the subject quickly, what happened with the verdict?"

Roger grins. "They were all found to be guilty as charged. Brandt and Hoffman were both sentenced to seven years in prison and, since he was the mastermind, McCallister got ten years. Plus, because he and his son are both detained, after seven days his licences will be revoked, and the claims offered to those he swindled, with the remainder being put back onto the market."

Ethan breathes a sigh of relief. "That's tremendous! We've effectively removed a bully and a rogue."

Roger tells him, "It also means we should be entitled to our original claims, and others who've been swindled can also be recompensed."

"That's poetic justice. Anyway, come in and see Lucy and have some refreshments with us, before your journey onward."

David says, "Thank you, Ethan, that's very kind, but we must make haste, as we have appointments this afternoon."

Roger responds, "I don't know, Dave. I think we ought to at least say hello to Lucy, not having seen her for all this time, even if we forgo Ethan's kind offer of refreshments."

Ethan opens the door wide. "Please come in. Lucy's with her friends Aurora and Rhys."

They follow him into the drawing room and greet Lucy warmly. Ethan then introduces them to Aurora and Rhys and relates the glad tidings about McCallister. He concludes, "The good news is, Rhys, that a large number of claims will be back on the market in a week's time and we must all be there, ready to bid for them."

Rhys grins. "That's good news indeed and very timely. Thank you, Ethan, for being the instigator of this."

"You're welcome. You're not the only one who'll be pleased that those two predators are now out of the arena. I doubt they'll ever recover their status and position, after folk hear of their crimes."

Lucy asks the brothers, "Can I get you anything to drink?"

Ethan says, "They weren't going to stop, but I've some champagne here and we've some celebrating to do." He lays out six champagne flutes and removes the cork from the bottle with a loud 'pop' and the bubbles overflow into the glasses.

He looks at his wife. "I'm sorry, Lucy, but I told them our secret. I just blurted it out, without thinking."

She smiles, shaking her head at him. "It doesn't matter. I know how excited you are."

"This means we've several things to celebrate, but firstly a drink to the healthy development of our little one."

Everyone raises their glasses with a chorus of "Cheers!" and "To the baby!", followed by sips of the sparkling wine.

"Secondly, a drink to celebrate the successful overthrow, conviction and imprisonment of the kidnappers."

Glasses up again and a chorus of "Hear, hear!"

"Thirdly, a toast to celebrate the sudden

availability of the McCallisters' Kimberley claims, meaning an ideal opportunity for Rhys to invest his company's money and new opportunities for the rest of us."

"Hear, hear!"

"Cheers!"

"Good news indeed!"

Ethan continues, "From across the world, people of all nationalities are lured by the glitter and sparkle of gold and gemstones. Gathered here today, we're among the brave pioneers who've given up their comfortable lifestyles at home for the unimaginable challenges that face the explorers and prospectors in the brave new world we now inhabit. I raise a toast to all of us present, to good health, happiness and good fortune."

All respond with enthusiasm.

A fortnight later an auction is organised in Kimberley for the re-issue of the McCallister claims. Ethan goes with Rhys to this event, held on the land at the cusp of the giant cavernous hole, alongside which is displayed a large plan of the individual claims, showing those that have become available. There are also similar claim plans of Klipdrift and Dutoitspan.

Here they see the huge round horse whims, from which ropes lead to the aerial trams and down to the working surface of the individual claims, the vast area over-meshed with a spider's web of ropes. At the bottom of the hole they see many stacks of rock, with valleys and walkways between them, the odd hut, a variety of ladders, barrows and countless men, from this height resembling a colony of ants. Ethan feels himself being drawn towards the edge and, feeling dizzy, he moves away quickly. It's astounding to him that in just the few years since he first arrived here, when this was the 'New Rush', this massive cavity has since been excavated, now known as 'the Big Hole'.

He catches sight of Roger and David Moss standing near the site plans and they make towards them through the gathering crowd. They greet each other affably.

Moments later the assembly are brought to silence with the rap of the auctioneer's gavel.

"Good morning, gentlemen. My first task is to designate claims, on the instructions of District Judge Metcalfe, to those who've been swindled by Simon McCallister en route to the fields. I'm pleased to offer first choice of the Klipdrift claims to brothers Roger and David Moss. Would you please make yourselves known to the clerk at the Klipdrift plan and select a claim each? You also have the opportunity of purchasing an adjoining claim, if you so wish."

Roger and David move to the front of the crowd to make their selection and pay the official for the additional claims they've selected, with the licence fees. They return to Ethan telling him, "We've chosen two more claims each, situated not far from those we already own, so we're both well pleased. Thanks, mate."

The auctioneer continues, "My next task is to offer a compensatory claim to Mr Ethan Hart, here at the Big Hole, plus the opportunity of an additional claim if you so wish. Please, Mr Hart, would you also come forward and speak with my clerk, standing beside the Kimberley site plan. Thank you."

Ethan goes to the edge of the hole and looks at the confusing muddle of men and stacks and ropes. He may as well take potluck and choose from the plan. He selects a claim in the centre of other unclaimed plots and purchases a second site beside it. Noting the numbers, he returns to Rhys. Once the compensatory claims have all been allocated, the auctioneer commences the auction proper and Ethan nudges Rhys to bid when numbers come up nearest to his own claims.

The auctioneer calls out groups of certain numbers, asking who wants to bid for eight claims, reducing down if no one bids. Rhys is ecstatic to get a block of four claims in the same area as Ethan. "That's fantastic. I can't wait to tell Rora. Between us, we've a group of six claims, so we'll be working alongside each other."

Roger and David congratulate them, and they all leave the auction together, feeling well pleased. Ethan can't help thinking, *That's one in the eye for the McCallisters!*

They go to the Star of the West saloon bar to celebrate with the brothers, before returning home to Lucy and Aurora with the good news.

Lucy throws her arms around him. "Oh, Ethan, I'm so proud of you, darling. This has all happened to our advantage because you wouldn't give up. If you hadn't thought about forming the MDU, we might never have captured the kidnappers. Roeli and his friends would be lost and McCallister senior would still be doing his dirty dealings unfettered."

Ethan grins, and says to her quietly, "We've all done our bit, Lucy. You shot at Simon McCallister until he ran off squealing, and even Kofi defended you with my revolver. We've stuck together through thick and thin and now we can at last reap the rewards."

Rhys puts his arm around Aurora. "Well, we're both extremely happy with the outcome. I'm sure

Hugh, my pa and Owen will be thrilled to hear Brecon Valley Mines have now added four diamond claims to their gold portfolio. I can't wait to write to them and tell them the good news." He turns to Aurora. "Also, we've some money left to buy a plot for our own homestead, but we'll have to unearth some gems, of course, to go towards the cost of building."

"Have no fear, you may both stay here with us until you're ready to move on. We love having you here. Don't we, Ethan?"

"We certainly do. Right, then, let's open another bottle of bubbly."

They hear the pop from the kitchen and Ethan shortly enters with the tray of fizzing, sparkling flutes. He passes them around and then raises his, saying, "Cheers everyone! Here's to all that glitters!"

They each respond, "All that glitters!"

THE EPILOGUE *(May 1876)*

Mr & Mrs Isaac Warren
Home Farm
Alvington Manor
Ivell
Somerset
Great Britain

14th May 1876

Dear Mama, Papa and All,

I have grand news in that Ethan and I are expecting a little brother or sister for Frankie, sometime in February. We are all over the moon and it is wonderful to have Aurora and Rhys here with us to share in our joy.

They have joined us from Australia to set up a subsidiary company to Brecon Valley Mines, so, as well as dealing in gold, they are now learning about the diamond trade.

We are all well and happy here. Ethan and his Miners' Defence Unit have managed to capture the kidnappers who stole some of our native children to send into slavery and return them to their families. The criminals have been charged, tried and convicted and so all the villains involved have been sent to prison.

This has meant that there have been a glut of claims to be re-issued, some of which have fallen into our hands, including one claim which Ethan was swindled out of on our arrival.

I hope you are all well and happy,

Please wish Daisy a happy birthday from us all here.

We miss you all so much.

With fondest love,

From Lucy, Ethan and Frankie

Lord Dryer Esq
Alvington Manor
Brympton
Ivell
Somerset
Great Britain

18th May 1876

Dear Mama, Papa, Gabriel and Lydia May,

It has taken several months, but, we have finally arrived safely in Hopetown and Lucy and Ethan have made us very welcome. Rhys has been working with Ethan, helping him erect his kit homes, but you will be pleased to learn, Papa, that he has now managed to purchase four claims at Kimberley in the name of Brecon Valley Mines.

I also have wonderful news in that Rhys and I are engaged to be married. As it is a leap year, on our voyage from Port Phillip to Port Elizabeth I took courage and proposed to Rhys, and thankfully he accepted. We're going to use the first decent diamond we discover for my engagement ring.

I hope you are all well and happy, and the two babies, Wilfred and Henrietta, are both thriving. Lucy has given me permission to tell you that she

413

and Ethan are also expecting a baby some time in February next year.

Please pass on our love and best wishes to everyone. Lucy and I miss you all back home terribly, but you now have something to celebrate for both of us. So raise a glass to your intrepid adventurers and wish us both well.

Your loving daughter,
Aurora

Mr & Mrs B Thomas
Brecon House
Waratah Street
Sandhurst
Victoria
South Australia

24ᵗʰ May 1876

Dear Ma and Pa and Owen,

We've arrived safely in Hopetown after an arduous journey overland and Lucy and Ethan have made us very welcome at Acacia Lodge. Our steamer chests arrived safely a week later. Thank you for organising that for us.

We are all getting along well, and Ethan is inducting me into the world of diamond dealing and valuation. We were fortunate in that a large number of claims became available just after we arrived, due to a man being arrested and charged with abduction and slavery, mainly thanks to Ethan and his Miners' Defence Unit. So, Brecon Valley Mines are now in ownership of four claims at Kimberley, that are alongside two others, now owned by Ethan and Lucy.

I was helping Ethan and his native friend Khumo to erect kit homes, but now we have the diamond claims, he has invited us to stay on with them at Acacia Lodge until Lucy's baby is born in February and rather than a kit home we hope to construct a comfortable ranch-style home nearer to Kimberley.

How are Hugh, Sarah and Gwyn? We are still both saddened whenever we think of poor Lewys. Please write and let us know how things are progressing with them and the business. Do you have any news of the Zhang family? We are still anxious and vigilant when it comes to Chinese faces.

But I have more good news in that Aurora and I became officially betrothed during our voyage from Australia, thus I am also on the lookout for a special Brecon Valley diamond to set in Aurora's engagement ring.

We miss you all, but we've settled in here very well, so please don't worry about us. I believe the distance between us has insured our safety, but it might be wise to destroy this letter just to be on the safe side.

With fondest wishes

From your loving son and future daughter-in-law.

Rhys and Aurora

Lord Dryer Esq
Alvington Manor
Brympton
Ivell
Somerset
Great Britain

My Dear Joshua,

I'm writing to ask you to please forgive my tardiness. I'm sorry that I myself didn't contact you at the time, and that Aurora didn't give you the whole story as to why they left with haste to South Africa in February. She probably didn't want to worry you.

I am afraid my son became involved with a Chinese girl and her family took against him. There was a fight between her three brothers and Lewys, Rhys and Owen. Tragically, Lewys was stabbed and Rhys hit his assailant with a rock in defence of himself and my son. Unfortunately, neither Lewys nor the Chinaman survived.

We all thought it best for Rhys and Aurora to leave the area for their own safety, before a Chinese vendetta caused any more harm. They decided to go to the diamond mines, where Rhys could find work and Aurora had a friend they could turn to.

You will remember the name Zhang Wei. Well, the girl is his granddaughter and we thought the family would be as much set against Aurora as Rhys.

I'm sorry we didn't inform you at the time, but we knew Aurora had written to you, and my family were grief-stricken and obviously we are greatly missing both Lewys and Rhys with regard to our business.

Forgive my thoughtlessness, my friend.

We've heard, as I'm sure you have by now, that they're well settled in Hopetown with Lucy and Ethan, and our company now have four diamond claims within the Kimberley mine, which have already been worked to the level of the bluestone and promise to be very productive.

I regret this incident as much as anyone; we grieve for our only son, but also Rhys, who I've known since a baby, and Aurora, who you'll be proud to hear had settled in very well and was a real asset to the business. This has affected all of us left behind. We love and miss all three of them.

Please pass on my kind regards to Louisa and your family.

With kindest regards,
Hugh

Telegram To:
Mr & Mrs Isaac Warren, Home Farm, Alvington Manor, Ivell, Somerset, Great Britain.

Mrs Helen Seymour, Bingham Manor, Sutton Bingham, Ivell, Somerset, Great Britain.

Mr & Mrs Laurence Hart, Durnford Manor, Salisbury, Wiltshire, Great Britain.

12TH FEBRUARY. LUCY DELIVERED OF A GIRL. LUELLA CORDELIA HART. 8LB 1OZ. MOTHER AND BABY WELL.

GLOSSARY

CHINESE WORDS AND MEANINGS

- *Chee Kung Tong Society* – Chinese Free Masons.
- *Gweilo* – Derogatory name for Europeans.
- *Hung League* – Chinese Secret Brotherhood, similar to British Freemasons.
- *Jian* – Chinese male name meaning: Strong, indefatigable.
- *Ju-i* – Goodbye.
- *Kung fu kuosha* – Chinese martial arts.
- *Ling* – Chinese female name meaning: Clever, intelligent, spiritual.
- *Longwei* – Chinese male name meaning: Dragon greatness.
- *Qíng rén* – Lover.
- *Qinyang* – Chinese female name meaning: Sunshine of my heart. Pronounced *Cheen-yong*.
- *Shangyuan* – The first full moon of the year.
- *Tián xīn* – Sweetheart.
- *Wei* – Chinese male name meaning: High, lofty, heroic, remarkable.
- *Weimin* – Chinese male name meaning: People's hero.
- *Xiǎnshì* – Display.
- *Yee Hing Company* – Chinese version of the British East India Company.
- *Yi Ho Chuan Society* – 'Fists of Harmonious Righteousness'– Emblem clenched fist, leading to the nickname 'Boxers'. Hence, in future years led to the 'Boxer Rebellion', which was an anti-imperialist, anti-foreign, and anti-Christian

uprising in China between 1899 and 1901, towards the end of the Qing Dynasty.

- *Yingjie* – Chinese male name meaning: Gallant hero.
- *Ying* – Chinese surname meaning: Clever eagle.
- *Yue* – Chinese girls' name meaning: Moon.
- *Zhang* – Family name or surname meaning: Archer or bowyer. Pronounced *Jong*.

XHOSA WORDS AND MEANINGS

- *Berko* – Boys' name meaning: Firstborn son.
- *Enkosi* – Thank you.
- *Griekwa* – Xhosa-speaking Griqua clan, sometimes referred to as *Korana*.
- *Idayimane* – Diamond.
- *Inkwenkwi* – Boy.
- *Isifundo* – Lesson.
- *Kaffir* – An insulting term for a black African.
- *Khoikhoi* – A member of a group of pastoral peoples of Namibia and South Africa.
- *Khoisan* – 'Khoi' meaning people, 'San' meaning forager. Bushmen.
- *Khumo* – African name meaning: Wealth and riches.
- *Kofi* – African name meaning: Born on a Friday.
- *Molo* – Hello.
- *Mpondo* – Nguni-speaking peoples from the Eastern province of South Africa.
- *Mpho* – African name meaning: Gift.
- *Roeli* – African name meaning: Wolf.
- *South Sotho* – The Sotho, or Basotho, are a Bantu ethnic group of Southern African people who speak Sesotho.

- *Tamela* – Girls' name meaning: She who is like a thunderbolt.
- *Tata* – Father.
- *Tswana* – Southern African people living in Botswana, South Africa, and neighbouring areas and one of the official languages of South Africa.
- *Ubhuti* – Brother.
- *Umama* – Mother.
- *Umfundisi* – Teacher.
- *Uncedo* – Help.
- *Usapho* – Family.
- *Usisi* – Sister.
- *Usale kakuhle* – Goodbye.
- *Xirikua* – Xhosa-speaking Griqua clan.

SOUTH AFRICAN WORDS AND MEANINGS

- *Appelbeignet* – A doughnut with a slice of apple within.
- *Blinke klippe* – Bright stones.
- *Kopje* – Areas of yellow ground that were minute flat hills, associated with the top of a kimberlite pipe. A small hill.
- *Kopje-walloping* – A slang term used in the early days in South Africa to describe a diamond dealer or buyer of rough diamonds.
- *Knobkerrie* – A form of club.
- *Malva pudding* – A sweet South African baked dessert, containing apricot jam.
- *Stoep* – Veranda.
- *Stroopwafels* – Dutch syrup waffles.

AUSTRALIAN WORDS AND MEANINGS

- *Warrigal greens* – Similar to spinach.
- *Wonga-wonga* – A large Australian pigeon.

ACKNOWLEDGEMENTS

I would like to take this opportunity to pay tribute to the following people whose meticulous work all helped enormously with my research:

The A to Z of Yeovil's History – *Bob Osborn – www. yeovilhistory.info*

The Death of Henry Turberville – *Newspaper reports in the Western Gazette and Western Daily Press*

Portland: An Illustrated History – *Stuart Morris (First Published 1985)*

1872 Chesil Shipwreck of 'The Royal Adelaide' – *Victorian Tales from Weymouth and Portland – Internet page by Cannasue Hogben – www. Weymouth history.org*

A Voyage From Southampton to Cape Town, In the Union Company's Mail Steamer 'Syria' – *Captain Charles Chapman (First Published 1872)*

Capital and Labour on the Kimberley Diamond Fields 1871–1890 – *Robert Vicat Turrell (First Published 1987)*

Alfred Beit: South Africa's Financial Genius – *Geraldine Auerbach – www.kehilalinks.jewishgen.org*

Bendigo General History – Department of Planning and Community – *www.yumpu.com*

Developing Trade and Port Histories – *State Library South Australia – samemory.sa.gov.au*

Xhosa words and phrase book – *Jeff Brown – www.wildcoast.co.uk*

Plus, thanks are due to Leigh McKinnon, Research Officer at the Golden Dragon Museum, Bendigo Australia, for her helpful information about the Yi Yuan Gardens, the Yee Hing Society Lodge and the Guan Yin Temple.

I would like to acknowledge Mr Don Gibson, at the Princes Street Dental Practice, who first told me about their past dental practitioner, Mr Thomas Maggs, who was accused in the Henry Turberville case, sensationalised in the newspapers in 1876. At that time, he worked from the old Medical Hall in the Borough, but he was eventually to take over the property, Glencairn House in Princes Street for his dental practice.

In addition to these erudite and eminent people, I am grateful for the help, support and encouragement of my family and friends, especially my husband, Barry Mazey, my sisters Maddy Sams and Bridget Overd and my friends Angela Hart and Kate Wood who took time out of their busy lives to read and comment on my manuscript, prior to publication. Their help and feedback is much appreciated. My gratitude is also due to all the obliging and professional staff at Matador: the production team, the digital team, the design team and the marketing team and especially my clever copy editor, Hannah McCall. I also truly appreciate all my loyal readers who have avidly followed my last four novels and are looking forward to *All That Glitters*. If you have enjoyed my stories, and can spare the time, please comment on my Facebook page: 'Shelagh Mazey Books' or on any of the various review pages. I am very grateful for your support. Thank you.

HISTORICAL NOTE

Richard Blackmore remained convinced his brother, Henry Turberville, had been murdered. He teamed with Charles Bradlaugh and together they disputed the verdict of suicide. The allegations went on with many acrimonious letters and accusations by Richard Blackmore to Dr Aldridge, resulting in a batch of libel actions.

In August 1876 the matter came before the Lord Chief Justice Coleridge in the Probate Court. Here it was disclosed that the last will of Henry Turberville was made out only shortly before his death and it was argued by Richard Blackmore, Charles Bradlaugh and others that for this reason it was invalid.

Richard Blackmore's claim to be the sole beneficiary was denied and thus his brother's £20,000 estate was divided as follows: Thomas Maggs, the chemist, was awarded £15,000; Charles Bradlaugh, the free thinker, was awarded £2,500; Richard Blackmore, the sole next of kin and the author of *Lorna Doone*, was awarded £2,000; and Henry Essery, the shoemaker, £500.

Hopefully I have not misunderstood any of the historical facts from the people or books above, but if so please understand that any errors are mine and accept my apologies, should you come across any.

POETIC LICENCE

In a subsidiary story line, Bingham Lake was mentioned in both *Legacy of Van Diemen's Land*, and *The Golden Fleece,* where I ignored the fact that Sutton Bingham Reservoir was not formed until the 1950s and made the reservoir a natural lake for poetic reasons. Thus, in this story I have continued with this fiction. Also, the position of the real Sutton Bingham Manor is hidden behind the church, but in my *Heart of Stone Saga* I placed it opposite the railway bridge facing the smaller part of the lake.

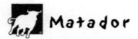